For Katherine

SONG FOR A SPY

a novel by

BERNARD TRAFFORD

Cover design by James Cave

Chapter 1

"As you wish, *Signore,*" replied the silky voice. "In order to remove all risk, we should silence him. But we could... merely teach him to fear us."

"Thank you, Bartolomeo." The huge man's voice was a deep rumble. "As ever you put my mind at rest. We shall take the latter course, and avoid the necessity of disposing of a body... though, God knows, that is easily done."

Naked I cringed against the plank, the straps holding me immobile as I awaited the torment they promised.

I know. It sounds like no more than the slick opening to a story. But have you ever found yourself, perhaps fifteen years old, bound helpless in a stinking prison while powerful men determine whether you should be quietly murdered, or flogged nearly to death instead?

I thought not. As my master always said, do not leap too quickly to judgment.

There - once again I have done it. My master, the most unusual master imaginable, used constantly to complain that I never started at the beginning: "You're always in such a rush, Lorenzo. Slow down. Think before jumping in."

Sound advice, often given, rarely heeded: that marks my whole, long life. Had I heeded that oft-proffered wisdom, I might have enjoyed an easier life, though it would have been a less exciting one.

Even in old age as I write this, the thoughts still tumble out in any order except the right one.

Nonetheless, I shall do my best to unravel my thoughts as I unfold my tale.

*   *   *

Naked I cringed against the plank, the straps holding me immobile as I awaited the promised torment. I could hear the Signore's heavy breathing as the two men began to lay into my

3

body with their heavy whips. There was nothing I could do but shriek my agony.

How can I describe a flogging of that kind to one who has not experienced it? The blows struck like a rod but then ripped the flesh from the bones of my back and tore my buttocks to ribbons. I bucked and howled and wailed: but I was held tight, mercilessly, by the leather straps. My body was a screaming mass of pain and, as I begged and pleaded, it seemed to go on forever. I think my tormentors took turns, finding it tiring work.

When they paused for breath, their master questioned me. "Now, Luca or Lorenzo, tell me again. How did you come by that name?" As I gave the same answer, he grunted and urged his men to further efforts. "Lay it on. Don't tickle him." At that they laid into me afresh. "Harder, boys, harder." He paused to pant between sentences. "You're meant to be teaching this street-rat a lesson about spying. Now, boy, one last time. Who sent you to spy on my men? Was it the Gatekeeper? Was it? Tell me only that and the pain will stop."

I had known from the moment I was seized that my only chance of survival was to plead ignorance, stupidity even, repeating over and over again the fact that it was just a name I had heard. In any case, now I was beyond any semblance of coherent speech. I mumbled amid my screams, and have no idea whether my inquisitor could make any sense of my nonsense. But I could tell he was enjoying my torment. Even as my two torturers struck still more viciously and I shrieked my pain anew, I could hear his heavy, laboured breaths.

When they slowed once more, his voice cut in one last time. "Well done, lads. He has nothing of use to tell us and, if he was indeed spying on us, we've taught him and whoever controls him a pretty lesson. Now I must go up and treat with the damned lawyer. Give him some more, say twenty more each, then throw him into the street. And," again the heavy breathing, "Send me a girl to my private chamber. Discreetly, as usual. That little blonde one: what's her name?"

"Laura, your honour."

"Laura. Yes, a pert little piece. She'll do nicely." I could hear him heaving himself up the timber staircase, and then he was gone. The two men chuckled.

"Poor little Laura," remarked one.

"Aye," replied his companion. "She'll be weary after a night of trying to satisfy him."

"Aye, gets his dander up, it does, watching a whipping. He'll be fair roaring for it when Laura gets upstairs."

"Does she tell you about it, then?"

"Pillow-talk. I'm saying nothing!"

"You want to have a care. The boss and Bardi see the kitchen girls as theirs to bed. They wouldn't take kindly to sharing with you."

"Laura's sensible. She knows a pretty serf needs someone in the household to look out for her. She'll keep her mouth shut."

"And her legs open!"

"Nothing comes free in this life. Still, she'll be pleased her hide's safe tonight: even he's seen enough blood for one day, so she won't be crying when she comes to me in the morning."

"Talk in the kitchen says it's the only way he can get it up now."

"You're right. At least, it's what Laura reckons. Still, look on the bright side. Time was, he'd have had the boy as well. Before the *Consiglio* got so particular about sodomy."

"You'll get yourself into trouble, the way you talk. He wouldn't have fancied this poor little bugger anyhow, the state he's in. What shall we do with him?"

"Give him a few more, like the boss said?"

"He's had enough."

"True enough. Just a few more, then, in case he checks."

As I closed my eyes (I could see nothing anyway) and braced myself for fresh agony, I heard a door open and footsteps approach. A new voice spoke, one I had not heard before. It was no man's voice, yet it seemed too harsh and grating for a woman. And it was angry. "What are you men doing? Why are you beating a child to death?"

The answer was grudgingly respectful. "Not a child," protected the man on my right.

"Not a man either," came the brusque reply.

"And not to death," came from my left. "Only to teach him a lesson for prying and eavesdropping. It's the Signore's orders."

"It's the Signore's orders, *Magister*." The emphasis was heavy: the owner of the voice expected to be addressed properly.

"Forgive me, *Magister*." Now the respect sounded genuine. "We're only obeying orders."

"And by the look of it you have carried them out fully and admirably. You may stop now. What was his fault?"

"He was snooping, *Magister*. And he seemed to know of the Gatekeeper and... and other matters."

"The Gatekeeper? How would he know anything of the Gatekeeper?"

"We don't think he does, *Magister*. In the end the Signore reckoned he just overheard the name somewhere, and was parroting it. So he insisted we teach him a lesson."

"Eavesdropper or no, if you put him out in the street now, he will most likely die. Have him brought to my house. I will tend him there."

"But, *Magister*, the Signore ordered..."

"The Signore ordered you to do what you have done. Now I will take charge of him. That is an end to it. You know where I live. Have him brought."

The same rough hands released the straps that held me and, as they moved me, the pain was so unspeakable that I lost consciousness.

Chapter 2

My next memory is of awakening slowly. I was lying face down on a bed, a real bed. My back and buttocks hurt, but not with the stinging, burning agony that I had known before. It was a dark, deep throbbing, but lacked its previous sharp edge.

"You are back with us, then," said a voice close to my ear. I remembered that voice: it was the last that I had heard before I passed out. A gruff, gravelly kind of voice, not deep enough for a man, but not belonging to any woman I'd heard. "Are you in pain?"

I considered the question. Afraid to move, I spoke into the pillow in which my face was buried (a pillow? I had never used one of those). "Yes, but it's... bearable. I'm very sleepy."

"The physician gave you poppy juice to help you sleep. You were screaming and fighting us: but I doubt you remember that." I shook my head, as far as I could, still afraid to move. The voice continued. "I must apply more unguent to your wounds or the pain will return. But I warn you, it will smart."

Gentle hands dabbed something onto my back. The voice was right. It did sting at first: but then brought some relief, returning the vivid pain to that same dull ache.

I lost all sense of time. I learned later that I had lain there for a month and more, though I had no perception of it. My memory is of one long conversation, punctuated by periods of pain. I slipped in and out of consciousness, partly helped by the precious poppy juice. At one stage I am assured that the household feared for my life as I developed a raging fever. At times I thrashed around, trying to tear at my own back, so much so that they were obliged to tie my hands and feet to the bed. At others I lay motionless and breathed so shallowly that I seemed likely to die. Or so they told me later.

Always the soft hands returned with the quiet yet grating voice, the hands anointing my back and buttocks, the voice strangely reassuring, explaining.

I first came to know the household only by its voices and later on by the strange view I had of those who tended me - always seen from knee-level, and never completely.

Gradually my lucid periods became longer, and I started to piece together the evidence of what had happened to me and where I was. "I'm not so sleepy now," I told my pillow one day.

"You're growing stronger, and the pain is less, is it not?" In response to the voice I nodded into the pillow, in the way that had become a habit. "It is some days now since we gave you the poppy for it. The physician was concerned that we should not give you overmuch, but your pain was too terrible to watch."

"The physician? I have no money to pay." I was suddenly anxious.

"No, indeed. You certainly have no money, nor any possessions. It appears you do not even possess clothes." I was suddenly aware of my nakedness, and embarrassed. I tried to move, bringing a sudden wave of pain. I groaned.

"There, that will teach you. No sudden movements, now. You cannot put clothes on those wounds for a while yet, in any case. And as for money, the physician does not require payment. He owes me some... *debt* of gratitude."

"I don't understand. Why are you doing this for me? You don't even know who I am."

"On the contrary, I know quite a lot about you, though you will not remember telling me. I know you are called Lorenzo: except when you go by the name of Luca. You might be called Giovanni. You could even be named Tommaso: though I suspect that is not you, but rather a friend. And you have come here to Bologna from Modena: but you disliked like it there. How close am I to the truth?"

"Pretty near." I was impressed.

"There are many other things I don't understand, most of all what you were doing in that terrible place being beaten nearly to death. Hush!" A soft hand touched the back of my head, gently, as I became agitated. "You are safe here and when you are

9

strong enough you shall tell me your story. But first heal yourself."

I started to garner some names. Michele belonged to the hoarse voice with a lisp, quite hard to understand at times. Michele limped as he walked: I could see his unsteady gait as he would bring a tray of food or drink and place it on a low table beside my bed. As I managed to turn my head further, I gradually saw more of him. He was old, grizzled, battered even. Constantly he complained at my nurse, his grumbling frequently rendered barely intelligible by his lack of teeth. "Another waif and thtray you've brought in, then," he would lisp. "Another mouth to feed."

"That's not your concern, Michele. Do you go short? "

"No, *Magithter*, of courthe not. But you're your own wortht enemy. Thith one will get thtrong again, eat you out of houthe and home and cauthe you nothing but trouble. Probably rob you ath well."

"As you did once, Michele, long ago, and yet, here you are still," came the inevitable retort. Michele left, grumbling.

Another voice was different again: male, certainly, but thin and weedy, a high-pitched nasal whine. This belonged to Mamolo, the cook. When I finally saw all of him he was as unlike a cook as I could imagine, for his meagre, effeminate frame matched his voice. Throughout my convalescence I would hear him wheedling at my carer: "*Magister*, leave this boy and have your dinner. I have some new cheese. I found it in the market, and spoke to the farmer himself. He was spinning me the usual yarn about how his buffalo were the best this side of Ferrara. But his cheese today was truly magnificent, so I bought it: soft yet firm; pure white; and the curd runs away from it. *And* a fresh load of ham came in today: all the way from Parma, the real thing. I nearly cried when I tasted it. Come away and eat your dinner. I have figs for after, just as you like them."

Always the same answer came. "When he's settled down to sleep, Mamolo: then I'll eat. My dinner will keep." And the cook would leave the room muttering about his fine arts being wasted on a master so unappreciative.

10

One day, after yet another such an exchange, the voice to which I'd become so accustomed sighed. "You would think, Lorenzo, that I would indeed be master in my own house. They call me *Magister*, but they nag and bully me all the time. I wonder why I put up with them."

At this I had to put the question that I had been burning to ask ever since I began to recover my reason. "You told me not to ask, but I must. Who are you? And why have you saved me?"

"The second question is easy to answer. You were in need, and I hate to see any creature suffer. Besides, I knew and lost someone a little like you once."

"As for the first, perhaps I should tell you now. But I had rather look you in the eye. Can you turn a little, onto one side? That would mark some progress." Gingerly I eased my right elbow under me and turned half onto my side. I expected the accustomed stab of pain, the burning agony: but none came. The strangeness of that absence of hurting, even for a moment, was startling.

For the first time I looked upon the face of my angel of mercy. It was a woman's face, though her hair was short, grey and severely cut above the collar in the style of a man's. She wore a sombre, dark habit, not quite a man's, but certainly not a woman's dress. She was thin and small, and her sharp, slightly hooked nose gave her a hawkish appearance. With its shrewd, penetrating eyes it would have been a formidable, even intimidating face (I saw it so on countless occasions later): but, as I looked into her eyes, her features instantly softened into a gentle smile.

"That's better," she said. "I am Bettisia Gozzadini, and you are right. I do owe you an explanation."

She continued, "I am a jurist. Do you know what that means? I thought not. The term signifies that I am both a student and a teacher of law: truly a servant of the law, indeed. I am a Doctor of Law here at the university."

I couldn't hide my surprise. "A lawyer? But you're... you're a woman!"

11

She sighed. "Yes, I am indeed a woman. And a lawyer: I prefer the term *jurist*, as I said. I am aware of precisely how unusual that makes me. Nonetheless it is the truth. My sex has not rendered it... *easy*, that is true. When I was young, and desperate to study, the priests insisted I should become a nun: like the blessed Hildegard, they said, I should devote myself to the study of the scriptures.

"But I did not want to lock myself away, deny my womanhood and read only those sacred books approved for my use, for what the priests deemed a *woman's* understanding. That would be a dry, sterile sort of study." Her tone was bitter. "No, I was determined to study here, at our university in Bologna: to learn about the law. Did you know that Bologna is the heart of the study of law? No? Well, it is so - thanks to the fact that our library here holds a precious, rare, perhaps the *only* copy of the *Codex Justinianus*, the first part of the Emperor Justinian's *Codex Juris Civilis*, his code of civil law. Seven hundred years old, it enshrines the essence, the very letter of Roman law, the model to follow even now for all jurists and all makers of law.

"And so students of the law have been flocking here to learn for the best part of two centuries. My father was the one man who understood my desire, my... *lust* for the law! As a result, and after many battles, I was, I am, the only woman to have attained her doctorate here. Oh, you'll hear all kinds of rumours that, when I started out, I used to lecture from behind a screen lest my beauty should ... *distract* the students – young men, I should say – from the message of my lectures. They are just stories. Even in my youth, I was not beautiful. But I did adopt a lawyer's garb rather than the finery of women, and I still do. It is... *easier* that way."

"But your title," I stammered. "Forgive me: I have heard people name you *Magister*. But all the Latin I have learnt tells me that they should call you *Magistra*."

"You may have come from the street, but I see you are educated, Lorenzo. And you are right: my sex should demand the feminine version of the noun, *Magistra*. But I find it more... *convenient* to employ the masculine form. Then, by the time people learn that the lawyer and master is a woman, it is generally too late for them to change their mind. I have a living to make, you know." She smiled, again adding a warmth that transformed that severe face.

I could not help but return her smile. "Is that what I should call you, then: *Magister*?"

"You should. And you will. Only my superiors, the grand signori, the *magnati* who pay handsomely for my services, call me something else: and even they generally accord me the dignity of addressing me as *Dottore*. I am... *known* in the city, and in others." She had a curious way of pausing before an important word, and then overemphasising it, perhaps formed from years of giving legal advice or lecturing to students. It certainly added gravity to her pronouncements. In all the years I knew her I rarely heard her raise her voice: but she always commanded attention.

She became brisk and business-like. "Now, Lorenzo, what are we to do with you? It seems your back is healing nicely, so we had better find you a shirt: you cannot stay naked forever." So fascinated was I by this woman, so intrigued to know in whose house I found myself, that I had again grown oblivious to the fact that I had worn not a stitch of clothes since my arrival. Embarrassed for a second time, I tried to cover myself.

"Don't be silly, boy," she scolded. "I have been tending your bare flesh for the past month and more, so it is a little late now to be concerned about your modesty." I relaxed a little at that, but nonetheless made sure I lay on my front, propping myself up on my elbows (another position I could newly achieve!) while we conversed. "*Magistra, Magister*, will you tell me? Why did you save me? And why have you cared for me all these weeks?"

"I have already told you. I cannot bear to see cruelty inflicted as it was on you. There was injustice and inhumanity in it, and I abhor both. To be sure, to me the law is a stimulating intellectual discipline: but it is also a wondrous instrument of righteousness, and of protecting the weak and helpless from the overweening powerful and unjust."

"You said too that I reminded you of someone? Who was that?"

"We will not speak of that. Certainly not now: probably never. There are... *chapters* in my life that I do not reopen. And there was a third reason, if I am honest, which I try to be when it is... *prudent* to be so. But that too must wait. Besides, we must look forward, not back. What is to be done with you now?"

A sudden fear seized me, a terror of being cast out, left to fend for myself in the streets whose danger I had learnt in all too short a time. I reached out to seize her hand: that *did* hurt, and I gasped. "*Magister*, please don't send me away. I'll do anything. Let me serve you. I'll earn my keep! I'll do anything. I'll be your humblest, lowliest slave: but don't send me away."

My plea seemed to amuse her. She raised an eyebrow. "My *humblest* slave? I suspect, Lorenzo, that humility is not your... *strongest* suit."

"But, Magister, I could work for you. I can read and I can write." She remained impassive. "And I can sing, too. I could entertain you when you dine, and cheer you when you're sad. I can do that."

"I was teasing you, Lorenzo. You are not well enough to go anywhere at present. Have you tried to stand? Of course not. You will find you cannot do even that yet. Look how thin you are: it was hard to feed you or even give you drink when you were lying on your face, let alone when you were raving."

As in everything - well, almost everything - she was proved right. Michele was summoned, and commanded to bring a shirt. Slowly, gingerly, I was raised to a sitting position: for the first time in weeks my feet touched the floor. I was instructed to raise my hands above my head, and a shirt was dropped over them. With the Magister on one hand and Michele on the other I stood. It felt strange, and my head swam, but I remained standing. I was clothed, and I was upright. It was as if, for the first time in an age, I had become human again. I laughed for the sheer joy of being alive: and the other two laughed with me. So began my convalescence.

Chapter 3

Young bodies heal quickly: moreover, I am blessed with a robust constitution. Nonetheless, it took some time for me to appreciate how weak I was. Imagine a boy of that age barely able to walk across the room, certainly incapable of concentrating on anything for more than ten minutes.

That changed with remarkable speed. Within a week I was walking about normally, though I still tired quickly. And, as I grew stronger, much of the time I spent resting, when not asleep, was passed in dialogue with my new master, who began to quiz me about my life. She claimed she was at pains to keep my mind occupied so that I did not become bored and then seek to over-exert myself: but it was clear to me from the start that she was desperate to understand the strange set of circumstances that had brought me to her. Undoubtedly she cared about me: she had almost certainly saved my life, after all. But there was something more: a hint of urgency, of anxiety, underlay her gentle but thorough questioning.

While I was at my weakest, I think she restrained herself from asking about the ordeal from which she had rescued me. Instead she took me back to earlier parts of my life. Recalling snippets that, she said, she had gleaned from my feverish utterances, she would quote a name or a place that I had raved about, and coax me to fill in the history.

"So, Lorenzo: I know that you came here from Modena. And you tell me that Lorenzo is your name, but I know you have lived under other... *guises*. How is that?"

I was ready to share much with her. I had no reason to distrust her – quite the opposite – and found the process of recounting my tale comforting: she was an expert questioner, as I learned later when I watched her applying that skill to the law.

"It was a new name, Magister: a new name for my new life in this city. I ran away from Modena and, because I feared I might be pursued, I came to the place that is Modena's enemy. I thought I'd be safe here." I laughed bitterly at that irony: a sharp pain in my back reminded me of my wounds, causing me to gasp.

"But why flee Modena, Lorenzo? How could a boy of your age feel himself in such peril that he must run away?"

Where could I start? "Magister, I think you know I was a musician. I was a choirboy, in Modena's cathedral."

"Indeed? A wonderful calling to follow, in a … *magnificent* building."

"It is magnificent, Magister. That is true. But it is not a happy place: not for me, at least."

"Are you a good singer? Or were you, I should say: I can hear that you have lost your treble voice."

Was I good? How could I express it adequately? I was – I had been – the best. So I told her. How Modena's *duomo*, and the monks who inhabited it under the iron control of its Prior, had sought to fill it with music of a quality to match its spectacular architecture. And how, in order to boast a choir to equal or better any in Italy, it had stolen from a rival cathedral a boy chorister whose fame had reached it. At the age of ten or eleven, I had been kidnapped, snatched away from the glory of San Marco in Venice, transported like a parcel, and delivered into the arms of the Prior of Modena.

Whenever I tell my story, it is greeted with disbelief. Yet my fate was not an uncommon one. Cities vie with one another for power and prestige. Just as the most powerful leader, even the Holy Roman Emperor himself, is quick to secure the support of the Almighty by demonstrating his piety in alms and good works, a city's cathedral is central to its rivalry with its neighbours. Offers of money and fame might lure an outstanding *maestro di cappella* from one great church to direct the music in another. By contrast, a voice such as I had as a little boy might not be bought: but it could be stolen, and it was, frequently. I was only one of many to suffer that misfortune: I am told the practice continues nowadays (more than ever, indeed), as ecclesiastical music becomes increasingly sophisticated and cathedrals more ambitious.

I had a dazzling treble voice. At High Mass on a Sunday or feast day, when the music was particularly sumptuous and the great families of Venice came to church, I touched hearts with my soaring top notes. To me was entrusted the task of improvising the counterpoint, shaping an ornamental second melody, a descant above the chant. And when the choir broke into the leaping, jagged rhythms of the *hoquetus*, it was my voice that led the way and made the vaults and domes of the great church ring. I was good: and I knew it.

Praise was lavished on my singing: after a particularly grand service I would even receive occasional gifts in appreciation from the great and good of Venice. Once the Doge himself spoke to me in warm tones. The Cardinal Archbishop used to stop on occasions as he was processing from the church, patting me on the cheek (how his great ring scratched!) and congratulating me.

My fame spread: that is clear. And the price of that celebrity was to be abruptly torn away from the life and the people I knew, and deposited in Modena.

Having tried, in fits and starts, to explain all this to my master, I fell silent. She, too, paused: then she exclaimed, "Monstrous! To treat a little boy so – and, I presume, justified in the name of giving... *praise*.. and *glory* to God." Her manner of speaking, with those curious emphases, made me smile. "But, in truth, they sought only the glory of Modena."

Again she stopped, deep in thought. Then, "But did no one try to find you? Did your family not come searching for you?"

"I had no family. As far as I know, I'm an orphan. Don't feel sorry for me on that score: I was always kindly treated at San Marco, and I had good friends, like any boy. But whether anyone from St Mark's looked for me, I have no idea."

She was indignant. "Barabaric! This was... *enslavement!* That is a topic on which I have strong views, as you may discover. But your absence of family perhaps explains, forgive me, your.. *complexion*. Yours is not a face of the North."

How delicately she broached the topic! She was right. My kin, whoever they were, did not originate from the region in which I have spent all my conscious life. My skin is dark, resembling the deep suntan of those who work all their lives in the fields: perhaps the Berbers and Moors I have seen working their merchant ships or even the Saracen captives I have observed for sale in the slave-markets. My hair, too, was curly, messy (I have always worn it long) and completely black, though nowadays it is silver-white. Such features stand out. Northern Italians, with their blue eyes and fair hair, betray the Viking and German blood that runs in their veins, and readily look on those who hail from the south (which I presume I do) as no more than peasants, or perhaps as slaves, a term of abuse constantly directed at me by my fellow-choristers in Modena.

She continued. "And your name? They took that away from you, too?"

I nodded. "I hated them for that. I was christened Giovanni. I assume it was a precaution to change my name, in case Venice did start searching for me. The Prior thought it amusing to replace one Evangelist's name with another: so Giovanni became Luca."

My name was not the only thing that Modena's Prior took from me, though I could not have explained it to the Magister at the time, so I did not try. Moreover, they did not merely take it from me: they tore it from me by violence and fear. They stole my innocence. Not that attractive childish trust in other people, particularly in adults, though that was lost too: but my innocence as a musician, my readiness to sing for sheer love.

From my start as a chorister in Venice I was assured that I was singing to the glory of God. I rejoiced in singing for the Creator: I believed that my song reached up to heaven, just as the incense filled the domes of San Marco. I was in no doubt that God heard my voice, as beautiful as I could make it, exercised in gratitude for the gift that He had given me, giving Him thanks and glorifying Him in it.

How naïve that sounds now! My early days in Modena dispelled that illusion, if illusion it was. This was truly a loss of innocence.

That arbitrary rechristening of their captive, for so I felt myself, kindled a deep fury inside me. Disregarding my helplessness in his hands, I defied the Prior. I gritted my teeth and declared that I would not sing a note for him or his cathedral. He merely smiled, and ordered his minions to take me "downstairs", assuring me that I would swiftly learn to obey him. How right he was!

I am wryly amused whenever I hear people speak of the indomitability of the human spirit. Whatever hardships it endures, they assert, whatever loss or privations it experiences, that spark can never be quenched. They are cruelly mistaken. I know differently. Father Prior said he would break my will: he did so brutally and efficiently.

I spent probably two weeks in a cell, a subterranean hole lit only by a narrow shaft of light filtering down from above. I guess it had been built as a storeroom: to me it was a dungeon. I say I spent two weeks there: but the task of breaking me did not require that long. Keep a boy on his own, locked in a cell in near-darkness, beat him soundly every day and feed him bread and water barely sufficient to sustain him: his resistance will crumble in only a few days. At any rate, mine did.

I do not need to go into details. During that period I inhabited a solitary hell of pain, fear and isolation. On the third or fourth day, after a particularly savage beating supervised by the Prior (he was not a man to get his own hands dirty), I flung myself down, clutched his feet and begged him to let me demonstrate my readiness to cooperate and to sing to the best of my ability.

His reply was cold. "No, Luca. Not yet. I know you *think* you want to: but you do not believe it yet, not deep down. This will continue."

It did. When the beatings stopped, the days became dark and interminable. My longing for a visit from the Prior, a craving for human contact, was tempered by the terror of not knowing whether it would bring further torment, or whether he would accept my affirmative answer to the question, "Are you ready to do your duty, Luca?"

It was a heartless, vicious thing to do to a young boy. I used to pray that one day I would have Father Prior in my power, see him cringe helpless before me and teach him in his turn the meaning of pain and fear before granting him the release of death. Years later I was finally granted that opportunity, having nursed my hatred all that time. Fortunately for him, and for my eternal soul, I resisted the temptation to visit that long-desired vengeance upon him.

Age and distance bring perspective. I can see now that there was a calculated logic even in his cruelty. For me the human cost was almost insupportable: for the Prior it was purely pragmatic. Though my subsequent adventures revealed that, all along, he had been up to his ears in political intrigues and machinations, not least with those who became my enemies, he approached the task of taming his new prize choirboy as if he were breaking a horse. He did no more than was necessary, but accomplished it methodically and without compunction.

He needed the result. He was under pressure to have his prominent new singer performing in the cathedral to the greater glory of the Bishop (I have no doubt that the glory of the Almighty was a lesser consideration): and his brutal method achieved the desired result swiftly. Had he bothered to consider the matter, which I am certain he did not, he might even have judged that it saved me months or years of turmoil: he put me straight in no time.

The young are resilient and recover rapidly. I am not convinced that the experience, terrible as it was at the time, scarred me in any lasting way, though it left me with an instinctive suspicion of the clergy and a particular susceptibility to the pleas of a child in distress. Like my master before me, I am what my friends call a soft touch.

When my tearful pleadings finally convinced the Prior of my sincere desire to do as he required, I quickly mastered the repertoire and learnt the cathedral's practices and customs.

I sang well. No, I sang superbly. Even the Prior nodded in affirmation while the Bishop, delighted to hear his choir so improved and adding lustre to the building that enhanced his power and status, would occasionally pat me on the cheek in the way that the Cardinal Archbishop of Venice had done.

I had been brought up in the belief that the music I sang, the finest work of human minds, complimented the architecture, the consummate creation of human hands. Once I had settled to the work in Modena's *duomo* and discovered by trial and error how I might cause its intricately-wrought marble to ring in response to my high notes, I could sometimes feel it as I had once done in Venice: but now I was even more skilled. I was singing directly to the Almighty, humanity's chosen vessel to carry its praise to the Throne of Glory.

Almost. Yet something had changed in me. I had become an actor. I was singing to God, but I was no longer singing *for* him: and I felt that He knew it. He had turned his back on me in that cell, and I was singing now not for joy or glory, but because it was my job. It was my side of the bargain: no more darkness, loneliness or pain, so long as I sang, and did so expertly.

In purely musical terms that change was the making of me. I became truly a professional. In time I could sing anything that was asked. I brought all my skill and experience to bear: by the time I was thirteen or fourteen, I had accumulated a great deal of both. My voice, my very talent, was like the sluices that I had seen controlling the canals in Venice: I could open the gate and the music, like the water of the *canali*, would pour forth.

The realisation made me effective. I knew how far to push an improvisation without confusing or unsettling the rest of the choir. It is not as hard as it sounds. The improvisation of a well-crafted *duplum* is a matter of aiming for the next cadence: at the end of the phrase the counterpoint must reach consonance with the cantus, a perfect interval five or eight notes apart – or a unison. In between it is all about creating a line that moves contrary to the cantus, even creating a passing dissonance with it, discord followed by perfect harmony, a metaphor for life and for our human relationship with the Almighty.

My judgment was keen, my ear as good as any musician's I have known. I could hear what was happening in the choir around me, every inflection, even whether my fellow singers were confident or uncertain: and I could temper my contribution accordingly.

Finely judged and calculated, my improvisation could simulate the very heights of religious devotion. I could replicate the ecstasies of the saints: but no longer did it come from the depths of my soul. It was cold, emotionless. Like a mercenary soldier who fights not to save his city or country, but because someone pays him, I sang because it was my job to do so. And, like a mercenary, that knowledge perhaps made me more skilful and reliable than those around me who sang out of religious fervour.

Perhaps I should explain how a choir worked in those days. We stood around an enormous wooden lectern upon which rested a great book. There in bold, black letters was inscribed the text that we sang and, above the words, a variety of marks and signs to remind us how the music went.

That sounds primitive nowadays. In this modern world, where musicians grandly describe their work as the *Ars Nova*, the New Art, every note and rhythm is precisely set down, so there can be no mistake. But when I was a boy (how often I say that, now I am an old man!), Maestro Guido d'Arezzo was still working on developing a notation that could be read by all: but it was as yet relatively new and remained far from standardised across the great churches and choirs of the Holy Roman Empire.

What a training this offered me, a set of techniques that I developed quite unconsciously, yet which have saved my life on numerous occasions. I learned to listen: to memorise; to discern and imitate voices and tones. Naturally I also learned to read and write, and to understand and translate Latin.

Some of this I explained to my master. Much was, back then, beyond my ability to put into words. Indeed, some of it I have come to understand only much later in life. And, as often happened in those early conversations, it felt as if we had reached the end of a chapter. Wearied by my account, I fell silent and, I think, dozed off in my chair, for when I looked up once more I was alone.

Chapter 4

Another few days of rest, healing and short walks, and there came another gently probing question from my Master. "Lorenzo, you may not remember it, but when you were talking in your pain and drugged sleep, you spoke much of someone called Tommaso. Who is he?"

How could I do justice to Tommaso, my sole ally in those early days in Modena? But for his friendship, offered spontaneously and generously, I think I might have gone mad. Once my harsh lesson was completed, and I had demonstrated that I could apply my singing skills diligently and to the Prior's satisfaction, I was permitted to sleep in the dormitory with the other boys; follow their regime, with the same freedoms and curbs; and live as, well, one of the boys.

I quickly learned that I had swopped one ordeal, loneliness, for the new challenge of establishing my place in the pecking order of a group of rumbustious and, compared to the choir in Venice, rough boys. There were eight other boys in the choir at the time. Five were little ones, learning the business of being a chorister from three who regarded themselves as seniors. The two eldest, named Guglielmo and Elio, saw themselves as leaders of the group and made it their business to render my life miserable. They knew I was the better reader and singer, and were quick to employ both their sharp, hurtful tongues and their fists in maintaining their position.

Next in the unofficial hierarchy came Tommaso: dear, dearest Tommaso. Younger than us seniors by a year or so, he was short, round and cheerful of countenance and the kindest, most generous person I have ever known - excepting, perhaps, my master. While the two eldest choristers bullied the younger boys, and extracted savage enjoyment from persecuting me, Tommaso was one of those characters who escape bullying: it was simply not worth trying to torment him. He was placid and content, the peacemaker of the group. If they made a joke at his expense he would laugh along with them.

I, on the other hand, have always been thin-skinned. Too concerned about what people think of me, my swift and angry reaction to any perceived slight offered Guglielmo and Elio an irresistible temptation. As our exchanges became more heated,

Tommaso would interposed himself physically between us. "Lads, that's enough. Luca, stop picking fights. And you two," he would wag his finger at Guglielmo and Elio, "Let him be." As often as not, they did.

Smaller than me, younger but infinitely wiser, Tommaso alone could calm my rages. "Why do you react to them, Luca? It's only because they see they've needled you that they carry on. Just ignore them."

"But it's so unfair. I'm better than them, and they know it."

"Of course they know it. They're scared of you, Luca, of how good you are. That's why they do it. Ignore them, and enjoy the fact that they're jealous."

It did not change immediately. It never does. But gradually I did learn to ignore them, even to smile when their own resentment and insecurity became so obvious. And always Tommaso was there, unobtrusively calming situations, pouring oil on the waters that we so readily troubled. We became inseparable. My younger companion loved to ask about my previous life in Venice, wondering at my stories of the seaport and the glories and civic pride of that great city.

Like all truly generous people he was modest. He admired my musicianship, always asking me how he could improve, convinced that he was barely up to the task set him each day. I did help him, where I could, and also with his reading and writing in which, never bad, he became stronger all the time. Meanwhile I in turn marvelled at the way he played the rebec, which he sat on his knee and sounded with a bow of horsehair.

Back then we called that little pear-shaped, three-stringed instrument with its bent neck a *lira*: nowadays it is generally termed a rebec. It played no part in church, but when we sang for the Bishop's great feasts, which occurred with some frequency, we would perform *conductus*, folk songs and even love-songs. Then his playing would sustain the key notes while the others held the melody and I would improvise descants. At such times I could occasionally forget my determination to sing for my own selfish purpose, lose myself in the music, and relish the joy of making it with Tommaso.

My friend made me ashamed, too, though he did not mean to. I had largely dispelled my anger, or at least controlled it: yet by contrast his patience and loyalty made me feel selfish and petulant. I loved that boy, loved him for his generosity and patience - but, above all, simply for being there. I had a real comrade for the first time and, for a while, my life became immeasurably happier.

Again I appeared to have reached the end of an episode, so I stopped and pondered, wondering how my friend fared in Modena without me – whether, indeed, he was even missing me, and praying that he did, although I would not have hurt him for the world. But my master had not finished her probing for the day. Gently, so quietly that I could barely hear her, she murmured, "And Rosalia? What of her? You spoke of her a great deal."

Rosalia. Why did my young heart, too young really to understand love, ache at the mention of her name? I grimaced, the warm memories associated with her name bringing with them the remembrance of loss.

"I'm sorry, Lorenzo. Do your wounds still pain you?"

I smiled at her. "No, Magister – or rarely, at any rate. But this memory brings hurt as well as joy."

So I told her how, one day early in our friendship, as the weeks of summer stretched out endlessly after Pentecost, with barely a feast-day to break the monotony, Tommaso was unusually diffident. "Luca," he ventured, "There's something I want to ask you." He fell silent, as if he could not find the words to frame his question. Eventually he continued.

"Luca, you have no family, have you? Never had a home, never had people to go and see, not even once a year?"

"No, Tommasino. No family. Not even any friends, real friends – except you." I paused, diffidently. Such confidences did not come easily to us boys. "Sometimes I try to picture what a family would be like, but I can't really. Though, if I had one, I'd want you to be my brother."

"I *will* be your brother, Luca: of course I will. I'd like nothing better: let's be brothers! And..." He was reaching the difficult part of his question. "Luca, perhaps you don't know that, the Sunday after the Feast of the Assumption, we boys are allowed home for a few days to visit our families. It's the only time in the year they let us go, partly so we can help with harvest. And I wondered, well," it came out in a rush. "I wondered if you would like to come home and meet my family."

I was astonished. I had never received any invitation of that kind, and did not know how to respond. Tommaso took my hesitation as reluctance.

"Of course, you don't have to. I didn't mean to ask too much."

As usual his kindness helped me to cope with an awkward situation. "Tommasino, forgive me. I didn't know what to say. No one's ever asked me anything like that. I'd love to come home with you: but I don't think I'd even know how to behave, what to do."

The tension immediately evaporated. Tommaso laughed, back to his usual, carefree self. "That's easy, I'll tell you! Just be you - except don't be an idiot, and keep your temper!" We laughed as I threw myself on him and we scuffled good-naturedly, as boys do.

It was agreed. As the weather reached its hottest, and we feared we should lose all grip on sanity if we had to sing even one more service, the Assumption arrived, that great feast on which the Church celebrates the Falling Asleep of the Mother of Jesus. We were granted a few days away, including the next Sunday, during which the cathedral would be without music, a long-standing tradition of giving the choir a holiday, albeit a brief one.

On the appointed day, Tommaso and I set out from Modena. His home was a day's walk to the northwest. "Just as well it's in that direction," observed Tommaso. "Many of the farms to the East were destroyed in the fighting with the bloody Bolognese." We took with us in a knapsack water, bread and sausage provided for our journey, plus his beloved rebec, wrapped in linen cloth for protection, and set out in good spirits. By the end of the day we were weary from our walk, having failed to meet any passing cart that might have given us a lift. But Tommaso knew the road and eventually, around sunset, he cried, "There's my home. I can see it!" Excitedly he broke into a run, which I did my best to match.

I had no idea what to expect: I had never seen a farm. In truth, it was a poor place, a low building of timber with a thatched roof, the animals living at one end, the family at the other. Every bit of the land around it, not a large patch, was tilled, sown or used for pasture. Agriculture was clearly a hard life.

Tommaso called out as he approached the door. Immediately two people appeared, whom I took to be his parents. He flung himself at them, and they hugged him to themselves, almost fighting to take turns to pull him close. I hung back, unsure of myself, a stranger to such affectionate greetings. Remembering himself, Tommaso pulled himself away from his parents, came back to me and said, "Papà, Mamma, this is Luca. He's my friend, and the best friend anyone could have."

I stepped forward and bowed, shyly, to his mother. Instantly I was enveloped in a warm, comforting embrace. "Luca, any friend of our son is welcome here. And we thank you for your friendship to him."

She released me, straightened up, wiped a tear from her eye and said brightly, "You boys must be starved after your journey. Now, wash the dust from your feet and sit here in the evening sun. And Papà and I will bring you food."

As we washed our hands and feet, I became aware that we were being watched. Three faces with big staring eyes peeped at us around the doorframe. Tommaso's delight was plain to see. "Tommasino!" cried the eldest. The two little ones, the youngest barely more than a toddler, echoed the cry of "Maso! Masino!" Gently prizing her hands from around his neck, Tommaso disentangled himself from the eldest girl's arms. "Luca, this is Rosalia."

We looked at each other. Shyly we both murmured, "Hello," and then fell silent. I had not seen many girls in my cloistered existence, and had never been introduced to one. In her turn I suppose she had never met a friend of the brother she adored.

It was more than mere strangeness that afflicted me. Even at the age of eleven or twelve Rosalia was exceptional. She was fine-boned, almost elfin, her slimness and poise striking beyond the mere skinniness of a girl-child. Her eyes were blue and lustrous, and she had thick, long hair of a startling deep-red colour. Red hair is uncommon but not unheard of in the north of Italy. As I came to know Tommaso's family I realised that all the girls, and indeed his mother, had a hint of auburn in their hair: but Rosalia's flame-coloured glory was a rarity indeed. So was her magical smile.

I know. It sounds as if I am just repeating the old saw about love at first sight. Yet what did I know of love? I was a self-centred, callow boy. The whole of my life had taught me that survival and negotiating terms with the circumstances in which I found myself was the only way to get by. What had I learned of giving my heart, or anything else, to someone else? Even the practice of giving alms, so often preached to us in church, meant little to us boys who had no possessions and were never paid for our work in the choir: we were told often enough that we were lucky to be fed, housed and educated. By the standards of our time, it was probably true: we *were* fortunate, though one should never expect a child to recognise the fact.

Perhaps it was simple shyness. There was an endless silence as Rosalia and I looked at each other. It was broken by Tommaso who called the little ones to him, gave them a hug and said, "Come on, girls. Show me the farm. Tell me how the animals are: and I want to know everything you've been doing since I was last here!"

With a happy shriek the two littlest girls seized his hands and mine between them and, pulling Rosalia with them too, showed us around their small-holding with such pride and excitement that it might have been a great country estate.

Tommaso's sisters insisted on pointing out and naming every living creature on the farm. Even the six lambs, identical to my untutored eye, had individual names. There had been a seventh, they explained: but (said Maria, the youngest, with a hint of reproach), "Papà killed him to feed you."

"Yes," added her sister, Rita. "Mamma said we must make a special feast."

Tommaso grimaced. "Every year I tell them not to make a fuss," he complained. "And every year they do this: I know they deny themselves in winter as a result."

That welcoming meal, like all those that we enjoyed during our few days with them, was a banquet to me, used only to the plain but adequate food that we received in the choir, and in Venice before that (though we observed enough fine foods being consumed when we served or sang for the Bishop). There was ham, cured from their own pigs. There were strips of thinly-rolled dough, satisfying and filling, a food we were fed in plenty in Modena, as it is a convenient way to fill the stomachs of growing boys: but never in such generous broth, thickened with pulses and flavoured with onions that hung in strings from every beam and herbs which we picked fresh or pulled from the bunches around the hearth. The chunks of lamb, spit-roasted, were of a richness I had never encountered: I think my lifelong partiality for roasted meats must stem from that visit. We boys drank watered wine, fermented from the family's own grapes.

In terms of food it seemed to me that the family lived like kings and queens. I said as much to Tommaso, who replied, "It's true that the good times *are* good. But if there is a harsh winter, and the cured meat runs short, or the crops fail, then there's hunger in this valley."

With hindsight I can see that the farm was a poor place. To be sure, everywhere in the colossal plain through which the Po meandered was fertile, so the trees were groaning under the weight of fruit: there were vines yielding grapes in profusion, row upon row of bean plants whose crop would see them through the winter, pigs rooting about in the muck, and chickens getting under everyone's feet. Yet Tommaso's parents looked old before their time. Farming was a hard life, even in a place where nature was generally kind to them. Similarly the house, which in high summer we entered only to sleep, was stark and plain. When we sat down to eat uproariously happy family meals, we sat on bench seats around a table erected from planks and trestles. As Tommaso told me, it was a simple way to live - but it appeared to me a wholesome one.

All these years later, I am still moved when I remember the family's hospitality, their open-hearted welcome to me, a strange and awkward boy, and the love all of them felt and showed for Tommaso.

During the evening there was uproar as more visitors arrived. Tommaso's two elder brothers had come home to greet him. They found work on larger farms whose owners, even in those days, mostly preferred to pay skilled labourers than rely on the half-hearted efforts of slaves. They still came home to help with harvest or ploughing, of course, and for the next few days we all worked from dawn till dusk picking fruit and vegetables so that the girls and Tommaso's mother could take them to market to sell.

Then we men (for so we boys termed ourselves) set to and harvested the grain. In truth, Tommaso and I lacked both the strength and the skill to achieve much, but his brothers wielded their sickles and reaped with an easy motion while we were put to threshing. That was hard, unskilled work, and we sweated and groaned through the task. Yet there was good cheer, and at night we rested aching limbs, tired but proud of our manly accomplishments, and feasted again. Then Tommaso fetched his rebec and asserted that we should sing and play to the family.

We gave them a few of the songs and *conductus* we would sing at banquets in Modena. I could see our audience was listening politely, but our music was unfamiliar to them. At last Rosalia put her hand on Tommaso's arm and said gently, "Tommasino, that music's too fine for us. Play one of the old songs, those that Mamma sings to us." He smiled, and started playing a pretty melody, a sentimental love-song about a woman who loses her love to battle. Immediately all the family joined in, the little girls in their thin, breathy voices, the men in deep, hearty tones, while Rosalia stood up, put her hands behind her back as if reciting and sang the words of the bereft widow, a simple, beautiful harmony.

I learned that evening that beauty need not be complex. On the contrary, ever since then, when seeking to create something of surpassing glory, I have striven for clarity and simplicity. Not when trying to impress in cathedral music, of course: there I mastered counterpoint in intricate patterns, achieving grandeur though complexity. Even now, though little remains of my once fine voice, if I want to move an audience I know it is a few notes perfectly placed that work the magic. Rosalia taught me that, unwittingly, all those years ago.

I sat and listened, captivated. Rosalia caught my eye and mouthed, "Sing with me." And she embarked on another love song, one that has been close to my heart ever since, and still touches my soul when I hear it: *Ti canterò lo meo amor*, I shall sing my love to you.

How could I refuse her invitation to join her in song? I forgot all my skill and training and lost myself in the music, singing along with her and ornamenting: not too much, just a little, creating – what? It felt like perfection. Perhaps it was merely rustic and primitive: but it moved all of us. Surprised, we were all silent at the end: but only for a moment. As constantly happened in that family back then, there was a spontaneous outburst of joy and laughter, and we ate, drank and sang some more.

Living their life for even a few days brought home to me the fact that this farm was not the rural idyll it appeared in a good time. The brothers' earnings were needed to help the family through the barren winter when supplies ran low and there was still rent to pay. "You stay in your smart city, Tommasino," they would say. "Become a great man there!" It was good-natured joshing, all the family joining in. They seemed convinced that his training in the city would somehow transform him into a *magnato*, a lord. He smiled, never boasted or made grand promises, but nonetheless let them have their way.

All too soon our six-day leave came to its end. Tommaso's father had located a drover who was taking an ox-cart of goods most of the way to Modena, so we were able to beg a ride, saving our feet the long, wearisome walk. As we left we all embraced, yet spoke scarcely a word, fearing perhaps that, if one of us started, we might all finish by crying. As Rosalia hugged me she whispered, watery-eyed, "Come and sing with me again, Luca."

As the cart rolled away, and we both waved from the back, I wondered how Tommaso could remain so calm. But when a slight rise in the road hid his home from our sight, I stole a glance sideways: great tears were rolling down his face, though he never made a sound. I put my arm around him, and he rested his head on my shoulder as his weeping continued.

Chapter 5

My new master constantly scolded me for being thin, and putting on weight to her satisfaction proved a challenge, since I was by nature a gangly, skinny youth. In truth, I ate like a horse. Mamolo, the sour-faced cook, was ordered to cook me every kind of meat: I gorged on beef, pork and lamb; sometimes there was fish; always a mountain of little packages of dough, painstakingly rolled from fine wheat flour, not the cheaper rice-flour to which I was accustomed, then filled with herbs, ham or cheese and cooked in rich broth.

I spent many hours watching Mamolo as he cooked, fascinated at his skill, worn down by his grumbling. He was one of life's self-appointed victims, always (in his view) put upon, misjudged and undervalued. Out of anger and resentment he had poisoned a previous employer and, it seemed, some members of his family. He was never clear about how the Magister saved him from the torture and death he had earned as punishment.

But here he was now, living out a sentence *sine die* of repaying the debt by serving her. He appeared not to resent that, at least, though he seemed incapable of displaying genuine gratitude. Periodically the Magister would appear in the corner of the courtyard he called his kitchen (and jealously guarded), and demand to know why I wasn't getting fatter. Mamolo would reply with a whine that I was eating them all out of house and home. "I can barely feed this gluttonous boy on what you give me, let alone the rest of us," he moaned.

My master would sigh. "If you need more, ask Michele. He keeps the purse. Just get that boy strong." And Mamolo would clatter his pots and pans tetchily, ensuring that the entire household was aware of his displeasure.

There would follow a squabble between Michele and Mamolo. The cook would cavil and wheedle, claiming that he couldn't possibly feed four mouths on the pittance he was allowed for food. Michele would call him a "mitherable, thieving, murderouth thtreak of pith" who was always "trying to poithon uth" with the muck he cooked. Mamolo would shriek abuse in return, calling Michele an ignorant brute who would eat a turd if he served it up to him in a garlic sauce. Each would threaten to kill the other:

then Michele would grudgingly hand over a few more coins, and the uneasy truce was restored.

It was pure theatre, and I delighted in it. All the while I became stronger, though I gained little weight. I was one of those boys who remain skinny however much they eat: through my adulthood and even in my current old age I may consume as much food as I like without getting fatter, to the dismay of those around me who worry about their spreading bellies.

Michele was assigned to getting me fit again. The regime began with exercises. If I failed to stretch my ruined back, he assured me, the healed wounds would shrink and the muscles tighten until I was a cripple, bent and deformed. So he would bend and extend me until I shrieked with pain and frustration: but every day I moved more freely and felt stronger. After a while I could hang from a beam by my hands and pull my feet upwards. Eventually I was able haul my whole weight up until my face was level with the wood. I could bend down and touch my toes. Every day it hurt less and I felt stronger.

I was impatient. Nowadays I look back at my young self and laugh at my eagerness to be fit and ready without delay. Still, if Michele was philosophical and knew the process would take time, he was nonetheless never satisfied. He had me running up and down the stairs (it was a modest, creaking two-storey house, not one of Bologna's great towers) for ten minutes, then for twenty. I would strip to my breeches, no longer shy about the scars on my back, gradually changing from raw wounds to livid red lines, and the sweat would pour from me, even as winter drew on.

Soon he decided that there was insufficient exercising space in the house and its little courtyard: so he borrowed a horse. My master and her servants appeared able to borrow anything at need: it was as if the whole city owed her a favour (which perhaps it did). We would head out east along the Via Æmilia, along the rough but timeless Roman paving. He would walk or trot, and I would be required to run beside him. After what felt like an age I could run for an hour, sometimes more, constantly threatened, bullied, cajoled, promised a beating, denied my supper. The threats were always empty, and made me laugh: but I was becoming stronger and fitter than I had been in all my life.

Next Michele decided that he needed to toughen me up. What was the use of being able to run for an hour or two, if I had no idea how to defend myself? So, when he judged I was strong enough, he taught me to fight. He had been a professional fighter once, wrestling and fist-fighting in taverns for bets and prizes: that was where he had lost his teeth. He had also been hired to provide protection for one or two of the great families of *magnati* (they all employed bodyguards), though he refused to name which.

He had certainly been a thief, because (inevitably) our master had found him languishing in a gaol somewhere, procured his freedom and engaged him, bound to her by the liberty he owed her, as her doorkeeper, protector, purse-keeper and general factotum. Certainly the tradesmen and vendors who came to the house hesitated to try anything on with him: anyone overcharging or being difficult received short shrift. And, just inside the door, there was a wicked-looking cudgel that he carried when he accompanied the Magister on her many trips out on business, for she was constantly in demand.

I cannot claim that Michele ever made a real fighter of me, not in his terms. But he taught me to defend myself, in the way he knew best. He invited me to punch him. I liked him, so I was reluctant. But eventually he goaded and persuaded me, and I swung a punch at his head, as hard as I could. Of course it never landed. Instead he was somewhere else, while a slap, apparently from nowhere, made my head ring.

Thus my training commenced. For weeks I never managed to land a punch or a kick on him or wrestle him to the ground: always it was I on the receiving end. But gradually I learned some of the tricks and eventually even made contact.

The days of healing turned into weeks, and then into months. It was not all easy, and I was constantly frustrated by the sheer feebleness that would engulf me while Michele was goading me onward. We became fast friends: you cannot wrestle, box and knock one another about without either falling out or becoming close. We achieved the latter outcome, though I rarely laid a finger on him.

Still those quiet inquisitions would occur, most often after my master had enjoyed her dinner, which I had served to her: by this stage I had become in effect a member of her household, though I was unaware of any such decision being taken or even discussed – least of all with me. "So, Lorenzo. You have told me much of your life in Modena, and even a little of Venice before that. And I know about your dear friend Tommaso - and," she smiled mischievously as I felt my face become hot, "The torch you carry for his sister Rosalia. But I have yet to understand why you left that city for Bologna: and how you came to be a captive and victim of torture in the tower of Massimo Lambertazzi."

"Lambertazzi? The great ball of lard told me that was his name before he had me nearly beaten to death. I shall kill him one day."

She laughed. "I do not think you will find it easy to approach, let alone slay, so...*grand* a personage. Nonetheless, this begs the question: why should so powerful member of Bologna's *magnati* have any interest in an orphan who, by your own admission, was begging on the streets of Bologna?"

Reluctantly, I began to retrace in my mind the path that had taken me to Lambertazzi's dungeon. Much of it I could share with her. But there were parts that I could not, dared not disclose – not even to the woman who had saved my life, worthless as it had appeared then, and given me the new one which already I so relished.

That first time at Tommaso's home remained the happiest memory of my childhood: though there were subsequent visits, the joy almost as great, Rosalia's presence increasingly intoxicating, but the parting harder each time. Generously Tommaso would swear that my presence made his homecoming all the better. Nonetheless one such episode gave rise to the only time we really quarrelled.

A few days after returning from my third or fourth trip to his home, and back into the usual routine, I could see he was not himself. "What's the matter?" I asked. "Are you feeling homesick? Missing your family?"

He nodded glumly. "Then why do you come back? Why not stay with your family? Every summer I see how happy you all are together: why don't you stay there, instead of coming back to this place?" The Cathedral seemed especially dull and gloomy on our return.

"Oh, Luca, don't you understand anything? You're so busy being this great singer that you can't see what's going on around you."

"I can see one thing. You're unhappy: so why not leave all this? Go home?"

"You see nothing! My parents can't feed all of us: they still have the girls to look after. Oh, I know the farm looked fine when we were there, with all the fruit and crops ready for harvest: but it won't be like that in winter, I can tell you. Besides, here I learn about more than just music. You and I are learning to read and write: we understand Latin. For families who are poor, my education is a wonderful gift. And you know, because they told you enough times, my parents think I'll become a great man!"

We looked at each other, pondering his impending greatness: and burst out laughing. That might have ended it, but my ignorance made me persist.

"Why doesn't your father rent more land? Your brothers could help cultivate it, and then you'd have a bigger farm, with more food to eat and even plenty to sell?"

"He can't just rent more land. All the land is controlled by the great lords, the *magnati*. A man like my father can rent only enough land to feed his family – and to sell the spare produce to pay his rent, if the harvest is good. But no more than that. The lords don't want people like us becoming rich: they keep us where we are, poor. That suits them perfectly."

"I don't see why."

"In God's name, Luca, why are you so stupid?"

I bridled at this. "I'm not stupid."

"Yes, you are. You don't seem to notice or understand anything. You're so bound up with your singing, so busy complaining that you shouldn't be here, that you're blind. And deaf! Don't you take any notice of what Father Prior and the Bishop talk about with their important guests? They talk of nothing but rents and the price of grain. It's all about money to them, and keeping hold of it."

"I've never noticed."

"I know. That's what I'm complaining about! We spend enough time serving at their table. Don't you listen while you're standing behind their chairs ready to fill their cups? You don't, do you? They spill all their secrets while they're stuffing their faces.

"You don't believe me? Let me give you an example. We knew about the plan to kidnap you and bring you to Modena weeks before it happened: we even knew your real name. Giovanni, wasn't it? I thought so. And they brought you most of the way by sea and river? You see, Luca: those who have nothing learn to live by their wits. You have far sharper wits than I'll ever have: but you don't use them."

He fell silent. Unusually for me, I did not feel like arguing further. In truth, he had made me feel stupid, and I resented it. I stared at my feet. After a few minutes' heavy silence, I looked at him. He was still flushed, angered mostly by the fact that his friend had failed to appreciate the reality of his life. There were tears in his eyes: when he saw that I had noticed, he wiped them away angrily.

For the first time in my life I felt someone else's pain. "So you don't want to be here, then?" He shook his head, not trusting himself to speak. "But you stay because your family want you to – need you to?" The merest nod. "And, when you go home, it makes it worse, because you have to leave again?"

His voice fell to a whisper. "This last time, I almost didn't go. Except that you wanted to. Then I thought I wouldn't be able to leave: but at least, when I leave now, one thing helps me to bear it. I have you. I have a friend."

Like a pair of young lovers we clung to each other, and both shed tears. When our sobbing abated we separated, embarrassed - as boys always are when they have revealed too much of themselves. We sat silently, lost in our own thoughts. Mine took a strange turn. I knew what Tommaso had been crying for: but what was *my* pain? I could not say, certainly could not articulate it.

A resolve hardened in my mind: while I was in thrall to Modena's cathedral and its clergy, for so I still perceived my service, I determined that I would learn everything I could from the adults who controlled my life. I would make the most of my lessons in music, in Latin, in writing. And, when performing those endless chores around the men who were oblivious to the service we provided at their tables, cleaning their rooms and emptying their chamber-pots, I would take Tommaso's advice and use my eyes and ears. I would use the knowledge and skill I gained to break out of that seductive, too-comfortable slavery.

We still did not speak: but, when I looked across to my friend, I swore to myself that I would share any advantage I gained with him. That was the first of many vows I have made in my life that I have broken.

Chapter 6

I put my plan into operation. We were by now the two most senior boys in the choir, and had charge of the little ones, teaching them the rules and the ways of the choir and leading them in the other duties required of us. We discharged these tasks with kindness, not bullying. In those few years, at least, we ensured that the life of all the boys in the choir was, if not entirely happy, at least free from fear.

As the eldest we were generally expected to serve together at meals for the Bishop's most important guests. Thus I was able to learn from Tommaso, and soon I became even more adept than he. My face completely blank, I would listen to every conversation. And when, out of some degree of natural caution, one of the interlocutors would drop his voice, I would lean forward to pour wine.

Our masters' conversation was, like most people's, largely banal. Yet, even when it was routine, even dull, I nonetheless gleaned much about local politics and came to understand more of Tommaso's family's world, that of agriculture. I discovered when to listen more carefully, without showing it. My musical ear helped me. So attuned was I to the varying tones and pitches of voices that I did not have to look to see who was speaking: very quickly I would recognise the voices and tuck them away in my aural memory.

The Bishop's most frequent visitors were the powerful landowners of the area, the *magnati* of whom Tommaso complained on behalf of his family. "How are your rents coming in?" the Bishop enquired one evening - more, I suspected, out of politeness than interest. The subject of his question was Signor Uguzzoni, a squarely built little man richly dressed in silks and furs, a regular guest at his table who helped himself liberally to the finest foods.

"You know how these peasants are. They pay late and grudgingly, forever making excuses about poor harvests. My bailiff threw two off their land last week: it encourages the others, at least."

"I suppose it's hard for the poor when the rains come late and ruin the grain," a churchman commented mildly.

"Hard? They need to work longer days. Or employ more hands: there are plenty needing work in these times."

"And what of your own lands? Are you still using slaves?"

"Aye, for now," sighed Uguzzoni. "My foreman swears paid hands do a swifter job: but always they want more money. My serfs (I prefer that term) cost little – and they know they won't eat if they don't work. However, my Lord Bishop, you must know more than I on this topic. Will the Pope support this move from the Bolognese, damn their eyes, to put an end to serfdom there – and here?"

"I am not privy to His Holiness's thoughts on the matter," replied the Bishop urbanely. "But we find ourselves at an interesting moment. Certainly here in Modena the big landowners such as you cannot imagine running their estates without serfs. But in Bologna they see things differently. It is the merchants, not the great families, who nowadays run things there. They see purpose only in buying and selling, making and trading: in their hard-nosed commercial world they see little value in owning serfs."

"But His Holiness will not support an overturning of the natural way of things? Men have always been masters or slaves."

"To be sure, the Church's teachings do not abhor slavery. Saint Paul is clear on the need for every man to know his station. But there are – how may I put it? - powerful factions. I know that negotiations are taking place, but I am not party to them. I suspect the Gatekeeper will play a role: the advice His Holiness receives from that quarter will carry weight."

"The Gatekeeper? How can one man wield such influence?"

"By being everywhere, and always well informed. The Gatekeeper moves invisibly between all the parties."

"Bah! Who is the Gatekeeper, anyway? It is just a silly handle, a nickname for a ghost."

I paused in telling my story, and looked at my master. "So you see, Magister, I had heard the name, Gatekeeper. And even I, merely a servant at the table of the great, could tell that this was a plot. And that the name meant danger."

"And you heard no more about him? Or of the import of the conversation."

"Alas, no, Magister. I... I was sent out to fetch more wine, and when I returned they had gone back to talking about farming."

It was lying to her. To my lasting shame, I withheld the meat of the information from my master. I know now – indeed, I understood all too soon – that, had I shared all that I knew with her at this first telling, I might have been spared much pain and sorrow. But I had learned caution, and exercised it now. Even to her, to whom I owed so much, I supplied only minimal information.

For much more had happened at that dinner.

"He is no ghost, my friend." A fresh voice cut in, an extraordinary voice. "We see evidence of his work, his meddling, wherever we turn. As to his identity, if we knew that, we might know what was about to befall."

From my vantage point behind the Bishop, I looked across the table. The speaker was a tall, elegant figure (even seated, his height was obvious). His shoulder-length black hair black was just beginning to betray flecks of grey: his garments were sleek and expensive, their cloth, leather and fur all jet-black.

His voice was more distinctive than his clothing, however. It was suave with a reedy edge, reminding me of the sound of the bass *cialamello*, the double-reeded Italian shawm. Yet that instrument's sound is harsher than that voice was, in truth. It was as if its owner mellowed its rasp with balm of oil and honey to furnish a silky timbre. One could imagine such a voice persuading, cajoling, comforting, always convincing its hearer of the wisdom of its argument.

I write this with the benefit of hindsight, of course. On first hearing, its tone might indeed have seemed warm and friendly. But for me the voice of the man who, though I had as yet no idea, was to become my implacable enemy has always been fraught with malice. It has rung in my ears on too many

41

occasions when, powerless in the grip of his schemes, I have faced torment and insupportable loss at his hands. Even in my old age, when I am reminded of it, I shudder. And, though long years have softened me and allowed me to shed most of the anger I carried for so long, the mere mention of Bartolomeo Bardi causes me to shake with hatred. I become another character entirely, the kindly old gentleman of whom my Bolognese neighbours are wont to speak generously engulfed in a moment by inchoate fury, cursing and spitting in impotent rage.

All that harm was to come much later. In my earliest encounters with my enemy I was a boy of no consequence, far beneath his lofty notice and of no significance to the intricate plots he wove.

"You are right, Signor Bardi," replied the Bishop who, finding his glass empty, turned to me testily. "Boy! More wine: don't just stand there!" Staring at Bardi, I had been neglecting my duty. As I reached forward to refill the Bishop's glass, he leaned away from me, across the table towards Bardi, and muttered, "God knows, we've tried to discover who the cursed Gatekeeper is. But none of my agents has come close."

"Nor mine." Uguzzoni made a gesture of helplessness. "Just the other week I received word that one was finally on the Gatekeeper's track: I heard nothing for days, and then his body was pulled out of one of the canals in Bologna. And so it goes."

"Bologna. Always Bologna." The Bishop was warming to his theme. "The damned Bolognese twist and turn to control us: after they captured the Emperor's son, they thumbed their noses even at him." He paused. "My apologies. I forget that our special guest is Bolognese." He inclined his head towards Bardi.

"Not at all, my Lord Bishop. It is true that I live there, by courtesy of our mutual friend to whom I have been privileged to be of service. But I was born in Florence, so by all means curse the Bolognese – as long as you except my noble patron from your imprecations!"

"Florentine, eh? Then you are all the more welcome!" laughed Uguzzoni, wiping a trickle of gravy from his chin and dabbing at the spreading stain on his shirt-front. He stretched his arm to spear a game bird with his knife, transporting it to his plate, already piled high with bones, as he continued: "As would be Signor Lambertazzi, should he feel able to make the journey."

Bardi made a warning gesture. "I think it prudent not to mention names."

The Bishop was dismissive. "Bah! Even here, among friends?" Bardi persisted. "Nonetheless, there are others within earshot, and I am a cautious man."

The Bishop looked around him as if noticing us serving-boys for the first time. "What, these? Signor, these boys spend their lives with their heads in the scriptures and exercising their voices. They know nothing of which we speak - and are too stupid to understand it. Boy! My glass, damn you!"

As I poured the Bishop still more wine, Bardi diplomatically returned to discussion of wider politics. "You mentioned Bologna's capture of Enzo. With his son held hostage in Bologna, Frederick certainly drew his horns in, Emperor or no. And since his death, who does rule the Holy Roman Empire?" His tone became ironic. "Germany or Sicily – or neither? We are in an interregnum, in an unholy mess, boasting either two emperors or none. Those with whom I work can get no sense from either contender, and it is not for want of trying. Which is why, my friends, you and your kin – for all your wealth and lands – have to dance at present to Bologna's tune.

"For now," snorted the Bishop.

"Indeed. For now." Bardi was emollient. "Yet I wonder if we might even beat those merchants and money-lenders at their own game. Modena has something that Bologna wants. It wants it very much, and in great quantities."

Uguzzoni leaned closer, intrigued. "You speak of the essence? The *balsamico*?"

"Precisely. The greedy merchants gorging themselves in their fine Bolognese houses cannot get enough of it. Have you seen the prices it's fetching?"

"Indeed I have. But the makers are producing more all the time."

"So they are. Yet it would not do to give the greedy Bolognese all they need. There is value in scarcity, my friends. You and your allies hold the power in this *Comune*. By all means let the barrel become larger: but be sure that you possess the tap."

"But how?"

"Find reasons. Insist that the makers buy licenses: that the essence must mature for so many years. Make rules. Take control. Render the commodity hard to acquire, and you will find Bologna readier to negotiate: all the more now that, through me, you have - how shall I put it? – so *particular* a friend in that city."

The entire company chuckled with glee, reloaded their plates and glasses and the conversation turned to more desultory matters.

That evening lodged itself in my mind because, after we had concluded our serving duties, Tommaso was out of sorts. Instead of exhibiting his usual even temper he was sulky, uncooperative and snappish. After making several attempts at conversation, to all of which he replied monosyllabically and with a bad grace, I snapped back. "For God's sake, Tommasino, what's got into you? Did you scoff too much of that belly pork they left?"

Even that provoked no more than a scowl. "No," he grunted. Then, with a sigh that lifted his shoulders a hand's-breadth: "I'm sorry, Luca. It's just that... You know the Bishop's guest tonight?"

"Who? That tall one with the funny voice? Bardi?"

"No. The other one. The little fat one. Turned out his name was Uguzzoni."

"Him? A mean and greedy bastard, I thought!"

"Bastard? You don't know the half of it, Luca. I'd heard he was coming, but I didn't know which of the fuckers was which until he started talking about his lazy tenants. Then I knew." I had never heard Tommaso so angry, nor so foul-mouthed. Ordinarily my language was infinitely worse than his.

"Uguzzoni, that fat, slimy piece of shit, is my family's landlord," he continued. "He squeezes rent and tithes from them, so much that they barely keep enough produce to live on, let alone surplus to sell."

"But when I visited everything seemed good."

"It was harvest-time, you idiot. The best time of year. Of course we all feel good then, unless the weather's been bad and the crops have failed."

"We had a great feast, though."

"Yes, in our honour. I bet you didn't notice how little Mamma ate, so as to leave enough for the girls."

"And that's why your brothers work away? So other farmers have to feed them?"

"At last! I thought you'd never understand!"

His tone was scornful, and piqued me in turn. "Well, I'm sorry I'm so slow. If you'd told me, I'd have spilt the soup in his lap!"

"And earned yourself a whipping! There's nothing we can do against a bastard like that. Besides, I didn't know who he was at first. I've never seen him before: I only heard his name later on. He doesn't get his own hands dirty. He sends his plug-ugly stumpy bailiff to demand our crops and our money. That's why I have to live here and hope to learn a trade to follow when my voice breaks - so that I can send them money." We fell silent, while I found myself for once pondering his misfortune rather than my own.

Years had passed, and nothing had changed in our lives. For a third and fourth time we spent those few precious days of harvest with Tommaso's family. The welcomes were warmer on each occasion, Rosalia ever more beautiful, the partings more grievous yet.

Tommaso and I were taller, growing up. I was starting to lose my voice. I must have been fifteen by this time, and nature was starting to turn me (too slowly, in my view) from boy to man. The process does strange things to a boy's voice. Some change from a high treble to deep bass almost overnight: others, like me, took two years or more to see the change effected. Drawing on nearly a decade's experience, I learnt to mask my lack of chest-voice. I developed a powerful falsetto, and anyone but an expert would be hard put to hear the difference. Besides, to this day the men in choirs make great use of falsetto, so the manner in which I masked my loss of high notes caused little comment - for several months, at any rate.

But I knew the end was approaching for my treble solos. What would happen? Ever since I had started using my ears, at Tommaso's bidding, I had also been applying myself to my studies, so my Latin was good, and my scribing more than passable. Would the Church look after me, as it did so many? It was hard to say. I was not born to Modena, merely brought in from outside, causing difficulty and resentment along the way. When choir matters were discussed at dinner, we boys listened for any plans for the future – in case they involved us.

Chapter 7

Tough as he was, Michele knew I needed to learn how to protect myself against people as quick and lithe as I was becoming, even if they lacked his long-acquired skill. I must have been around seventeen years of age when he brought in Paolo, a young man about my age to whom he introduced me with unusual formality. Paolo stood still and looked grave: since ceremony appeared to be required, I bowed, at which Paolo threw a punch and knocked me down. I was immediately back on my feet, and hurled myself upon him. The scuffle turned ugly, until we were separated by Michele, cackling with glee: he gave us both a dressing-down for losing our tempers and forgetting all the techniques that he had painstakingly taught me - and, it transpired, Paolo.

Under his tutelage our fierce rivalry was transformed into a keen yet friendly competitiveness. So my bruises increased in number, as I was floored and pummelled - until eventually I learned to give as good as I got. Always Paolo and I would shake or embrace at the end, and laugh at one another's mistakes. Paolo had a carefree, devil-may-care attitude that made everyone, including me, want to be his friend. In no time at all, he was bringing along two other friends, Giacomo and Salvatore.

None of the three boasted a permanent home, as far as I could tell, yet they always appeared adequately fed. They got themselves occasional casual work in the market, loading and unloading wains for the stallholders: at other times they gained employment as hired muscle when a merchant needed to transport a rich load of fabrics to Ravenna, or collect a precious cargo of *balsamico* from Modena. I did not believe half the tales they told, but they were such engaging company that I nonetheless encouraged them.

When I was allowed out - infrequently, for reasons I shall explain - I would go with them to a tavern. Michele would argue, then huff and puff, and finally, grudgingly, give me a few coins to spend there. We lads would drink and boast and try to chat up the serving-girls. Giacomo, in particular, was always boasting of his success with girls, and of his sexual prowess: I am not sure that he was ever any more successful than the rest of us, which means that he never persuaded one into bed. In those boisterous times with the three I heard more tavern songs that I filed away in my musical memory, and learned to speak in the dialect and accent of Bologna ("like a Bolognese ruffian", my master would say, shaking her head indulgently).

If my new-found friends had only limited time for relaxation, busy as they were making a living with no evidence of families either to support or to keep them, I had even less leisure. I do not mean I was overburdened with work, because I was not: but the household seemed never to stand still. I am not sure now whether I offered or was expected to become, in effect, my master's personal servant. My role in that small household of four seemed to evolve naturally.

In the morning I would bring her hot water: she was fastidious about cleanliness. She liked to sleep in fine linen sheets, which I would regularly change and wash. I washed all her linen, except her undergarments, which she insisting on doing herself. I would bring her breakfast in her room, and empty her chamber-pot into the river Idice that ran beside the house – as everyone did in our quarter of the city. She would spend hours reading and writing, as the scholar she was: at such times I would continue my training with Michele.

At lunchtime I would be there again, serving her food, pouring her wine. Sometimes she would be in conversational mood: "Sit down, Lorenzo. Tell me more of your past and what brought you here." Sometimes the stories would be repeated: at others I would remember new facts or events. Yet on other occasions she was bound up entirely in her own thoughts, and would not even bid me sit. Then I would stand behind her chair, ready to serve and slightly piqued at being excluded from her thoughts.

On studying days (as she called them) the afternoon would be the same, her quill-pen scratching away while I would go outside and train some more with Michele, perhaps run an errand or go shopping in the market with Mamolo. In the evening I would serve my master once more, and again she would sometimes bid me sit and talk, at other times ignoring me.

If I thought she looked careworn, as she frequently did, I would offer to sing for her. According to her mood, I might sing sacred pieces I remembered from Modena or even Venice: at other times I would sing a comic song from the tavern, or even one of the country songs I had learned from Tommaso. When I sang those I would frequently be reminded of the happy times with him, and with his family. I would recall Rosalia, her clear voice and her blue eyes staring into mine, and I would be overcome with guilt that I so rarely called them to mind, and had never found a way to send word to my friend that I was safe and well.

My master claimed she liked my singing, but she never wanted to hear more than one or two songs: I never believed she was much interested in music. I watched her while I sang and, while for a verse or two she might be enjoying the melody, I could see that her keen mind was soon racing away down some juristic by-way, and frequently convinced myself that she was barely aware of my singing. Yet, as in so many things, she quickly proved me wrong. One evening she interrupted my song abruptly and accused me of "going through the motions" instead of singing properly. Affronted, I asked her what she knew of it.

"Lorenzo," she said, "You have told me how Modena robbed you of your love of singing. You comfort yourself by boasting that, without feeling anything, you can nonetheless perform with consummate skill, so that no one can tell the difference. You can indeed do so: almost. Yet I *can* tell that difference. Fortunately. And you do me honour – no, don't interrupt me: I have no time for your false modesty - I feel you honour me when you sing to me out of love: but I would be insulted if I suspected that you were singing for me merely out of duty.

"Do you know anything of St Augustine? Augustine of Hippo, that is, not the curious one who went to convert the English: such a thankless task. He wrote: 'Singing belongs to one who loves'. Do not pretend that the beauty you create comes from anything but love, even if the cruelty of others towards you has rendered it harder at times to find that love within you. Your art is a thing of beauty: that comes only from love. Never, never bury or forget that love."

It was only one of countless occasions on which I was left abashed, silenced: angry, certainly, but uncomfortable because she had seen straight through my vanity and pretence. Yet I was at the same time calmed because, while she mercilessly dispelled my illusions, I never felt that she condemned me.

After a pregnant pause, she fixed her eyes on mine, a ploy that always disconcerted me. "Now, Lorenzo, you told me some time ago how you came to hear the name that put you in such danger with Signori Bardi and Lambertazzi, that of the Gatekeeper, though I suspect you omitted some details that might have proved... *illuminating*." I averted my eyes and hung my head, feeling both ashamed and somewhat humiliated that she could read me so easily. "But you have yet to explain," she continued smoothly, "How you came to be here in Bologna, and at the mercy of the two most dangerous men in this city. I must presume that the memory is full of pain for you and, notwithstanding my... *anxiety* to know, I have exercised... *unusual* patience in refraining from questioning you. But perhaps you now feel strong enough?"

She left the question, almost a plea, hanging. I could not deny her. Yet, once again, I did not dare tell her the whole story.

If it had been easy to develop the habits of an eavesdropper with regard to local politics, we boys found it less simple, as we waited at table, to find out what was going on in the Cathedral itself. Even after plenty of wine, the Prior and Bishop in particular were tight-lipped. It was as if we were invisible when they talked about the wider world: but we shadows behind their chairs became once more choirboys when they discussed internal matters.

Nonetheless, between us Tommaso and I gained at least some early warning of the next challenge that was to confront me. In their conversations we started to overhear mention of the city of Paris, and the great church of Notre Dame. "When I was last in Rome all the cardinals were talking about Paris, and the glories of its music," exclaimed the Bishop. "We need to learn how they do it."

"We must indeed discover more of this, my Lord," responded the Prior, and then flicked his eyes warningly towards me. The Bishop took the hint, and fell silent.

Later, in one of our few moments of privacy (people rarely understand, in my experience, how little time the religious and institutional life allows for private conversation), Tommaso and I compared notes on what we'd heard, but could deduce little. To be sure, Paris was the name mentioned all the time, and there seemed to be something special happening in the music there: but at that point our masters' conversation invariably became guarded.

Then, one day, Tommaso came running from his duties to find me: for some reason I hadn't been serving at table that day. "Luca, I know what they're planning. And it's bad news." His face was ashen.

"What is it, Tommasino? Tell me."

"Luca, it's as bad as it could be. I think they're going to send you away, to make you go to Paris to learn about the music there."

I have described how I came to terms with my enforced if comfortable life in the great Cathedral of Modena. I did what was required of me and in return was fed, clothed, housed and safe from punishment or threat. Moreover, I had received considerable praise.

As I have said, I had convinced myself that I now sang not for the glory of God, and certainly not for the that of the Bishop, but rather for myself, for sheer survival. Yet that cynicism had faded as my friendship with Tommaso had developed. We were happy in each other's presence, relaxed, open and frequently laughing. We supported each other through the inevitable ups and downs, hurts and pains of life.

This latest news brought back, in a rush, all those horrors, the way in which the Prior and his henchmen had stolen away my very soul. A cold determination came over me. I know my face hardened, because Tommaso noticed.

"What? Luca, what are you thinking of doing?"

"I'll tell them I won't go. They can't make me go to Paris. This is my home now, even though I didn't choose it."

"Luca, you know you can't defy them. They'll break you. They did once before..."

I reacted furiously. "I won't let those bastards beat and starve me again. They did it once: but I'm older and stronger now."

"Luca, you know you're not as tough as them. None of us is. That's why we have to do their bidding. God knows we don't have to step far out of line to spend a day or two downstairs. When you first came, when you were down there for two weeks or more, I thought they might kill you."

"They'll have to kill me, then. I won't go."

"Luca, I know you're strong. I've always admired you for that. But they would break anyone. They'd break the spirit of one of the holy martyrs, if they had him there! You can't beat them."

"What can I do then? How can I stop them sending me to some foreign land? I don't even know where Paris is."

"I know it's in somewhere called Francia. They say the food's good. It's not cold and miserable like England. But I don't think it'll be as warm as here: and God knows we shiver enough here in winter. "

"But it's another strange place. Why does this keep happening to me?"

To that he had no answer. We both fell silent.

The summons to the Prior came within hours. That same evening I found myself again standing in front of his great chair, a burly brother to each side of me. In the corner, standing at a writing-desk, a monk was writing on a scrap of vellum. The scratching nibbled constantly at the edge of my consciousness, somehow irritating and distracting.

"So, Luca," growled the Prior. "I concede you have done well. Since those early, ah, difficulties you have performed your duties to my satisfaction. The music of our Duomo has gained quite a reputation, in large part due to your contribution – even if your voice is now not what it was." I bowed: there was nothing to say.

He continued. "Now we must look to the future. You may have heard talk," at this he looked at me searchingly, as if he knew exactly what I had overheard, "That there is a new musical style coming out of France. At Notre Dame in Paris, of which you may have heard, they tell me that the late Master Perotinus developed a way of expanding the *organum duplum*. They talk of *organum triplum* and even *quadruplum*, three and four parts winding above the cantus. Do you know anything of this?"

"No, Father. I can imagine how more than one part might weave together above the chant: but it might not be improvised. I think it would have to be written down or the result would be... chaotic."

" You have learned your trade well, boy. They tell me that, before Master Perotinus died, he helped to produce a great book, the *Magnus Liber*, and that all the wonders of this style of music are contained in it.

"We must look to the future. Your days as a treble are numbered: yet you have mastered the skills admirably, despite your early stubbornness. So I propose to send you, with a few of the brothers, to Notre Dame in Paris. You must spend time there: a year, perhaps. Hear the music, learn the style, transcribe the works from the *Magnus Liber*. You can scribe competently, I suppose?"

"Well enough, Father, I think."

"Good. We shall make preparations, and you will leave after Pentecost. The weather will be good for travelling, if hot."

I tried to protest. "But Father, Modena is my home now, and has been for four years. I found being uprooted from Venice hard: I fear another upheaval."

"Don't be absurd, boy. You're no longer a child, and are well fit to travel. Besides, you shall be doing a great service to the Cathedral and, through that, to the glory of God: no man can seek a higher calling."

I thought quickly. It was clear there would be no diverting him. "Then, Father, it occurs to me that it will be a great labour to copy sufficient music to bring back to Modena. Should you not send two of us, so that we can both labour at the transcription? Tommaso, for example: he writes almost as well as I do." It was true: I had helped him.

The Prior appeared to consider it for a moment, then shook his head. "No, that will not do. Tommaso is a year or so younger than you, and his voice remains good, if less glorious than yours at its height. He must lead the choir in your absence: the others are too young. Besides, this is not an adventure for friends to share: it is work, God's work. My mind is made up. You will go within the month."

He looked at my face. I had learnt to hide my feelings in most situations, but he undoubtedly spotted a hint of rebellion. "Do not think to disobey me in this, Luca. You know the price of disobedience: I do not think you will wish to pay it a second time."

But I did wish it. Something in the ruthlessness with which the Prior wielded his power caused me to set my jaw in defiance: indeed, I was on the point of telling him so when, unusually for him, he gave a deep sigh. "Luca, I believe you are the most foolish boy I have ever had to deal with." He nodded to the brothers who flanked me and, in response, seized and pinioned my arms.

As I struggled, futilely, he raised his voice. "I will be merciful, Luca. Spend tonight downstairs, locked up as you were once before, when you first joined us. Pass the night in contemplation. In the morning you may submit to my instruction without further fuss, and I shall overlook this latest disobedience. If you continue to defy me, however, you shall suffer the consequences. And you will indeed suffer." Then, to the brothers, "Take him down."

He had, of course, omitted to tell me that the process of being taken downstairs involved a savage beating on my arrival in the cell. When that was complete I was left, sobbing in pain and fury and curled into a ball of misery on the floor of the dank cell. I heard the heavy door slam, and the key turn in the lock.

I paused as I recounted the tale to my Master. Frequently during such accounts of my past, she was content to allow a period of quiet. But not on this occasion. Indeed, there was an unaccustomed urgency in her question. "So what then, Lorenzo? Did you defy them further? Is that why you ran away to Bologna?"

I thought for a moment. I had reached another part of my story that I dared to share, not even with her. But she had involuntarily furnished me with a plausible answer. "No, Magister – and yes. The Prior, damn him to hell, had been right. I couldn't face another period in the cell like the last one. So, when they came for me in the morning, I told him I was sorry, and that I would do as he instructed, and go to Paris. And then, before it was time to leave for Francia, I ran away – with Tommaso's help."

My voice caught. It had been a hard parting from my friend, and I hoped my master would ascribe my inability to continue to that. In truth, though, I had stopped because that memory also reminded me of the danger I had been unwittingly dragged into, a peril which, for all I knew, was stalking me still, and which prohibited me from telling her the rest of the story.

Chapter 8

The subsequent episode of my tale contained but a single element that I could share with my master: I was able to describe my next conversation. I was aroused from my welter of self-pity by a quiet knocking on my cell-door. "Luca! Luca! Is it you in there?" It was Tommaso, speaking in a hoarse, urgent whisper.

"Of course it's me!" I replied, delighted to hear my friend's voice in my loneliness. "Who else would it be?"

"Well, there are three cells here in a row, and I didn't know which one you were in." I made no reply: I had not even noticed the other doors on the two occasions on which I had been hustled to my place of punishment.

"Luca, don't... don't be a fool. You can't beat them. Do what they say. Go to Parigi, Paris, whatever it's called. Just do their fucking work there and come back as quick as you can. They'll kill you otherwise."

"Kill me?"

"Or good as. Please, Luca. Please. I couldn't bear it if..." Even through the thick, though ill-fitting, door, I could hear him sniffling.

I knew he was right. There was no way in which I could win a battle of wills with the Prior. I thought for a moment, as Tommaso scratched at the door and begged me to be sensible. "All right, Tommasino. I know you're right. I was stupid to think I could fight him: but I was so angry."

"Same old Luca, stubborn as ever! So promise me? Promise you'll say yes?"

"Yes, Tommasino: I'll give in to the old bastard, yet again. He always gets what he wants."

"Good. Thank God. I was afraid you'd really done it this time. Luca, I, I've got to go. I can't let them find me here. So just say yes in the morning, Agreed?"

I sighed. "Agreed."

"Good night, Luca." And he was gone, before I could even reciprocate.

If only the story of that night had ended there! Yet what ensued rendered me the carrier of danger, not only to myself but also to whole cities. So, although I felt I was betraying her kindness and her trust, I could not tell my master what else happened during that long night in the cell.

It was pitch black, but the cell was devoid of any furnishing, so there was nothing to see. I groped around the floor, bundling up the few scraps of straw I could find to make some sort of bed, and settled down to sleep.

Whether I had slept or not, I had no idea. But I was startled by a man's voice – or, rather, a ragged, gasping imitation of a voice.

"Boy! Boy! Are you there?"

"I, I... Who – where are you?"

"In the cell next to yours, you fool. Did you not see the gap in the wall between our cells?"

"How could I?" I paused, "It's pitch dark in here."

"You have a point there, boy." He laughed, and then caught his breath, clearly in pain. "I thought they'd only locked you up tonight. But in the morning you'll be able to see a little, though not much. You'll see a space, high up between the top of the wall and the ceiling. Higher than you can reach, I'll warrant. And I'm chained." A rattling sound reached me. "Did they hurt you much?" I considered for a moment, but he was impatient. "Eh, boy? Eh?"

"A beating always hurts,... sir." Something in his damaged voice commanded respect. "We boys are used to it. But I hate those bastards. God, how I hate them." The way my voice cracked betrayed the impression of fortitude I had tried to convey.

"They know how to inflict pain, I'll give them that," the voice replied. "They've been working on me for two days."

"Working on you?"

"Do you understand nothing, boy? I've been tortured for two days."

"Tortured? But why?"

He sighed. "Finally they put someone in the cell next to mine, and I find it's a simpleton. Listen, child. I don't know why you're down here, but I imagine it's not for the good of your health."

"No. It's because... because I won't do what they want. First they kidnapped me," it all came out in a rush: "They made me sing for them here. They beat me till I did. And now they want to send me to the end of the earth, away from everyone and everything I know. So I defied them. God knows why I tried. I'll have to do as they tell me. There's no beating them." Again I could not prevent a little sob from escaping.

"So..." his tone changed, became a little wheedling. "So you really hate them?"

"With all my heart."

"Would you like to take your revenge on them?"

I pictured the Prior and his henchmen at my mercy, pleading to be spared some horrible fate. "Yes, I would. I'd like that very much."

"Then carry a message for me. Tell them you'll do as they say and, at the first opportunity, run away. And take my message."

"That doesn't sound much like revenge to me."

"God!" he muttered to himself. "A mere boy, and a stupid one at that." Then, louder, "Listen, boy. Hm. I can't keep calling you Boy. What's your name?"

"Luca."

"Well, Luca, carry a message from me to the right people, and you won't just put one over on these bastards here. You'll destroy them."

"Destroy them? How?"

"Because there are people, powerful people where I come from who, when they know what this little cabal is planning in Modena, will put an end to their plots – and to them."

"So why don't you tell them yourself? Oh...."

"Ah," his exclamation turned into a painful, hacking cough. When he had recovered, he continued: "Now you're beginning to understand. Not so stupid after all."

I bridled. "If you're so clever, how did you let them catch you?"

"Fair question," he conceded. "I would have said it was through bad luck. But the more I lie here and think about it, when they permit me to, the more I am convinced it was treachery, that one of my contacts here in Modena betrayed me. And now," he coughed again, "Now they will not let me go, nor cease from tormenting me until I tell them what I know of their intrigues – and of those of my own side."

There was a long silence. "So, boy - Luca. Will you take a message for me to Bologna and deal these treacherous scum a blow from which they will not recover?"

I hesitated. "I, I don't know. I don't know what to do. I don't even know where Bologna is."

"Fool! It's due East along the great Roman road. A blind man could find it!" He sighed dramatically. "Still, so be it. Let them kill me, and cow you until you are truly their creature, their slave. Hearing you talk to your friend, I thought you might put up more of a fight. Clearly I was mistaken."

"How could you understand?" Now I was angry. "First they stole me from my home. Then they forced me to sing for them. Now they want to send me to Francia: they always get their way!"

"Precisely. So why don't you let them think they have done so once again. Humble yourself, grovel to that damned Prior. Say you'll go: and then run away to Bologna with the message I shall give you. Frustrate their small plan for you – and their grand scheme to bring down Bologna. That should be sufficient revenge even for you."

I pondered for a while. Then, "If I take that message, what will happen to you?"

The response was so quiet I could barely hear it. "I will make sure that they learn nothing from me – nothing of your involvement either. You have my word on it. So will you bear my message?"

Something in the insistence of his tone decided me. "Yes. At least, I'll do my best."

"Good. Now, let us sleep a little. When it's light – as light as it gets in this damned hole – we'll speak again, and hatch our little plot. Good night, Luca. You're a brave boy."

Brave? The unexpected compliment served only to awaken fresh fears in me. Why did I need courage? Was I placing myself in danger? Yet the temptation to strike back at my captors, if only in a small way, was irresistible. As I settled down to sleep on my filthy straw I could hear his chains clank while, restless and clearly in pain, he constantly coughed and stirred.

Nonetheless, I must have slept soundly, for I was awakened by my neighbour's agonised, insistent voice. "Boy! Luca! Wake up!" A pale light seemed to creep into my cell from the gaps around the door, between the walls and the rough wooden beams of the ceiling, gaps large enough to admit a hint of dawn but not, I could see at a glance, to permit even as skinny a youth as I was to wriggle through them and escape.

"Luca, quickly! We have little time. Are you still ready to be my messenger?"

"Yes, I think so."

"Good. Do you have a good memory?"

"Of course!" I was indignant. "I'm a musician. That's my training."

He was oblivious to my reaction. "Now, listen carefully. In Bologna you must find the Gatekeeper: you hear, the Gatekeeper."

"The Gatekeeper. Yes. But where...?"

But he had rushed on. "And the message: it's just four names. In Modena, Uguzzoni and the Bishop: you've got that?" They were familiar to me, of course, though he could not have known. "Repeat them!"

"Yes. Uguzzoni and the Bishop. I heard you."

"Good. And in Bologna the traitor, God damn him, traitor to the city of his birth, the city that makes him rich, he is Lambertazzi. Say that name back to me!"

"Lambertazzi. Lambertazzi. I heard you!"

"And the greater villain, the slimy, scheming worm who does all Lambertazzi's dirty work, that's his so-called advisor, his friend and confidant, Bardi. Have you got that? Bardi."

Another familiar name. But he had not finished drilling me and testing my memory. "Say the names back to me, boy."

"Very well. I find the Gatekeeper. And I tell him that in Modena his enemies are Uguzzoni and the Bishop, and in Bologna Lambertazzi and Bardi. I said I could remember. But you haven't told me how or where I find the Gatekeeper."

"That's the difficulty. I don't know. He covers his tracks well. They say that there are some lawyers who have his ear, but I have no name to give you. Find an honest one: they're rare enough!" Again his laugh was quickly transformed into a cough. "You will have to be careful, and use your sense. But I judge that here you've learnt to keep your own counsel and move cautiously. You will work out who are enemies to Lambertazzi and Bardi: and in time they will lead you to the Gatekeeper. Be patient."

"Patient? I thought you said I could just deliver the message and be free of it. I thought your friends in Bologna would help me to make a new life. But now you tell me I won't even know who your – or my - friends are!"

"That's true! We'll make a spy of you yet!"

"You will not! This isn't fair! You didn't warn me of any of this!" I was outraged.

"Had I done so, would you have agreed? I think not. But now, Luca, you possess dangerous knowledge: so hazardous, indeed, that if you want to live a healthy life, you will have to bear my message to Bologna."

"I will not! I shall just forget about it."

"But will you be safe? For all you know, under torture I might tell them what I have told you, and you'll be the next one they come for. No, Luca. I am sorry I duped you, truly sorry: but I had to make sure you took the message, once I decided you were capable of it. And you are. So now, because you're sharp, you know that the road to safety for you lies in Bologna."

I was lost for words. But he quickly filled the silence. "Now, Luca. I have one more thing to do. Do you have a knife?"

"Of course," I carried it tucked into my girdle. "Just the little one we all carry for cutting fruit and things."

"That will have to do. They took mine. Can you pass it to me through that gap at the top of the wall?"

"I can't reach that high!"

"Of course you can't, you fool! You'll have to throw it – but carefully!"

"What do you need it for?"

"Never you mind. But I need it. Now throw it, and make sure it doesn't get stuck."

I tried several times, but each time the knife failed to clear the tiny space and bounced back, and each time the man who seemed to be taking control of my life became more exasperated. "For the love of Christ, Luca. Is it so difficult?"

I took a deep breath: otherwise I might have said something rude. Then I stepped back, gripped the little knife between my teeth and ran at the wall. I leapt as high as I could, and just managed to seize its top. For a moment I hung there, then let go one hand and, before my remaining hand slipped, managed to take the knife from my mouth and thrust it through the crack below the ceiling. The sound of it falling to the floor in the next cell was followed by an exultant shout. "You did it! Well done, boy."

I must have been as stupid as he had suspected. I had not even asked what he needed the knife for. Instantly I realised that I did not need to enquire: but I did so, nonetheless, a sense of dread growing in my heart. "Sir, you're not going to harm yourself, are you?"

"Of course I am, Luca. It's the only way. Those swine have tortured me for two days. They only left me alone tonight because they know they'll break me tomorrow. No one, not the greatest saint or hero can hold out indefinitely. And they must not know what I know – what you now know."

"But," I was too horrified to consider the threat his words contained for me. "It's a mortal sin to take your own life. You'll be damned to hell, forever!"

"My, my, Luca, you have been well schooled by these priests who rule your life!" His tone was gently mocking. "It's good of you to be concerned for my eternal soul. But I'm hoping St Peter will know that I was only doing my duty, and let me in those gates notwithstanding." He paused. "I'm sorry. I shouldn't tease you: you're a good boy, and you have a big heart. But this is the only way. Tell you what: you can say a prayer for me at the tomb of San Geminiano in your splendid cathedral here. Ask the saint to intercede for me. Will you do that for me?"

"Of course I will," I replied, miserably.

"And then run away. Take my message and let Bologna protect you. Tell me you'll do it." I nodded, too overcome to speak. "Will you?" he insisted urgently. In my confusion I had forgotten he could not see me.

"Yes, I will. I promise." Truth to tell, I was by no means convinced that I would do as he asked and set off on a wild goose-chase to a city I did not know in search of a mysterious figure whose identity was shrouded in secrecy.

"Don't let me down. Don't let evil triumph. And these people are truly evil." His tone became brisk and business-like. "Now, they've chained me to the wall, but my hands are free, so I can use your knife. Thank you, Luca. I'll hide it so they don't know it came from you. Now, whatever you hear, keep quiet and just be an innocent little choirboy. You hear? We don't want them thinking that you and I have been talking, do we? It would go ill for you."

Now I could not speak. I was about to hear a man kill himself, and all I could do was sob in dismay. But now he was about to perform the dreadful act, my interlocutor seemed unable to stop talking. "So, Luca, I must say goodbye – and thank you, Luca. Luca?"

I controlled myself. "I'm still here. Where would I be?" A thought struck me. "Sir, will you tell me your name. To... to part without knowing who you are, let alone to pray for you, it seems wrong."

"Well," he pondered for a moment. "I have put you in enough danger: perhaps that knowledge cannot hurt you further. Very well, Luca: my name is Giovanni. It's a common enough name, I know. But I was a leather-seller, with a stall in the Old Market in Bologna."

"Giovanni. Would I be able to find your people in the Old Market? Would they lead me to the Gatekeeper?"

"Alas, no, Luca. They're all dead. For reasons that led me into this game, and to this end. Which must come now – before they come for me, and perhaps for you. Goodbye, Luca."

As I murmured as tremulous "Goodbye… Signor Giovanni," I heard him shifting and grunting, and shuddered as I imagined, horrified, what he was doing with my puny knife.

He did not speak again. I thought at times that I could hear him breathing, and was constantly on the point of calling out to him: yet always something held me back.

Chapter 9

I was rudely aroused from my trance, or perhaps it was sleep, by heavy feet descending the stairs outside my cell. I guessed they belonged to two men, who were chatting as they approached. All the determination, the sheer bravado that Giovanni had somehow kindled within me, dissolved in an instant and, fearing another beating, I leapt to my feet and backed against the wall that faced the door. But the steps went past my cell to that of my neighbour. I heard the key rattle in the lock.

Close behind them, however, I heard the voices of my regular guardians, who greeted them with a rough camaraderie. As these two opened my door, an uproar broke out in the next cell. There was shouting and cursing, and I could make out the word "blood". Through the doorway I saw a figure scurrying up the stairs, spurred on by more shouting behind it.

A rough-looking man in a leather apron, his hands and arms covered in blood, came into my view, his eyes wide in shock. Alarmed, my gaolers turned to face him. What's up?"

"Our prisoner's done himself in. Clever bastard: opened his wrists and slipped away in the night. Should've kept an eye on him. He knew we'd crack him today. Now there'll be hell to pay." He noticed my open cell door and spied me cowering in the darkness, and bellowed, "What the hell are you doing here, and with this?" He pointed at me. "This is no place for a child!"

"Prior's orders. Cooling off one of the choirboys overnight."

"Well, get him out. No, better still, get in there with him and close the door. Bardi's coming, and he won't be happy."

"Why?"

"Just get in and don't make a sound till he's gone. It'll only make things worse if he spots you."

"Well, don't be long. Prior hates to be kept waiting."

We cowered together in that cell, behind the closed door: I think the brothers were almost as scared as I was. In the next cell voices were raised in blame and counter-accusation – and silence fell. Then I heard that voice, its shawm-like tone still vibrant when raised in anger, cracking like a whip across those he blamed for the loss of his valuable prisoner. Their voices by turns cringed and pleaded – for their jobs, for their very lives.

When it seemed that their master was satisfied by their grovelling, the shawm became commanding. "You fools shall get rid of the body: be sure to bury it deep. Meanwhile I shall see the Bishop and *try* to explain how your utter incompetence has lost the very information we needed, that we had in our grasp."

We heard his long strides take him to the stairs and ascend them, two at a time – and the three of us breathed again. "Right, my lad," said the elder Brother, "We're off to see Father Prior, and I *advise* you," he twisted my ear so hard that I yelped, "to give him the answer he wants." I nodded my assent: I already knew what I must do. "Especially after all this," he added, jerking head to indicate the neighbouring cell, "Which you'd better forget all about. If you want to see another dawn." They dragged me unceremoniously from the cell, as was their wont: nonetheless, all three of us paused involuntarily in order to avoid the pool of blood forming on the stone slabs outside the row of cells.

As I described it, I shook my head to clear from it the memory of that night. It had come flooding back to me even as I tried to erase it: I was determined to place neither my master nor myself in danger. So I continued the part of my story that I could safely share with her.

I found myself standing once more before the Prior's great chair, flanked as ever by my two guardian angels, the Prior's scribe scratching in the corner as ever. But something had changed since my last interview. The brothers and the Prior alike were nervous. He lacked his usual poise and air of omnipotence, and appeared to regard my presence as an interruption to more important work.

Sensing that his attention was elsewhere, I hoped that the task of convincing him of my penitent obedience would not prove arduous. In that I was proved right. I bowed low, and spoke quickly and earnestly. "Father, forgive my earlier disobedience. I sought wilfully to follow a path of selfishness and ungodliness."

Had I overdone it? I looked up but the Prior, accustomed to getting his way in all things, was not in a mood to be suspicious. "Yes, yes, boy. Get on with it!" he responded testily.

"Father. I accept your ruling that I should go to - to Parigi?" Uncertain that I had the name correct, I looked up again. The Prior merely nodded. "There I shall seek to learn about the music of its Great Church," I could not recall the name of that city's fabled cathedral, "And transcribe what I can. I will do my best – for Modena and for the glory of," I could not resist it, "Our Bishop."

The Prior's face hardened. "Don't be impertinent, boy. It shall be for the glory of God and of Him alone. Any lustre that may be reflected onto our city or our Bishop is purely coincidental. Now go, and prepare yourself for your journey, which we shall bring forward. You will leave in two days."

I was dismissed. I almost ran from his study, but quickly slowed as I realised a harder task awaited me. That of telling my friend, my only true friend, that I must run away – either with him or alone.

My spirits sank as I saw his delight at seeing me released from my captivity: this conversation would be still crueller than I had feared. As always when I was troubled, he sensed it immediately, and insisted that I tell him. I took a deep breath and began. "Listen, Tommasino. You were right. I can't beat them. Whatever we do, they're going to part us. Try as I might, I cannot think how to prevent that. There's only one thing to do. We must escape from here."

"You mean run away?" It was something that had never occurred to him. I might not have done to me: but I had been both schooled and placed in danger by Giovanni the leather-seller and the burden he had laid upon me in the form of a message – though I was careful not to mention the fact.

"What else can we do? I cannot stay here, because they'll send me to Paris. And they won't let you come. If we want to be together, we'll have to run away and find a life somewhere else."

I could see the uncertainty in his face. His fear was palpable. "I, I don't know if I can, Luca. My parents, my family depend on me being here. Oh, I know I can't do anything for them. It isn't as if I can earn money and send it to them – or not till I'm grown up, when perhaps I might help them pay their rent to that leech Uguzzoni. But they're proud of me being here. I think it keeps them going through the hard times. What would they think if they heard that I'd run away from this? They'd say I'd disgraced them."

I was angry, unreasonable. "Well, maybe you have to choose between them and me," I said harshly. "You can stay here and be comfortable. It's me that's being uprooted again. I can't stay here: so either I go to Paris, or I run away. "

"Where would you go? You have no one to go to."

I pretended an inspiration had struck me. "I'll go to Bologna."

"Bologna? Why?"

"Because it's Modena's enemy. If I can make it to Bologna, no one will follow me there. And even if I am discovered, there's such bad feeling between the cities that no one will send me back: they'd see keeping me there as a further way of annoying Modena. Besides, it's only a journey of a day or two." My mind was suddenly made up. "Yes. I'm going to go to Bologna, and you can come if you want to."

I could see that Tommaso was about to cry. "Luca, you know I can't. I can't do that to my family. I'll, I'll just stay here. But maybe, one day, one day when I finish my time here – I'll come and look for you in Bologna." He was weeping now.

"I'd like that," I said quietly, stricken with remorse. "I'm sorry, Tommasino. I had no right to ask you to choose between your family and me. I'm so selfish: you make me feel ashamed. No one ever cared for me before I met you. And now the one thing I can't do is stay with you. So I'll run away."

He nodded miserably. "I know, Luca. If you really won't go to Paris, then you have to run away. There's nothing else to be done."

"I'll miss you, Tommasino. I've never missed anyone before: but I'll miss you."

"I know." He flung himself on me, and we hugged, cheek to cheek, our tears mingling. The parting from my only real friend marked the loss of the last part of my childhood innocence.

We made our plans quickly, not least because there was little to plan. We agreed that I must make my escape the very next day, market-day, when the main square was full of stalls and the roads in and out of the city jammed with carts and wagons. We choristers were generally allowed out in the afternoon to wander around the market and spend the few coins we might have accumulated, occasional (and far from generous) gifts from those whom we entertained with our singing at dinner. Before we went to the market Tommaso and I went through our plans once more.

"What are you taking with you?" he asked.

"I have nothing: just the clothes I'm wearing." In a purse I had a few tiny coins: they might buy me food for a day or two.

Tommaso made a typically generous offer. "Luca, you know they'll question me. They'll assume I know where you've gone, and they'll punish me. I'll hold out as long as I can, to give you time to get away."

"Tommasino, don't play the hero for my sake. If you can buy me a bit of time, that's all I ask." An idea occurred to me. "You can make out that you're angry I've left you: pretend to betray me. Tell them I've headed north, trying to get back to Venice. They might believe that, more readily than if you tried to deny that I'd gone. And then they might leave you alone. Tommasino... I don't want you hurt for me. I swear I'll never ask that."

"I'm not a hero, Luca! I'll just try to gain you some time. After all, what are friends for?"

"What are friends for? Tommasino, you're the only friend I've ever had. I cannot bear to leave you."

"Send word to me, will you? Somehow. Just tell me you're all right."

"I will. I promise." I could not know that I had just sworn another oath that I would break.

With the other members of the choir, when we were permitted, we went out into the marketplace. It was easy enough in that great square to wander off towards the edge, down an alley: and then I was off, running, ducking through archways and round corners, always heading towards the eastern gate of the city.

I was out. Ahead of me stretched, straight as a die, the great Roman road, the Via Æmilia, that would take me to Bologna. I felt exposed on the road, so I walked on the edge of fields: yet that slowed me down, and I needed to put as great a distance as I could between me and Modena.

I came across a wagon. Its driver had been selling his wares in Modena, and was travelling home light, if slightly the worse for wine. He offered me a lift and readily shared his bread and olives. He knew where he was going, and showed no interest in my destination. My vague suggestion that I had family some way down the road seemed to satisfy him.

When he turned off the road towards his farm, I thanked him and bade him farewell. If I had worried about how any strangers I met might react, my fears were soon allayed. Several times during the next two days I begged a lift in a cart, either in the back with the produce or in the front with the driver. People were friendly but incurious, and ready to share a crust in the season of plenty, so I did not go hungry – or, at least, only a little. My single night on the road I spent in a barn, creeping in after dark and leaving early, disturbing no one. I may have been lucky: or perhaps people were just busy with their own lives and one lone boy on the road was not worthy of notice.

Towards the end of my second day of travelling I caught my first sight of Bologna. At the time I was travelling on a cart full of watermelons, and sucking on a large, juicy slice. From a distance it assumed a strange aspect. It resembled no city I had seen before (though I had seen few enough). As we neared Bologna the shapes emerged from the haze, and I realised I was looking at countless tall, slender towers. "Don't you know about Bologna and its towers?" asked the driver. "They all have them, all the big families: every one of them trying to build their tower taller than the rest. If that's a city, give me the country. They're all fucking mad."

That is how I first perceived the great city of Bologna, the place that has been my home ever since.

Chapter 10

How may I adequately describe Bologna? There has never been a city like it, though I am told there are pale imitations elsewhere. At its height, which was about the time that I first saw it, the city boasted nearly a hundred towers within its wall, less than a league across.

It was a sight both extraordinary and terrible. Every tower was taller than any building I had seen, certainly loftier than the elegant *campanile* of which Modena was so proud. There was a daunting beauty about it: and a sense of horror. Not without reason did my friend Dante Alighieri take Bologna as his model when trying to conjure a vision of the Seventh Circle of Hell. (But that was decades later: at the time I am describing he was not even born, let alone immortalised. How I mourned when we buried him, only a year or two back! One day I shall tell the story of my turbulent friendship with the great poet).

I entered the city through its western gate. There were guards on duty: but I walked in amongst a group of wagons and, with so many people coming and going, I was not required to account for myself. Once through the gate, I craned my neck to take in the detail of these extraordinary edifices.

The towers stretched upward, up as far as the eye could see: and at the tops, connecting them, I could see slim walkways. They looked perilous in the extreme, and the few people I saw walking along them from one tower to another looked tiny, smaller than birds. Above them the sky was blue and clear: it was like looking up to a discrete, heavenly world bathed in sunshine and fresh breezes.

At ground level it was very different. With so many towers, so close together, there was little full daylight. Here and there were bigger spaces between them, accommodating a canal, for example, but otherwise the shadows they cast were deep and black: the streets were full of ordure and filth, and they stank. Down here was a world of poverty, fear and crime: it was a threatening place, and crowded too (someone told me recently that some fifty or sixty thousand people live within Bologna's walls nowadays, a number hard to picture, and there cannot have been many fewer back then).

Up there, I thought. Up there was where I would live my life in Bologna. Somehow I would make my fortune, and enjoy clean air, freedom and beauty in the vertiginous world at the top of those towers. Only later did I discover that there lurked more wickedness, more perversion of law and humanity and more stench of corruption than I would ever encounter in the noisome streets below.

I continued to stare up at the delicate platforms far, far above me, fingers stretching between the tops of those great towers: I turned this way and that until I was dizzy. So mesmerised was I that I paid no attention to the sound of running footsteps behind me. Something, or someone, slammed into me. I fell to the ground, striking my head with a force that made my ears ring. A body pressed itself on my head and shoulders while a voice hissed, "His purse. Quick!"

It was over as soon as it had started. I rolled over to see two boys, perhaps my size, maybe smaller, running away down an alleyway. I reached for my purse to find only the leather thong that had attached it to my breeches. It had been cut, and my meagre money was gone. I sat up and spat from my mouth the filth that had been forced into it. I had been robbed. The few tiny coins they had taken would not buy them much, I thought: but I was left without the means to buy even some bread to eat.

I cursed my stupidity. I had been so proud of my plan to escape from Modena: I had travelled without difficulty down the Via Æmilia and reached my goal. But I had not given a moment's serious thought as to how I might live. How would I earn enough to feed myself, let alone find anywhere to live? In my dreams, while I had been planning my escape from Modena, the great city had taken on the gleaming aspect of the New Jerusalem of which I had sung so many times, but in this case one built especially for me. By contrast, Bologna in the flesh was revealed as entirely out of reach, far above my head, leaving me lost, penniless and rolling in a shit-filled street.

It was tempting to sit there and cry. Nonetheless, much of my earlier resolve remained. Indeed, the blind self-belief that has got me into so many scrapes throughout my life was barely diminished. After all, the last time I had been completely alone I was locked in a cell and being bent to the will of others: this time I was free. I had succeeded in escaping to a place where even the omnipotent churchmen of Modena would hesitate to follow. Besides, in this new life I would not draw attention to myself by singing in a cathedral. I would keep my head down.

Yet the question remained: what would I do? For the time being, I had no idea. For the rest of the day and far into the evening I wandered the streets. I kept in the shadows and avoided drawing attention to myself, watching and listening as I had taught myself. I found myself in a square by a large church which looked old and was built of warm-coloured orange-red bricks. I asked a passer-by the name of the church, and was told it was San Stefano. A succession of curious bulges and apses created little nooks and indentations that were relatively free of filth: I settled myself in one and watched the world go by.

I was hungry, to be sure, but not starving. I thought I would save my strength and, on the morrow, find stalls and shops and offer myself as a boy-of-all-work. Someone, I reasoned, must need a reasonably robust lad to fetch and carry: and I could impress potential employers with the fact that I could read and write.

As evening fell, the streets, which had fallen empty, filled up again. There were groups of young men, apprentices and journeymen, finishing their long day's toil. Some were clearly making their way to the tavern: others must have been there for some time, as they sang and burped, occasionally relieving themselves in the street.

From time to time a larger group would appear. In the lead, a dozen big, strong, fierce-looking men armed with cudgels and knives clearing the street ahead of the richly dressed group: a man with his wife and family, beautifully clothed children following their parents a respectful distance behind. Without exception the adults ignored me. One or two of the children in tow caught my eye: but, when I smiled at them and, plucking up courage on one occasion, put my hand out in a begging gesture, they looked away abruptly. A couple of the bodyguards spotted the movement, detached themselves from the group, approached and stood on either side of me, large and intimidating. "Oi, scum," hissed one. "Keep yer thieving hands to yerself."

"Yeah. We don't let dirty little beggars bother the quality."

"Stick yer fucking hand out again and I'll cut it off. Understand?" Cowed, I nodded without speaking, and a tremendous kick thudded into my ribs. I curled into a ball as the two brutes rained kicks and blows on me, hands protecting my head as the silent assault continued. Then, as abruptly as they had started, the blows ceased. One of the men spat on me as he turned, and they both stumped away, muttering to themselves.

Slowly I straightened my limbs. I was bruised, and shocked: I was encountering sudden, casual violence too often for comfort. Yet nothing seemed to be broken. Either I was fortunate or, more likely, the two knew their business, and their blows were calculated to scare me without causing real hurt. I decided to remain in the relative safety of my corner and, drawing myself further into the gap between the brick buttresses, I settled down for the night.

As dusk gave way to full darkness, I could see lighted windows above me, stretching high up in the towers that surrounded that square. The streets fell silent. The only passers-by were cautious, or furtive: I guessed they were either fearful of footpads, or up to no good themselves.

With my plan fixed for the next day, I turned my thoughts to my identity. The name Luca had been given to me against my will when I arrived in Modena. Should I revert to my given name, Giovanni? I decided against it. This was another new life for me, requiring another new name.

I considered various possibilities. Then I remembered the story of a particular saint. Modena's cathedral, truly the architectural marvel of its age, was built of lustrous marble and embellished with exquisite carvings by the renowned Maestro Wiligelmus. I had kept my promise to Giovanni before I made my escape, and crept down to the vault below the cathedral's main altar where the city's patron saint lies.

We boys must have processed past the pillars that supported the chancel floor more times than we could count, and never accorded a second glance to the way in which the sculptor had cunningly woven Biblical stories around them. Yet on that last visit, I had at last noticed those illuminated tales, and one in particular had intrigued me. It was that of San Lorenzo, Saint Lawrence, who had distributed the riches of the early church to the poor rather than surrender them to the Roman authorities, and was martyred by being cooked on a large grill. I was mesmerised by the figure of the saint sculpted, faintly comically, stretched on his griddle, as a torturer with wicked glee on his face stoked the red flames beneath him. I shuddered as I wondered, briefly, what torments had been inflicted on Giovanni the leather-seller.

Lorenzo. That would do for a name: after all, I had undergone a few trials myself. I would be Lorenzo of Bologna. And that name, apart from those occasions when I have been obliged to assume another identity on a temporary basis, I have kept until the present day. Lorenzo da Bologna: I liked the ring of it. I curled up where I had been sitting and, tired from a long day full of new experiences, I fell asleep.

I cannot claim I slept well. Whatever else I had lacked in all my years in a cathedral dormitory, I had never been without a straw mattress. I found the hard street, a packed-down surface of dried mud and stones, an uncongenial bed. I had chosen the corner of a church to sleep in because it was familiar: and maybe I thought it would afford some kind of safety. If so, I was mistaken.

Several times in the night I was forcibly awakened. Once or twice someone passing by kicked me: when I groaned sleepily, they grunted and moved on. They may have been checking that I was alive, or maybe they hated beggars: having known homelessness, I frequently note how those who enjoy prosperity feel threatened by the presence of the dispossessed on their doorstep.

At other times I woke from my fitful sleep to find hands rummaging through my clothes. Even when I woke and protested they carried on: would-be robbers were not deterred by my stirring. On each occasion, though, they left with a curse and a kick: I had nothing for them to steal except my very garments.

After one such episode when, in the pre-dawn glow, I was lying awake, too scared to allow myself to drift off again, a sudden uproar erupted from a nearby street. Four men burst into the square, knives drawn, shouting. In a moment they were pursued and part-surrounded by a much larger group, some twenty at least. There was a clash of weapons and a scream. Amid the yells and shrieks I made out a cry of, "Lambertazzi bastards! You'll not take us." Another urged, "Split up, lads!"

Flashing their knives at those closest to them (and apparently drawing blood, for there were fresh screams), two of the pursued broke free and ran for a street across the square, a dozen or so of their enemies at their heels, hallooing as if it were a hunt. The other two ran towards me, heading for a narrow alleyway running down beside the church. As they passed me something whistled through the air, striking the hindmost of the pair. With a groan, almost an expression of surprise, he fell to the ground beside me: I could see the knife-hilt protruding from his back.

The other never slowed, but disappeared down the alley. Most of his pursuers followed him, shouting as they went, but two halted by the body. "Good throw!" commented one, as he checked that his quarry was dead and proceeded to check thoroughly through all his clothes. "A purse: I'll take that," he muttered. "Nothing else, though. I'd have sworn I heard him say he was taking something to the Gatekeeper."

"Curse those *gonfalonieri*! The Companies of Arms are always making mischief," replied the other. "Still, this one won't make any more." Terrified by the proximity of these killers, I just wanted to be ignored, so I lay still, feigning sleep or death.

"Who's this?" Now they had noticed me. Rough hands groped me, checking my clothes too. Pretending to sleep was useless now, so I uttered a sleepy, complaining kind of grunt. "Nah, just some street-urchin. Leave him: we'd best get away." With a cuff round the head, he dropped me.

I was left alone with the corpse. I was shocked by the fatal intensity of such sudden violence. Moreover, I had swiftly learned that men were ready to kill in response to the merest, most casual mention of the Gatekeeper. Dark thoughts teemed in my mind: yet, in recounting my tale, I realised once again that I could not tell my master half of it. I was resolved never to disclose the other names I knew, not even to my rescuer and confidante.

That decision was made on that alarming first night alone in Bologna. It was clear that knowledge of the message entrusted to me by Giovanni was deadly. Even to seek to find the

Gatekeeper would be foolhardy: to deliver the message, close to suicidal. So I would not do so. I would forget all about the Gatekeeper and the other names I was carrying in my memory. I would become Lorenzo, and make a new life in Bologna.

My hand was resting in something dark, sticky and warm: a pool of blood had formed under the body, and was spreading towards me. I shivered and pulled away from it. Knowing that no good could come of being found there, I got up and ran away, taking care to choose a direction that none of the combatants had taken.

Sunrise found me in the city's main square, feeling groggy, sore and stiff. I washed the blood from my hands, splashed my face and drank greedily from the marble fountain in the corner of the square. That feature is charitably provided in many city squares, clean water keeping people in my situation alive and, so they say, reducing bellyache and sickness among the population.

Shopkeepers were opening their shutters. Stallholders were setting up and laying out their wares. Even after my disturbed and alarming night, I felt a surge of optimism in the morning of a new day. Having rehearsed my lines over and over in my head, I tried them on one shopkeeper after another. "Please, sir. Excuse me, ma'am. I'm newly arrived in the city. Do you have some work for me? I'm strong. I can work hard: and I can read and write."

Responses varied. Some ignored me and turned their back. Others threatened or chased me away. The women I approached were more likely to spare me a word. I lost count of how many times I heard, "I have enough mouths to feed already, boy, without adding you to them." But some were kind, and pushed a crust or a piece of fruit into my hand.

Even an incurable optimist may be worn down by constant refusal. After a whole day of it I was truly despondent, even if the disappointment had occasionally been tempered with a small gift of food. Nonetheless, by evening I was weary beyond belief while hunger gnawed my insides. Still wandering the streets aimlessly, I stopped beside a tavern. At tables and benches spilling out into the street sat a cheery group of men and women who seemed to be celebrating. I loitered, mostly because the smell of roast meats from within the tavern was irresistible and my stomach was rumbling.

Then, as people do in convivial company, one of the women started to sing. It was a melody I immediately recognised, that song, *Ti canterò lo meo amor*: its haunting melody transported me in memory straight back to Tommaso's house where his parents, brothers and sisters – above all, Rosalia - had sung while he accompanied them on his rebec. Tears started in my eyes. Without thinking I joined in, and sang along with them.

What possessed me? On arrival in Bologna I had vowed I would not sing again: partly in order to remain anonymous, and partly because I was sure that I would never again sing for love. Yet, just as the happiness of Tommaso's family home had made me forget my cold-hearted resolves, so hearing these people sing for sheer joy, enjoying a tune I had sung with my friends, I could not help myself.

When the company embarked on a second verse, I added a descant, in my mixed treble-and-falsetto voice, just as I had last done with Tommaso nearly a year before. It was a plaintive melody, telling the story of a lost love, and as I improvised a counterpoint, almost unconsciously I poured into it my own sense of loss and loneliness.

At the end of the verse there was a silence. I had been singing with my eyes closed, using my ears and my musical instinct even while I wept. When I opened them every member of the group was staring at me: abruptly they burst into spontaneous applause. "Come here, boy," exclaimed a matronly woman. "That was beautiful. Where did you learn to sing like that?" Fortunately she was too busy talking to listen to any answer I might make. "Do you know any more such songs? Sing them with us."

So I did.

Food and drinks began to arrive, which they shared with me. They made a fuss of me, saying, "Feed that beautiful voice. Have some wine for that descant." They were not curious about me, but they were welcoming. In their company I relaxed, and certainly ate and drank my fill. I probably drank a little too much wine, as my head started to feel fuzzy. As the evening progressed, the singing died down. As often happens, the party fragmented into small conversations, some desultory, some intense. From being the centre of attention, I was gradually excluded: not that I minded. Although slightly befuddled with wine, I had the good sense to know that I needed to feed up as much as I could, in case the following day was another long and hungry one. Quietly, greedily, I picked up a board of meats and bread, and moved to a quieter corner of the tavern.

As I sat and munched my way through the pile of meat in front of me I became sleepy and hardly aware of what was going on around me. I ignored two burly men, both with knives at their waists, who sat down at the table next to me. They were talking quietly, earnestly, and I paid no attention to them, staring vacantly in front of me, lost in my own thoughts.

Then I heard a word that instantly grabbed my attention. I was sure I had heard one of them say, "Gatekeeper". I turned my head slightly towards them and, continuing to eat, started to listen intently.

"The Gatekeeper? What about him?" asked the other.

"The *Padrone* is nervous. This damned Gatekeeper's got under his skin. He's convinced he knows what he's doing even before he's planned it. Take that scheme to bankrupt Orso: you know, the tapestry-weaver. The boss had it all lined up so that he'd scare off all the clients and leave him with a pile of expensive silk he couldn't pay for. But what happened? Orso turned out to have a line of credit. He could bide his time and wait for them to come back to him."

"Someone must have tipped him off. And found someone to stand surety for him."

"It'll be one of the guilds. When those tradesmen band together, even the families can't win against them."

"Or the Gatekeeper, stirring trouble between us."

"The Gatekeeper? You reckon *he* fixed things for Orso?"

"Seems most likely. Everything the boss tries, he seems to be headed off. It's really rattled him."

Tiredness, the wine, the unaccustomed volume of meat: I don't know what caused it, but my usual caution had deserted me. Overhearing that name again, I neglected to appear blank and vacant, focused on nothing, as I had learnt to do in Modena. Instead I must have been staring at the two men. One signalled to the other and they fell silent, finished their wine and left. The tavern had fallen quiet by this stage: the landlord and two girls were clearing up, putting stools on top of tables and clearly wanting me to go. Disappointed that the cheery party who had enjoyed my singing had broken up and departed without asking me to join them, I stood up and left, resigning myself to another solitary night in the corner by San Stefano.

Chapter 11

As I turned the corner a hand grabbed me and slammed me against the wall. In the darkness I could barely make out the face pressed close to mine, while a hand squeezed my throat. "Why were you listening to us? Who sent you?"

"I didn't. No one," I stammered. "I was just eating."

"Who are you? What did you hear?"

"My name is Luca. I mean, it's Lorenzo."

"What? How many names do you have? Don't dare to lie to me."

The face pressed even closer to mine, as the point of a blade pressed under my chin. I could feel it begin to break the skin.

"What did you hear, boy?"

"Nothing, sir. I swear. I was just eating."

"Well now, Luca or Lorenzo. I think you're a liar. And I'm going to make you tell me the truth." A fist was suddenly rammed into my stomach so hard that I doubled up. He let me go and I vomited my supper all over his boots. He hauled me to my feet again as I gasped for breath.

"Honestly, sir," I gasped. "Please don't hurt me. I just heard something about a Gatekeeper. Only that, a Gatekeeper."

My answer failed to satisfy him. "What else? What more did you hear? I'll skewer you, you little…"

"Nothing, sir. I just heard that word."

If only I had been truly as unaware of conversations in Modena as I had always taken pains to appear! Still, having accidentally let slip that single piece of knowledge, I quickly determined to admit to it, but to no more. Assuming a mask of blankness, even idiocy, would, I prayed, convince them that I was harmless to them.

"I don't believe you. What does a street-rat like you know about someone like the Gatekeeper?"

"Nothing, sir. I don't know anything. It's just something I heard. Please let me go. I didn't mean to stare - or to listen."

The other man intervened. "Not here. We'll take him back to the tower. No one'll miss this little runt. We can take time to find out what he knows."

Still incoherent, gasping, "Please! No," I was dragged down the street towards one of the great towers. If anyone saw a boy being taken against his will, they did not intervene. There was nothing remarkable in that around those lawless streets.

They hammered on a large, forbidding gate which was swiftly opened. Inside was a courtyard of timber buildings on two floors. A fire was burning in the middle, and a number of men were sitting or standing around it. Others were leaning on the rail of the balcony that ran around the first floor, chatting and laughing. It might have been a cheering sight, had I not been scared out of my wits. No one appeared to take any notice of our arrival.

From the corner rose the massive base of a great stone tower. I was pushed through another doorway into a lofty but dark space which narrowed towards the top in shadows that were not penetrated by the few lamps and torches around the walls. I was dragged to a wooden staircase. Again I was held by the throat. "Listen, boy. Either you walk up those stairs without making trouble for me, or I knock you senseless and carry you up. What's it to be?"

I indicated that I would walk, though in my terror my legs were unsteady at best. Between them they dragged and pushed me up the stairs. Up, up, up we went, through storerooms, one above the other, packed with bales and barrels containing what goods I could only guess. On we went, ever upwards. Some of the rooms, always square, one above another, were entirely empty. One, as far as I could tell from my captors' flickering torches, contained chains, manacles and other strange constructions of metal, as if it were a prison, though there was no one confined in it. I had no idea how high we had climbed when the men stopped me, though we were all sweating and out of breath. Again I was pushed roughly against the wall.

"Now, my lad. On the next floor's the Signore's chamber. That's Signor Lambertazzi. You're going to tell him what you know about the Gatekeeper. And why you were eavesdropping." Again I shook my head and babbled that I knew nothing. Again my head was pounded against the wall, making me dizzy. "I'm tired of you lying to me, boy," he said. "If you don't tell me the truth I'm going to start hurting you."

I was too terrified to think coherently, let alone to point out that he had been hurting me ever since he grabbed me. "Sir," I replied, "I've heard the name, and that's why you caught my attention. But I don't know what it mean or who it is. I've just heard it spoken."

"Spoken? By whom?"

"By the Bishop. Of Modena." I cursed myself as I heard the words tumble out. Though it was the truth, they would never believe it. My head was banged against the wall again.

"The Bishop of Modena? You expect me to believe that scum like you would ever hear that great man speak, let alone of such private matters? Now tell me the truth before I slit your throat."

The blade was at my throat again, pricking the skin till I felt the blood run. I was shaking with mortal terror: I think I wetted myself as I swore that I really was telling the truth.

"So you heard this at the Bishop's table, in Modena?"

"I did. Honestly." I panted. "I was pouring his wine. Serving at table. In Modena." The words were tumbling out now: I seemed incapable of holding them back.

"So if that was in Modena, what are you doing here, in Bologna?"

"I ran away. They wanted to send me to France. I escaped. Please, you must believe me."

There was a silence as the knife continued to press against my neck. "Well," one of the voices came slowly: by this stage I could not tell which of them was speaking. "He's an idiot, and probably mad. But maybe he's saying what he thinks is true?"

"We'll take him upstairs."

I was dragged up a further floor, and bundled through a door. After the darkness of our ascent, the light was dazzling. There were beautiful lamps all around the wall, which made the rich hangings on all the walls glitter. I was thrown to my knees in front of an enormous man seated in what seemed an immense chair. As I crouched abjectly before him, I could see a huge face sitting above several chins. But it hurt to look up that far, so I fixed my eyes on the large, pudgy hands, heavy with golden rings and sparkling stones.

I knelt, quaking with terror, while my captors outlined to their master what had ensued. When it came to my explanation they concluded, "He's either mad or a good liar." From the depths of that immense body rumbled a deep voice, "Ah, but which? We need to know." One of the immense hands cupped my chin and forced me to look him in the face. "Now, boy, I am Massimo Lambertazzi. I want to know, I *will* know what you know of the Gatekeeper."

Cowed beyond terror, almost in a trance, I found I could not speak. As I shook my head in desperation, a silky, smooth voice cut in from my right, quietly yet with authority: I had heard it before. "If I may advise, Signore?" I looked round and my heart sank as I recognised the lean, tall figure clad in black above pointed, highly polished black boots: Bardi. The big man grunted. "And what *do* you suggest, Bartolomeo?"

"Merely that we should test the truth. Let us take him outside – for some air." In response he received a wheezy chuckle: "Very well."

I was seized again, and dragged to a door – or was it a window? The shutter was pulled open, and we were out in the open, a cool, brisk wind whipping around us. Just as I realised that we were on one of those bridges between the towers that I had seen from the ground, my ankles were seized and I was dangled over the thin rail. In front of me – no, below me - the tower stretched away, down into blackness, a dizzying, vertiginous perspective. Only the strong grip on my ankles held me from plunging headlong into that void. The wind lashed my face and blew my hair into a wild plume as I pictured my fall, tumbling helpless, turning over and over till I was dashed to pieces on the invisible hard ground. I howled my anguish.

"So now tell us the truth, vermin," said one of my captors. I stopped screaming, and hung limp and helpless in that relentless grasp.

The velvety voice took over. "What do you know of the Gatekeeper, boy? Tell me the truth and I might let you live." Even in my perilous predicament, there was a comforting note to his speech. "If not, I wonder how long it will take you to hit the ground when we let you go? How long did we count, the last time we dropped a spy over the edge? I forget."

"It *is* the truth," I whined. "Please, sir, I just heard the names, when I was serving wine. That's all."

"Hm," he pondered for a moment. "Have I seen you before, perhaps?"

I assumed my blankest, most guileless face. "I don't think so, sir. I, I'm sure I would remember a *grand signore* such as your worship, if I had served at your table, though you might not remember a humble serving boy. No, sir. Sir, I beg you, please let me go."

"Let you go? That might be the best thing."

"No, I mean... please," I wailed, and then screamed again as the hands holding my ankles pretended to let me go and I felt myself falling into that immeasurable abyss. Amid rough laughter I was hauled ungently over the rail and thrown back into the room. I curled into a ball and lay snivelling.

"He's telling the truth, I think," murmured Bardi, "Or what he believes to be the truth. Nonetheless, to be entirely safe we should kill him."

A new voice broke in, a childish girl's voice. "Don't kill him, uncle. He's a pretty boy."

The fat man grunted. "He's a dirty ragamuffin, Livia. I don't know why you would say a piece of rubbish from the street like this is pretty. Even if he were cleaner. Besides, I suspect he's a spy,

87

though I cannot imagine who would send an idiot child to attempt to discover our secrets."

"Please, uncle. Don't kill him." It was a voice with an edge, both child-like and petulant, used to having its way.

I looked up and saw the most beautiful girl I could have imagined. About my age, she had pure white skin, full sensuous lips, brown eyes and long, straight hair as black as jet. I stared at her as she cast her cold, appraising glance over me. Did I say cold? Her look was icy. "He's too pretty to die," she repeated, pouting. I could not know then the extent to which Livia, niece to the infamous Massimo Lambertazzi, would dominate my thoughts, my very life, for years to come.

Her uncle looked uneasily across the room. "Bartolomeo. Should I follow your advice, as I always do? Or should I indulge my niece's whim, as I do - all too frequently? I confess I find myself leaning toward the latter course."

"As you wish, *Signore,*" replied the silky voice. "In order to remove all risk, we should silence him. But we could... merely teach him to fear us."

"Thank you, Bartolomeo." The huge man's voice was a deep rumble. "As ever you put my mind at rest. We shall take the latter course, and avoid the necessity of disposing of a body... though, God knows, that is easily done." He laughed indulgently. "Very well, my dear. You have your wish. We shall whip him soundly, until we are satisfied we have the truth from him, then throw him back into the street."

He turned to the tall man in black. "Bartolomeo, would you make a start on our business with that damned lawyer? Stand no nonsense, mind." He sighed. "In the old days, notaries would simply do our bidding and make the law work for us. Now it seems we must argue and wrangle over every little issue, and be put in our place by some puffed-up jurist who presumes to use the weight of the law to tell us, *us*, how to conduct our business." As he warmed to his theme, his face grew red and his vast bulk shook with fury.

"Do not be troubled, Signore. I shall be firm." The smooth voice was infinitely reassuring. "Indeed, given the tenor of recent conversations, I suspect this may be the last time you will wish to employ the services of that particular adviser. I have another, more malleable character in mind."

"Thank you, Bartolomeo. As ever you put my mind at rest. Now, I shall see this urchin questioned and properly whipped: that will put me in a better humour. And then I shall join you above." Bardi bowed and headed up the stairs.

I wasn't dismissed so much as discarded, a piece of refuse identified and thrown away. This time I was hustled down the stairs two, maybe three floors into the room that I had suspected was a prison. There they tore my clothes off me: they were poor rags, and flimsy enough. They strapped me to a rough plank, and set about whipping me.

I stopped, looking my master in the eye. "And now, Magister," I concluded, "You have heard the whole story."

"Or nearly all, Lorenzo, at any rate. And I thank you for it."

Chapter 12

Those long recitations of my personal history took place on the rare days when my master appeared to have time on her hands. Her busy days ran to a very different rhythm. She was truly revered (and in demand) as a lawyer. Whatever the truth or otherwise of the tales of her lecturing from behind a screen in her youth, so fine a speaker was she, and so lionised, that she could not hold her lectures in an ordinary university teaching room, a *studium*. Instead a small platform would be set up in one of the squares, frequently that beside San Stefano where I had spent my first lonely night in Bologna.

Students of all ages and, it seemed, from all cities and nations would crowd into the square and jostle for a position close to her. And when she began to speak, a respectful silence fell. Any interruption, even a cough, earned the crowd's weighty disapproval. And at the end, however much she had berated her audience for not working hard enough, for not properly absorbing the detail of the text, for not interpreting with sufficient originality or rigour, they would applaud her, something almost unique in the university which was, for one thing, stiffly formal and moreover, as far as I could tell, frequently dull when it came to the other lecturers.

It was uncommon for my master to entertain visitors, but she frequently stayed up late to work: thus the nights were rare, when I had seen her safe to bed and received my orders for the next day to pass on to Michele and Mamolo, that I could slip out to meet my three friends at the tavern.

Occasionally the Magister would decide it was time to entertain, and invite guests to dine with her. Her regular, if infrequent, guests were fellow jurists, and from time to time some of the lesser merchants who were part-friend, part-client, even part-dependent. The welcome of the house was always warm and the fare sumptuous, notwithstanding Mamolo's constant whining that he could not be expected, at the notice he was given and on the budget he was allowed, to provide food worthy of anyone above the status of a beggar. The meals he served were a delight: there was pungent ham mellowed with figs in season, or olives in brine; rich stews of meat with fruits or dried plums; meats roasted with herbs or lemons, or perhaps a suckling pig; more of his tasty dough parcels; followed by sweet delicacies of every kind.

I would stand behind my master's chair, filling the cups with wine as required, fetching and carrying the next course as Mamolo demanded. My mouth would water and my stomach rumble as I watched the guests dine. When they had eaten their fill, I would be instructed to remove the platters: naturally, as soon as I had the opportunity, I fell on the leftover meats and sauces.

Never one to pay lip-service to etiquette, the Magister did not invite guests out of mere politeness: nor did she do so for business reasons, to gain any kind of advantage. She asked people whom she liked, and with whom she could have what she termed a lively debate, always about the law. Discussion, which would often become heated, would range from the niceties of a particular point to consideration of the entire purpose of the law.

A frequent dinner-guest, and undoubtedly the Magister's preferred company, was a lawyer whose reputation I soon discovered was even greater in Bologna than hers. Rolandino de' Pasaggeri was a big lump of a man, about the same age as my master. His large, coarse hands and round, florid face betrayed his humble origins: his very name came from his late father's occupation as a toll-collector at one of the river crossings. Even his accent belied his education: perhaps that suited him, since an opponent who did not know him might be deceived into underestimating his mighty intellect.

He liked his food, and would tuck into Mamolo's creations in hearty fashion, washing them down with copious amounts of wine: in this he was the opposite of his host who would invariably pick at her food and drink sparingly. When it came to legal debate, however, they were alike, neither giving ground. Over dinner they would contest points of law so fiercely that at times I feared they would come to blows.

"*Idiota*!" she would exclaim. "Even the newest, most callow of my students knows better than to argue from that standpoint!"

He would storm in return, "Saving your sex, *Dottore*, I would beat you over the head with one of your scrolls until you saw sense!"

"And how would you recognise sense when you saw it, *Maestro Notaro*? The ruling is in the Codex, as Irnerio determined beyond any doubt a century ago. That is immutable."

"Immutable? Surely you jest? To you everything is open to challenge. You use the law as if it were merely a philosopher's fancy, to be stretched and distorted according to your whim!"

At this point Mamolo would cough loudly and announce the next course. The two formidable antagonists would subside, muttering, and my master would order, "Lorenzo! More wine for our guest!" Moments later they would be swapping stories of minor legal triumphs, of battles of wits lost and won, of the foibles of other prominent lawyers, the storms replaced by gales of laughter. At the end of the evening, Rolandino would lurch unsteadily to his feet and embrace her with a warmth that she returned. "Forgive me, Bettisia. I am an old boor and should not abuse your hospitality."

"Nonsense, Rolandino, *caro,*' she would retort. "I should not provoke you in my turn – but cannot resist the temptation, you old devil!"

He would laugh uproariously, bellow for his servant (who had also made the most of the food and drink on offer, passing his time in Michele's company) and stagger off into the night, still chuckling over one of the more elegant arguments that one of them had fashioned during the evening.

When he had left, the Magister would smile at me apologetically. "Ah, Lorenzo, were there ever two bigger fools than we, who spend all day wrestling with the law and then all evening arguing about it? Now, to bed. There is much to do tomorrow."

It was always the same. I confess I used to resent the fact that her friend seemed better known than she was, and taxed her with the fact one night, after I had served at yet another combative meal. "Magister, I always thought you were the finest lawyer – jurist – in Bologna. But it seems Master Rolandino is yet more highly considered than you."

"Indeed he is, Lorenzo. In truth, he does not lecture as convincingly as I, though I... *forbear* to remind him of the fact. But his knowledge of the law in detail and depth is beyond even mine. We studied together: he received his doctorate a year or two after I. What he does not say, choosing instead to shout and bluster," she smiled indulgently, "Is that he has written a book, the complete compendium of the art of the jurist – though he insists on terming his work that of the... *notary*, a word that I consider makes us sound little more than mere... *clerks*.

"No, do not be jealous of him on my account, Lorenzo. He is a man, and I am but a woman, and fortunate to gain as much acceptance as I do. Besides, it is sometimes... *convenient* to be able to hide oneself in the shadow of a greater figure." I asked what she meant by that but, as usual, she declined to explain and went to bed, reminding me that we had "much to do tomorrow."

When I first joined her household, my master invariably took Michele with her when she went to lecture, or to visit the homes of the many rich and powerful people who employed her expertise: the clustered great towers of the *magnati*, the old aristocratic families; the grand and ever-growing houses of the bankers and merchants in their enclave around the Piazza della Mercanzia; and the modest craftsmen's dwellings where groups of tailors, ironworkers, furriers and the like would gather by trade.

To journey with protection, even a short distance, was commonplace. No one of note walked Bologna's streets unaccompanied: they were too lawless and violent. Although she was held in awe by great numbers, and knew too much for their comfort about the shady reputations of the rest, even the Magister rarely failed to take that simple precaution. And Michele, the old, scarred ex-fighter, remained a formidable protector with that heavy cudgel at his belt.

When I was feeling strong enough, I asked her, indeed I pestered her, to allow me to go with them: naturally that meant that Mamolo was obliged to stay at home (then as now, no one of substance left their house and thus their wealth unguarded, particularly in a city as lawless as Bologna was back then). Leaving Mamolo in a paroxysm of self-pity ("I might as well be back in prison for all the freedom you grant me!" he cried), that was how I first witnessed her acclaimed lectures.

When she visited her clients I sometimes went too. If we were visiting one of the towers of the magnati, Michele and I would wait in the courtyard surrounding its base. The Magister would disappear alone into the massive edifice, returning an hour, sometimes as much as three or four hours, later. The merchants and money-lenders seldom kept her so long: Michele would comment drily that they, unlike the aristocrats, understood that an hour spent discussing a contract was time stolen from making money.

When she returned to us she would usually be carrying a purse of money which she would give to Michele for safekeeping. I divined that the deep trust between them stemmed from the fact that he had been a criminal whom she had saved from a dreadful end: but whereas Mamolo spoke of his past almost unceasingly, Michele's was never mentioned.

Nonetheless, Michele was growing old. His right leg and hip troubled him, and in the cold of winter he became quite lame. He coughed and dribbled unceasingly during cold weather, too, and I could see that my master was becoming concerned for him.

That winter, Michele fell sick, and developed a fever. We feared for his life. It was at such times that the Magister transformed herself from the ruler of the household to servant and nurse. She cancelled all her engagements: she even sent me to a couple of the great families to announce that she was unavailable for the foreseeable future. To my surprise, they accepted the bald announcement without a murmur.

For three days and nights she never left Michele's bedside, bathing him, feeding him thin broth and administering medicines and potions brought to her in person by her physician of choice. Always nosy, I was desperate to find out what was the great debt that the physician owed her, to the extent that he would come running at any hour of the day or night when the summons came. But, as with all my enquiries as to who brought the finest foods, rare wines, even furniture or other gifts (though she had no time for finery), my query was blocked with a gentle smile.

Michele recovered, though it was clear that it would be long before he could once more play the part of protector as the Magister walked Bologna's chaotic streets. Still puppy-like, ever eager to please, I was desperate to take his place. "Let me accompany you, Magister. I'm tall now."

"And still skinny as a rake," she retorted with a smile.

"But Michele has taught me to fight, and to wield a cudgel. No one will molest you when I'm by your side. And they'd better not try," I added with a growl.

I was sitting beside her at table, when we had this conversation. As usual she had picked, sparrow-like, at a succulent piece of beef fried to rare perfection by Mamolo, and bathed in a thick, black balsamic sauce; and after half a dozen meagre mouthfuls, as usual, she had passed it over to me so that I could wolf it down. She reached across and tousled my hair, a maternal gesture that had become more common of late. "Bless you, Lorenzo. I do not need a bodyguard."

"Yes, you do, Magister. The streets are dangerous. Let me be your protector!"

"Have you not yet learned that we stay safer *not* by looking threatening, even though Michele can appear fierce, but by avoiding trouble, lowering our eyes and never appearing to confront."

"Magister, I've never seen you lower your eyes, nor back down from an argument."

She laughed. "No, perhaps not. But that is what we scholars term academic debate, even if with some professors it appears more akin to a street brawl. Very well. You shall become my protector - but only until Michele is strong again."

My heart leaped, and yet it seemed suddenly a solemn moment. I slipped to my knees beside her, seized her hand, and kissed it. "I would give my life for you, Magister, if it were required."

She pulled her hand away and put it on my head. "I believe you would, Lorenzo," she said softly, "But I trust it never will be called for." Her tone changed abruptly, and resumed her brisk, bossy manner. "Now, you must look the part. Stand up."

I stood before her, towering over her. "I fear you will never impress with sheer bulk, Lorenzo," she observed. "But you must appear commanding so that, when you stand on the podium in the square and call for silence, they take notice. Those clothes, now." I looked down at my clothes. They were well-worn - few ordinary folk wore new garments - but they were passable. "No, you're too young, and you're too lanky: we shall have to make you look more important! We shall buy you a new leather jerkin, brown I think; breeches, perhaps a light tan? And boots. Yes, you need proper boots up to your knees."

For much of my life I had gone barefoot, as did all boys except the rich. We were mostly barefoot in the cathedrals of Modena and Venice, sometimes wearing sandals in winter, just a roughly shaped piece of leather clasped to the feet by thongs. At the time, I was wearing some light shoes of the thinnest, meanest leather, cast-offs from somewhere that Michele had retrieved when the household had first fed and clothed me.

"Boots, Magister? I won't refuse." I was already picturing myself strutting proudly beside the Magister as I made way for her: proudly announcing her presence to her students or clients; banging on the gates of the magnati, calling loudly, "Pray, open for my master, the jurist Dottor Bettisia Gozzadini!"

"Yes, Lorenzo. I believe you will do it... *adequately*: if a little theatrically. Now, I know just the man who will make you those garments and boots. I believe he is in my debt."

She gave me the address and I hastened to the worker's little shop. The owner's surly indifference turned instantly to anxiety to please when I mentioned who my master was, and within a few days he was proudly bringing the items to the house for me to try. I twirled and preened in my finery, until my master twisted my ear and bade me stop. "Lorenzo, you are there merely to protect me and announce me; you are not required also to sing and dance!"

I grinned. She knew me too well, always ready to get carried away and show off. But she was also aware that I was desperate to serve and please her, and I took delight in my new role, as much as anything because it was another way to prove my devotion to her. Was I to be her protector? If so, I hoped, desperately in my imaginings, to put my body, my life even, between her and danger. I too felt that debt to her that so many appeared to share; and I bore it not as a burden but as a privilege. That was her incalculable power.

Chapter 13

One thing I learned then, which still makes me laugh when I think about it. If you want to transform a stripling boy into a man, give him a pair of stout boots. I felt as if I had grown a hand's breadth. I strutted about the house, and lorded it dreadfully over Mamolo and Michele – or tried to. It made little difference to Mamolo, whose sourness and complaints continued unabated. Michele, restored to some measure of health but no longer strong enough to tramp the streets with our master, took it in good part, merely taking the opportunity to cuff me around the head if I came too close or enquired too solicitously about his health. He continued to mind the house and the money, but now stayed at home.

Thus I became bodyguard, announcer and, eventually, scribe. I had eventually persuaded my master that my reading and writing might measure up even to her exacting standards. One day, after weeks of wheedling, I persuaded her to let me copy a contract for her, a simple indenture for an apprentice. When it was done I presented it to her with a flourish. She grunted and looked through it carefully, holding it up close to her face as she tended to when reading. I stood motionless, silent: that is what I had learnt to do if I was seeking her hard-won approval.

After an age, it seemed, she grunted again. "That is well written, Lorenzo. In the matter of writing, at least, you have not overstated your skill. Very well, then. When I need something written or copied you may do it: but woe betide you if there is a single mistake. This is the law, immutable and unbending. It binds men's lives, and must be correct to the very last letter."

In my delight at receiving her approval, I could not resist teasing her. "But surely, Magister, it is not entirely immutable, as Master de' Pasaggeri said to you the other night. Otherwise, why do people pay you so much money to bend the law in their favour?"

Fortunately she was in a good humour that day. "Damn you for a rogue and a trickster, Lorenzo! You know full well I never bend the law."

"But Master Rolandino said…"

"That old buffoon will say anything after a few cups of wine, simply to needle me! No, Lorenzo, you have my word: I merely... *interpret*," she lapsed into her legal mode of speech: "And offer guidance in favour of my client. Unlike some of my colleagues, I may add. No, the law itself is implacable and must not be open to doubt. Why," she continued, "That is the reason why I am here, and why the university came to be founded in Bologna."

"I know, Magister, I know. You constantly remind me of it. The university preserves the Codex of Justinian: the Emperor commanded that Roman law be written down for all time."

"Precisely, Lorenzo. Perhaps I do somewhat frequently ... *stress* the importance of the Codex. Yet it is timeless, and irreplaceable, the foundation of all law. No one knows now how many copies were made: but ours, kept here in Bologna, is the only one known in our modern world."

I was in argumentative mood. "But surely custom and practice change? You always say in your lectures that times change, cities adapt, and people and customs must, too."

"You've been listening to my lectures? Good. Perhaps we shall yet cram some sense into your empty head! It is true that times and customs change. But the law stays, timeless and perpetual: and it is the task of jurists such as me, following in the footsteps of our great founders, the *glossists* (you see their grand arched tombs by the Church of San Domenico), to ensure that the law is relevant to our times, without sacrificing its eternal truths."

"But, Magister, your clients *do* pay you to gain the ruling that they want: even if you have to go and argue for them in the *Consiglio*."

"Yes, Lorenzo, I do. And sometimes I go to the council to prevent an injustice. As I did once for Mamolo, and again for Michele. Both had done wrong, but neither deserved the maiming or death that threatened them."

"And me: what about me? Why did you rescue me?"

"It was pure chance that I saw you: and why should I not stop two brutes beating a child to death at the bidding of their master? Signor Massimo Lambertazzi, a monster and a bully."

"Lambertazzi, that bastard! But, Magister, If you thought so ill of him, why did you ever do work for him?"

"One cannot always choose one's clients, Lorenzo: yet your reproach demands a fuller response. It... *suited* me to advise him for... *various* reasons. But I did not like him, nor approve of his spoilt and perverted ways. Moreover, to answer your previous question, perhaps I enjoyed thwarting him by saving you: though in consequence I will not receive instruction or money from him again. Never forget, Lorenzo: from any action, particularly a rash one, flow consequences. Now, let us go to work." The subject was closed abruptly and she moved on, as she often did.

I loved that time. Through the winter and into the spring I strutted ahead of her, clearing a path in the streets, shouting for order at her lectures, hammering on the doors of the great towers or the merchants' enormous homes to announce her - sometimes being permitted to climb high up into those towers or to penetrate the depths of what seemed to me palaces to find myself with her in the private chambers of her powerful employers.

Attending the magnati in their towers was frequently absurd, even comical. Too grand to descend to receive us at street level, they would require us to climb stair after stair, sometimes mere ladders, until we were far, far higher than any church roof. Eventually we would arrive in the great family's rooms, dripping with sweat and out of breath. If the manner of our arrival amused our illustrious clients, they did not show it - while my master's pride would not permit her to acknowledge weakness, or even to wipe the sweat from her brow, as she outlined the nature of the day's legal business.

If it had been a particularly arduous climb, however, with servants hurrying us all the way, she would express herself forcibly – once we were safely out in the street. "How ludicrous is the fearfulness of the powerful, Lorenzo! They build enormous towers in which to hide their families, each one higher than the last. Having removed themselves to that great height they next require us to wear our legs out attending to them. Perched in their lofty nest, few stoop to... *descend* to the real world. Instead they build precarious aerial connections between the towers of their *consorterie*. I distrust those flimsy structures and avoid them at all costs: if I must enter the realm of birds to do business, I prefer stone around me and solid beams beneath my feet."

"They say they dig tunnels between them, too, Magister, so that even when they do come down they need not find themselves in the streets. Except when they go to church, I suppose."

"Yes, even they have not yet succeeding in summoning the Almighty to their towers, Lorenzo: they still must go to *him* on a Sunday or feast-day. I dare say you are right about the tunnels: I have heard tell of them, too. The great families are rich and mad enough to do such things. Fortunately, even though they can... *immure* themselves against the world, they still need to pay me, pay *us* - and handsomely - to protect them from and through the law. No tower is high enough to place them... *above* the law."

When I say that I accompanied my master whenever she went out into the streets of Bologna, I mean *every* occasion. Indeed, from time to time she would evade our vigilance and contrive to slip out discreetly to visit colleagues or friends nearby: on her return she would be greeted and scolded by the three of us. Mamolo would be shrilly outraged, protesting the fears and nightmares he had had while she was away, imagining her abducted, robbed and left for dead. Michele was more blunt: he would tell her she was foolish, had no sense of her own worth or how much others depended on her, and showed no more sense than this whippersnapper here, at which he would nod towards me. For my part, unable to get a word in, I did my best to look wounded and offended at being denied the chance to do my duty in protecting her.

She would have none of it, muttering under her breath throughout our expressions of outrage, "I thought I was the only old woman here." Then she would dismiss us and set off to her room to do some work, asserting as ever that there was "much to do".

In addition to accompanying her to her lectures, and to the houses and towers of her clients, I also went with her to church. The Magister normally chose to attend Mass at San Stefano, the very place where I had found a dubious kind of sanctuary on my first and only night living on the streets of Bologna. That ancient abbey was inhabited by an obscure community of monks: I never fully understood the esoteric tradition from which they hailed, but it was not one of the powerful orders, such as the Benedictines or Augustinians, with all their influence and their links to Rome, nor the followers of Francis who in recent memory had caused Rome itself such heartache and soul-searching.

San Stefano was not generally visited by the smarter families, although in its ancient circular chapel it housed the tomb of San Petronio, a magnificent construction based, it was said, on the Holy Sepulchre in Jerusalem itself. Liturgically the church was something of a backwater, not given to excessive displays of spectacle, light, incense or even music. My master disliked those aspects of cathedral worship with which I had grown up while, in my new life, I was content to avoid such complexities. So, on a Sunday or a feast day, I would accompany her there, in my now customary role of protector.

I would not say that I was devout: I am certain she was not. But going to church on the appointed days was something that everyone did. Not to do so would attract comment and, for so public a figure as the Magister, some hostility: so we went. It was as if, for both of us, there were other arguments to engage in, other battles to fight, without wrestling with our own faith or observances.

However one Sunday, for a reason I forget, my master had agreed to go to Bologna's Cathedral for Sunday Mass. As we approached that great church, larger than that of Modena though lacking its intricately decorated columns and carvings, we could discern a formidable crowd gathering. This, then, was where the families went to worship – and to be seen. It was the patronal festival of the Duomo, the feast of Saint Peter, and the Cardinal Archbishop of Bologna himself was presiding over the service.

All the major families were there: my master reeled off their names as she saw them approach, each great man surrounded by his family and, around them, his retinue. Some were clerks, servants and assistants, many clad in livery. Some were slaves, carrying goods and even the money that the aristocracy would distribute, amid great show, as alms to the poor. Surrounding them, as ever, were their armed guards, hired bruisers so lumpish and threatening as to make Michele look relatively harmless.

There appeared to be an order of precedence, pointed out to me with amusement by my master as the families jostled for position without appearing to push. One of the first to enter the great west doors of the Cathedral, with much bowing from other families, was a group at whose heart I recognised figures who still occupied my dreams, and my nightmares. A massively fat man waddled in the centre of his group, sweating under his rich robes in the summer heat and wheezing as he walked: it was Massimo Lambertazzi, lord of that tower in which I had been tortured nearly to death. Beside him walked the tall figure of the advisor with the smooth, silky voice – Bartolomeo Bardi, who had enjoyed tormenting me by threatening to throw me from the top of the tower. Then, just as hatred and resentment were about to consume me, my heart leapt instead: for there, with the other women of the household, was Lambertazzi's niece, Livia.

Livia. I had seen her for but a moment, when I was cowering in front of her uncle, awaiting his judgment. She had pleaded for my life, claiming that I was too pretty to die. Now she stood before me, Livia, pale, with jet-black hair, slim, her back straight, her body taut as a bowstring. And my heart leapt again.

She turned and looked towards me. I swore she caught my eye, and recognised me. I was transfixed: she smiled and walked on.

After that I was a regular attender at the cathedral, at least on the bigger Sundays and feast-days. If my master thought I had succumbed to an attack of religious fervour, she said nothing. Yet I constantly found excuses to go, always in the hope of seeing Livia. Frequently I was disappointed: but from time to time I would spot her. Always I was tall enough to look across the Duomo towards her: and always I was certain that she had caught my eye, smiled and looked away. We never spoke - of course we could not - and I could not prove that she ever really acknowledged me: but I convinced myself that she did, and a glance from those eyes would pierce me.

Lovelorn and foolish, I could not keep away from the Duomo. Like a gambler constantly drawn to the dice, no matter how much he loses, I was forever in hope: yet, when I set eyes on her, I was more wounded by my inability to speak to her and profess my devotion than if I had not seen her at all.

I should explain the nature of the work that my master undertook for her clients. Much of it was simple by her standards: bread-and-butter work, she called it. There were marriage contracts between the great families: deeds for exchanges of land and farms; even (she sniffed at this base work, but nonetheless took the money) agreements of rents for farms, some just outside the city, some in distant places, so that I marvelled at the extent of the lands held by her noble clients. However, she steadfastly refused to notarise the sale or purchase of slaves: "I will not stoop to … *bartering* with human flesh," she would say.

For the merchants there were bills of sale of all kinds, and complex agreements between moneylenders, merchants and craftsmen who needed the wheels of commerce to turn so that they could borrow, invest, trade and augment their riches. This was rarely the simple matter of buying a bundle of furs, or even a wagon full of wine-barrels: rather they were complicated chains of consequences binding the value of a shipment of precious spices from the East to the profit on a cargo of ivory and ebony from Africa; tying a prodigious quantity of raw silk contracted to be woven at vast expense and worked into the gorgeous hangings that would cover the walls of an entire palace to the cost of a wagon-train of the precious *balsamico* of Modena. Always there would be the checks and balances: the costs and values measured in the finest detail, with bonuses for early delivery and penalties for default. And there must be either two copies of every contract, signed and kept by each party or else one, torn in two, half retained by each.

It seemed that a jurist's work encompassed more than merely ensuring the accuracy of the paperwork. At times a rich client would explode with rage, complaining that the terms were unfair, that he was being cheated by their business partner, his cousin, his closest friend or his worst enemy. Always my master would calm him and repeat, as she did so often, "The law is the law. There must be give and take. We may not apply the law to gain advantage, solely to achieve equity."

Within a few months she was allowing me, if not to draft the contract, then to complete it and to produce the duplicate. I lived in awe of both her wisdom and her microscopic attention to detail: in terror of failing to meet her exacting standards; in delight when she declared herself satisfied with my work.

Only slowly did I come to understand that her work also immersed her deep in the city's politics. On most occasions she was the only lawyer in the room, no matter how many other advisors and counsellors her clients, whether aristocratic or a merchant-class, might surround themselves with. But when she was summoned to a meeting of one of the many guilds that were emerging at the time, her friend Rolandino de' Pasaggeri was frequently also present. In public their dealings were marked by grave formality, bowing and referring to each other as "My learned colleague", "My esteemed fellow-jurist." Only the flashing of their eyes in surreptitiously exchanged glances betrayed, to me but to no one else, a shared knowledge or private joke.

When I quizzed her about the need for the two of them to be there, let alone the cost to the guild, my master chided me for my lack of understanding. "Lorenzo, these are great and perilous matters for the city. The tradesmen have learned that they are stronger when they band together and are protected by statute: not only to protect their trade and their ability to earn money, but also to give them, as a body, a voice in the city. As a result Master Rolandino and I are constantly occupied in translating the urgent desires of these men into a language and structure that will satisfy the *Consiglio* and persuade its members to pass the statutes into law.

"The work is laborious: you will have to start working on these statutes too, as will Master Rolandino's assistants. The guildsmen are hungry for change and always in a hurry. It is all the two of us can do to convince some of them of the wisdom of the old saw, *festina lente*: more haste, less speed. The statutes must be correctly drafted and approved in detail if they are to hold force."

"Then, Magister, why do you have only me to assist you, and no one before me, if he has several scribes?"

"This is more his territory than mine. The guildsmen can be... *conservative*, suspicious of a woman acting for them. Besides, he is well-established in working with them. Did you not know that Master Rolandino represents the guilds in the College of *Anziani e*

Console, the elders and consuls? He has the title of Pro-Consul, so in matters of their statutes I merely assist him."

Once again I was jealous on her behalf, resenting what appeared her lesser status: "Why are you not also a consul, Magister?"

"Bless you, Lorenzo, I have no desire for a position of... *power*. I am content to advise and interpret, to move between the many factions and try to establish agreement."

For a moment, and for no reason I could afterwards fathom, the message from Giovanni the leather-seller, by now long-suppressed, forced itself into my consciousness. "Is that where you come across the Gatekeeper? Do you keep him informed?"

The question unsettled her, and her eyes flashed: "You are sometimes so sharp that you risk cutting yourself, Lorenzo. Why would you raise that name again?"

"Because it seems to come up every time city politics are mentions – and whenever I find myself in trouble," I replied.

"To avoid such trouble, then," she retorted, "You would do well never to use or hear the name again. No!" She held up her hand. "I will not speak of it." I found myself half irritated by her dismissal of the subject, but relieved in equal part that I was able to relegate it to the back of my memory once more as my master continued.

"As for Master Rolandino, he is to some extent... *compromised* by representing the guilds as Pro-Consul. The great families, most of them, refuse to have anything to do with him, since he is so clearly aligned to the bodies they see as their opponents. The Lambertazzi, for example, will not let him come anywhere near them: while I, until I found you and lost their trust, was able to work for them and ascertain at least some of their subversive plans. No, I am content to retain my relative independence and serve the law as my master, rather than any one faction." Thus I began to appreciate a little of the constant political intrigue that simmered beneath Bologna's surface, at ground level as well as at the top of the towers of the *consorterie*.

Chapter 14

The first time my master took a draft set of statutes to the *Podestà*, I was beside myself with excitement: I would be required to announce her to the greatest personage in the city, the Governor himself. "Make no mistake, Lorenzo," she warned. "Notwithstanding the Podestà's title, his sphere of influence is severely circumscribed."

"But, Magister, he must surely be the most powerful man in Bologna!" I was capering by her side as we walked up the Via Æmilia to the main square.

"You must surely understand by now, Lorenzo, that such power is illusory. His position depends entirely on the support of the magnati. Yes, he is appointed by the Consiglio, but only by that section controlled by the old families. As the merchants and guilds tighten their grip, he is at best compromised. He cannot enforce his will except by the acquiescence of his opponents, the *Popolo*, who have their own *Capitano* – and he is at least as influential as the Podestà."

I was bewildered afresh. "Magister, this city is like an onion. Every time I think I understand its workings you peel off another layer and show me yet another underneath."

"Indeed, Lorenzo. That is an apt description. Today you may understand more."

The Palazzo del Podestà formed one-third of a recently-constructed, magnificent building which shared its great arches, under which lurked countless stalls and shops, with both the luxurious prison created for the captive King Enzo and, on its far side, the Palazzo del Capitano del Popolo. We climbed the stairs at the eastern end and were ushered into a hall with benches for some forty people: it was the council chamber for the *anziani*, the elders. The Podestà himself, seated in a large chair, almost a throne, cut a disappointing figure. A small man, as apparently lost inside his rich robes as in his chair, he had a nervous manner and a querulous voice, and completely ignored me. "Well, Magister: what do you bring me this time? More demands from people who should be content with their station, not seeking to aggrandise it?"

She was unabashed. "It is merely an expression in legal documents of the desire of hard-working people to protect their trade and their livelihoods, Podestà," she replied mildly. "May I outline the major arguments to you?"

With a bad grace he listened as she explained the documents in her customary style, with the economy and clarity that always amazed me. He did not argue, merely grunting when she finished. "The great families will never agree, of course."

Tartly she rejoined: "If it is the will of the Consiglio all together, they shall be obliged to."

He sighed. "And still more ordinary workmen will come to believe that they should have a voice in the running of this city above that of their betters."

"In this city, Podestà, *all* men who make wealth for themselves and furnish livelihoods for others have a voice. That is as it should be."

"Magister, you know I cannot agree. But I dare say you will have your way when you have swayed the Popolo to your way of thinking. I shall see you, I suppose, at the meeting of the college when this is discussed?"

"I believe I shall be asked to address the College in order to clarify the chief legal points, though merely assisting Maestro de' Pasaggeri. I am grateful for your time." We both bowed deeply and took our leave. As we skirted the square, passing Enzo's palazzo-prison to reach the adjoining Palazzo del Capitano del Popolo, I thought she might express herself forcibly on the subject of the Podestà's ill-concealed hostility, but she said nothing.

We ascended the grand staircase that led up to the *piano nobile*, its majesty diminished to my mind by the bodies of executed criminals rotting on gibbets as a lesson to those who might be tempted into wrongdoing. Their eyeless sockets appeared to glare at me balefully, and I suppressed a shudder. On the first floor we entered the *Sala*, built to house the College, the section of the Consiglio which held real power, a grand and elegant room which would hold perhaps a couple of hundred elected officials.

"Magister. You are welcome." The man who greeted us with a cheerful wave and a courtly bow could not have been more different from our previous host. He was tall, athletically built and looked about forty, with an easy confidence and gravitas born of experience. His hair and beard were dark and flecked with grey, and the creases at the corner of his eyes were suggestive more of laughter than of anger. His dress was understated yet elegant, and at his waist hung a sword which, despite its finely-wrought and jewelled hilt, looked as if it had seen hard use.

"Capitano, I thank you for seeing us." If my master effortlessly included me in the opening exchanges, the Capitano del Popolo did not fail to notice the nuance.

"So, a new bodyguard? What has become of that old rogue Michele?"

"Michele begins to feel his age, and minds the house. Lorenzo is perhaps less fearsome, but he reads and writes and assists me ably."

The Capitano looked me in the eye. "Lorenzo, eh? You are fortunate in your employer, young man. And you are welcome here."

Accustomed to being ignored by the Magister's clients, I was shocked to be noticed, let alone spoken to. "Th - I thank you, Signore," I stammered, then found my tongue. "And, yes, I appreciate my good fortune and seek to repay it in some measure through good service."

"Well answered, Lorenzo. Now, Magister, to business. You have the statutes for the new guilds in draft? Good." At a gesture from my master I reached into the scrip in which I carried her papers and handed over the relevant documents. The Capitano appeared to read the legal Latin with ease: so he was an educated man as well as, by repute, a soldier of distinction. "Magister," he concluded, "I know these statutes will all be in order: I do not need to check your work! But the question is, will the College accept them and recognise the new guilds? Two more will weaken the position of the magnati still further: even the merchants may feel themselves similarly threatened."

My master grunted her agreement. "Yet there is precedent in law and, if the tailors and millers have their own guilds, it is hard to see why such significant trades as the furriers and ironworkers should be denied the same voice and protection. The other guilds will support them, and I think the merchants and bankers will appreciate the wisdom of doing so. But you, Capitano, will have a better idea than I of how the Companies of Arms will cast their votes. They are beyond my influence and do not use my services, nor those of our friend Rolandino."

"No, indeed. They are unpredictable, and frequently unbiddable. My task as Capitano, balancing the two camps, guilds and *gonfalonieri*, is frequently a tricky one. But if we – no, if *you* - can persuade them that strengthening the voice of the guilds will add to that of the Popolo as a whole, and will truly weaken the position of the old families still further, they will support us, even if we are obliged to take the matter to the Great Council."

"I hope it will not come to that," replied my master.

"Yet it may, as might our bigger battle, the slavery proposal. There have been developments."

At the mention of slavery I recalled that conversation overheard in Modena, now years ago. Perhaps I gave myself away, for my master looked sharply at me and gestured the Capitano to caution. "I think that is a topic best kept... to *ourselves* at present. Lorenzo, wait for me in the courtyard, if you please."

I knew better than to argue, or even to embarrass her with a display of disobedience. But I was angry. There had been other occasions when, to my chagrin, I was excluded from my master's discussions. From the top of a family's tower I would be sent downstairs to wait for her, descending stair after stair, ladder after rickety ladder, to ground level. As I left I would see the head of a great family leaning close to her in urgent, whispered conversation.

At such times I knew there were great treaties being planned, far beyond mere trading between families. Here were territories, cities, bishoprics, countries and empires under discussion, all so secret that not even her servant, to whom she entrusted almost everything, could be allowed to hear it. Yet I hated to be shut out. Once I remonstrated with her, complaining that she should trust me even in the most confidential matters, that I would never betray her. "Lorenzo," she would explain with a sigh, "Some of these weighty matters are perilous indeed. If you have no knowledge of them, you are in no danger. But once you are privy to them, your life could be snuffed out in an instant."

"But, Magister, are you not in the same danger? Why do you make so light of your own life?"

"I have a... *position*," she replied, adopting her legal mode of speech once more. "On both sides, where there are indeed two sides, my value is known, and it would be unwise of one to seek to do me harm. Besides, in my world one is able to put in place certain... *safeguards*. I know too much about those who might wish me dead. No, I do not have to fear for myself. But I would fear for you, Lorenzo."

"I'm not afraid," I retorted. "I owe you my life: why would I not offer it for you?"

"I know you would, and readily. I thank you for that, Lorenzo. What I would fear for you, and what you should fear above all, is not a swift death, but days and weeks of torture if you fell into the wrong hands, and if your captors were determined to extract information from you. Believe me," she shuddered, "I have seen the results of such torments. And the fate from which I rescued you is nothing to what you would suffer there. I will not put you in peril of that."

I made a face and continued to argue, until, eventually and almost to my surprise, she relented. "Oh, very well, Lorenzo. You are wearying me, and I see I shall have no peace. I shall share this one secret with you – at your peril, mind. You want to know why the Capitano mentioned a proposal regarding slavery?"

"I do, Magister. I was intrigued when he mentioned it: you refuse to have anything to with buying or selling serfs."

"Indeed I do: the practice, the entire concept of one man owning another as if he were an animal is abhorrent to me."

"Yet men have always owned slaves – or have been slaves themselves."

"Custom and practice, however long, do not render a wrong acceptable, Lorenzo," she retorted. "Have I taught you nothing?"

I grinned. "You have taught me that I must work very hard to squeeze information from you, Magister!" I replied cheekily.

She laughed. "You truly are a wheedling trickster, Lorenzo! Very well, though I warn you that in taking you into my confidence, on this matter above all, puts you at risk in precisely the manner that I have just described. In short, Maestro Rolandino and have spent many years framing a law that will, if passed, put an end forever to slavery in this *Comune*."

I was astonished. "But, Magister, even the Church defends slavery. Your plan is like turning the world upside down!"

"To many that will appear the case, Lorenzo. But while Bologna enriches itself from its flourishing manufactures and trade, there are growing numbers among those who both create that growing wealth and benefit from it – particularly the merchants, the bankers and the skilled tradesmen - who are beginning to see that they are better served by willing men than by slaves."

"But is not the use of serfs, in the fields, say, a less costly way of producing crops?"

"Not necessarily. A serf must be fed and housed: yet will frequently be an unwilling labourer. The guilds, for example, see more value in a skilled apprentice who works hard to learn his trade in the hope of himself becoming a master in time: he will fabricate better goods than a slave who is without hope of ever changing his station."

I thought for a minute. "I can see how that might work: and that is why the guilds are forming and making rules about apprentices?"

"Precisely, Lorenzo."

"But those great families who own hundreds of slaves: they will never see this as wisdom, surely?"

"No, indeed. There will be much argument and wrangling. In truth, it is more Master Rolandino's work than mine. He is drafting the text of such a law: he calls it, presumptuously in my view, the *Liber Paradisus*, the Book of Heaven. No, it will not be easily achieved: but it is right and virtuous, and he will receive my support, and my aid and advice whenever he seeks them. It may yet take years for us to achieve our end but, if that is one lasting change that I help to achieve, my life and my work will not have been entirely wasted."

I was still full of questions. "But how...?"

She held up he hand in her customary gesture. "And now that is enough. I will say no more of it at present."

If my pride was hurt to some extent by my occasional exclusion from her most confidential dealings, I was delighted when she relented, as on this occasion. More and more I enjoyed my work with the Magister, especially when it involved the affairs of the *Comune*. Indeed, so involved had I become in it all that I saw less and less of my three friends, Paolo, Giacomo and Salvatore. It was rare now that we went carousing together, and they rebuked me when we succeeded in meeting. But I was absorbed in my work, and knew how much I was learning: about the law, certainly, because I heard the Magister's lectures as well as helping her to deal with her clients. But I was also learning about life, commerce, and even a little of politics. And I was happy.

So it continued for many months, until the next interruption to the even tenor of my life. That was when, for the first time, I met Sordello.

Chapter 15

Sordello: or, to give him his full name, Sordello da Goito; troubadour; sometime soldier; notorious womaniser; mercenary; braggart; spy. I suspected that he was an assassin at need, too, though I never witnessed it.

First and last, though, he was a troubadour. He had a deep, sonorous voice, and could work magic with a harp in his hands, but it was as a writer of songs that he excelled. People still sing them now, long after his death. Mostly, though, those are the songs he wrote in French, in the service of Charles, Duke of Anjou. They are every bit as marvellous as everyone claims they are. But for me they have never had quite the magic of the songs he wrote in his native Veronese dialect.

People say the latter are all lost now, that he must have destroyed the few manuscripts he made. He did not: I have them still. His writing is distinctively spidery, the original verses faint and barely legible for all his scratchings-out and amendments. Yet I can read them. When my end comes, I have left instructions that they should go to the university here in Bologna: the academics there keep manuscripts safe and dry in their library, rather than allowing them to moulder away in a cupboard in a crumbling church.

My friends say that I should deposit them there now, in case they should meet with a mishap in my keeping: but I cannot bear to part with them. Sometimes even now when, in my extreme old age some sixty years and more after the events I am recounting, a sense of loneliness and longing for the past overwhelms me (I have spent a lifetime succumbing to those weaknesses), I reach down those precious rolls of vellum from the high shelves in my study, spread them out – oh, so carefully, now they are fragile – and hum through them.

My servants think me as cracked as the parchment: "The old man's humming and muttering gibberish," they complain. I hear every word: my hearing is almost as good as it was when it was my means of gaining information and of staying alive. But they do not know the lovely northern dialect that I learnt from Sordello (it was not very different from my natural mode of speech, learned from my earliest years in Venice): nor did they ever hear him sing his love-songs, so poignant and beautiful that they would make a statue weep. They still reduce me to tears, confirming my servants' view that I am in my dotage and prone to crying without reason.

I am frequently lachrymose nowadays, it is true. But there is always a reason, invariably a memory of someone I knew: Sordello could weave magic out of words and music, creating a spell that entranced those who heard it all those years ago, and which even now transports me back to those wild, dangerous, heady times.

There, I have done it again. I have leapt five or six decades in one bound, and I have failed to describe yet how I met Sordello.

It began with uproar in the household. Michele was bustling about, as quickly as his poor health allowed him, going to the door and shouting into the street for urchins to run errands for him to fetch and carry all manner of goods and foods. Mamolo meanwhile was beside himself with outrage at being required to produce food and drink for a special guest at only a day's notice. We were not unused to entertaining, as I have said, but this furore was of an unusual degree. "What's all the fuss about?" I asked Michele. "Who's coming?"

"Sordello, of course," came the irritable reply. "Who else do you think we would go to all this trouble for?" I had never heard of him. His style of music had not penetrated to the sanctuaries and holy rituals of the cathedrals whose repertoire was almost all that I had known till then. But, back then, he was a hero, a genius, to the ordinary people who readily sang his songs in taverns, as much as to the rich *signori* and merchants who would pay gold to have him entertain at their great feasts, weddings or banquets.

When he arrived, he did so in style. There was a peremptory knock at the door. Michele flung it open and, with Mamolo, formed a two-man honour guard as he strode into the courtyard. I watched this at a distance, bemused.

Following Sordello were two shabbily-clothed individuals carrying between them a variety of bags and boxes, musical instruments slung on their backs. I heard Mamolo mutter under his breath, "Even more mouths to feed. How am I to manage that all on my own?"

As his retinue scurried around, Sordello stood stock-still, his cloak flung back over his shoulder, his right arm extended in a dramatic gesture, as if he were the hero in one of the dramas we would occasionally see performed on a stage built in a city piazza at festival times. His jerkin and breeches were brightly coloured, cut in extravagant curves to display his tall, slim physique: and inexplicably, although he had been walking through the filthy streets of Bologna, his high leather boots gleamed. He knew how to make an entrance.

A voice cut across the courtyard. At the top of the steps that led to her chamber on the first floor stood my master. She rested her hands on the rail, smiled and uttered a single word, "Sordello." It was not an exclamation, nor a question: it was a statement, almost an expression of satisfaction.

His response was theatrical. With an exaggerated bow he swept off his hat, held it high in the air and replied, "Magister! Dottore! Bettisia. I am come."

She smiled sardonically. "I see that. You had better come up. Lorenzo, some wine for our guest, our very… *special* guest!" I scurried away to do her bidding and brought a jug of the finest wine up to the table at which they were sitting, facing each other across it – already, it seemed, engrossed in retelling old stories and laughing at shared memories.

Having poured the wine, I lit more candles, at the Magister's behest. She stared into Sordello's face, as if checking for signs of age, guilt, or damage. "You look well, Sordello. Older, but well." To me he looked of an age with her, forty or fifty years old, not more: like her, slim and hale, and with a similarly hawkish expression that betrayed keen intelligence. For the first time, Sordello acknowledged my presence. "You have a new servant, then."

"To be sure. This is Lorenzo, a young man with an interesting history."

"Another of your rescued birds, then?" enquired Sordello sardonically.

"He is… *useful* to me." Her legal manner of speaking, yet again. "He is strong and clever, but headstrong and foolish. All young men are the same. Some grow out of it. Others... are as you were, or are. And never really grow up." As he guffawed good-naturedly, she reached across the table and took his hand. "How are you, old friend? Tell me what you have been doing in the years since you last visited Bologna."

It was quite a tale. As I listened I could hardly believe my ears, and assumed he was making most of it up. In the months and years during which I got to know him, I came to understand there was not an untrue word. He was an adventurer. He described fighting in battle for the Duke of Anjou: recounted how he abducted a noblewoman – not on his own account, he insisted, but at the request of a powerful prince.

And all the while he was caught up in the politics between two rival emperors and a third, French, claimant to the throne, meeting cardinals and bishops as emissaries from the Pope. It sounded like one of the ballads that minstrels sing about the heroes of old, of Roland and Oliver. But my master took in every word, nodding and questioning. It appeared that she knew he was telling the truth.

I was kept occupied even when listening intently. Naturally there was one fine dish after another to be brought to the honoured guest: olives, cheese and succulent ham cut so thin as to be almost transparent; little twists of dough filled with boar and truffles; pork belly roasted and with rosemary and lemon; figs, pears and sweet things too numerous to count. They talked incessantly, frequently laughing at one another's tales. Then, abruptly, the laughter would stop: they would both lean towards each other across the table while the conversation became earnest in tone. At such times their voices dropped so low that even I could make our hardly a word.

A few evenings after Sordello's arrival the two of them were again seated at the table, and I was hovering as usual, pouring wine and helping Mamolo to serve food. Their conversation seemed unusually tense, and there were muttered comments between them that I could barely hear. Then, as she did whenever taking someone into her confidence, she leaned forward across the table to Sordello. As she had done before, she took his hand: looking into each other's eyes, they could have been lovers (I always assumed that they had been, in the past, though neither ever vouchsafed any such information to me).

My master looked anxious, and dropped her voice so low that even her dinner-guest, I reckoned, could barely make out what she was saying. Standing behind her chair I caught only odd words. The few I could discern caused me to start. "Lambertazzi" was the first name I caught. I adopted my long-developed habit of appearing uninterested as I stood, holding the wine jug: but all my attention was focused on their conversation. I picked out other snatches: "There cannot be two emperors," murmured Sordello.

"There is only one with a realistic claim," retorted my master: even in a near-whisper, she was forceful in debate. "God knows, I taught Manfred as best I could, but he was a dull student at best. And now he styles himself King of Sicily."

"If neither of those sons should succeed Frederick, what about Enzo? He's still in prison not a league from here."

"Enzo? No, his health is ruined. Besides, he's a spoiled popinjay who will only pander to the old aristocracy. That is why Lambertazzi is so eager to see him freed, because he reckons he can control him."

"Lambertazzi. Always Lambertazzi, at the heart of every conspiracy. We need to get into his house, into his confidence. You are in his house frequently enough, as his lawyer."

"I was: but no longer. I continued to take his money, grudgingly enough paid, only in order to get inside his tower. Yet, when I was there, he and his silver-tongued advisor were more tight-lipped than you would believe possible. I learned nothing."

"His advisor? Still that slimy devil's spawn Bardi?" I felt myself tense at the memory of the tall man in black who had his men hang me over the parapet at the top of the tower.

"The same. Together they push constantly at the bounds of what is legal: they were forever pressing me to use the law to threaten their rivals by means of unfair contract or, indeed, plain misrepresentation of the value of their goods or lands. On the last occasion they pressed me to act for them in what I regarded as a blatant contravention of equity.

"I spoke my mind, and have not been invited to return. I hear they have engaged one of my fellow jurists to advise them, that fool Oseletti with whom I crossed swords in debate last month." I could not help smiling as I formed a mental picture of the learned Professor Oseletti wilting under an assault from my master's acid tongue.

"We need to get a spy inside that household, Bettisia. We cannot wage this war blind. The Gatekeeper must be kept informed."

Gatekeeper? There was that name again. Perhaps I let my guard drop, and allowed my interest to show: maybe the timing was coincidental. But abruptly my master turned to me and barked, "Lorenzo. Fetch more wine."

"We have plenty of wine here, Magister."

"This stuff isn't good enough for Sordello. Bring us a jug of the very best: the old skin. Do as I say." Her voice was like the crack of a whip, a tone she adopted when she would not be gainsaid. Grumpily I shrugged, put down the nearly full jug I had been holding and left the room. I found another jug down in the store and filled it from the skin in the corner, a dusty, misshapen thing that the master had claimed to be keeping in reserve for a special occasion. Perhaps this was that event, though I could not see why.

As I stood up straight from pouring and turned away, I was abruptly seized and pushed up against the wall, dropping the wine-jug which shattered noisily.

It was Sordello. With his left hand on my body he held me still. His right hand held the knife with which I had so recently seen him cut his meat, now pressed to my throat. "Who are you spying for? Tell me!" I shook my head in bewilderment. "No one. I'm not a spy. I serve the Magister."

"Don't lie to me. Tell me who you really serve, or I'll slit your throat." A year before – no, nearly two now - when I had been in a similar position, I had been paralysed by fear. But I had learnt a great deal since then. At the hands of Michele I had picked up some idea of how to defend myself.

Sordello was clearly stronger than I was, and the knife pressed hard on my windpipe, so I dared not use my arms. Instead, I stamped down hard, raking my boot down his shin and smashing into his instep. He swore, and loosened his grip on me. That was all I needed. I tore myself out of his grip, pushed him away and ran for the door, screaming for help.

Sordello was fast, unbelievably quick. As I ran into the courtyard, deciding where to go, he flung himself on me from behind, knocking me to the ground. One arm wrenched my left hand behind my back, pushing it so high that my muscles screamed their agony. A knee was planted in the small of my back, the knife pressed into the indentation between my jaw and ear. This time I was helpless.

Disturbed by the commotion, Mamolo and Michele ran into the courtyard. "Stay back!" Sordello ordered. "I'll kill him. You know I will."

Bringing his face close to my ear, he hissed, "This is your last chance. You lie your way in here, taking advantage of her, a little piece of shit worming your way into the household of the finest woman who ever lived. Why are you betraying her? Who are you working for?"

Fear gave way to fury. "Let me up and I'll tell you who I'm working for!" I yelled, pushing his knife-hand and spinning away as far as I might, my anger rendering me heedless of the peril of the blade against my neck. He released me, but stood poised with his knife in case I tried to escape him entirely.

I stood before him, incandescent with rage, refusing to be intimidated. "Yes, I'll tell you, damn your eyes," I shouted. "I work for only one person." I wrenched off my jacket and pulled my shirt over my head, turning my back to him.

"Look, *Signor* Sordello, *gran trovatore.* Look at my scars. Feel them, if you like. They're real enough. Who rescued me from that torture? Who nursed me day and night to save my life? Who offered me a home and gave me back my dignity? Who treated me with respect for the first time in my life? *Damn* you! How dare you suggest that I would ever betray the Magister! My life is hers, and she knows it. Accuse me once more of betrayal, you bastard, and I'll kill you. I'll do it now. Put that knife down and fight fairly!"

As Sordello gave a wry smile, but made no answer, her voice came from the top of the stairs, cutting through the commotion, imperious, not to be denied. "Enough! That is *enough*. Sordello, let the boy be. Bring him up here to me. Lorenzo, put your shirt on: you look ridiculous half-naked!"

Chapter 16

It was as if she were admonishing two small boys. Out of the corner of my eye I could see Mamolo smirking as Sordello frogmarched me swearing and protesting up the stairs. Once in the master's chamber, he shoved me onto the chair that he himself had occupied so recently and stood behind me.

"So, Lorenzo: what have you to say?" She was staring deep into my eyes.

I was almost incoherent with rage and fright. "What have *I* to say, Magister? I have done nothing but serve you faithfully. What this lunatic thinks I've been doing I have no idea. He would have killed me."

"No, Lorenzo. He would not: not unless I asked him to. And I shall not do that. Nonetheless, you were listening intently, perhaps too closely, to our conversation. Why?"

I breathed heavily and tried to collect my thoughts. "I heard the name Lambertazzi. That animal would have killed me but for you, and one day I shall take his life from him."

"My, you are full of threats today! To kill that powerful personage will not be easy," she replied with a smile. "But, yes, we were speaking of Massimo Lambertazzi. What else?"

"Magister, you were talking about how there are two emperors – or, at least, two men who think they should be emperor. And Enzo, still kept prisoner here in Bologna. Everyone knows that: but, but when I was in Modena I heard the Bishop talking about them, too. It seems that everyone starts talking about them, at least, all the powerful people like you and the Bishop, and then you start talking quietly as if you're plotting."

"That is perceptive of you, Lorenzo. I congratulate you. But I think there was one more name, one that interested you perhaps more than the others. What was it?" Her eyes seemed to drill into my consciousness. I felt Sordello's hand on my shoulder and made to turn, but at the smallest gesture from her he removed his arm. "What was it, Lorenzo? Tell me."

"It was that name again. The Gatekeeper."

The Magister nodded. "It is true, we were speaking of the Gatekeeper: we frequently do. And you have mentioned the name to me before now. Why is it of such great interest to you, Lorenzo?"

"Magister, I'm not *interested* in the name. In fact, I've learned to hate it. It's come to rule my life. Every time I hear it, I get into trouble. I hear the Bishop mention it in Modena, and end up having to run away. I hear it in Bologna when I'm sleeping in the street and someone's murdered in front of me. The next day the men in the tavern talk of it, and I'm flogged nearly to death. Then you use the name, and a moment later this madman here is all set to skewer me. I don't know who the Gatekeeper is. I wish I'd never heard the name. All it seems to do is bring me pain and misery." I was beside myself with humiliation and rage.

She put her hands on mine, which were clenched before me, and spoke softly. "Lorenzo, I think – no, I am... *convinced* – that it is time for you to put your trust in me. You have told me much of your story, and I thank you for that. Tell me the rest now, those parts that I know you have withheld for your own good reason: and I think you will be free of that which is tormenting you."

Suddenly I knew that she was right, that I must trust this strange woman who had entered my life when it had seemed lost, and had enriched it in ways that I could never have dreamed of. And, in sharing the secret I had been carrying for the best part of two years, I hoped I might relieve myself of the burden placed on me by Giovanni the leather-seller in the last hour of his life.

I have no idea how long I spoke for, as I recounted the conversations I overheard while serving wine in Modena: how I saw Bartolomeo Bardi for the first time at the Bishop's table, and heard his distinctive voice a second time, when Giovanni had taken his own life after entrusting his message to me; how Bardi's name and that of Lambertazzi were linked, as Bologna's traitors, to Modena's plotters, the Bishop and the hated landlord of Tommaso's family, Signor Uguzzoni; and how all of that cabal walked in fear of the mysterious Gatekeeper, whom Giovanni made me swear to seek out.

As I reached the end of my tale, this time without the cautious omissions of my previous account, a thought struck me. "Magister, before he died, Giovanni said I should find a lawyer in Bologna, an honest one whom I can trust to pass his message to the Gatekeeper. I know you match his description, though Maestro de' Pasaggeri would also, so I have shared this with you because my heart tells me it's the right thing to do. If you are indeed the one of whom Giovanni spoke, although he did not know your name, then I have finally delivered his message, and am free of it. If not, then let Sordello kill me and make an end, for I am tired, and weary of living with it." I hung my head in resignation.

My master looked above my head and was clearly exchanging glances with Sordello. "Very well, Lorenzo. You honour me with your trust. I see no lie in your face, and I thank you for your honesty. But..."

My feeling of exhaustion gave way to a fresh wave of resentment. I interrupted her, something I normally hesitated to do. "But what, Magister? Now I suppose you'll send me away. You'll throw me out, when I was so happy here. And all because of some phantom, some mystery man who keeps popping up and ruining my life. And *this* one, this Sordello, puts you up to it." I was feeling sorry for myself now, and looked daggers at the man I blamed for my latest predicament.

"My, Lorenzo," she relied, as Sordello remained silent. "I fear we have deeply upset you. Forgive me. I didn't intend to anger you with our little.. *masquerade.* Though it is true we sought to... *frighten* you a little. To test you."

"Test me? Why?"

She looked over my shoulder again. "Sordello, for the love of God, sit down! You make the boy nervous, and you're giving me a stiff neck. Pull up a stool, give us all a fresh cup of wine – Lorenzo too – and let us talk this through."

He did so. My hands were shaking so much that I could barely drink without spilling the wine, but eventually I composed myself, though I kept directing sideways glances of hatred towards Sordello. He laughed every time he saw me glower at him, making me still more angry. At last I subsided. Sordello poured me more wine and, though I did not know it at the time, I had embarked on another phase of my life.

My master leaned towards me across the table, just as she had done to Sordello over dinner. I felt the full intensity of her gaze, an unspoken force to which my poor words can never do justice. "Lorenzo," she said, "You frequently ask me why I rescued you from the Lambertazzi tower that evening."

"No I don't. It's just that..."

She held up her hand. "Of course you do. Whenever you feel unsure of yourself or threatened, you ask me – and, the Lord knows, that is often enough! Yet I do not blame you. Until now I have furnished you with only a... *partial* answer." She was back to her lawyer's manner. "It is true that I first intervened simply because I cannot bear to see pain inflicted needlessly. Why would that man, that monster, want to see a boy maimed, perhaps even killed? So I bade them cease. But then those... *torturers* explained why you had been taken: you had overheard and responded to their mention of their master - and of the Gatekeeper.

"That made Massimo Lambertazzi nervous, which is why he overreacted: only a frightened man would use something so circumstantial as an excuse to beat a boy nearly to death. That and his... *insatiable* passion for inflicting pain. Now, since everyone in Bologna wants to know more about the Gatekeeper and his... *activities* (and I am no different from the rest), it seemed that I could both rescue you and perhaps find out if you really did know anything. So I insisted that they release you, and brought you here."

She continued "But why, you still want to know: why did I keep you in my household when you were well on the road to recovery? Partly, in truth, because I have grown fond of you. You sing beautifully: of that there is no doubt. I find you useful, as you also know. You're clever, quick: you write well and your Latin is... *passable*. And you make me laugh: both when you are humorous, when you joke and trick – and when you are cross and difficult and cannot see how ridiculous you are!"

I tried to protest, but she held up her hand again. "But there was something else. Indeed, there were two things. First," it was as if she were addressing the council of the *Comune*. "First, you have a habit – more than that: a skill, a talent even - for eavesdropping. For listening carefully. And for noting names and facts of importance. You cannot know how much you told me when you were so hurt that we thought you might die, in such pain and fever that you were raving. I spent many hours tending you, anointing your wounds, comforting you, hours that you will not even remember. And here I must confess that I... took advantage of you, a fact of which I am not entirely proud. You told me a great deal about yourself: I knew probably all of your history before you chose to tell me a... *portion* of it, when you were well enough to do so.

"Thus it is that I already knew that you listened to your masters and to the Bishop in Modena. At times during your fever you would recount the whole of the conversation throughout dinner. Your memory is remarkable, and you mimicked the voices and tones so faithfully that I feel I almost know the Bishop, the Prior, and those important dinner guests, some of whom I *do* know a little. Indeed, I have met the odious Signor Uguzzoni more than once: all three of us know Signor Bardi, of course, but your recreation of his distinctive voice invariably made me smile.

"I knew you had overheard their plotting about how to control the flow and thus the price of *balsamico*. I knew they were talking about the imprisonment in Bologna of the old Emperor's son, Enzo: and you revealed how intently the Modenese plot against Bologna and scheme at ways of removing the yoke placed on them after that disastrous battle at Fossalta. Disastrous for them, that is."

There was so much I wanted to say. But she held up her hand again, that same imperious gesture. "You raved about the Emperor and the interregnum. Many powerful people are devising stratagems in order to make one or other of the sons of Frederick, legitimate or bastard, the next Holy Roman Emperor – unless Sordello's potent patron, Charles of Anjou, has his way instead."

I sat amazed: she sighed. "I fear, Lorenzo, that you could have spared yourself the pain of harbouring for so long the message from the late Giovanni, with whom I was acquainted both in his previous occupation as leather-seller and, later, in his guise as a spy. He was a brave man, alas for him. In your fever you had rehearsed most that that conversation in your cell. And if all that were not enough, you shouted time after time about the Gatekeeper."

Once again I started involuntarily. She continued. "Yes, he is clearly something of an... *obsession* of yours. Yet you do not know even what the name means, do you? Or who it may be? Nonetheless, it seems to be a name that is inextricably bound up with your fate: and it leads you into peril on every occasion. It was your reaction to that name, was it not, that betrayed you to Lambertazzi's men? No need to nod. I knew it, although you... *glossed over* the fact in your earlier account. You remain easier to read than you imagine, Lorenzo: but we might improve on that.

"Shall I tell you about the Gatekeeper? In truth, I cannot tell you much, for... *no one* knows the identity of that elusive figure." She paused and exchanged a meaningful glance with Sordello: he nodded, as if giving her permission to continue. "You have benefited from an education, Lorenzo. Who was the Gatekeeper of Roman legend? No? You are forgetting those lessons in Venice and Modena! Janus was the Roman god of beginnings and endings, and therefore of gates, doorways and passages. He had two faces, so that he could look two ways at once, both in and out, and thus protected the gates of Rome itself. And, while this city and region tie themselves in knots with conspiracies and intrigues, it is believed that there is someone at the heart of all these conspiracies, looking both ways, to the empire and to Rome; to the next Emperor; to the Pope; perhaps at once to Modena and Bologna.

"Always he is playing off one party against another: one powerful family against another; the aristocrats against the merchants; the merchants against the moneylenders; the *Popolo*, especially the Companies of Arms, against the rest of the *Consiglio*. You learned of this when you met the Podestà and the Capitano del Popolo. Whoever he is, the Gatekeeper is a master strategist who, depending on your point of view, can save this city - or has it in his power to plunge it into chaos and bloodshed.

"So now you see how you put yourself at risk by appearing to recognise the name. All of us would like to learn the Gatekeeper's identity, those up to their elbows in blood and intrigue even more than the rest. Then," she sighed again, as of all these intrigues and subterfuges pained her, which I always believed they did. "There was another reason for keeping you close to us. We might have simply dismissed you or even.. *disposed* of you, despite my fondness for you." I took some small comfort in her evident dislike of the notion of having me murdered. "But you also possess particular qualities which we could not overlook. You are a survivor, a fighter against fate. Most people are not. To your credit, when you find yourself in a ... *predicament*, you stubbornly refuse to roll over, or meekly to accept it.

"Were you of that latter disposition, you might still be singing in Modena. Perhaps you would be Maestro di Cappella by now. Or a renowned troubadour like Sordello here: who knows? Or you might have fallen by the wayside in France, had they succeeded in sending you there. But you have something about you that I like and admire. You are strong, belligerent, pig-headed even: that makes you tiresome on occasions, as I well know. But you are also resilient and resourceful at need. So I think you might be of use to me – to us." She included Sordello in her glance.

" For that reason, and because we knew that the name of the Gatekeeper possessed great significance for you, we were obliged to test you. We set a trap for you this evening, Sordello and I. And you fell into it."

Again I tried to protest: once more she held up her hand. "Yes, we did ensnare you. We knew the names that would interest you, and we dropped our voices so low that, if you were to overhear our conversation, you had to betray yourself to us. Yet it was also a test: a test that you passed. We knew that you would eavesdrop, and were fairly sure which words would interest you.

"Had you shown no interest, we would have had to make a judgement. Were you so good that you could deceive even us? Or were you, after all, just an ordinary boy who did not care about anything beyond where his next meal would come from and when he would first have his way with a girl? Don't pretend to be shocked, Lorenzo! I've seen the way you stare at the girls we see in the great towers we visit, both the serving girls and (shame on you!) those far above you in station.

"Be that as it may, you took our bait, and you stuck your head into our snare. Then I sent you down for more wine, and Sordello took you by surprise. You did well there: he will not quickly forgive you for the injury you did to his foot."

Sordello gave me a wry grin, and reached for some cheese from the middle of the table. "I'd have paid you back ten-fold, boy, if the Magister had allowed me. But she seems to have taken a shine to you. Me, I'd have given you a thrashing you wouldn't forget for striking back at Sordello!" I shrugged, uncertain of how to respond.

"So now, Lorenzo," continued the Magister, "What *are* we to do with you?"

Chapter 17

My master continued. "It is curious how frequently I appear to ponder your future. You will have understood by now, because you are certainly not stupid, even if you are vain and excitable, that Sordello and I are... *involved* in the intrigues that I have outlined, as is Maestro de' Pasaggeri. Indeed, we have been so for a decade or two now. So I think your own curiosity has brought you to a crossroads at which you may take one of three turnings.

"First, you may forget this conversation and leave my service now. I will give you money for your journey and merely warn that, if you ever breathe a word of what I have said, Sordello will find you and end your life. It is that serious a matter."

Once more she waved away my protestation. "Second, you may continue exactly as you have been, as my servant, my scribe - as my helpmate in many ways. You have done well, and I value your service. But, if you do not wish it, I will not involve you in any of these dealings which are, at the very least, perilous.

"Third, you will continue with your duties as you have done. But you will also become my eyes and ears. You will listen out for plots and conspiracies: in the squares, in the marketplace, and in the houses of the great and powerful to which we gain access. You will report back to me everything, absolutely everything that you hear and learn: but again, if you tell another person, Sordello will find you and kill you. These precautions are designed to protect not *my* life, but the health and wealth of the city I love and serve.

"Those are the hard choices, Lorenzo. There are no others, so consider well. Now, which is it to be?"

For a moment I was nonplussed. I could scarcely believe the offer that was being made to me. But my decision required no pondering. "Magister, you know me too well. You already know my answer. I will be your eyes and ears, and I will die before I divulge anything I know. Yet will you not tell me? Who is the Gatekeeper?"

She paused before answering. "Even I do not know that, Lorenzo. It may be perhaps your prime task: to discover, and tell me, who the Gatekeeper is. And, while we seek for that deep truth, we will between us, God willing, lay bare the secrets of the enemies of Bologna."

Abruptly she turned to Sordello. "And now, Sordello, I must tell you of another of Lorenzo's skills that I have omitted to mention until now. He is a fine musician in the making, if a little rusty at present. While you are in Bologna, I believe you can train him, make him known as a troubadour in your mould so that, when you depart once more on your travels, he can gain access to the houses and revelries of our friends and enemies alike. You know how well your skill has served you. The musician at the banquet is invisible, yet he hears and sees everything. We will train Lorenzo to be the new Sordello."

Sordello grunted. "The new Sordello? He has much to learn then, and not only about music."

"I can sing," I retorted "I can improvise descants. I can hold my own in any musical company."

"I dare say you can, boy," replied Sordello. "But I doubt whether you can do that, listen to what's going on, bribe and threaten to gain information, and handle a knife when things get dangerous – all at the same time. Can you? I thought not. Then you have, as I said, much to learn."

Thus I entered into yet another apprenticeship. My master and Sordello, acting in unison, had meticulously planned this whole scene, then, entirely a confection of play-acting, all based on the fact that they already knew the secret I had been carrying for so long. It had been a test that, fortunately, I passed. In the following days we planned my training, not that I had much say in it. What was I learning to be? A spy, perhaps: certainly an agent, working secretly and always reporting back to the Magister.

She was particularly solicitous towards me. I suspected she felt that they had pushed me too hard: in truth, I had been sorely tried. But, as my anger and resentment at that harsh treatment subsided, those feelings were replaced by one of exultation and deep excitement.

I had little real idea of what I was becoming involved in. But Sordello was entertaining company: moreover, when he was with her, the master was quicker to laugh and less severe than usual. Besides, what eighteen year-old boy, anxious to be a man, could resist the allure of conspiracy, danger and intrigue? I was beside myself, and wanted to get started immediately. As always, though, whenever I badgered them I was scolded for my impatience. "But what am I to do?" I demanded. "What part do I play in all this?"

"Your part is to shut up and stop asking damn fool questions," growled Sordello. "When you are ready – and that's when I say you are, because the Magister is much too soft with you – you'll be our ears. And you'll recount to us every conversation that you overhear."

It had been decided that I would sing alongside Sordello: all his troupe sang, though his two shabby fellow-musicians, Filippo and Andrea, mainly played the rebec and drum. Filippo was a mournful character with a thin face and long, lank black hair. He played the rebec proficiently - though, whenever I heard him play, I couldn't help thinking that Tommaso would have shaped the phrases more elegantly. His miserable character added a plaintive tone to his playing: this became more pronounced when he had been drinking, something he did prodigiously when we performed.

By contrast, Andrea looked precisely as a drummer should. He was round, bald and unquenchably hilarious. When he had been drinking (which he also did to excess, to Sordello's disgust), he became uproarious. He still played well: but always, as drummers will, he pushed the music faster and louder. The audience loved those moments, clapping and cheering him and demanding more, while we singers were close to expiring.

Every performance ended in a row between the three of them. Sordello would berate them for drunken sots who could not earn a crust without him to keep them in order, so poor was their musicianship. Andrea would curse him in turn for a miserable killjoy whose views on music were too highbrow and whose songs were far too intellectual to appeal to ordinary people. At this stage Filippo would usually burst into tears and then fall asleep. Thus I could tell that they were proper musicians!

I loved the work. At first it was hard. The musical language of Sordello's songs was entirely different from everything, both sacred and secular, that I had learned in my previous life. Where the cathedral music had been necessarily austere and rarefied, Sordello's music possessed an earthy vigour. Moreover, although many of the turns of phrase and underlying rhythms of his melodies were rooted in the kind of folk music I had learned from Tommaso and his family, and appealed readily to the audience (whatever the drunken Andrea might say), there was a subtlety, an added layer of sophistication, that made them great.

And the texts! How I came to admire Sordello's poetry – once I had got my tongue round both his Veronese dialect and his songs in French, a language entirely foreign to me. He was a ruthless taskmaster, repeating over and over again until I was word- as well as note-perfect. By the time I knew the text, the melody too was well fixed in my memory, and only then was I allowed to improvise a counterpoint to some verses.

Demanding though he was, he gave me credit when I contrived a particularly elegant contrary movement in the approach to a cadence: not that he said as much, confining himself to a grunt and a nod. From some people, though, that is enough. Like my master, he did not waste empty words on praise: from both of them a mere hint of approval was all I needed, or expected.

The training did not end with music. That was merely a matter of time. Sordello confessed, as far as he would admit to anything, that I possessed sufficient technique to satisfy him. I was merely required to learn the repertoire (it is surprising how many songs a troubadour needs to fill an evening's music).

But Sordello had plans for increasing the range of my skills. "Have you ever handled a knife?" he asked me one day, in his brusque manner. "You don't look as if you have."

"No," I replied. "I've been threatened with plenty, not least by you, and I've felt them against my throat more often than I'd like. But I've never handled one. The Magister's not keen on weapons. When I started carrying Michele's cudgel to accompany her in the streets she said, 'I looked... *ridiculous*'," (he laughed at my imitation of her manner of speaking), "And forbade me to take it. Yet I've often felt that some kind of weapon would be useful if ever she were threatened."

"You must learn, then" he concluded. "I would argue that a musician needs a knife. At some of the feasts where we entertain, things can get nasty after a lot of wine. But in the work we're preparing you for, things could get a lot more dangerous, so you had better learn to protect yourself. And her," he added as an afterthought.

"Don't you care about what happens to me, then?" I asked innocently.

"Of course not, you idiot!" he snorted. "But we don't want you killed before you've spilled the information you've gained."

Thus a new aspect was added to my training: how to use a knife.

I have always felt there must be better ways of teaching the young than slapping or bellowing at them until they master the subject. Sadly, no one ever tried such novel methods on me: certainly not Sordello – or not at first. He drew his own knife and put it in my hand. "Now," he said, "Try to stab me."

At this early stage in our association, I had not yet learned to love the great troubadour: indeed, I still harboured an intense dislike for him. But I had never handled a murderous weapon, and this invitation seemed extreme and somewhat absurd. I lunged at him half-heartedly. He immediately stood back and snorted with derision. "Come on, you milksop. Make an effort. Stab me!" I tried again, still without conviction, but this time the response was a stinging slap on my cheek. Then the slaps rained on my face, as he hurled abuse at me. "Come on, you weakling. Is that the best you can do? I thought you were tough and brave, the Magister's great protector. Come on, show me what you can do!"

The slaps continued, and the goading, until I was genuinely riled. I hurled myself at him, the knife pointed directly at his breastbone. I have never been an instinctive fighter, being quicker with words than with fists or weapons. Back then I was clueless. Unsurprisingly the wicked blade, longer than the span of a hand, never touched him. Instead he was suddenly beside and behind me. His left hand was round my throat while his right twisted my wrist so sharply that I dropped the knife with a cry of pain.

Sordello put his hands on my shoulders and looked me in the eye. "You really have no idea about using a knife, have you?" I shook my head. "Perhaps that's a good thing. You have nothing to unlearn, and everything to grasp. We shall begin now."

Once again I was made to feel a novice. Yet, to my surprise, Sordello was gentle and encouraging. While we were learning to sing together, he had always been demanding, treating me (with some justice) as a fellow professional. By contrast, understanding that I was neither naturally disposed to violence nor experienced in it, he showed his skill as a teacher.

We started with basic techniques: how to hold the knife; how to approach my antagonist; how to feint and parry: and how to watch my opponent's eyes as well has his knife-hand. We practised again and again, Sordello always demanding more, yet giving credit for progress. "You're doing well, lad. But you've much to learn. It's fortunate that your singing's good: we haven't time to put that right too."

We took to using wooden daggers so that we could fight in earnest, and even wrestle for possession of a blade. I learned how to deceive my opponent, and to disarm him. I even achieved that feat once or twice with my mentor, though I always suspected that Sordello had allowed me to. However well I learned the skills, and he was a good teacher, I never had his speed or eye, so I knew I would never truly have the edge over him.

Some weeks on he finally declared himself satisfied. He reckoned I could take care of myself at a pinch, though he issued one warning. "Lorenzo, I know you're not a killer. That's to your credit. Too many of those already roam the streets. But remember this: the first time you face an enemy with a knife, he will be trying to kill you.

"You can only defend yourself, however much you might think you're good at disarming someone, if you are truly ready to kill him in return. All this work we have done with our toy blades is mere play. When the real thing happens you must have no scruples, no hesitation. Be like an animal, like the wild boar at bay: even when the spear is embedded in his entrails he will do his utmost to gore the hunter."

I must have appeared unconvinced. "Look inside yourself,' he continued. "Deep within all of us lies the mean, vicious side that we dislike and try to hide. If you want to live, you must search for that dark piece of your soul. No scruples, no regrets, no compassion: find the cold-blooded murderer within you, and put him to work. Make no mistake: you must kill your enemy, or he will assuredly do for you. Wound him merely, and he will come back at you, doubly intent on slaying you."

It was a sobering thought. "I shall try," I replied.

Chapter 18

Sordello declared me ready to go to work, and announced that we should have a trial. He arranged that our troupe, now playing and singing as an effective, tight ensemble, should perform at one of the tavernas that surrounded the Piazza Maggiore. Word spread like wildfire throughout the city. Sordello was back in town, and performing free for patrons. When we arrived to set up, not only that hostelry but the whole square was thronged with people. As usual, most of the customers were spilling out from the cramped hostelry into the open space, some on benches around tables, some on stools, many simply standing.

Everyone wanted to be there. My first musical performance in Bologna was thus very different from my debut in Modena, but no less daunting. Few of the crowd could have heard Sordello in the last five years, because he had been away from the city: my master frequently, if fondly, berated him for his long absence. Yet his reputation went before him: and he knew how to play a crowd. He started on his own, accompanying himself on the beautiful fifteen-stringed harp he carried.

It was a simple love song, one of his compositions in French. I had presumed the crowd would expect something boisterous as an opener: but always Sordello surprised his audience and won it over. A silence fell. People even stopped eating and drinking, a rare enough response in Bologna: they strained to hear him when he dropped his voice to the soulful, heart-rending finish. Instantly the applause erupted amid cheering and stamping. "Sordello! Maestro! You've come back to us!"

Before the applause had died away we launched into a roistering drinking-song, Andrea pounding the large, flat round drum held firmly in his left hand, using both ends of a stick with his right. Even Filippo projected joy into the playing of his rebec as Sordello and I sang the melody together. In the third verse I added a harmony part above Sordello's melody, and in the last two verses I created a proper descant, swooping and turning in contrary motion, exploiting my high falsetto to the full. Again the reception was rapturous.

And so it continued. The crowd loved the music, whether it was fast or slow, high or low, loud or soft, happy or sad. Sordello's artistry encompassed a dazzling range of styles and moods, yet I was not merely equal to the task: I was inspired by the challenge, and excelled in his shadow.

As the evening drew on, the nature of the audience changed. Families had headed off towards their homes and, by the end, there were fewer listeners, those who had been eating meals or drinking steadily throughout our entertainment. Judging the mood nicely, Sordello changed the music to match it. The songs we performed now were more tender. We were singing directly to the thirty or forty people closest to us.

As we continued (even taking occasional breaks, we had been performing for well over three hours), I became aware of a florid, bearded face at the table close to us. Far from enjoying our music, he seemed to be scowling. When others cheered and banged the table, he turned away in disgust. As we sang and played I could see him address his neighbour and point at me, his expression and gestures unmistakably hostile. As we embarked on another song and I added an appropriately emotional descant, he raised his voice so that I could hear him sneer: "What's that caterwauling? Is that boy some kind of eunuch, wailing like that?"

I ignored him. Performers must learn to do so, knowing that they cannot please everyone. Yet this heckler persisted, at times calling out during a song so that everyone could hear it. His dislike appeared to intensify, and it was directed not at the group as a whole but particularly at me. His gestures became more animated. Sordello indicated that this song would be the last before we took another break. I was relieved, because my self-appointed critic was starting to get under my skin. Throughout that song he was mouthing obscenities at me, and, as we reached the final cadence, I was sure he said, "Fucking eunuch."

As we stopped I could bear it no longer. I walked over to him and asked what was troubling him.

"Nothing much, boy," he replied. "Just that your voice sounds like a cat wailing at night, and you're ruining Sordello's songs."

I was angered. "Ruining them? The maestro says he's delighted with what I'm doing."

"Sordello's losing his touch, then. He used to have a good band: not this rubbish. He needs to sack you for a start."

As we argued I could feel the anger rising in me: he was making a deliberate attempt to get under my skin, and it was succeeding. Eventually he said, "You aren't listening to me, lad. Your voice is horrible: you're wrecking the music, and I suggest you piss off home and leave it to your colleagues who know what they're at."

I have confessed often enough how easy it was to goad me until I lost control. By this stage I was beside myself with fury. I drew the dagger I now habitually wore at my waist and pointed it between his eyes. "My friend, I think you'd better take back that comment, or you'll regret it." He laughed in my face.

Suddenly my right wrist was seized, the knuckles of my knife-hand smacked repeatedly on the table until I let the knife drop. I turned to see Sordello, furious. He picked me up bodily by my shirt and hurled me across the room. I leaped to my feet, both enraged and astonished. "What?" I demanded.

"You fool. You bloody stupid little idiot! What do you think you're doing, pulling a knife on someone?"

"He was insulting me, and all of us. But me especially. He has no right to speak to me like that."

"And did he threaten you?"

"Well, no. Not exactly. But he..."

"So you pull a knife on a man in a tavern because he doesn't like your voice?"

"It wasn't like that."

"Yes it was. I knew I couldn't trust you. Your temper's too wild. You lose control. I don't mind if you get yourself killed: but you're not dragging us down with you." He turned to my bearded antagonist, who was now grinning from ear to ear. "Thanks, Francesco. You did a good job on him."

The bearded man chuckled. "Never found an easier one! You want to watch that temper, sonny. I played you like the maestro does his lyre."

"You mean... you set this up?" I was abashed.

"Of course I did," snorted Sordello. "It's another lesson you have to learn. You're no use to me if you cannot keep your temper. As soon as you lose it, you're at risk. Had you been in need of defending yourself, you would have been useless. In our work – and I don't just mean musical – you must never, *never* lose control." He seized me by the collar, and looked into my eyes. "Do you understand? Do you really understand?"

He released me. I felt ashamed and stupid. I dropped my gaze and stared at my knife, lying on the table, hating it and myself. Unable to speak to him, I nodded. Then, mastering myself, I turned to Andrea and Filippo: "I'm sorry, boys. I've let you down." I picked up the knife, turned and left.

Disconsolate, I walked slowly back to the Magister's house. She greeted me as I entered the courtyard. "Lorenzo! How was it?" I made no reply, but shook my head. "Ah, I see. Another lesson learned, perhaps? I am sorry, Lorenzo. They are hard ones. But... *necessary*."

"So you were in on it too, Magister? Is everyone setting out to make a fool of me?"

"No, Lorenzo. I expect you did that all on your own. But I hope we shall have taught you not to do so again. Go to bed, and we shall speak in the morning."

Even now the reminiscence of my youthful follies causes me on occasions to squirm with embarrassment. That episode in particular still has the power to wake me from slumber, foolish old man that I am! That night, I slept badly. Indeed, I hardly slept at all, tossing and turning instead, cursing myself for a fool who could be manipulated so easy and, in equal measure, blaming Sordello who, once again, had set me a trap into which I had fallen headlong.

I was both morose and desperately tired when I rose to perform my usual morning ministrations to my master. We completed our morning rituals without speaking, I sullen and silent, she impassive. Only when I had served her breakfast did she speak to me.

"Well, Lorenzo, what did you learn last night?"

I hung my head in shame. "I learnt two things, Magister. First, I'm an idiot who never seems to learn. And, second, whenever I'm tested I let my friends down."

She looked at me in that searching way of hers. "Do you count me your friend, Lorenzo?" She asked softly.

"Yes, Magister. I do. But then, it doesn't seem the right word. It doesn't mean enough." I was suddenly overcome with emotion and, partly to hide the fact and partly because it seemed so natural at intense moments of this kind, I dropped to my knees beside her. "I owe you my life and – I know, you tell me not to keep saying so, but it's true. But it's more than that."

One minute I was tongue-tied: the next the words were tumbling out of my mouth. "You know I never had a mother or father, or at least, I never knew them. I didn't miss them, because I hadn't known what it was to have parents, to have people who loved and cared for me. Not until I met Tommaso. I went to his house and saw how his parents loved him, and how they sent him away to Modena not because they did not love him, but because they wanted the best for him. They denied themselves the joy of having him in their home – because they loved him so much. Yet he was never happier than when he was in their home, for one short week in a whole year."

I stopped, embarrassed.

"Go on," she murmured.

"Well, now I have a home. And on your own you have become to me mother and father, brothers and sisters. I know I can never truly repay your kindness to me, though I try to serve you as well as I can. But I always mess it up. I do something stupid and thoughtless. I disappoint you, when I desperately want to please you. And I let you know that at bottom I'm useless and untrustworthy and that I shall never deserve your confidence.

And I shall never make you proud of me." Like a little boy, I pushed my head into her lap and cried my heart out.

There was a long silence. Then she took my head in her two hands and pulled it upwards so that I was looking into her eyes, her hands cupping my cheeks. "Oh, Lorenzo. When will you learn not to take yourself so seriously?"

Her tone was gentle, chiding me certainly, yet with love and kindness. "None of us is perfect. We all get carried away by our emotion, our pride, our greed, our ambition. We become like a pig's bladder filled with air, until something pricks it. And what happens then? It is instantly deflated, with a… loud *fart*!"

I looked up: I had closed my eyes, but opened them at this, startled by her use of a coarse word, something she never did.

"Lorenzo, you are not so different from anyone else, displaying both strengths and weaknesses. Indeed, you are clever, amusing, a lovely singer, and a quick learner. Why else do you think Sordello and I are training you? You can do all that we ask of you and more: and I can always be certain that you will do my bidding. You silly boy, you please me all the time. It's just that I am too sour an old sow to acknowledge it. I merely grunt and take you for granted.

"Don't interrupt: you know I do. We have tested you cruelly, the two of us. And each time you have passed the test. Sordello set out to teach you a lesson last night: but I think you learned it, and that was its purpose. So dry your eyes. Compose yourself. And then we shall call Sordello in, and see if you can convince him that you have learned to control your temper. Can you do that?" I nodded, still unable to speak. "Good. A few minutes, then. And we shall go to work again."

Chapter 19

As if on cue, Sordello entered the room. It probably was a cue: everything in this period of my training seemed to have been planned and orchestrated by the two of them. As he entered, I stood. "Signor Sordello," I said stiffly, "I believe I must thank you for teaching me another lesson. I am grateful for it, and can assure you that it has been well learned."

To my surprise, his austere, haughty demeanour suddenly softened. "I am sorry, Lorenzo," he replied. "It was another hard lesson for you: but one you needed to learn. There's passion in your heart, something I recognise and admire. It's why you are such a good musician – no, no false modesty. You are outstanding. I recognise much of myself in you. The Magister will confirm that I was wild and frequently out of control when I was young." She smiled and nodded, but said nothing. "And it nearly cost me my life more than once.

"You've seen how fights happen in the street. God knows, Bologna has enough armed gangs roaming the streets, whether they represent the old families or the new Companies of Arms: they're certainly flexing their muscles nowadays. They stand up to one another, shout insults and goad one another until the fight starts.

"But responding to that is the best way to get yourself killed. To win, to stay alive, you must keep a cool head, antagonise your opponent and let him make the first wild swing. I've taught you enough to help you deal with an idiot bent on violence. A real assassin, now that's another thing. But the average bully should be no danger to you now."

I bowed. "I'm obliged to you."

Sordello laughed. "How stiff and formal you are! Lorenzo, forgive me. I humiliated you: but I think you will never forget yourself again. And one day, perhaps, you'll thank me for it." He strode across the room towards me. "Come, let us be friends as well as colleagues. Take my hand."

What could I say? The man was a consummate musician, spy, courtier – and he was offering me his friendship. In that instant I stopped resenting him, his superiority born of age and experience, and his closeness to my master. "Thank you," I responded. "Friend and colleague: I should like that very much."

"Good. And now let us get to work. Bettisia," I never used the Magister's name, and still found his familiarity shocking. "What must our next move be?"

She sounded downcast. "I have forfeited my influence with the magnati. It started with Lambertazzi, as you know. Now he has spread word around the great families that I am siding entirely with the merchants and the guilds. He is correct, in a sense, because they have right on their side. I fear I shall be welcomed inside the towers of but few of the *consorterie* for some time, so I shall hear no news from there – beyond the occasional informant whom I still pay."

I was shocked. "You pay spies in their households?"

"How naïve you are, Lorenzo! Of course I do. Or, rather, I did: but I earn less now, since being... *shunned* by the aristocracy. Fortunately I am still appreciated in the university, and well rewarded by the guild of students: otherwise we should have to live more... *frugally*."

(Indeed I was innocent in those days! Even now I still pay one or two well-placed officials a small retainer to keep me informed: just in case the city's authorities decide to enact some kind of retribution, even against an old man, for some of my shadier activities in the past). I was still puzzled: "Magister, I understand how you have fallen out with the Lambertazzi. But, since you are so careful with your words, how have you so offended the other families?"

"Not all of them, in truth, Lorenzo. Indeed, although most are now highly suspicious of us, our good friend Master de' Pasaggeri remains very much favoured by the Geremei, one family (and an important one) that supports our work." I continued to look bewildered.

"It is the new law," she explained with unaccustomed patience. "That which, God willing, we shall pass here in Bologna within months. I spoke of it to you briefly, Lorenzo." I nodded. "If we win the argument in the Consiglio, we shall finally put an end to slavery in this city – and in those places under our influence, such as Modena."

"I know we talked about this before, Magister. But I am still confused. Surely," I protested, "Lambertazzi for one will never agree to it. His family owns hundreds of slaves."

Sordello cut in. "Of course he won't. None of the families will – save one. Only the Geremei will support the new law, thanks to work over years by Rolandino – Master de' Pasaggeri."

"But the Geremei must keep slaves too?" I was having difficulty in comprehending all this politicking.

"They do indeed." My master was warming to the theme: "Almost as many as the Lambertazzi. But they will accept the compensation offered by the *Comune*: they see the wisdom of the move, for the good of all. Yet they are the only family so far to agree: every other one of note is against us."

Sordello interrupted. "So if both the Magister and Maestro Rolandino are now excluded from the counsels of all the other magnati, then we must get into their houses. Where jurists or notaries cannot tread, musicians may! Let us roust out the rest of the troupe, Lorenzo, and go to work. I guess those two rogues are still sleeping off last night's excesses somewhere."

And so we did. For a while I began to inhabit that rarefied world created by the ancient families high above the streets of Bologna. We found ourselves within the enclaves of the Accursi, the Alberici, the Toschi and the Ghisilieri, all engagements that flowed from our first few appearances which had been engineered through the good offices of Master de' Pasaggeri with the Geremei, one of the oldest and most powerful families, overshadowed only by the Lambertazzi and the Asinelli, yet disposed pragmatically to support the growing power of the guilds and the Popolo.

In all there were twenty or more families who each formed their own *consorterie*, their great towers clustered close together. At ground level they were like fortresses, stout timber walls with heavy gates surrounding the base of each, or occasionally encompassing two or three towers at once. There were stables, kitchens and accommodation for their retainers, as many as two hundred men or more with their women and children. As musicians hired to perform at a banquet we would arrive at the gate, to be admitted by a group of surly guards. Then we would embark on the wearisome climb, some fifteen or twenty minutes' breathless ascent (although Michele was still keeping me fit, it remained sweaty work) before we arrived at the family's luxuriously appointed rooms at the top.

The families, accustomed to fighting feuds with one another (though at this time more frequently building alliances against what they saw as the threat of the growing power of the merchants and the Popolo), felt appropriately fortified and secluded in their aerial world: yet they lived a cramped existence. Their towers, absurdly tall, were necessarily narrow, so that the family's apartments at the top of even the greatest towers were only some eight or ten paces across. Thus at a banquet, or wedding feast, the closest members of the family might eat in one room, the food brought up laboriously from ground level: then we musicians, having sung and played for them, would be sent across one of those perilous links to the adjoining tower in order to entertain the lesser members of the family.

I discovered that there was a pecking order among the families. The height of the tower reflected the status of the family, so that the Lambertazzi and the Asinelli gloried in their possession of the highest towers in Bologna, sneering at the lowlier families – at least, until they needed their support or wished to conclude a favourable marriage contract. I always suspected that the greater height of their towers also reflected the degree of their insecurity: from the taller building they could fire arrows at need onto their inferior neighbours, though I never saw it done.

Among the great families, only the Geremei appeared to hold a different view of their lineage, and of their family's place in the ever-growing, rapidly changing *Comune* of Bologna: as a result, in retaliation for siding with the merchants and the Popolo, and notwithstanding their great wealth and influence which must have rivalled those of the Lambertazzi, they were largely isolated.

Wedding feasts provided our most reliable source of engagements. At one celebration after another I would look with pity at the terrified expression on the face of a twelve or thirteen year-old girl, beautifully dressed and wed to a husband three times her age, her youth and virginity sacrificed on the altar of family politics, mastered entirely by the imperative of retaining power within that tiny aristocratic circle.

There was a steely purpose behind our work as musicians, that of infiltrating the great families and discovering secrets and plots against the wellbeing of the city (from the point of view of my master and Maestro de' Pasaggeri): yet I will not pretend I did not enjoy myself. As that spring progressed, warm and sunny as always in our part of Italy, the alliances between the great families, and their celebrations of them, multiplied endlessly. For a while we hired entertainers seemed nonetheless to live the life of the great families.

While our work was the same as that of any group of troubadours, to entertain the aristocracy while they gorged themselves on rich foods and fine wines, talking and shouting above the music to which they paid little or no attention, we found vast amusement in this alien world. So high were some of the towers, so far above the kitchens in the courtyard below, that truly hot food must have been unknown to our employers and their guests, for all their wealth. We would watch trains of servants toiling up the stairs, staggering under heavily-loaded platters of roast meats, cheeses, fruits and other delicacies.

Some families, I remember particularly the Guidosagni, had identified this shortcoming and, on the top of their tower, had cultivated a garden within the sturdy stone parapet that prevented drunken guests from plummeting to an early death: the space boasted a tree growing in the middle while, on a charcoal brazier in one corner, large chunks of wild boar and new season's lamb crackled and spat in the flames. The smell was so alluring that, at times, the rumbling of my stomach threatened to drown out our music.

We would lead grotesque processions lurching along those insecure walkways from one tower to another. After dark, torches would be placed in sconces above the doorway at each end of every bridge and frequently at its mid-point. There were handrails on either side, or those bloated and drunken guests would never have made the crossing safely. Yet, high as they were, the stone towers themselves swayed in the wind. Moreover, the connections between them wobbled and creaked alarmingly when too many people crossed at once, occasionally spitting out splinters that spun crazily down into the void below, while their anchor points at each end similarly ejected mortar and even lumps of stone.

As if anyone cared! They believed themselves to lead charmed lives. Andrea and Filippo, Sordello's trusty if bibulous colleagues, would lead the way, frequently roaring with laughter as they played their drum and rebec respectively. Andrea would beat out a rhythm that was impossible to resist and dragged the guests to their feet, while those narrow spans squeaked and groaned their protest. We would arrive in the adjoining tower, finding ourselves in yet another richly-hung room with more tables bending under the weight of food, and the banquet would begin afresh.

Always full of mischief, Andrea and Filippo would seize every opportunity to nose around the family rooms at the tops of the towers. Sordello made sure that they never stole anything, but they pried habitually, while Sordello and I followed their lead, searching for any documents that might give us news of the machinations of the great families. Always in vain: perilous matters were rarely committed to vellum and, if they were, would have been securely locked away in the chest which, bound with iron and padlocks, stood in the corner of every family's great chamber.

On occasions our two fellow musicians could not resist the temptation of pissing off one of the walkways. So high were we that we could never hear any reaction from below, and it was always too dark to see: but they joyously imagined the ruination they had visited on some grandee's fine clothes, giggling hysterically until sharply rebuked by our leader.

Notwithstanding all our efforts singly and together, we never learnt anything of our enemies' plans: nor did any opportunity occur for us to get inside the Lambertazzi house. At first we assumed that it was merely a matter of being patient, until a chance encounter in the towers of another of the *consorterie*, the Catalani. We were performing a routine drinking-song when the evening was well advanced: Sordello had dropped out to rest his voice while I carried the melody, as there was no need for a descant or other complexity.

A voice spoke behind me, silky, oily and etched so firmly in my memory that I nearly forgot myself and stopped singing. But my training reasserted itself, and I continued while straining my ears to hear. The words were addressed not to me but directly to Sordello, standing to my left.

"My, my, Maestro Sordello, you are very much in demand these days: Bologna has not seen so much of you in many years."

"Signor Bardi," Sordello replied evenly, bowing. I allowed myself one quick glance at the tall figure, immaculately dressed all in black, that I had twice observed in Modena, again encountered on my night of agony in the Lambertazzi tower, and subsequently spotted accompanying Livia on those precious occasions when I spied her attending the cathedral.

"So you still serve Lambertazzi?" Sordello was teasing.

"I have that honour. As you well know, I am not the first exile from another city to appreciate the freedoms and tolerance of Bologna. And Signor Massimo Lambertazzi is kind enough to offer me his protection in return for my counsel."

"And do you counsel him well, Signor?"

"I furnish him with excellent advice, particularly urging caution as to whom he trusts. And I would warn you, Sordello," I noticed that he dropped any title of courtesy, "To keep your distance and resist the temptation to spy for your *particular* friend. Make no mistake. If you care for the esteemed Dottor Gozzadini - and I think you do, perhaps all too much – you will advise her against any further interference in the affairs of the family I serve. She and her notary friend are becoming a thorn in the flesh of the great families."

"I dare say they will be gratified that their efforts have been noticed," responded Sordello dryly. "But they do not seek to interfere with anyone's business – merely, so they assure me, to serve and preserve the rule of law in the *Comune*. Surely no family, however great, would seek to put itself above the law, especially here in Bologna which sees itself, more than any city, as its guardian?"

His interlocutor's veneer of urbanity dissolved instantly. "Don't bandy words with me, Sordello. It will take more than a mountebank and a brace of scribes to bring down the family that has made this city what it is. Bologna is become rich, and immensely powerful, and will not be swayed by a few scribblers with the support of the rabble. You have heard my warning, and if you are wise you will pass it on."

Sordello tried to intervene, but was cut off immediately by Bardi's tone, now harsh and hostile. "If it is not heeded, things will go badly for your friends – and for you, particularly if you are unwise enough to set foot on our territory. Do not think for a moment that I do not see how you spy while you sing, and meddle while you play. I know you, Sordello. Have a care."

After what seemed like an eternity the song came to an end. I turned to Sordello: there was no sign of Bardi. Hearing that voice, so close, so threatening, had brought back memories that I had tried to suppress, yet which still recurred in my nightmares. But Sordello was apparently untroubled. "You heard him, then, Lorenzo? Bardi, I mean?" I nodded. "Don't worry. His threats are empty: yet the fact that he makes them suggests that we have them rattled. Perhaps that is progress. We'll finish here as soon as we can, and report back to Bett... the Magister."

Chapter 20

Back at the house we talked far into the night. Even Sordello had lost some of his usual certainty and optimism. "Lorenzo has done a good job," he said, putting some rare praise my way. "Between us we have heard much – and learned nothing of note."

"It's true, Magister," I added. "Everyone's talking about the work you and Master de' Pasaggeri are doing on the law to end slavery. In the places we've been singing, many people seem to approve, even if they have some reservations."

"But then," cut in Sordello, "Someone will always add that the old families aren't happy. They mention the name Lambertazzi, and the conversation stops dead. We have discovered nothing."

"Has he told you that Bardi warned him off tonight, Magister?" I asked.

"No one warns off Sordello," he grunted. "But, yes, she knows it all."

My master was silent for a while. Then she said slowly, "We are sure they are plotting... *something*. We have no information, merely... *suspicions*. When the Lambertazzi, Asinelli and others were indulging in their usual small, mean tricks and subterfuges to get their way in the Consiglio, we used to hear about it: that is the way in any city. But it is the very silence, the barrier that we constantly strike, that makes me suspicious. What are they plotting? Does Lambertazzi think he can intimidate the council itself? Time was he could: but surely not now? Now that the guilds and the Popolo have tasted power and liked what they found."

"Can he not bribe and extort? That used to be his way."

"To be sure, it was how he operated – how they all did. But times have changed. No, I fear something altogether bigger. I suspect that Lambertazzi and his close allies will try to take control of the city by force."

"By force of arms?" Sordello scoffed. "Those families have maybe a thousand men between all their retainers, guards and downright bruisers. That's not enough to take control of a city the size of Bologna."

"No, indeed. But it is the nucleus of a powerful force. They might achieve it: if Lambertazzi could buy support from elsewhere and hire a small army."

"An army?" Sordello scoffed. Even with all his wealth Lambertazzi could not achieve that. Where would he find an army? Not in Bologna."

"In Modena!" I surprised myself by interrupting. "Of course. That's where I first saw Bardi, as you know. I was serving the Bishop's wine: and he, the Prior and that Modenese lord, Uguzzoni, were talking about having a powerful friend in Bologna. When they named him, Lambertazzi, it was Bardi who stopped them and said they shouldn't, not even among friends. You know how he speaks." I could not resist showing off a little. "It's a bit like a shawm, a bass cialamello, but warmer." I changed my own tone to mimic my enemy. "*If I may humbly suggest, Signori.* He could charm the birds from the trees with that voice, if his heart weren't so black underneath it."

They laughed momentarily: it had been a good imitation! But Sordello instantly reverted to interrogating me. "But they never discussed details of what they were planning?"

"No. Bardi wouldn't let them. But they complained about the Gatekeeper and how they couldn't find out who he was." I glanced reproachfully at my master. "It *must* be the plot you're suspecting."

My master nodded. "I believe you are right, Lorenzo. With Uguzzoni's enormous wealth added to his own, perhaps Lambertazzi could seriously consider an armed... *intervention.* With troops and arms from Modena, he could detain the consuls, the Podestà and the Capitano del Popolo, take control of the administration, and bully the *anziani* and the College into submission. He could free Enzo and declare him King, gaining the support of whoever is the next Emperor, when that matter is resolved."

"And what of the Pope?" Sordello remained sceptical. "He would never agree."

"Nor would he have the power to prevent it. The Emperor's faction would be delighted to see both the *Comune* here and the Pope at a distance humbled. No one would ride to Bologna's rescue."

I was bewildered. "How can you know all this, Magister? Did the Gatekeeper tell you?"

"I... *know* nothing, Lorenzo. But I suspect much."

"So what can we do about it? We can't just sit here and talk."

"Ah, Lorenzo, you are always in such a hurry. But perhaps for once you are right. If Lambertazzi really is planning the kind of move we suspect, and Bardi takes the trouble to threaten Sordello, his plans must be close to fruition. He will be obliged to lay out a great deal of money. Therefore we should try to find out where he is spending money in large sums, whether it is in gold and silver or indeed hidden in his trading. There are more goods passing in and out of the city in the name of Lambertazzi than of most of the merchants put together."

"Aye, that's true," commented Sordello. "I've heard as much. You must have done too, boy, amid all that inconsequential babble we've been trying to follow."

"It's true, I have. But I thought families like the Lambertazzi believed trade beneath them."

"Do not underestimate the magnati, Lorenzo," warned my master. "The old families still maintain their wealth through land and slaves, and their power through collaboration, but they are ready to learn from the merchants whom they fear and profess to despise. If, by buying, selling and controlling supplies of goods, they can maintain or increase their influence, they will do so – however much they may publically... *sneer* at what they term 'trade'."

I had a sudden inspiration. "If you want to find out what they're trading, Magister, then I know how we can find out." The other two looked at me in surprise. "My friends. You know: Paolo, Giacomo and Salvatore."

"Your disreputable drinking companions," she commented drily.

I grinned. "Not that disreputable. But yes, I do sometimes drink with them - when," I added pathetically, "I have a moment to myself. They make a living mostly by loading and protecting traders' wagons. I only have to ask them to make sure that the next few jobs they get are guarding Lambertazzi's goods. But they might need, you know..."

"Some money for a drink, perhaps?" asked Sordello wryly.

"They have a living to make," I replied, somewhat defensively of my friends.

"They shall be paid," my master confirmed. "And handsomely, if they find us the information we hope for. Meanwhile we must not give our enemies time to plan and seize the initiative. On the contrary, we must keep them on the defensive. We shall push on with the change that Lambertazzi hates most, that makes him most angry. We must bring forward the law to end slavery. Lambertazzi is no fool, but this proposal has rendered him incandescent with rage when it has been discussed in the College."

"Is he not more dangerous when angered?"

"More dangerous, perhaps: but less likely to plan his response coolly and logically. I fear Lambertazzi, but less so when he is furious than when he is cold and calculating – which is when he will listen more readily to that snake Bardi, whose intellect is twice that of his master. So we shall do Lorenzo's bidding, and hurry things along in the hope that an ill-considered response from Lambertazzi will be more likely to go amiss. Truly a hasty solution... *typical* of Lorenzo, indeed! But a shrewd one. I know that Rolandino has all but finished the draft of the legal document: the *Liber Paradisus*, the *heavenly book* that will put an end once and for all to the inequity of one man thinking he can own another.

"Lorenzo, you are proving yourself more valuable in our counsels than I dared hope." I preened, until I caught sight of Sordello's raised eyebrows and mocking grin. "You must see your three friends tomorrow and ensure that they position themselves guarding Lambertazzi wagons. As for me, I shall speak to

Rolandino in the morning. Then you and I, Lorenzo, will go to visit our friend the Capitano del Popolo and lay plans so that the full council will meet to ratify this law."

"The *whole* council, Magister? Which do you mean? I confess I don't understand all the colleges and councils that claim to run the *Comune*."

"This is one you have not yet seen, Lorenzo. It is some years since it last met, but we shall ensure that it is obliged to do so in order to consider this matter. Master de' Pasaggeri and I will go to the smaller College and ... *contrive* matters so that they will conclude with a demand that the Podestà call a meeting of the *Consiglio dei Due Mila*. That will be a grand spectacle, Lorenzo: you will enjoy it."

"The *Due Mila*, Magister? You mean two thousand people?"

"Precisely, Lorenzo. Normally a busy city must do business through smaller councils, some of which you have encountered. But for a great change like this, the full council must be summoned. It may require some few weeks to arrange. But we *shall* take the law against slavery, Rolandino's *Liber Paradisus*, to the Two Thousand, the guardians of our great city and *Comune*, one man speaking for twenty or thirty in his Quarter. And our suit shall prevail!"

The plans were quickly set in motion. When I sent word to my three friends that their help was needed, they arrived with alacrity, perhaps drawn by the chance at last of meeting my enigmatic master. Their arrival was interrupted by one of Mamolo's frequent outbursts from the kitchen, this time because he could not lay hands on any of the essence of *balsamico*, "Not for love nor money." He was complaining that the price had more than trebled in recent months, and now he could not find any at all. "How am I to make the Magister's favourite sauces now?" he whined. "She doesn't eat enough as it is, not enough to keep a sparrow alive." A thought, or perhaps a memory, nagged at me for a moment, but was swiftly gone again.

As was his wonted response, Michele roared at Mamolo to stop disturbing the household: and my master herself was firmly pacific, assuring Mamolo that whatever alternative sauce he produced would be entirely satisfactory. That was when Paolo,

Giacomo and Salvatore arrived, bubbling with excitement and good humour.

The Magister briefed them on their task. They were to do all they could to attach themselves to any wagonload of Lambertazzi goods, wherever it was travelling, and find out everything they could. Above all they were to look for any large sums of money being transported, anything unusual about the goods delivered or collected, and they were to be particularly vigilant for any hint of secrecy in the transactions they witnessed.

It was little to go on, but it was the only hope we had. The three of them were well known among the regular wagonners as extra pairs of hands ready to help with transporting and guarding goods. As long as they were fortunate in attaching themselves to a Lambertazzi convoy, there would be nothing to arouse suspicion.

I could see that the master was wary of entrusting sensitive information and, indeed, so important a mission to three ebullient lads. It was Sordello who broke into her third admonition to them about taking this task seriously, commenting quietly, "Magister, these young men know their way around, and are familiar faces amongst the wagon trains. They have Lorenzo's trust, and that must be enough for us." I looked at him in surprise, flattered by the compliment he paid me.

To my further astonishment, the Magister readily accepted his advice. "Very well. I thank you for your help, gentlemen. Lorenzo, obtain payment for them from Michele and show them out." Impressed to learn that I really did have proper employment with this eminent lawyer, my friends bowed awkwardly to her and to Sordello as they prepared to leave. As I was showing them out of the gate, I took Paolo aside. "Paolo, where do you think the next parcel of wagons is most likely to go?"

"To Ravenna, perhaps, or even Ferrara. But my bet is that it'll be Modena: that's where nearly all the Lambertazzi wagons are going at present, so I hear."

"I thought as much: and the Magister will be delighted if that's where you end up going. She reckons any plots against Bologna will be hatched there. But will you do something for me, my friend?"

"You're suddenly very serious, Lorenzo? What is it?"

"Paolo, your task is to follow those Lambertazzi goods and men, and not to take your eyes off them for a second. But if you do have a moment..." I stopped, in confusion.

"Come on, Lorenzo. Spit it out. What do you need me to do for you?"

"If you can slip away, I need you to... No, I must just ask you. If you can. You know I came from the Cathedral in Modena?" Paolo nodded. "Well, when I ran away from there I left a good friend. I've never sent word to him about where I am how I'm doing, although I promised I would. Don't talk to any of the priests, whatever you do. But - if you can find someone who has to do with the choir, or one of the choristers perhaps, could you try to pass word to him?"

"Of course, if I can. What's his name?"

The name almost stuck in my throat as a wave of remorse overcame me. "Tommaso. I used to call him Tommasino. Don't use the name Lorenzo for me: I was called something different then. If you have to send him a message, just say that the choirboy from Venice sends greetings and is well."

"The choirboy from Venice? Lorenzo, I think there's more about your past life that you must tell us one day. In the tavern - and you're buying the wine, after all we're doing for you!"

I laughed and clapped him on the back. "I certainly will: and I won't even complain about paying, although you and Giacomino drink twice what Salvatore and I manage! Thank you for doing this - all of it."

He looked me in the eye. "Lorenzo, it's when you trust a friend to do something important that you know he's a real friend. We'll do this for your master - and the other thing for you. You can count on that." And they were gone.

Chapter 21

The next two weeks were so busy for us that we barely gave my three friends' mission a thought. We heard that they had gone to Modena, which served to fuel my master's suspicions that any conspiracy in which the Lambertazzi were playing a leading role must involve our neighbouring city, so frequently and so violently at odds with Bologna.

We had much to do on our own account. A couple of days after they had left, Master de' Pasaggeri appeared unannounced at our door to report that the Capitano del Popolo had succeeded, more quickly than he had expected, in persuading the Podestà that he must call a meeting of the College to consider the proposed law to end slavery. Moreover, although he was the author of the draft, he was anxious that my master should accompany him in order to provide support and offer a second opinion on points of law. "For we know," he added, "That our opponents will bring to bear every opposing argument they can."

And so I found myself at my first meeting of the College. As always I accompanied my master through the streets to the Palazzo del Podestà. Once we had climbed the stairs to the *gran sala*, I expected to be sent out with all the other assistants, bodyguards and hangers-on, leaving the College alone. But, to my surprise, my master barked (betraying how nervous she was), "Lorenzo, you will stay. Be seated at that table, equip yourself with quill and paper and be ready to hand me any of those scrolls or papers in your scrip when I require them: particularly that copy of Master de' Passageri's document with my annotations. We may need to think on our feet."

Delighted, I settled myself down and rifled through my scrip to check which document was which, in case she asked for them. The table was situated at the edge of the dais at one end of the great chamber, affording me a grandstand view of the dignitaries and important functionaries of the council – the Podestà and four each from among the *anziani* and the *consoli*. My master and her colleague, to my surprise, were not to be seated on the dais. Instead they sat among the ordinary members of the College at floor-level, on hand to offer expert opinion when called upon.

Once all the benches in the hall were occupied, two pale and ink-stained men appeared and bustled their way up onto the platform, carrying sheaves of vellum, bundles of quills and bottles of ink. Peremptorily they pushed me to the very edge of the table while they arranged their equipment on it. Clearly they were the scribes, deputed to record the discussions and decisions of the meeting. Equally clearly they were full of their own importance, liked to make an entrance and resented ceding any space to me at their table. In order to play my part convincingly I reached into my scrip and pulled out a few sheets of vellum and the quill and small bottle of ink I always carried in case my master needed me to draft a clause or contract. They sniffed disapprovingly but ceased to push me any further.

As I looked across the dais, the Podestà, seated on a chair which rested on a small podium, raising it a little above the height of those around him, rose to his feet and cleared his throat.

"Gentlemen of the College," he announced, "I have called this Council because it appears impossible to delay it further. It concerns a piece of proposed law which, were I able to act entirely according to my inclination, would never have seen the light of day." He spoke as if he had a bad taste in his mouth. "I refer, of course, to the proposal to put an end – no, I shall say it plain - to *outlaw* the long-established practice of slavery."

The four anziani, or elders, to his right - among whom I noticed with a start the unmistakeable figure of Massimo Lambertazzi - murmured their agreement. On his other side, it was clear that the four consoli, the consuls who represented the guilds, felt very differently, just as their appearance was at variance with that of those with whom they were in disagreement. The latter were unmistakably magnati, aristocratic in bearing and haughty in demeanour, their robes trimmed with expensive fur, silver and white for the most part, large stones sparkling in the rings that adorned their hands. Whereas Lambertazzi was enormous, the other three ranged from diminutive to tall and lean - almost skeletal, indeed. All exuded an air of arrogant irritation at being called together at all, let alone to consider a proposal so preposterous to them.

By contrast, the consoli were dressed soberly, as if consciously eschewing the trappings of wealth. Yet their expressions were shrewd and calculating, their hawkish eyes scanning their opponents and the rest of the gathering. These were men who had accumulated considerable fortunes without the privilege of birth, and they would not permit old vested interests to thwart them, nor miss an opportunity to increase their wealth. Unimpressive as he was, for a moment I felt some sympathy for the Podestà, caught between such formidable sets of antagonists. Raising his hand towards the anziani, the Podestà continued. "Notwithstanding your disquiet, gentlemen, with which I have much sympathy, it is clearly the will of at least *some* of this assembly that we now consider it fully. Our esteemed notary, Master de' Pasaggeri, tells me that he has now drafted the document in full. Accordingly it must be placed before you and opened to scrutiny and debate."

He gestured towards my master's friend. "So, Signor Notaro, will you read the text to us in its entirety?"

The eminent notary rose to his feet, bowed and spoke deferentially. "Podestà, I would be happy to do so. However, as is proper in any legal document, the text is written entirely in Latin. Nonetheless, with your permission I would translate it for you in brief, and provide a gloss of its main articles - if that would suit?" A murmur of assent rippled around the hall, and the Podestà nodded his agreement.

"Gentlemen, as the wise and elected guardians of this city of Bologna, who in this college represent and advise the greater Councils, I believe you have both the right and the duty to consider this matter in which I act solely as a humble scribe, instructed by previous resolutions to explore how in law this city might bring an end to the practice of slavery within its territories and dominions." A steady rumble of muttering, a confusion of approval and disapprobation, started to grow in the hall as Master Rolandino continued.

"In law, it is quite simple. This College and the greater Councils have indicated that they wish the Comune to reappraise the value it places on human life. To be sure, some are greater in station than others. Some hold rank and wealth through family and position. Others have achieved wealth and influence through their success in *mercanzia*, in banking and commerce.

"The guilds represented here also now have their place in the Councils of the city, as they should, representing as they do the craftsmen, the makers of tools, of goods, of finery and luxury that fuel the commerce on which this our city thrives.

"And the Companies of Arms, they who protect their respective Quarters of the city, and who serve at need in her defence – as they did with distinction only a few years ago at Fossalta, ensuring that decisive victory: they too demand a voice in the governance of Bologna, the city they bear arms under oath to protect.

"The will of this city's various Councils is, as I understand it, that all men – and, indeed, the women who serve them – should be paid according to their station, their skills, their knowledge, their experience and their labour. It is by adopting that righteous path that the city has rendered itself both rich and powerful. Its mills and its farms: its workshops and its forges: all are best worked by free men, offering their labour in return for a fair wage. And in this haven of honest trade and fair reward, there is no longer any place for a man to be demeaned by being owned by another, as if he were an animal."

The hubbub grew almost to a roar, as the notary raised his stentorian voice above it. "And therefore, with the assistance of my learned friend Dottor Gozzadini, I have drafted the legal instrument which, if approved, will allow this city and *Comune* to abandon forever the practice of serfdom. Slavery, for such it is, shall no longer have any place in the life of our great city and its territories."

There was uproar. Most of the men in the body of the hall were on their feet, shouting towards the dais. It was clear that opinion was divided. Some were roaring their approval, while others bellowed defiance. There was even pushing and jostling in the crowd. On the platform, Massimo Lambertazzi was on his feet, too. Somehow, above all the noise, his deep, stentorian voice made itself heard. "So you will rob us of our rightful possessions? Our serfs are as much our chattels as our houses, our lands and our beasts. You shall not tear them from us and leave us destitute!"

The Podestà seemed powerless to regain control. Beside him the Capitano del Popolo leapt to his feet and roared, "Silence!" Slowly, reluctantly, the noise abated. "I demand respect for this College, and for the position of the Podestà," he continued. "Gentlemen, this matter must be debated properly, and with dignity, or we shall all be the poorer for this, this mayhem." He turned to Master Rolandino. "I believe, Master Notary, that Signor Lambertazzi has put a question to you. What of the loss of wealth to those who keep serfs? Will he and others like him be recompensed?"

"Indeed, Signor Capitano. I believe that Signor Lambertazzi," he bowed in his direction, "Knows full well that ample compensation is planned, paid from the coffers of the city. The proposal is that the owners of freed slaves be recompensed to the tune of ten of our Bolognese *Lire* for each adult slave: and eight for each child, girl or boy." The murmuring began again. "Since I believe Signor Lambertazzi's family owns more than seventy-score slaves, it is clear that the Comune will be making a more than generous payment to him. I would estimate it in the region of some fifteen thousand Lire, a handsome sum by any measure."

There was a gasp, and then another loud reaction from the crowd, again split into supporters and opponents. The notary held up his hand, gesturing for silence, which slowly descended. When he could make himself heard he continued: "The will of the Councils, as it has been expressed to me, was that this wise and just move in freeing slaves should not be achieved at the expense of any one party, except of the *Comune* itself which, in turn, believes that former slaves, working as free men and women and paid fairly according to the rules laid down by the guilds, will work more readily, produce more goods, and contribute to the trade and taxes which will swiftly repay the city's liberality and see its prosperity grow.

"The *Comune* has therefore set aside fifty thousand Lire for the manumission of the six thousand serfs estimated to be presently owned by some four hundred lords." This time the sheer scale of the expense planned reduced his audience to a muttering near-silence. He continued: "It is furthermore my contention that the name of every freed slave should be appended to this legal document in order to enshrine and protect their liberty: and that, when it is complete, it should be given the name *Liber Paradisus*, the Book of Heaven."

There was another outburst. The elders, representatives of old families, and their allies on the floor expressed their outrage again, snorting with derision at the proposed title. "Book of Heaven? It'll drag us down to hell," shouted one.

"Why," called another, "This notary is declaring himself a priest, speaking for God!"

"He'll be proclaiming himself Pope next!"

Once again it took the Podestà some time to regain a semblance of order, with help from the Capitano del Popolo. "Gentlemen," said the former, "We must now determine how this matter should proceed. I know that the anziani, our elders who for centuries have guided this city, see this change as unnecessary and dangerous, undermining the very social fabric of this city and this traditions." A roar of anger from the consuls and guildsmen greeted this comment. "But," he raised his voice, "I am aware that others do not share this view. Yet we cannot enact law when our College is so bitterly divided. To do so would rend the very fabric of this city and reduce us to warring factions."

"We already have those!" came one shout from the floor.

"Lambertazzi's men are out every night breaking heads!" came another.

"The families are only protecting themselves from you damned *gonfalonieri*!" bellowed another of the elders. This time it was the Capitano del Popolo who established sufficient quiet to make himself heard. "Gentlemen, amid this furore I believe we cannot even agree to disagree. We must have calm. To resolve this division in the College we must obtain proper counsel: and who better to give a second opinion, I suggest, than another jurist. I call on Dottor Gozzadini to advise us in this matter."

The shouting died down to a rumble, then to a murmur. My master rose to her feet and slowly, deliberately, climbed onto the podium. I suspected this moment had been rehearsed between her and the Capitano. She was calm, serene and, as at her best when lecturing, authoritative.

"Gentlemen of the College," she said, her scratchy voice cutting through that charged atmosphere, "Our leaders, both Podestà and Capitano, are correct. No decision can be made on so weighty a matter when passions are aroused and you are coming almost to blows. Good law may not be created in heat and anger, only in calm and with reason. First, then, I would advise that you calm yourselves." I could not resist smiling. It was as if she were admonishing a bunch of naughty boys: I suspected that she felt she was doing precisely that.

"Second, this is a long document which cannot be debated line by line by a full meeting of any of the Councils of the *Comune*: it is simply not practicable. I suggest therefore that the four anziani and four consoli here each nominate one lawyer of their choice, and that those eight be instructed to examine minutely Master de' Pasaggeri's *Liber Paradisus*, that they may satisfy themselves that the law proposed therein is not only right and equitable but also capable of being put into statute and made to work: for law, however lofty its intention, must be practical and functional."

Now she had the attention of the whole room: there was not a sound. It was an uncanny effect that she seemed always able to work on crowds, even disagreeable ones. "If what Maestro de' Pasaggeri has drafted, with my humble assistance, has thus satisfied our fellow jurists, they must say so, publicly and under oath, giving their assurance that this work is well done. Yet, even then, I believe that so mighty a law may not be passed by this College, notwithstanding its gravity." Again disapprobation began to grow.

"Nor even by any of the larger Councils," she continued. As she reached the end of her proposal, she could barely make herself heard above the growing noise. "I believe this College must call a meeting of the *Due Mila*, the Council of the Two Thousand, where each man may speak for his part of the city, and where lots must be cast and counted publicly. That way," she raised her voice again, "That way there can be no cheating, no bribery, no coercion."

As she said these words she looked directly at Lambertazzi. "No vested interest shall sway this, and the true representatives of this *Comune* shall have their say. That is my advice."

Now it was clear that the supporters of the new law, not its opponents, were in the ascendency. There were cheers and stamps, roars of approval for my master's proposal, until the rafters rang with the noise. While it continued, I could see the Podestà and Capitano del Popolo in urgent, fierce conversation. It was clear that the Podestà was unwilling to continue: and equally evident that the Capitano would brook no further delay. I was sure I could hear him as I could see his lips move: "Do it. You must do it."

Eventually the Podestà raised both hands, appealing for silence. Slowly, grudgingly, the noisy crowd fell silent. "Very well," declared the Podestà. "Though I personally retain grave reservations about the wisdom of this proposal to change our law, it has been drafted and endorsed by two of our most esteemed lawyers. The means of determining the outcome has been suggested, again by a respected authority. I shall call a meeting of the Two Thousand four weeks from this day, and at that meeting lots shall be cast and counted to determine the outcome.

"In the meantime, eight jurists shall be nominated to examine the document, as the Magister recommends, and at the meeting of the Two Thousand they shall be required to give their opinion as to the worthiness of this document. If they declare it fit to be enacted, then the vote will be taken as to whether it should be passed. And now, I declare this College closed."

There was a sigh of relief followed by the distinctive sound of forty opinionated men all speaking at once as the Podestà and the Capitano stepped down from the dais and made for the door, closely followed by the consuls and elders. The two lawyers remained together, in intense conversation. As he walked past them, Lambertazzi stopped abruptly and turned to them. "Have a care, you two scribblers," he hissed. "You may pull this College hither and thither with your clever words: but remember where the true power lies in this city – where it has always lain. It will take more than the machinations of two word-twisters to wrest power from those who have ruled this city for centuries. Have a care, I say, lest you find yourselves without friends and unprotected."

"Is that a threat, Signor Lambertazzi?" asked my master. Her tone was sardonic, mocking.

"Only a fool fails to see the snares he sets for himself. Or herself." He snarled, turned on his heel and left.

"He is right in one thing, Bettisia," sighed Master Rolandino. "You should take care, and refrain from provoking the great families."

"Bah!" she replied. "He is both powerful and dangerous, I grant you. But he does not control *all* the great families: the Geremei are with us, for example, though the head of that family was not here today."

"Nonetheless, I beseech you. Be careful," urged her friend.

"I shall. You know I am never reckless, old friend." She smiled and turned to me. "Come, Lorenzo. I did not need your assistance after all, but at least you were able to enjoy that... *performance*. Now let us go home. I am weary."

Chapter 22

It was late afternoon, and most members of the college had dispersed. My master and I made our way through the busy streets as the shadows lengthened. We did not talk. She was clearly tired, while I was perturbed, at a loss to know whether she had put herself in further danger by ignoring Lambertazzi's threats, or whether they were as empty as she appeared to believe.

It was as well that we were not conversing: otherwise I might not have heard the running footsteps behind me. I had been taken by surprise from the rear once before, on my first day in Bologna's crowded streets: since then, I had received the benefit of intense and exhaustive training from my two teachers, and would not be caught out a second time.

Instinctively I barged into my master, shoving her against the wall, and turned to my right so that I protected her with my body. I had just time to see a man running at me as a knife in his right hand stabbed at my belly. Thanks to Sordello's training, I did not have to pause to consider my reaction. With my left hand I pushed his knife-hand away from my body. Turning to my right, I drew my own knife as I stepped into him and stabbed upward under his ribs. My knife must have pierced his heart, for he went instantly limp and fell away from me, his weight tearing my knife, still stuck in his body, from my grip.

Before I could relax, a forearm was clamped against my throat. My left arm was pinioned, my right unable to loosen the pressure that was preventing me from breathing. Only as I realised that I was dealing with a second attacker did I consciously remember Sordello's stricture: "Be like a wild animal. Kill or be killed." Unable to break that grip on my windpipe, I hurled myself backwards. My assailant was not expecting that move and was flung back against the wall (mercifully my master must have discerned my ploy and moved out of the way). There was a grunt, and the grip on my throat loosened momentarily.

I wriggled free and turned to face my attacker. He was older and bigger than I, and I knew that only speed would save me, since I would certainly lose any trial of strength. I had no weapon now so, calling to mind Michele's lessons in the uglier forms of street-fighting, I feinted with my fist and kicked him in the groin.

Surprised, he doubled over in pain. As his head went down I seized it in both hands, pushed it up and away from me and thumped it hard against the wall. His hands came up, battering my chest and face but I would not let go.

With all the strength I could muster I kept smashing his head against the wall, time after time until the bricks were red with his blood. Eventually he managed to land one stinging blow on the side of my head and I staggered back, dazed. He seized his opportunity and ran away down the street, scattering bystanders as he pushed them to one side, swiftly disappearing down a side-alley. I was too breathless, dizzy and bewildered to follow him.

A crowd had gathered, forming a circle and staring at me. I was covered in blood: some of it was mine, and some my second assailant's, but most came from the man I had killed. To my left stood my master, pale and breathing heavily, but composed. While I stood and puffed, she took charge. "You!" she cried, pointing to one of the bystanders. "Do you know who I am?"

"I do, Magister," he replied. "Everyone knows you."

"Good. Then run to the Palazzo del Capitano del Popolo. Demand to see the Capitano in person, tell him what has happened and ask him to send one of his sergeants. Tell him I will attest that my servant killed this man and wounded another while preserving my life. And that I will see him tomorrow … *personally*. Do you understand? Now go."

As ever her natural authority brooked no disagreement. The man ran off and the other bystanders gradually moved on, leaving a respectful, or perhaps fearful, space around the body that was still leaking its life-blood onto the ground.

"You had best retrieve your knife, Lorenzo. It served you well."

"Magister, I..." I simply could not find the words.

"You did well, Lorenzo. Very well. Sordello will be proud of you. And I am... *grateful.*"

When we eventually arrived back at the house there was uproar. Michele, Mamolo and Sordello were all beside themselves with a mixture of rage and guilt. They scolded my master and me for putting ourselves at risk, for being out in that dangerous street and, above all, for being nearly killed. Then they heaped blame on themselves for not being there to help and finally started blaming us again.

For a moment I was offended. Had I not put into practice all that training they had given me, and saved her life? Soon I did not care, as I started to shake and feel dizzy. So busy were the other men with their recrimination that they did not notice: but the Magister did. With that uncanny knack of hers, she cut through the hubbub and ordered sharply, "Lorenzo. We should go upstairs and have a cup of wine. Mamolo, bring us some food. It has been something of... *a day*."

As always, when The Magister took command, the whole household responded. She led the way up the rickety stairs to what I always referred to as her chamber, though it was the only room on the first floor. As I followed her I stumbled, feeling suddenly weak. I felt Sordello's hand under my left arm, gripping me tight and supporting me. In my ear I heard his voice, speaking quietly so that only I could hear: "You did well, Lorenzo. Very well. We're all upset because we weren't there: but I thank God that you were."

In her room the large table was covered as usual with manuscripts. When these were thrown unceremoniously into a corner of the room, my master uncharacteristically failed to protest. I looked at her in wonder: even she, never known to be flustered, had been shaken by the experience. Then, as she had ordered, Mamolo and Michele loaded the table with food. Fortunately the former could produce a meal – hams, cheeses, fresh bread and olives – at a moment's notice. To my surprise my master tucked in more hungrily than I had ever seen her. She caught my gaze and smiled: "We have had a shock, Lorenzo. Eat and drink heartily, and the effect will pass."

As always, she was right. I helped myself from an enormous platter full of food and then, uniquely, the Magister ordered not only Sordello but also Mamolo and Michele to sit and eat. "Come," she said, "Let us eat together and celebrate our deliverance. *My* deliverance, I should say. Thanks to this brave young man. Lorenzo, I salute you." She raised her cup to me and the others followed suit. I was abashed, nonplussed. It was, I think, the proudest moment of my life until then, to receive such praise from the people I regarded as my family and, above all, from the woman who was to me mother, father, master and teacher.

Even she could not resist some gentle mockery, however. Looking at me quizzically she commented, "Heavens! Is Lorenzo lost for words? Come, my friends," she added with a twinkle, "Let us make the most of this... *unaccustomed* silence."

To my astonishment Michele, who rarely entered the master's chamber and never, in my experience, spoke when he did, addressed me directly: "They thay you did well, boy."

"It was pretty knife-work, certainly," interrupted Sordello. I was amazed at the flow of compliments.

"Bah! Kniveth: nathty thingth," he lisped. "I wath talking about the other chap: that wath good bare-handed fighting. Though I'm thorry you didn't kill the bathtard."

I shrugged. "I'm sorry, Michele. I mean, I'm sorry I let him get away: he slipped out of my hands."

"You did what you needed to – and that'th to thave thith one." He nodded at the Magister.

"But I'm frustrated that I let him escape," I continued. "We could have found out a lot from him."

"You would have learnt little or nothing," interposed my master. "They will have been hired killers, not a regular part of anyone's household. And we would not have been able to complete the chain linking him to the person who gave the orders."

"Lambertazzi!" I exclaimed. Of course it was he.

"Or Bardi, at his behest," suggested Sordello. "It makes no odds. We know who it was, but even capturing an accomplice would not have proved it to us. We know those two are planning every kind of skulduggery, yet we can prove nothing. Any word from your friends in Modena?"

I shook my head. "Not a peep, yet: though they won't let me down. If there's anything to be found, they will find it."

"That may be, but we cannot sit on our hands doing nothing while our enemies regroup. We must uncover something."

A hush descended heavily in the room. A feeling of dread, and of inevitability, stole over me as an unwelcome thought grew in my mind. Finally the understanding dawned on me that I could no longer remain on the fringe of these intrigues. I knew that I must commit myself fully and put myself at greater risk than merely acting as bodyguard to one of the main protagonists, even though that lowly role had already proved more hazardous than I had imagined.

I felt the silence press in upon me and, eventually, it was I who broke the silence, my voice sounding odd - distant, almost as if from a stranger - because I volunteered the suggestion against my better judgement. "We must get inside the Lambertazzi tower," I said, reluctantly. "They know both of you. So it must be me. I will do it," I looked at Sordello. "And you must get me in, somehow."

My master looked up in alarm. "Lorenzo, you nearly died once in that tower. Will you seek torture and death there again?"

I laughed humourlessly. "No, Magister. I don't seek any such fate. But I am a nobody. When Bardi threatened Sordello he didn't even glance at me. Neither he nor Lambertazzi could possibly recognise me as the street urchin they took for a spy nearly three years ago. The magnati and their circle take no notice of mere entertainers, so there's little chance of anyone connecting me with you."

"But a possibility, nonetheless. I will not permit it."

"He may indeed fall into a trap." Sordello's tone was more earnest, more considered than I had ever heard it. "But we have had no success in any other direction, and no word from Lorenzo's friends in Modena. So perhaps we have to take that chance. But, Lorenzo," he looked me in the eye: "You know what those devils are capable of. You have suffered once at their hands. Do not go into this lightly: you must weigh the cost to you if it goes amiss. No one will think the worse of you if you consider the risk unacceptable."

171

I confess that a sense of dread overcame me. He had offered me a way out. I could heed my master's words, and Sordello's warning, and abandon my plan as sheer foolishness. Again a hush fell on our company, a silence that was unsupportable. Again my voice sounded not like mine at all, as if it came from elsewhere, somewhere outside me. "No," I said, the words booming in my head. "I must do this. I don't fully know why. But I must. And I will."

So it was decided, though not without a great deal of muttering from all the menbers of the household. In the end, it was easily arranged, too. Naturally no group of musicians gaining access to the Lambertazzi family towers might be associated with Sordello: Bardi's threat had made that clear. But all the families regularly hired in musicians for their feasts and banquets (which were frequent), unless the household kept its own musicians, a rare thing indeed. Thus all Sordello had to do was to use his contacts to find a relatively obscure troupe of musicians whom I could join the next time the Lambertazzi required one.

All fell into place swiftly. Within a day Andrea, whom Sordello had deputed to put the plan into operation so that he was not seen to be involved in any way, came back with the news that, the very next week, the family would be celebrating the name-day of Massimo Lambertazzi's wife, the matriarch of the dynasty. One of his old musical friends had been booked, and there was no difficulty, once some coins had changed hands, in substituting me for another singer.

We rehearsed together once in advance of the event. I cannot claim that we were good: there again, none of the families at whose feasts we performed listened to a note we sang. I have rarely compromised on musical standards: but I may have bent my principles on this occasion.

Deeming ourselves competent, we arrived at the Lambertazzi tower, ready to go through the usual routine, beginning with that endless climb. To our surprise, we were directed to another of the *consorteria*'s adjacent towers. This cheered me. Since my mission was to find my way to the great chamber at the top of Massimo Lambertazzi's tower and hope (almost beyond hope) that they may have been careless enough either to omit to lock the great chest or to leave some papers lying around, it would be impossible to achieve if the topmost rooms were full of people.

But if the party were in another tower, probably moving between a number of them along those elevated catwalks, my chances of finding myself alone in that room appeared enhanced.

It worked like a dream - almost. Arriving at midday, we knew we were in for a long stint. A midday meal would give way to a somewhat somnolent afternoon and then, when evening fell, the drinking and feasting would begin anew. Even musicians are permitted a break from time to time, so I was confident of being able to snatch an opportunity to conduct my clandestine search.

We started in one of those attractive little gardens on top of a tower, and could look across the Lambertazzi territory. There were four towers in all, all connected by walkways. That in which I had been so close to death a few years before was the highest by a significant margin. From its immediate neighbour, a distance of only some twenty paces, I could see that it was in poor condition, a fact that surprised me. There were cracks in the stonework, particularly where not one but two walkways from other towers had been attached, their ends rooted in doorways that had been crudely hacked into the stonework. In my time performing with Sordello we had rarely arrived for events during daylight hours, so I had received few opportunities to observe close up just how crudely built the walkways themselves were, too: poorly constructed, rough structures added to overextended stonework; ambition, vanity and perhaps expense all combining to exceed the wealth even of the magnati.

Our performance was adequate. All of us were accustomed to providing music in the background while guests arrived and drank in the rooftop garden: moving down to the host family's great chamber while the principal guests ate; crossing the catwalk to reach the next tower in order to entertain the lesser guests, always squeezed into those rooms that, compared to some of the great halls being built by the merchant class at ground-level, were small, poorly lit and claustrophobic. Yet up here was where the power in Bologna still resided, or believed it did.

We continued moving around between courses. At one stage I found myself in the room that was my goal so, while I was singing, I was able to spy out the room. There, to be sure, was the great coffer, a heavy oak construction bound with iron, and locked with three padlocks. There was no sign of any discarded paperwork: yet I did not give up hope. I could see that neither Massimo Lambertazzi nor his advisor Bardi was joining in wholeheartedly with the celebrations. Whenever we found ourselves entertaining a group containing those two, they were to be observed in quiet conversation. Perhaps if I could get close, even if I could find no evidence, I might overhear what they were saying.

Suddenly it seemed my chance had arrived. Darkness was falling: we were back in the tower where we had begun: Lambertazzi and Bardi were standing in one corner of the room, deep in discussion. Lambertazzi gestured, a flick of the head: he seemed to be suggesting that they went back to their own tower, which was precisely what they did. My fellow troubadours continued, but they were singing a simple song which did not require the addition of my descant. If I could make my way across and at least overhear what the two were plotting, my mission might be accomplished.

From the far end of the bridge I watched them disappear into the tower, straight into that chamber. Gingerly I crept across, fearful that the shaky timbers would squeak or groan: but I am light and, whereas it had reared and bucked under Lambertazzi's enormous weight, it took no account of me. As I reached the far side I could hear their voices, speaking low and urgently: "We must conclude it this evening," I heard Lambertazzi say.

"All in good time," came the reply in Bardi's silky, smooth voice. "There is one thing yet to achieve."

I could not resist it. I crept closer, my head in the doorway but still, I reckoned, invisible to the interlocutors. Suddenly a large figure confronted me in the doorway. It was one of Lambertazzi's men: in a flash I recognised him from my previous visit to the tower. He grinned at me, and a fist lashed out, striking me in the face. Pain exploded in my nose, my head struck the wall behind me. Blackness engulfed me.

Chapter 23

Darkness. Pain. Blood in my mouth. Something was preventing me from breathing, something wrong with my head. Then light, a light so bright it hurt my eyes. Voices. A confusion of memories. A return to a nightmare. Panic.

A bucketful of water struck me in the face, leaving me wet, spluttering, and very much awake. I felt strangely stiff. A voice, a fat, deep, rumbling voice that I remembered all too well, spoke in front of my face, though I could barely see it for the dazzle of the burning torch held between it and me.

"Our guest is awake, then."

Comprehension and memory returned. I knew whose the face was. And I was afraid, very much afraid, that I knew where I was. I tried to move, but found my arms and legs stretched out to either side. I should have fallen over: no one can stand like that. But I was not truly standing: I was spreadeagled against a wall, the stones pressing into my back and buttocks. I tried to move, but was prevented by ropes biting tightly into my wrists and ankles. I was helpless and realised that I was naked - and in great danger.

Another voice that I instantly recognised cut in: "If he is back with us, then perhaps he will tell us why he is here."

The light moved away from my face. As my eyes adjusted, I recognised where I was: I was indeed in the dungeon where I had been tortured two or three years before, and which had occupied my nightmares ever since. In front of me were the two faces that populated my feverish nocturnal imaginings – and still do, to this day.

"So, as the dog returns to its vomit, the spy returns to my house." The anger in Lambertazzi's voice was unmissable. "Do you take me for a fool? Does that witch who owns you think she can send spies into my house whenever she likes? Does she?" Beside himself with rage, he pushed his face close to mine while drove his fist into my stomach with immense force. Unable to double up as my body begged to do, I could only retch and hang in my bonds.

The oily voice of his advisor interposed, soothing and reassuring. "Calm yourself, Signore. If the ordinarily wise Dottore is so deluded as to send her own servant in to spy on us, she must be at her wits' end – or else her judgment has entirely deserted her. Which is it, I wonder? May I question this boy?"

"Of course, Bartolomeo. But do not be gentle."

In one hand he held his torch, guttering and smoking. He tangled the other in my hair, pushing my head back tight against the wall. "So, Lorenzo, you have returned to us. Was that always your name, or did you have another one on a previous visit? No matter. We know who you are, whatever you may call yourself: the Magister's famed choirboy. Yes, I keep myself informed. Besides, you have quite a reputation. Did you really think I would fail to recognise you? You were at Sordello's side when I warned him: and I knew you were listening. Do you regard us *both* as fools? I think you will regret that."

Lambertazzi broke in again. "Make him tell us what he knows. Let us teach him the meaning of pain."

"Oh, I think we can learn all we need from him before we have our entertainment at his expense. So, young man, the last time you were in here you half-convinced us that your presence was all a misunderstanding. But this occasion, this is more than a coincidence: it is a conspiracy. You will tell me of all your machinations: yours; those of your friend Sordello; and, of course, of your master."

Summoning all the courage I could muster, which was little, I spat the blood out of my mouth and swore at them, muttering all the vilest, filthiest words I could think of, adding, "You will learn nothing from me."

Lambertazzi pushed Bardi aside. Again his massive fist pounded my stomach, and once more I retched, agonised, stretched tight instead of being able to curl my body around the pain.

"On the contrary," came Bardi's even intonation. "You have already told us much. Your very presence here is an act of folly which betrays the desperation of your associates. What were you trying to discover? What our plans were, what plots we might be hatching? Am I right? You need not answer: you are entirely transparent. And you have learned nothing, a fact you may report to the Gatekeeper, if you can still speak when we have finished with you. Though that, I'm afraid, is much in doubt."

"The Gatekeeper?" A tinge of anxiety crept into Lambertazzi's tone. "Is he reporting to the Gatekeeper, not that lawyer bitch?"

"I am unsure, Signore, as yet. You heard the question, boy. Is your master working with the Gatekeeper?"

I tried to shake my head, but that hurt too much. My nose and face throbbed, and I still could not see clearly. Bardi continued. "So you will tell us his identity, and in return we might give you a swift death rather than a slow and painful one. Does that strike you as a bargain?"

But for the severity of my predicament, I might have laughed. It was the most absurd of inquisitions. My miserable attempt at burglary had been a fishing expedition at best: I had discovered nothing. Yet I did not want to let them know that we had nothing beyond a mere suspicion that they were planning to act against the city. As for the Gatekeeper, I had no more idea of his identity than on the day I had first found myself at the mercy of these two. So I shook my head, more slowly this time, reckoning that silence might keep me alive longer than revealing my ignorance.

"Cat got your tongue?" enquired Bardi. He turned to Lambertazzi. "Signore, I suspect this boy knows nothing. We can put him to the torture." Involuntarily my body became rigid at this suggestion. "But Dottor Gozzadini and her circle are unlikely to have trusted so lowly a functionary with such valuable information as the identity of our chief antagonist. Nor with details of their plans - if they have any of substance, which I doubt. Besides, under torture I fear he would merely babble nonsense in order to end his pain."

"Then let us entertain ourselves at his expense. If he has nothing to say," suggested Lambertazzi nastily, "He will not need his tongue. Shall we cut it out, just as a first step? Let me call my boys in. They are adept at this work." As he spoke he held his torch close and ran his right hand over my torso in a proprietorial way that made my flesh creep. "In any case, I should like to observe how this handsome body bears the pain: I think it will stand up well." His intrusive hand fondled my left buttock, pressed against the wall. "Yes, he will suffer long, and I shall enjoy hearing him scream and beg for release."

"Hm." Bardi appeared to think for a moment. "Signore, if I may suggest. As I said, I believe this boy has nothing useful to tell us. But he can tell his master, and those for whom she acts, a great deal. No," Lambertazzi reacted anxiously, "He can tell them nothing about our activities. He knows nothing: his silence is a feeble and unconvincing attempt to conceal his ignorance." I began to despair. He had seen straight through me, and through my witless efforts at guile: he had divined that we knew next to nothing of their scheming, and had even guessed that I had not a clue as to the identity of the Gatekeeper. "But he can bear a message from us. If we were, say, to return him to his friends…"

Again there was a reaction from his master, which Bardi overrode in his urbane manner. "Returned to his friends, as I say, but – how shall I put it? - *altered*. Would that not send a powerful message that your house, your family is not to be trifled with?" This appeared to arouse Lambertazzi's interest, and something more. He grunted his assent. "Very well," continued the silky voice. "Let us blind him and castrate him as an example to other spies: then return him to his master."

I strained against my bonds, but could do little more than wriggle my toes. My panic was clear for them both to see, and they took pleasure in it. The torch came close to my face again, as Lambertazzi chuckled: "Your face seems changed. I think one of my men broke your nose when they struck you. But we shall send you home in a very different condition."

I hissed my hatred. "I will tell you nothing. I owe the Magister my life, and I will not betray her confidence. No matter what you do to me."

Now it was Bardi's turn to laugh. "You have nothing of note to tell me. But you will bear a message from Signor Lambertazzi. We shall leave you your tongue, so that you may endlessly express your sorrow and loss. You may even sing them to that bitch, your *Magister*." His normally urbane tone had become venomous. "But you will not see light again."

"Be grateful I leave you your life: though you may wish that I had not. Spy! Filth!" Lambertazzi's voice rose from his customary rumble into a near-scream. "And you will tell her why your lost eyes will not permit you to shed tears for them. And why," he gripped my testicles, wrenching them painfully, "Why you will never know the love of woman, the touch of female flesh, because you have lost these. And you may ask her whether your loyalty to her was worth that loss." I gasped in pain as he squeezed and twisted my balls again. Then, abruptly, he released me.

"Enough for now, Signore," resumed Bardi. "We must return to the festivities. I suggest we finish our dinner and enjoy the music, though without this one to add to it. And, when we have bade our guests farewell, we shall attend to our business with this... spy. Who knows, he may even sing to us!" He wrenched my hair and put his face close to mine. "But it will have to be a fine song indeed, if it is to save your eyes and your balls. Consider well, boy. And ponder what foolishness led you to sacrifice your sight and your manhood in blind allegiance to an overweening notary and a ragtag of tradesmen."

Each carrying his torch, they left my dungeon, plunging me into total darkness, matched by the depths of my despair. I heard their footsteps clatter up the stairs away from me. And I hung in my bondage while my body shook uncontrollably in a paroxysm of terror.

How long I was left there, stretched tight against the wall and unable to move more than my head, I have no idea. I was dazed, and perhaps I drifted in and out of consciousness. A dull ache developed in my shoulders and hips, unused to bearing my weight in that position. Blood was still dribbling into my mouth from somewhere, and I could not breathe through my nose: there I remained suspended, snuffling and spitting. I was in total darkness: the dungeon had not a single window and no glimmer of light penetrated even from where I knew there must be a door and stairs.

It felt like hours later when I heard footsteps. Not the heavy tread of Lambertazzi and Bardi, nor of their henchmen, they were the light footfalls of a child or a girl – and, moreover, one taking considerable care to tread softly. I heard the door open, again with every impression of someone trying to make as little noise as possible. Then came the light of a candle. It came towards me and, as my eyes adjusted, I could see that it was indeed not borne by any man. The bearer of the light was a strikingly beautiful young woman: it was Livia Lambertazzi.

"Livia. My lady..." I stammered. What was there to say?

Her face came close to mine, the candle held in her left hand. "So, pretty Lorenzo. You are here again." It was a statement, not a question. It was as if she were not surprised.

"My lady, how do you know my name?"

"I never forget names. You were here before, years ago. My uncle was determined to kill you but I said you were too pretty to die. And I have seen you in the Duomo, have I not? Looking for me, I expect?" She giggled. Her manner was strange: fey, or perhaps merely drunken? I could not tell which.

"I wouldn't let them kill you that time, Lorenzo. You were too pretty. Had you stayed we might have had fun. But that sour-faced old lawyer took you away. I'm glad she doesn't come here anymore."

"They nearly killed me anyway, my lady. But I thank you for intervening. And, yes, I have been watching out for you in the Cathedral. I think you are very beautiful."

Chapter 24

I felt a strange sensation, then realised that she was running the fingers of her right hand over my body as she spoke. "They've made a mess of your face, Lorenzo. I can't see it properly: you're all bloody. And your nose is a funny shape."

I laughed at that, though it hurt. "I know. I can't breathe through it."

"Can you kiss, though? Let us try." And her lips were pressed to mine, her tongue pushing insistently and searching my mouth. I could barely move my head, and nothing else. But I could not breathe while her mouth was clamped to mine. Eventually, after what seemed an eternity of desire which I reciprocated, while nonetheless wrestling with a fear of suffocation, she moved her head away and I sucked in deep, whooping breaths.

"I like kissing you, Lorenzo. Though you taste of blood. I think perhaps I like that, too." Her conversation was like that of a wayward child: but her lips and her hand, which still explored my nakedness, were not those of a child, rather of a knowing woman familiar with a man's body.

"Why *are* you here, Lorenzo? Why have you come back? You know they'll hurt you again. They'll kill you, and I shan't be able to stop them this time. Were you spying again?"

"This time I was, though not the last time. But," I could not maintain the façade of bravery anymore, and my voice cracked as I continued. "They don't want information from me: they know I have none to give. They say they'll blind and castrate me, and send me back to my master as a lesson."

"Poor Lorenzo!" Her tone was not one of genuine anxiety for me, but of the kind that one might adopt to an injured lapdog or a poorly child. "Will they do that to you? Your eyes are lovely." The roving hand moved to my face, carefully avoiding my injured nose yet touching me around my eyes as she stared into them. "And castrate you? Geld you? Like they do to animals?" I nodded heavily, hanging my head in, what? Dread? Shame? I could not tell.

Her hand explored my body again, stroking my chest, even teasing my nipples. "You have a fine body, Lorenzo. You seem fit and strong."

"I suppose I am. Was."

"And will they really..." Her hand crept lower and lower. "Will they really cut these off? These lovely things?" Her hand cupped my balls. "Oh...!"

Her surprise was feigned. She knew what she was doing. How would any young man not respond to those presumptuous fingers, teasing and exploring? I may have been pinioned to the wall, helpless and in mortal fear of maiming or worse: but a beautiful girl was handling the parts that a man prizes dearly, and my reaction was involuntary. She breathed heavily and ran her forefinger the length of my erection. I moaned. Her right hand holding me, her left still clasping the candle, she pressed herself to me and whispered in my ear: "Lorenzo, I want you, you pretty, lovely boy."

She stepped back and, spotting a sconce on the wall, placed the candle in it. Then, standing directly before me, she put her hands to her throat and loosened the laces that held her finely embroidered collar around her slim neck. Impatiently she pulled out the laces down the length of her bodice, pulled it apart and let her dress fall to the floor. She stepped out of it, nude, to my fevered eyes shining like an angel in the flickering candlelight. She was beautiful beyond compare, and I wanted her.

I had never seen a naked woman before. Oh, of course, like all boys I had enjoyed looking at the female forms painted or carved in churches and in the fine houses of the rich. I had chuckled at those many representations of Adam and Eve expelled from the Garden of Eden, understanding for the first time the nature of their nakedness: Eve using one hand coyly to shield her bosom while the other concealed the intimate parts of which she had just become aware.

With my friends I had tried to see everything I could of the serving girls we would find in the taverna, the hint of a breast, the flash of a thigh as they climbed the stairs. But here was the girl of whom I had dreamed for years, baring herself before me, more like a harlot than a lady of gentle birth. Women of her class might never fully expose themselves in the act of love, not even to a husband: yet Livia knew what she was doing. Lasciviously, wantonly, she put her hands behind her neck and displayed herself, aping the most shameless of whores displaying her charms. "Am I fair, Lorenzo? Do you desire me?"

As she stood before me in the light of that single candle I greedily drank in the sight of her body. From her high cheekbones downward she was slim, nearly but not quite to a fault, and her skin was pure white. Below her long neck two small, perfectly round breasts rose and fell barely perceptibly with the breathing. Her nipples, like her lips, were pale pink, as if understated. Below her almost impossibly narrow waist her hips broadened in a slight but infinitely seductive curve.

My eyes were drawn to her pudenda, dark hair and shadow combining to conceal a region of mystery to an untried boy like me, and the source of near-insupportable lust. She revelled in my hungry gaze. "Do you not find me pleasing, Lorenzo?" she teased, and turned slowly round so that I could see her straight, jet-black hair fall down her back to the swell of her buttocks, soft, glorious and, bound as I was, to me frustratingly untouchable.

She knew precisely how desirable she was. She had a power over men, and would not hesitate to use it cruelly, without mercy. She had me entirely in her thrall, almost maddened with lust, yet helpless. "Don't you want me?"

I could barely speak. "My lady," I croaked. "I have never seen anything or anyone so beautiful. Yes, I want you, desperately – but I cannot move." It seemed time to point out my predicament to her.

She pressed her bare body up against me, her lips nibbling my neck, my ears, her hands all over me and then both caressing my buttocks. She began to pant. "I want you, Lorenzo," she murmured. "I want you to possess me."

It is possible to make love in a vertical position and, though I have never been an adventurous lover, I can recall doing so. But to achieve the act, both participants must have their hands free. Livia positioned herself, and tried to manoeuvre herself onto my erection, which by now made me feel as if I must burst. She was gasping – with desire, I presumed, though being inexperienced I could not be sure.

Try as she might, however, she could not manoeuvre herself onto me without my help. The situation would have been ridiculous, laughable, but for the intensity of her desire and my virgin urgency. Moreover, I was still bound to the wall. Even in the depths of passion approaching climax, aware of the danger I was in and of the fact that this might be the first and last time my manhood would be put to use: perhaps that too merely served to add to the piquancy of the overpowering need I was suffering – yet enjoying.

Angrily she pushed herself away from me. "It's no use, Lorenzo," she snapped petulantly. "No use at all."

"Untie me, my lady. Livia. Untie me!" Immediately she reached up to my right wrist, and tried to wrestle with the rope that bound me to a metal staple in the wall.

Breathless she complained, "I cannot do it. I'm not strong enough. The knots are too tight."

"Then cut it," I pleaded. "Find a knife. There must be something. Look for it! Just look!" Her urgency was communicating itself to me now. Then I had an inspiration. "My clothes, my lady. Livia, find my clothes! My knife should be with them."

With an exasperated sigh she grabbed the candle from its bracket and searched the dark room. Sure enough, there were my clothes, boots, jerkin, breeches, thrown aside into a corner. And, thank God, my knife, still attached to my belt.

Livia seized the knife, and returned to face me. The candle, once more on its bracket, threw a feeble, flickering light which illuminated her bust and reflected from the blade which, on Sordello's instructions, I kept wickedly sharp. With that distracted expression to which I was becoming accustomed, she looked at me quizzically. She ran the blade of the knife across my chest, not enough even to scratch, but sufficient to alarm me.

She looked down, my physical desire for her still evident, despite the bizarre situation. She touched the tip of the blade to my balls: "Will they really cut these off? Hm." Even that comment failed to quench my desire. Without warning she leapt to my left wrist and sawed at the rope that held it. Then to the right.

With my ankles still spread far apart and secured to the walls, I could not stand, and fell forward, crying out with pain as the ropes refused to allow my ankles to move. She quickly cut those ropes too, so that I was on all fours, groaning as the blood returned to feet and hands. But there was no time for recovery.

She knelt in front of me and pulled my face hungrily to hers, adding fresh pain to my broken nose as she pressed against it, her lips seeking mine once more, forcing them apart with her tongue. Swiftly she pushed away again, lay back on the hard floor and pulled me urgently to her. Her experienced hands took hold and pulled me inside her, hot and wet with her need.

As all young men know, that first coupling was alarming. As she writhed beneath me, feral and noisy with arousal, I feared my member might be torn from me. Then I was pushing in turn, responding to that same animal urge with no thought but of my own fulfilment. All too quickly, suddenly, it was over. I was spent, breathless, and paused to look at the body beneath me. I ran my hands over that alabaster skin, felt the heavy softness of her breasts and marvelled at the fact that I had finally known this flesh, this goddess, the object of my desire for so long. I leaned forward, rested my head on her shoulder and sighed.

My normal senses began to return to me. I became aware that both her hands were gripping my buttocks, so hard that the nails were digging deep into my flesh. I did not know what to say to her. Had I satisfied her, or had my youth, inexperience and the swiftness of my climax proved disappointing? It was clear I was by no means her first lover.

I pulled out of her: drops of my seed and her arousal glistened on the floor as the candlelight caught them. She stood up abruptly, wordlessly, reached down and started to replace her gown. I knelt in amazement, still looking at her, worshipping her. "I must go," she said again. There were no words of endearment, no promises, no regrets.

"What about me?" I asked.

"You? You had better escape while you can. Do you want them to geld you?"

"No. But, I mean, what happens to us now? Shall I see you again?"

"To escape should be enough for you, Lorenzo. No. I cannot see you again. How could I? If my uncle sets eyes on you he will have you killed. You may not stay in Bologna."

I was feeling brave and reckless. "He will not drive me from this city, nor from you," I replied.

"Then you're a fool," she said. "A bigger fool even than I took you for. I must go. They must not know it was I who released you."

"My lady: if you ever need me, send word. I will come for you."

"You truly are a foolish boy, pretty Lorenzo. I shall not need you. I look after myself."

"But if you do. Please heed me. Send word for me at the Magister's house."

"Silly boy! I shall not." Once more she took my face in her hands and kissed me. "Goodbye, Lorenzo." She retrieved the candle and was gone.

I was alone once more. Still naked. Still in pitch darkness. But I was free of my bonds. My hands and feet throbbed as the blood returned to them fully, and other parts of me felt strange. There was something wrong with my nose: still I could taste blood in my mouth, and could not breathe properly. My stomach, too, was sore from the punches it had received. As for my testicles, first tormented by Lambertazzi and afterwards teased by Livia as a prelude to our lovemaking, they produced a dull ache that was not altogether unpleasant.

After that episode with Livia, already receding into the semblance of an erotic dream, the reality of my situation returned to me forcefully. I was still in great peril. I knew I must escape before Lambertazzi, Bardi or their henchmen returned to carry out their threat to rob me of both my sight and the ability to repeat what I had just experienced with Livia. Gingerly I felt my way back to the wall against which I had been bound: sure enough, above my head I could feel the metal ring to which one of my hands had been tied.

So my clothes must be to my right, I reasoned. I felt my way to that corner of the room, falling over objects on the way: a stool here; something metal there, which felt like a brazier, mercifully without the glowing coals that might yet be used in operating on me, but sufficiently jagged to tear my shins. Further to my right, at last, I felt the soft material of my clothes, which had been simply thrown in a heap as I could only presume they had been taken off my unconscious body.

To my joy I even found my shirt, and then my boots. I dressed swiftly and, once stoutly shod, felt less vulnerable. Next I needed to find my knife. That was less easy, for I could not recall where Livia had dropped it after cutting my bonds. There was nothing for it but to search the dark dungeon methodically.

Again feeling the wall from which I started, now I crawled along the floor, my left hand just touching it, my right stretched as far as it would go, while I edged my way along the floor. Once more I collided with unseen objects, some of which fell over with such a crash that I froze in anticipation of the attention the noise might attract. Eventually my fumbling fingers located my knife, which I tucked thankfully into my belt as I stood up.

Chapter 25

What now? Escape, of course. It was clear the door was not locked: what need was there, when the prisoner was pinned immobile to the wall? However, to find the door would be another task. I remembered that it was in the corner of the room, on the far side and to the right. I hugged the walls, following the wall of my bondage to the end and then turning left. Sure enough I reached what resembled a large box in the corner and, fumbling around it, eventually located the door and a latch.

With trepidation I opened it and looked out. It was dark on the other side, too: but not the total blackness of my dungeon. My eyes, by now fully accustomed to the absence of light, could make out the tower's seemingly endless stairwell. Steps climbed up away from me: my memory from my first unfortunate visit reminded me that there were three or four floors above me, though I could not see that far. As for the downward stairs, I could discern little pools of light in the far distance, presumably where moonlight penetrated the occasional tiny window.

Down it must be: so, tiptoeing as lightly as I could, I began the long descent. It took all of my concentration, with the treads so uneven, to avoid losing my footing in the dark and clattering down a flight or two: some were more like ladders, where I would turn and descend backwards for fear of falling. Though I had to concentrate on every step, I knew I must plan my escape. I guessed my face was covered in blood, so my sudden appearance in the courtyard would immediately arouse suspicion.

A stratagem was suggested to me by the appearance of three or four retainers. Toiling up the stairs under barrels and skins, all presumably full of wine, they made such a clattering and banging that I had plenty of warning of their coming and was able to slip into one of the many storerooms on the lower levels. They were wheezing and cursing as they puffed aloft with their load, directing curses at their employers' demands for more drink at this late hour. "You'd think they'd have had enough by now," complained one.

"Or had enough brought up earlier so they didn't run out."

"Still," said a third, "I'll be helping myself to a stiffener when I get to the top."

"You've had enough, friend," responded the first. "You want to have a care if we have to go across to one of the other towers with this load. Them bridges wobble enough as it is. I don't care if you fall off: but I don't want you bringing us down with you."

"Relax," came the response. "I've never dropped a barrel, have I? Even when I've had a few."

"Nah, but one day the boss will spot that you're pissed as a priest on his wine."

"The padrone won't notice: he'll be too busy feeling up the kitchen girls."

"Bardi'll see. He don't miss nothing."

"What do I care what that nosy bastard thinks? One day I'll tell him what I think to him and his spying ways."

"Yes, you will: and you'll be out of a job and out on your ear – you and that whore you keep. Come on, let's get this over with and then we can all have a drink."

Continuing their good-natured grumbling, they plodded on upwards and I hugged myself in my relief. I reckoned I could bluff my way through the courtyard, and had an idea what I would say if challenged.

When I reached the bottom, I pulled the door ajar and squinted through the gap. There was the same sort of courtyard scene as I had seen when I had been dragged unwilling through it those few years ago. There were a couple of fires, cooking pots, women chattering as they cooked, a few children still running about although it was late (how late? I had no idea). And, thank heaven, few men in sight. Across the courtyard I could just make out what I was looking for so, eschewing all secrecy, I barged the door open and ran in an unsteady gait across to the horse-trough, plunging my head into it and surreptitiously wiping the blood from my face, as far as I could. A couple of the women looked up from their work, and called across sharply: mercifully I could see no men taking any interest.

"What are you doing here?"

"Why are you sticking your head in the trough like that?"

"Are you drunk?"

I slowly stood upright, using my elbows to lean heavily on the trough. In my thickest Bolognese accent, with an added alcoholic slur, I replied, "I might have had a drink or two." I consciously mimicked the lads I had seen heading upstairs. "It'sh good shtuff they're sherving up there. And that bugger Bardi shaysh he wantsh even more! Can you believe it?"

"You idiot!" they cried. "The lads have just taken another load up. You must have bumped into them!"

I looked puzzled. "I fell down a few shtepsh. Knocked me head. Musht've mished 'em." I shrugged my shoulders. "I don't even know where I am!" I sniggered. "Thish ishn't my tower. Where am I?"

"You fool, you're in Signor Massimo Lambertazzi's tower. Where are you from?"

I waved vaguely at one of the other towers. "Oh, you know, I'm from..."

"Well, you'd better get back there, before there's trouble."

"I'm not fucking climbing all the way back up there. I'll walk acrossh to mine. Can you let me out?"

"Giovanni will," came the reply. "Oi, Giovanni! Let this drunkard out, will you?"

With a grumpy snort an elderly retainer came out of the shadows, holding a large key which he inserted in a lock. "Go on, piss off back to your own tower, and stop bothering me."

"Thank you," I replied, with an extravagantly drunken bow. "It'sh been a pleasure!"

Then I was out the gate, and haring down the road towards my master's house.

As I approached, I glimpsed the lights of many torches. From closer I could see a crowd of men heavily armed, spears and other weapons glinting in the light afforded by the torches. Alarmed, I quickened my pace still further. When I arrived at the house I saw there were some forty men in the street outside the house, standing around a fire they had lit in the street for both light and warmth. I started to push through the crowd towards the gate, but was quickly stopped. My arms were seized by two men, while a third confronted me. "Who the fuck do you think you are, pushing through as if you own the place? What's your business here?"

"I serve the Magister, the jurist Dottor Bettisia Gozzadini. And I might ask in turn what the bloody hell you men are doing here!"

"Less of your impudence. We are here sent by the Capitano del Popolo expressly to guard the Magister. So now we'll just check whether you're known here." And my questioner called to one of his men:"Oi! Daniele! Rouse that old rascal Michele and see if he knows this whippersnapper." The man addressed as Daniele rapped on the gate to be answered by Michele's grumbling tone, a voice and lisp that, after my ordeal and near-mutilation, I could not have been more pleased to hear. "Let me have a look, then. Aye, we know him. The Magithter'th been fair worrying about him thinthe he didn't come home. Let the young idiot in, and he can account for himthelf."

With some reluctance I was released, and found myself in that familiar courtyard which, given that it was the middle of the night, should have been quiet and sleepy: but the whole household was awake. The moment I entered my master appeared on her little balcony, Sordello behind her. Any relief she may have felt at my return was quickly masked by a peremptory order. "Lorenzo, where have you been? We have been... *worrying* about you. Come up here at once!"

She cares about me, I thought. Suddenly weary, I slowly climbed the wobbly steps.

Both of them were rattled, firing questions at me, chiding me and arguing with one another all at the same time. I held up my hand in a feeble attempt to quiet them so that I could speak. Eventually they became quiet and I said, "I'm tired beyond belief. Might I sit down and have a cup of wine? Then I shall tell you all that has happened." With unusual attentiveness my master led me to a seat and poured wine for me herself. Then I told my tale – leaving nothing out, as I was firmly instructed several times. Except one thing. I told them, of course, that it was Livia who had released me: but I did not feel they needed to know of our particular intimacy after she had cut the ropes that held me. And they laughed at my account of feigning drunkenness in order to bluff my way out of the Lambertazzi gate.

"I still don't understand why the lady Livia should put herself at risk for you. Her uncle would be beside himself with rage."

I shrugged. "She recognised me from before, as they did. And she thinks I'm pretty!" I grinned.

"She has seen you staring at her across the cathedral frequently enough, at any rate," remarked my master, tartly. I was amazed. Yet again she proved that she knew precisely what was going on, even when I thought I had concealed that part of my life from her. "Nonetheless, Lambertazzi's rage will know no bounds if he discovers it was she – as he surely will."

"She's unusually strong-willed," I opined. "He's indulgent towards her."

"Not for much longer, I fear," replied Sordello. "But in any case, we have been fortunate. You're lucky to have come away in one piece – and not to have lost…, you know." As he gestured graphically, I shuddered.

"Lucky?" interposed my master. "Yes, he is. And we have been very foolish. They knew who Lorenzo was before he even entered their house, and I… *castigate* myself for putting you in such peril, Lorenzo. They have been running rings around us, mocking us at every step. We are no further forward, and they are in no doubt that we are attempting vainly to uncover their stratagems. They have all the dice in the game, and we have none. And now, we had better do something about that nose of yours."

I was suddenly alarmed. "What will you do with it, Magister?"

"Idiot! They broke your nose. Have you not realised that? We shall have to reset it."

"Will you send for your tame physician?" asked Sordello.

"No, I can do this myself. I must warn you, Lorenzo. There will be pain: but thereafter you will possess something like your old nose, rather than the flattened mess we see now."

"Very well," sighed Sordello. He knelt swiftly behind me, and held my arms and shoulders while the Magister gripped my nose and, it seemed to me, tried to tear it off. I screamed at the agony that shot across my face, and squirmed in Sordello's iron grip. But in an instant, almost miraculously, apart from a residual ache the pain was all but gone.

"There, Lorenzo. I'm sorry to have hurt you, but you will look better. We must protect that nose for a while – a leather mask will do, I think, for a week or two. And then you will look almost as handsome as you did before: indeed, the slight bend in your nose might furnish you with an additional rakish charm. Now, it is dawn, and we should sleep a little. There is much to do today."

Exhausted as I was, I slept little. My rudely re-set nose, indeed the whole of my face, still pained me and, whenever I closed my eyes to sleep, the crazy sequence of the day's events crowded in upon me: my capture and helplessness; the prospect of mutilation and emasculation; my first experience of knowing a woman, relishing the act of love while terrified of being discovered and consigned to the grisly fate planned for me; the rush and drama of my escape; all crowded in upon me in a cascade of whirring visions and emotions so vivid that, even now, they return to me three-score years later. No, it was not a restful night.

Did I say night? It was already becoming light when we went to bed, so even those who slept can have managed only two or three hours. All too soon we were up again, and planning the next steps.

Yet what step could we plan? We had learnt nothing new about Lambertazzi, except that he and his crony Bardi had known from the start who I was, that I was servant to the thorn in their legal flesh, and had set out to trap me in order to hurt her. The threat to her was now obvious to all, including the Capitano del Popolo who, unbidden, had sent those men-at-arms to protect her house. That guard remained outside the gate, changed regularly, organised and fed itself, so there were no calls on the household, for once depriving Mamolo of an opportunity to grouse about spongers and his inability to feed everyone adequately.

My master's plan had been to push forward the law to end slavery in an attempt to provoke Lambertazzi into hasty action. There could be little doubt as to who was behind the attempt on her life: yet we had no proof of that – nor of any scheming. Exasperated, I asked why there were no other sources of information. "What about the Gatekeeper?" I asked. "If he is at the centre of all the conspiracies, can we not learn from him the details of what Lambertazzi is planning? Surely he would help those on the side of Bologna?"

My master looked uneasy, even evasive. "Information does not travel in... *that direction*, Lorenzo," she replied after a pause. "We know how and where to pass on what we know, something I have not shared with you in order to protect you. But we cannot contact the Gatekeeper directly, nor gain advice from that quarter."

"He seems a fat lot of use, then, "I commented huffily. "I begin to wonder why everyone makes such a fuss about him."

"He is... what he is, and that is enough." My master clearly wished to put a stop to the direction our conversation was taking. We carried on, but it was clear to all three of us that we were going round in circles.

Chapter 26

At last, however, we struck some good fortune. A commotion at the gate announced the arrival of Paolo, Giacomo and Salvatore, clearly determined to make an entrance, while flanked by suspicious guards who were unwilling to let them through until Michele, still theoretically holding the gate, confirmed that they were known and should be admitted.

As we had pondered the situation we were in truth close to losing hope of finding a solution. But my friends' noisy arrival changed the mood in an instant. Paolo was clearly bursting with news, while his two companions grinned and bobbed respectful bows at my master. They did not know what to make of Sordello: but that was nothing new, for few did. Paolo was determined to make a big entrance. Sweeping a bow at my master, he proclaimed, "Dottore, I have news. In fact, I have such news as you hoped for. I think we have found the link that you seek."

He was all ready to tell us, out loud and in the courtyard, but my master and Sordello were too canny for that. Gesturing him to silence, she beckoned him to join us upstairs in the chamber, from whose doorway we had greeted him. She instructed Mamolo to feed all three of them, which he set about doing with his usual bad grace, leaving the other two downstairs while she sat him at her table.

"So tell me, young man. What is your great discovery?"

"Magister," he looked at me to check that he had used her preferred title this time. I nodded encouragement. "Magister, in these last three weeks we have been to Modena and back four times." He paused and looked at me: "Lorenzo, what happened to your face?"

"Lambertazzi," I replied curtly. "But I escaped. And he will pay."

"By the Holy Virgin and all the Saints!" exclaimed my master, rarely given to summoning beatific aid. "Will you two young men stop preening like peacocks and get to the matter in hand? Now, tell me. Why so long? Why four trips to Modena and back?"

"Simple," he replied. "The first three times we found nothing. We took various goods from Lambertazzi's estates, and other loads on behalf of various families. There was nothing untoward about any of them."

"And the money? Were they taking large sums?"

"Not at all," came the disappointing reply. "They took a few purses of coins for city taxes and for settling the balance on the merchandise. Mainly barrels of *balsamico*: we brought back a lot of that."

"That might be significant," commented Sordello, but my master gestured him to silence.

"The *balsamico* may have some small significance, I grant you. It is… *impossible* to obtain it in the city now."

"I remember now!" I exclaimed. "That's what's been nagging at my memory. At that dinner in Modena, when I was serving at table, the Bishop, Uguzzoni and Bardi were plotting together how to starve Bologna of the *balsamico*, and push the price up at the same time."

"Uguzzoni?" Now Paolo's interest was piqued. "I've got things to tell you about someone of that name."

"Enough, enough!" The Magister sounded weary. "Let us cover the events in the order in which they occurred. You mentioned the *balsamico*. Perhaps Lambertazzi is accumulating a considerable store of it, either to push the price up or merely to deprive his fellow-citizens of the pleasure of using it. But whichever is his aim, it is merely small mischief. More important, young man, you are certain those barrels were all of *balsamico*? Nothing else concealed in them?"

"It certainly was the essence, Magister. You know those small barrels they use? There could be nothing much hidden in them. So shall I tell you what we found in the end?"

"Of course, you fool!" I exclaimed. "Get to the point, man!"

Ignoring me he embarked on his tale with relish. "We began to think there was nothing going on. Maybe they didn't trust us, and only let us go with innocent wagon trains. Even the return journeys weren't all *balsamico*. There were loads and loads, full

196

of stuff just for Lambertazzi and his *consorteria*. The usual thing: you know, hams, mountains of beautiful hams, flour – they say the grain's better over that way. Just domestic stuff.

"But after the fourth trip, it all changed. We knew there was a big consignment going out the next day, but we were told we wouldn't be needed. No explanation: they just said they had their own men and didn't need any extra hands. We blustered a bit, saying how much we needed the work, but they got a bit unfriendly. Well, you know the saying: when the devil drives. So we made sure that three of their regular men weren't fit to travel the next day."

"How did you manage that?" I asked. "Let me guess!"

"Of course! What could be easier? We got them drunk, falling-down pissed." He glanced at the Magister's face, which was inscrutable: "I mean, begging your pardon. And we managed to slip some bad wine into their cups so they were sick as dogs the next day. They weren't fit to travel."

"And you three just happened to be on the spot when the wagon-masters found they were short-handed?"

"Precisely, Lorenzo. Listen to me, and you learn from an expert! Mind you, there was some expense involved: we had to buy them a lot of wine."

Again a sidelong look at my master, who appeared to lose patience once more. "Yes, yes," she responded testily. "We shall settle the score. Get on with it!"

"Sorry. Where was I? Yes, we did get on board the last wagon, and had a good look through it as we travelled. But there was nothing: in fact, we were travelling light. A suspicious man might have felt that the goods we were transporting this time were just put in there to make the wagons look full. There was nothing of any worth, nor anything that couldn't be bought in Modena in any case."

"Go on," urged Sordello quietly.

Paolo warmed to his tale. "Well, on the first four trips we'd delivered different wagons to different places, though most went to one big house in Modena. Apparently it belonged to the richest man there whose name was, you know." We almost screamed our frustration at him. "You just mentioned it, Lorenzo. Ug, Ugu..."

"Uguzzoni, you donkey!"

"Yes," said Paolo decisively. "That was it. Uguzzoni. All the wagons went there except one. And that was another strange thing. We took that one to a place we'd never been before: the Bishop's palace. It was odd. For a start, bishops don't do trading."

"So what was in the wagon? What did you deliver to the Bishop?"

"Nothing special. That was what was most peculiar about it. A couple of sides of beef: but why would you transport that from Bologna? Some cheese: they reckon to make better stuff in Modena. We'd made sure we split up when we realised that this was a different kind of load. I stuck with the wagon that was bound for the Bishop's palace. The other two went to Uguzzoni's.

"Well, we get to the Bishop's courtyard and they goad the oxen through, with all the farting and grumbling as they do. So I follow it in, ready to help unload: those sides of beef are heavy. I go round to the front of the wagon, looking as if I want to help but really because I haven't seen what's stowed at the front: and there's Lambertazzi's foreman and one of the men he keeps closest. They're lifting a strongbox out: it looks heavy, really heavy for its size. They see me looking and turn nasty. Ask me what I'm looking at. So I say nothing: just trying to help.

"Next thing I know, the foreman pulls out a knife, points it at me and says, 'Nothing? Keep it that way. We won't need you from now on. You'll have to make your own way back to Modena. Here's money for it.' And that was it. He gave me about three times what he needed to, paid me off. I didn't see them again. At least, they think I didn't see them again, because I made sure they didn't spot me watching them."

"Are you sure that box contained money – silver?" asked my master urgently.

"I can't be sure," came the reply. "But it was strong, well made: even those two hefty men were having a job to lift it. And I think there were letters, too. All the way out to Modena the foreman seemed to be hanging onto a satchel. Never took it off his neck, and it looked like documents in it."

"What about your two friends?" Sordello interrupted.

"Yes," I chipped in. "What did they find at the Uguzzoni house?"

"Much the same," replied Paolo. "Giacomo got closer than I did: just the one chest, which he tried to lift. He couldn't open it, of course. It was sealed. But he was sure it must be silver – or gold. Then they were paid off, too – and warned off a bit more unpleasantly. They didn't want us outsiders with them at all."

"A plague on Lambertazzi and all his schemes!" exclaimed the master in a rare outburst. "His minions go where he pleases to send them and we can only run to keep up. So perhaps he is paying money to *two* people in Modena. Lorenzo told us long ago that the Bishop and Umberto Uguzzoni were thick as thieves. It was the Bishop's scheme – and Bardi's, if Lorenzo's memory is to be credited - to hoard and control the supply of *balsamico.* Why should they not plot on an altogether more ambitious scale? As for any letters, they have been already delivered, and unless we intercept a reply – of which there is little chance – we shall discover nothing. Bah! We are little further forward." She paused in thought, then looked up at Paolo, that shrewd expression back on her face. "So you did not see what they transported back in those empty wagons?"

"Of course I did," laughed Paolo. "We kept watch on both houses, and soon enough the empty wagon left the Bishop 's palace and went round to the Uguzzoni house. It went inside: the gates closed. We could see nothing. But we could hear a fair bit. It was a heavy load being lifted into each wagon. They made a fair old fuss about it, and there was a lot of clanking. There was certainly metal involved."

"Weapons?" asked Sordello.

"That's what I wondered." Paolo was thoroughly enjoying himself now. "So I had an idea, a stroke of genius if I may say so. Lorenzo, you know that big bell-tower by the cathedral?"

199

"The Ghirlandia? Of course. We choirboys used to go up a lot. We could see into people's houses. Ah, I see..."

"Precisely. I told you you could learn from me, Lorenzo."

"Oh, get on with it!" exclaimed my master.

"Sorry. Yes, I sent Salvatore up it. He couldn't see into the Uguzzoni place: but he did signal to us when the wagons left. And we positioned ourselves so we could have a good look at them. They really were heavy: the oxen were straining to move them away. The men guarding them were nervous. They set off just before dawn, so they could get clear of the city as soon as it got light."

"But how could Salvatore get into the tower at night?"

"He hid there before they closed it for the night! We gave him a loaf of bread and a blanket. I don't think he slept well!" Paolo chuckled with delight at his ingenuity. "Giacomino managed to get onto the roof of a taverna near the East Gate, so he got a good look down into the wagons without the guards seeing him. There wasn't much to see, of course: everything was in bundles and they tried to muffle the noise with rags and sacking. But there was still metal clanking all the way. Some of the bundles were long. We reckon there were pikes, swords: I'm sure they were weapons."

Sordello exploded. "Why didn't you get word to us so that we could intercept them? You could have hired horses and travelled much more quickly than heavy wagons drawn by oxen."

"We tried," Paolo grimaced. "All day we tried. But we couldn't find any for love nor money. The stables we went to offered excuse after excuse. Someone had made sure that no one leaving Modena travelled faster than those wagons. The next day there was no problem. We did what you say, hired three fast horses and came back here like lightning: but there was no sign of the wagons on the road. Maybe they reached Bologna within the day, though that would have been pushing it with ox-carts. More likely they left the road and hid them up somewhere. We saw no sign of them."

We three listeners groaned our disappointment. Yet another dead end, it seemed. Paolo noticed our change of mood, which seemed to dampen his enthusiasm too. Then he brightened. "I heard news of your friend, too. You know, Lorenzo, your friend Tommaso?"

I had forgotten my old friend once again! "News? What about him? Tell me!"

"We were killing time, waiting for Salvatore to signal that the wagons were on the move. So Giacomino and I did as you asked, and went and asked around the cathedral. Don't worry: we were subtle. We saw a few choirboys in the square and asked them if they knew him. None of them did: until we found one who was a bit older. He remembered him, all right. Remembered you, too: Tommaso's friend who did a runner. I knew you had a story to tell! Anyway, Tommaso's been gone from the cathedral for a year or two now."

"A year or two?" I was aghast. "What happened to him?"

"Nothing bad that they knew of. But he got a job. And here's another funny thing. They reckon he's working as a clerk – for the Bishop."

"For the Bishop? Did you go and find him?"

"Of course we didn't, you dolt! I'd just been warned off from there: I couldn't show my face again. So there was nothing I could do. We were trying to plan a way of making contact without drawing attention to ourselves, when Salvatore whistled from the tower. You know the rest."

There was a silence, another of those long, heavy pauses while everyone in the room considered how to frame the unpalatable proposal. Then the Magister spoke, slowly and deliberately. I knew what she would say, and dreaded hearing it. "So, we believe that Lambertazzi is buying weapons. He is paying vast sums of money to Uguzzoni and the Bishop of Modena – more, I suggest, than the value even of those wagonloads of arms. He is hiring himself an army, I am sure of it.

"Yet we have still no proof. Not a shred of it. Even if we could find where he is hiding the weapons, that would not be sufficient.

We have to find something to link him to Modena. We need a letter, a contract, a promise: or a witness, a traitor perhaps."

She looked me in the eye, unflinching, that stare that bored into me when she chose. "We need that proof, Lorenzo. And you know someone who can obtain it for us."

I knew it to be true, and my heart sank. With that crazy confidence of the young, I did not mind putting my own safety at risk. But now I would have to re-enter Tommaso's life and, whereas I should have been delighted at the prospect of being reunited with my oldest and closest friend, I feared I would finish by dragging him into the intrigues that had already bemired my other friends and me and imperilling him. Indeed, had I known how much danger I would place him in, nothing would have persuaded me to make that journey.

Chapter 27

The next morning we were on our way. It had been agreed that only Paolo and I would travel back to Modena. With fine woollen cloaks hanging from our shoulders, spread out across our horses' rumps, we felt like noble knights going into battle. We aimed to appear well-born young travellers, with fictitious connections to a great family in Bologna. My cloak also boasted a hood in order to hide my face at need, for now I sported a mask – or, at least, a triangle of leather that covered my nose and was tied by a leather thong at the back of my head. This had been carefully sculpted by my master's tame physician to hold my nose in the desired shape while the bone healed. I could not decide whether I looked sinister or comical: from time to time I glanced anxiously at my companion to gauge whether he found it amusing.

I had never ridden a horse before, and it took all my performer's instinct to feign mastery of the beast. I did not like to ask Paolo whether he too was bluffing: he seemed to know what he was about, and I tried to imitate him. With saddlebags stuffed with two days' food and enough silver to pay tolls and bribe the occasional official, we departed.

To begin with we headed due west along the Via Æmilia, the great Roman road down which I had travelled a few years before to start my new life in Bologna. But, when we reckoned we were only an hour or two's travel from our destination (on horseback, at any rate, Modena is only a day's ride away), I pulled up.

"Paolo," I said. "I have a suggestion." A thought had been growing in my mind all day, "Modena and its inhabitants are suspicious of Bologna, and may doubt the intentions of two young travellers coming from there. Why don't we head north for a while, then continue west and enter Modena from its northern gate? We're less likely to arouse suspicion."

He considered for a while, then signalled his assent. So we headed off along a drover's way that looked promising, and indeed it took us between farms and smallholdings for a couple of hours until we came upon a larger track which, like the Roman road to the south, travelled east to west. My thinking had developed further as we rode through this rich farmland, though now bare and stripped after harvest and being transformed by degrees to furrowed strips of ploughed earth.

"Paolo," I said again, "If we take this road east, we might yet be in Modena by early evening. But it may be hard to find somewhere to stay. It occurs to me that, if we quicken our pace a little, I might be able to find the road that heads north-west from the city. If I can find that, I should be able to spot Tommaso's house – at least, his family's place. It would ease my conscience, if we saw them. And we might find a little more about him - and take him news of them."

"I thought this was going to be a two-day trip, but you're certainly stretching it out, Lorenzo," he replied. "Yet you may be right. We don't know that Tommaso will have any evidence: nor yet that he will share it with us or be prepared betray his employer to us." That shook me. Notwithstanding my unease at involving him in our intrigues, I had not stopped to think about where Tommaso's loyalties might lie. In my mind I had been relying on the ties of old friendship: but he would doubtless owe a duty to his employer.

"Precisely," I commented, trying to give the impression that his idea had been in my mind all along. "Let's try it."

We were successful, surprisingly so. Fewer than two hours must have passed before we had found a large track which emerged from the city, now just visible in the distance to our left, and headed away at an angle to our right. I was sure I recognised it, and spurred my mount to the northwest. I had only travelled the road to visit Tommaso's family a few times, but I recognised its gentle undulations (necessarily gentle ones, for we were still amid the flatlands that comprise the colossal valley of the river Po): then came that rise that I remembered and, at its crest, I could see their house. I recalled Tommaso's joy when we first went there: when he first took me to meet his family; when he caught his first glimpse of home and ran all the way to hurl himself into his mother's arms. "That's it, that's the place!" I exclaimed. I urged my horse into a canter in my eagerness to revisit the place where I had briefly known such happiness.

We approached the old farmhouse which, with my more recent experience of living among affluent city-dwellers, I recognised for the first time as truly poor and run down. Our horses' hooves made a clatter as we pulled up outside, and I spied movement within it. A harsh aggressive voice called from inside, though no face showed: "What would you fine gentlemen be wanting here? No good, I'll be bound. Be on your way!"

I dismounted, as elegantly as I could (another technique I had yet to master) and approached the door. "It's me. Do you not know me? It's Lorenz... I mean, it's Luca, Tommaso's friend. Do you remember me?"

The door was flung open, and there stood two figures etched in my memory from when I first visited. I would have recognised Tommaso's mother and father anywhere: but I was shocked to see how changed they were. Their faces were pinched with poverty and hard work, their hair was grey and even white in places, and they looked older, weary beyond belief. Nonetheless their good-hearted faces burst into smiles. "Luca? Is it really you? How tall and grand you are! And you've brought Tommaso with you! Oh..." Then they saw Paolo's face and knew that it was not their beloved son.

Their disappointment was palpable. Paolo descended from his horse and bowed low. Trying to hide her feelings, Tommaso's mother asked, "So do you bring word from our son, Luca? How is he?"

"In truth, we have not seen him, though we are on our way to do so. We have come straight from Bologna, where my master is a lawyer, a famous notary," already I could see that I was describing a world completely alien to theirs. "But we had to make a detour, so we came to see you first." Again that look of disappointment. I tried to take the conversation in a more positive direction. "As I say, we are on our way to see him. We hear that he is now an important man, working as a clerk for the Bishop."

"Indeed," added Paolo, sensing the situation. "It was I who told Lorenz... Luca," he gave me a searching glance, "Of this. I was in Modena just last week and heard news of him, although I did not speak to him in person."

"But we shall see him tomorrow," I added. "And can take to him any messages that you would like. Meanwhile, might we stay the night with you? Of course we'll pay for our board."

With something of the old mixture of briskness and warmth that I remembered, Tommaso's mother wouldn't hear of payment, returning to her old insistence that "a friend of Tommaso's is a friend of ours, and always welcome." Then she brightened. "You must meet our girls again, Luca. They have grown almost to young women since you were here last. Rita! Maria! Come and see who's here. It's Luca."

On my previous visits, the two youngest girls had hurled themselves on me. Now they were infants no longer, but slim girls on the brink of womanhood. They emerged shyly from the house, but their embrace was warm, and then they bowed gravely to Paolo who returned the greeting. Yet someone was missing.

A sense of foreboding struck me. "And what of Rosalia? Is she well?" A shadow fell across the faces of all four.

"She is... she has... employment elsewhere. We shall speak of it when you have eaten. Come, see to your horses. Wash yourselves from your journey and then we shall eat and talk. You must have much to tell us, for we have heard nothing of you since Tommaso said you left Modena."

As twilight fell, Tommaso's father went to see to his livestock while we fed and watered the horses. Tommaso's mother busied herself with a cooking-pot, all the time chivvying her daughters as mothers do, and before long we were sitting down to eat, six of us squeezed around a table near a fire in the chimney: at this time of year it was too chilly to sit outside as I had done with Tommaso on our summer visits. We ate a stew fortified with beans: if there was any meat in it I did not find it. We broke coarse brown bread. It was the food of hardship endured, not of harvest celebrated. A shadow hung on the place and the family, and, when we had eaten and politely expressed satisfaction, I could bear it no longer. "Tell me, Signora. What news of Rosalia?"

Tommaso's father coughed and stared at the embers of the fire. The two girls looked at one another but were also silent. It fell to his mother to reply. "She is – we believe she is near Modena, working for the overseer, the bailiff of our landlord. She... it had to be that way. He came for the rent, you see." She seemed unable to continue.

Her husband's voice broke in harshly. "That short-arsed bastard Cortino came at harvest, demanding even more rent than usual, and the usual tithe. Did you know it had been a poor summer? Most of the crops failed after all that unseasonal rain. We have always managed to find the tithe, which leaves us little enough to live on over the winter. But the bigger rent? We had no money. So he cast his eyes on Rosalia. The scum, he's always wanted..."

"Hush!" his wife interrupted. "He proposed that Rosalia should go with him and, by working in his house, pay the rent in kind. My husband refused, of course," she said with an indulgent smile. "That's how fathers are. Rosalia was more practical."

"As she ever was," added her father in a broken voice. "She looked at me and told me not to fuss. 'It must be this way, father,' she said to me. Then she went with him, holding her head high as she walked in her bare feet, holding onto the stirrup of that bastard's horse. And I did nothing. I sold my daughter into slavery."

"Not slavery, husband. You know it is not. It is but the payment of a debt, and she will return to us when it is paid. Yet I fear for her. I fear for her safety among those rough men. And I pray to God every day to return her safe to us."

Maria and Rita were holding one another and looking at me with their big eyes. "If that bastard has laid a finger on her," grated her father, "I'll..." His wife put a hand on her husband's, and hushed him.

The table fell silent. We avoided catching one another's eye. A monstrous injustice had been perpetrated on the family, and the wrong of it hung in the air. To me it felt like a reproach. I had been leading my exciting city life, congratulating myself on the way I was mixing with the rich and the powerful. I had given barely a thought to my friends, the only real friends I had known before I made my new life in Bologna. And all the while they had been suffering grinding poverty, the viciousness of a crooked bailiff and the loss of their beautiful daughter. I could still picture the first time I saw her, that red hair glowing in the sunset, the eyes fixed on mine and the love in her regard for her brother, so readily shared with me.

I found myself suddenly speechless: the words would not come. At last I managed to say, thickly, "I will find her for you. I swear I will return her to you."

I prayed that it would not prove to be yet another of the promises I had made in my life and failed to keep.

There was no singing that night. We were tired after our journey, and the family seemed exhausted, though whether by loss and sorrow or by sheer physical labour it was impossible to tell. We young men slept in the barn with the animals, but with fresh straw for our bed. That is how it was done then, and still is in country areas.

Wearied from our long journey and from my own lack of sleep, I slept soundly for a few hours. But soon, too early, I was awake again, not least because my body was starting to complain about spending a day on horseback. My bottom felt bruised beyond belief while my thighs, unaccustomed to straddling a mount, were stiffer and sorer than ever Michele's exercise regime had made them. As I tossed and turned, vainly seeking a comfortable position, I turned over in my mind the tidings I had heard of Rosalia. I pictured that warm smile, those full, soft lips which, now I was a man rather than a boy, I realised I had been longing to kiss, and that lustrous hair falling in deep red coils (as I pictured them) to her waist. And then I imagined her in her current situation: ill-treated, worked day and night and, I feared, abused and even raped by Uguzzoni's bailiff. The thought was unbearable. Yet I had no idea what to do.

I was in no doubt that Cortino's action was illegal. Under the laws of Bologna – and I guessed it must be the same in Modena, since that city was now ruled by its more powerful neighbour – no free person could be bonded or enslaved for a debt. Nor, indeed, could any such arrangement be made, if at all, without proper legal process and written contract: that much I had learnt from working for my master. Yet Uguzzoni, the landlord sitting on his vast wealth, would have no interest in the detail of how his bailiff collected the rents, so long as his wealth continued to grow. And Cortino himself would ensure that the books added up: I was certain of that. He would extort extra rent from the next few farms, while making the most of his hold over Tommaso's family and his power over Rosalia.

It was equally clear to me that Cortino had been planning this for some years. He would have had an eye on Rosalia since she was a child, watching her grow to womanhood and waiting for his chance, the first bad harvest, when he could threaten her family, as he had surely done to others before them. He probably calculated that Rosalia would willingly, generously, sacrifice herself to save her family and her younger sisters from being thrown off the land. It was so simple and, in the scale of things, just another small, mean act characteristic of the world controlled by the great landowners and particularly typical of their venal henchmen: they readily enriched themselves and extorted creature comforts while ensuring that their aristocratic patrons also saw their fortunes increase year on year.

What would Uguzzoni care about a little embezzlement here, a private deal there? He was already as rich as Croesus, and constantly becoming wealthier, which was why he was also prepared to play political games with the Bishop in Modena and Massimo Lambertazzi in Bologna. Dangerous games, certainly: but likely in the end to bring him still more money, even greater power. I ground my teeth and determined to bring down both Cortino and Uguzzoni, if it was the last thing I did.

Chapter 28

When he was awake, I shared some of my concerns with Paolo. It is curious how often we feel that our worries are unique to us: yet Paolo understood immediately what my main concern was. Clearly we needed to find Tommaso. Equally clearly we would have to tell him the fate that had befallen his sister. And then, I guessed, when we had completed our urgent business, I would need to set out, perhaps with Tommaso, in order to effect the rescue of Rosalia from her servitude and restore her to her family.

I was worried about Tommaso, too. Paolo had heard that he was in the employ of the Bishop, presumably a safe enough job in that prosperous household. I knew how efficient and skilled a clerk Tommaso would be: his writing was perhaps not quite as good as mine, but he had always had a better head for figures and could manage accounts and transactions impeccably. Yet his family, so they had said the night before, had heard nothing from him. Why? Had he fallen into misfortune? Or perhaps (and I prayed this was the more likely reason) his employer kept him busy, paid him poorly (it seemed all the men of influence in Modena were fundamentally mean) and allowed him no time to visit. Nor could he have sent a letter, since none of the family could read.

It was Paolo, not I, who suggested how we might solve two of my numerous concerns. I wanted to help that proud but desperate family, ground down by their inability to make all their grinding labour pay sufficiently. And I wanted to reassure them about their son, although I had no firm news of him. We decided on a deception that we hoped would prove harmless.

Accordingly, when we bade the four of them farewell, Paolo pulled out a purse of money (we had been well furnished with funds for the trip). When they once again refused payment for the night's lodging, Paolo said brightly, "I almost forgot. Although I have not yet met Tommaso, I did get a message to him. His important work for the Bishop would not permit him to come out and meet me: besides, he did not know who I was.

"But when I mentioned Lorenzo here, I mean Luca, Tommaso sent a servant out with this purse, begging me to ensure that he received it. He was sure that Luca would come to see you when he was able, and he did not feel able to entrust the money to anyone else. I hope you will forgive me for not remembering yesterday – and, indeed, for forgetting to give it to Luca. Now I make amends: this is from your son."

The parents were overwhelmed. "Look, husband," declared his mother. "I told you that Tommaso would become a man of importance, and that we could look to him for help when the time came." She turned to Paolo. "Thank you, sir, for honouring our house and for bringing this gift from our son. We are in your debt."

Paolo responded with his most courtly bow, then skilfully helped me into my saddle so that I avoided making a fool of myself by betraying my inexperience on horseback, not to mention the fact that I could barely move my cramped legs. We waved a cheerful farewell and cantered up the road towards Modena. Once we were out of sight, we slowed to the ambling walk that our horses preferred and which added less aggravation to the bruising on my behind. Paolo looked at my face. "What's the matter? You look as if you've swallowed an onion."

"I don't know. I worry about that family. I feel guilty: I've not been in touch, barely thought about them, for three years and more. My life has moved on - while theirs has, if anything, gone backwards. The place is a lot poorer and their plight more desperate than I remember."

"Lorenzo, you must stop feeling guilty about everything! You cannot take the woes of everyone on your shoulders! Besides, you have brought them joy in seeing you again and bringing news of Tommaso, even if some of the tidings were fabricated. Sometimes a little deception's justified if it brings happiness or avoids hurt. And we've left them better off than we found them. You can do no more: stop fretting."

"But I shall have to tell Tommaso about his sister, which will break his heart, I think. I can't bear to think of her, taken and ill-treated. Will they rape her? Treat her as an animal or a whore? I can't bear to think."

"Were you fond of her?" Paolo asked gently. "Was she beautiful, or one of those sturdy farming types?"

I remembered her face that last time, asking me to sing with her one more time. "I think she was the most beautiful girl I've ever seen. Oh," embarrassed, I added quickly, "I don't mean some kind of childhood infatuation. I mean she was... remarkable. And, yes, I think I loved her, as much as one child can understand loving another."

"Was she more beautiful than the lady Livia, then?" he asked mischievously.

"Livia? What do you know of her?"

"Only how much you have *not* said about her, but sighed whenever her name was mentioned. Yes, Lorenzo: you have mentioned her quite a lot, between calling down curses on the heads of all the other members of the Lambertazzi clan. And then, of course, you've never quite said how she came to release you from your captivity two nights ago. However did you repay her?" His eyes were twinkling with mirth, but I was unable to see the funny side.

"Damn you for a fool, Paolo! Do you think I'm like an open book to read?" He nodded, and grinned infuriatingly. "Well, I confess I think of Livia a great deal. And she is beautiful - though distant, unreal, like a goddess. But Rosalia: that was something else. We were just children, but her smile, the love for her brother, her affection for me, her warmth – those were real to me, not a dream as Livia seems. They were things I can never forget. I must find her. For Tommaso's sake. For his family's. And for the love I bore her - I still bear her."

"Lorenzo," replied Paolo gently. "I can't resist teasing you, because you're like a lyre. Whenever I touch your strings, you play music! But I have feelings, too: I do understand, you know. Cheer up! We have a job to do. Let's move on quickly." And he spurred his horse to a trot and then a canter.

Somehow I persuaded my mount to something like a trot. When eventually I caught him up I asked: "If you understand, then what shall we do?"

"It's obvious, isn't it? We must find Tommaso and conclude your master's business. We must tell him the bad news as gently as we can. And then we shall have to see what we can do about rescuing your Rosalia. Though the Magister's business must come first. Is that agreed?"

"Agreed," I nodded, both grateful and relieved, and we set off at a pace for Modena.

We made good time. The journey had taken Tommaso and me all day as young boys walking home, or enjoying the equally slow luxury of a lift on an ox-cart: by contrast, on horseback we had covered the distance by midday. As we clattered through the north gate and into the great square, Paolo asked, "What now?"

"Now? Go and find Tommaso – at the Bishop's palace."

"And how are you going to find him?" Paolo enquired sarcastically. "Are you going to knock at the front gate and ask for him? You already look like a brigand with that mask: and they don't know you from Adam in any case."

"If they don't know me, that's all the better. Remember, I ran away from here without permission, what, three or four years ago."

"So, if they don't know you there, they won't admit you. And if they do, you'll find yourself in trouble. What's the plan now?"

I was irritated by Paolo's unhelpfulness. Back in Bologna, I had imagined it relatively easy simply to search out my old friend and enlist his help. Now everything seemed to be slipping away from me. "I don't know, Paolo. Perhaps you'd better ask."

"I can't go there. Remember, I was warned off. Oh, I know it's unlikely that there will be any of Lambertazzi's men there today. But what if there were? Or one of the Bishop's men remembered I'd been sent away from the wagon-train because I wasn't one of the trusted few? It's asking for trouble."

I paused. In truth, I was stumped for a moment. Then an idea began to form in my mind. "Paolo," I asked, "do you know anything of the layout of the palace? For instance, do you know where the Bishop's clerks and bookkeepers would work? There must be several of them. I can't believe Tommaso is his only clerk: he's too young to be entrusted with the task on his own."

Paolo considered for a moment. "I guess... yes, I think, when we were in the courtyard, Lambertazzi's foreman, the one carrying the letters, went up some stairs to the right and towards the back. Yes. I'm sure of it. It's only just down this street, and we'll find ourselves at the palace."

He was right. As I had anticipated, the Bishop's palace was indeed close to the centre of the city, almost adjacent to the Duomo and only a stone's throw from the palazzo where the Podestà exercised his power (power deputed and sanctioned by Bologna in those years) and where the council of the *Comune* met. Where else? The Bishop would not be far from the centre of things so that he could exert his influence and play his political games.

We found ourselves facing the gate of the Bishop's grand dwelling. Down each side of it ran a small alleyway, narrow and dark on account of the high buildings on either side. "The right, you said?" Paolo nodded. "Then we'll go down there." Our horses' hooves clattered and echoed as we went the length of the alleyway, until we were at what appeared to be the back corner of the bishop's immense house. At street level there were no windows: but high above us there appeared quite large openings. "Maybe that's where they work?" I wondered. "Where the light's good. For reading and writing," I explained.

"So what now?" demanded Paolo. "Do we just shout his name?"

"Better than that," I replied, smugly. "We sing. Or, at least, I do."

As we had ridden through the streets of Modena I had kept my hood over my head: the city, the Cathedral and its Prior still held some terrors for me. But now I threw it back and, reaching behind my head, undid the thongs that held that grotesque mask firmly on my nose. I started to sing. It was the song that I had first sung in happy times at Tommaso's house, blending my voice with that of his sister Rosalia. I began softly: *Ti canterò lo meo amor*. Even quietly my voice rang from the high walls surrounding us and, my confidence grew, I sang more loudly. No longer was I singing in a treble voice: nor did I adopt the falsetto I so frequently used when performing with Sordello. This was my natural voice, sung from my chest, a warm (if unexceptional) baritone, but still I was moved by the emotions that the song still aroused in me.

Paolo sat astride his horse, a look of bemusement on his face as I launched into the second verse. Louder still I sang, and Paolo was just starting to gesticulate, to urge me to be quieter, when a voice called from high above us. "Who's singing that? Who would know that song? Is it? Surely... Luca, is it you? Is it really you?"

I looked up and saw, at a window two or more floors above us, the round face and curly hair that I remembered so well. Older, of course: perhaps a little plumper. But it was unmistakable. "Tommaso!" I laughed for sheer joy. "Tommasino, it *is* me. Who else?"

"Luca. I don't believe it. Don't move. Stay there. Don't move an inch. I'll be with you." The head was withdrawn and we waited. A minute. Two, perhaps. To me they seemed an eternity. And then, running from the front of the building down the street towards us was my friend, my dearest friend Tommaso. I slid from the saddle, and was nearly knocked flat when my old friend hurled himself at me with such vigour that I barely managed to prevent him from causing further damage to my nose. We hugged and disengaged. With our hands on each other's shoulders, we looked at each other. "Tommasino," I said. "You're just the same. But you're fatter!"

"Well," he replied. "You know the food's better here than the swill you must be obliged to live off in Bologna! And as for you, Luca. You're... I think you're taller. But you're still skinny: and what happened to your nose?"

"It's a long story," I laughed. "Can I tell it now? Can we go and eat? Can you escape from your work?"

"For you? Of course I can. Just give me a few minutes, and I'll ensure I can spend the rest of the day with you. I can fix it with the chamberlain." Then he was gone again, rushing up the street until he disappeared around the corner.

Half an hour later we had stabled our horses and were sitting with Tommaso at a table at a comfortable inn, a log fire roaring at the end of the room. Tommaso, delight written all over his round face, demanded to hear all my adventures, which I recounted at length, though necessarily glossing over the parts I could not share and interrupted occasionally by a wry commentary from Paolo who stepped in whenever I risked becoming self-congratulatory. Then it was Tommaso's turn: how had he ended up in the Bishop's household? I wanted to know.

"It's simple enough, Luca. Sorry. I must learn to call you Lorenzo now. My voice broke and I never developed any kind of falsetto so, really, I was of little use to the choir: they needed no more men's voices. Still, the Church looks after her own. My writing had become good – almost as good as yours, Lu-, Lorenzo – and I'm good with figures. I really can do numbers. So the Prior had a word with the Bishop. He'd just been made *Arch*bishop, would you believe, so apparently he needed another clerk. And here I am!"

"Do you ever get home to see your family?" I asked, earning myself warning glances from Paolo.

My old friend's face fell. "No. We have the occasional free day for major feasts, but I don't get the week's holiday that we choirboys used to. Do you remember those visits to my family, Luca?"

I didn't correct the name, but nodded. "Tommasino, they're the clearest and happiest memories of my time here. Why do you think I sang that song?"

"I'm glad. I remember them too. I cling onto those memories when I'm unhappy or lonely: which I am from time to time. It's dull work, the dealings and accounts of a Prince of the Church. And, though I am paid, I receive so little that I have not saved even one purse-full to send to my family. I think they may have abandoned hope of my ever becoming an important man, as they hoped!" He caught my eye, and we both smiled at our shared memories of those family discussions of his outstanding prospects in the city of Modena.

Chapter 29

Our conversation ebbed and flowed and, at last, Paolo and I knew we must broach the reason for our visit. When Tommaso asked innocently, "So what brings you back to Modena now?" I was obliged to tell him.

"Tommasino, it's a serious matter, and I need to ask for your help."

"Anything," he replied, apparently astonished that I should even have to ask.

So I outlined the legal wranglings in train in Bologna. I explained how we were convinced that Lambertazzi (whose name he had already heard as the villain of my own tale) was plotting, perhaps even aiming to seize power in the city: and how, following Paolo's investigations with Giacomo and Salvatore, we were sure that the Archbishop and Uguzzoni were preparing to raise a small army to support him.

"Uguzzoni, eh?" commented Tommaso. "He'd stoop to anything. I try to have as little as I can to do with him or his clerks, though there are many dealings between them."

I leaned forward, my tone more urgent. "Tommasino, do you remember last week, a wagon coming in – just one – from Modena with some kind of special cargo?"

"It's funny you should say that, I do. It looked pretty ordinary stuff, but there wasn't the usual bill of exchange to sort out. It was all kept a bit quiet, well away from us clerks. The chamberlain dealt with it himself."

"We think there was a shipment of silver, to pay for weapons that Uguzzoni was supplying."

Tommaso made a face. "I'm pretty sure no weapons came through the Archbishop's household: I'd have known about them."

"That's the point. We think the Bishop, the Archbishop, is keeping his hands clean, but he's passing on money and acting as intermediary. Tommasino, this is important: can you find us a letter from Lambertazzi, some kind of agreement, anything that we can use as proof back in Bologna that he's plotting to overthrow the *Comune* there?"

Tommaso's manner changed abruptly. "Luca, Lorenzo: You know I'd do anything for you. Well, almost anything. But this is one I cannot. You're asking me to steal a document from my master. I'm a clerk, in his service. He's not generous, but he's not a bad employer, and I have a roof over my head. Besides, here in Modena, what do we care about your problems in Bologna, ruled by it against our will? Modena has lost her pride, and you'll never hear a good word about the Bolognese here. I'd be betraying my city *and* my master. You're asking too much, more than I can give."

I was nonplussed. Not for the first time in our long friendship, Tommaso had seen through my wiles and self-deception. Why had it not occurred to me? We certainly enjoyed the bonds of friendship, which remained as warm as they had done the day I left Modena those years before: but he owed nothing to my master, nor to a city which was alien to him, had beaten his own in battle and now ruled it from afar with the arrogance of a conqueror and scant respect or concern for its inhabitants. As Paolo started to argue, I laid my hand on his. "No, Paolo. Tommasino is right. I have no right to ask him to betray his employer, however much he may be our enemy."

"His loyalty?" replied Paolo harshly. "To the Archbishop, perhaps. But what about Uguzzoni? You haven't told him what he, or his men, have done to his family, have you, Lorenzo? When were you going to tell him that?"

The effect on Tommaso was electric. "What about my family? What's he done? Have you seen them? Why didn't you tell me?" He was angry now.

I sighed. "We went there yesterday: stayed there last night. Your parents and sisters are well, although it's hard. The harvest was bad. We didn't see your brothers. But..."

"What? Tell me." His tone was urgent, his anxiety palpable.

Paolo tried to explain. "The harvest failed, so when the bailiff came, they could not pay the rent."

"I guess that bastard Cortino was trying to screw extra money out of them?" queried Tommaso.

"I think so," I replied. "And they couldn't pay. So he..."

"Go on. Don't spare me. For the love of Christ, just tell me the truth," pleaded Tommaso.

I realised my tears were starting. "Tommasino. He took Rosalia. Cortino took Rosalia."

Tommaso was aghast. "But he can't do that. No one has the right..."

"No one has the right. I should know: I work for a lawyer," I retorted angrily. "But there was no one to help them. Cortino was cheating his employer, of course. He said that Rosalia would work for him for a year in place of payment, and earn the rent and tithe that your parents couldn't pay."

"And she agreed to this?"

"You know Rosalia. She offered herself, so that her parents and sisters would still have a home. She walked beside Cortino willingly as he rode off laughing. Your mother wept as she told me."

Tommaso was lost for words. "But he will... she, she's not safe with an animal like that. Everyone knows about him. He's a rapist."

I nodded miserably. "I know."

Tommaso leapt to his feet. "What are we waiting for? We have to go and find her. Get her back from Cortino: kill him if we need to. He's not taking my sister, the filth. He's bullied and cheated and... violated," his voice cracked, "For too long. It's time to put an end to him." Other customers were looking round, disturbed by the uproar. Paolo put his hands on his shoulders and pressed him back into his seat.

"Tommasino," I said gently. "If I've learnt one thing, it's that we must tread carefully." Knowing my reputation for over-hasty action, Paolo snorted at this. I ignored him. "We need to rescue Rosalia. But we need to make sure that neither Cortino nor anyone else can treat your family like that again."

"If my brothers knew, they would already have torn Cortino's throat out."

"Perhaps that's why they don't know. Maybe your parents didn't even tell them, for fear of what they would do, putting themselves beyond the law."

"So what can we do? Leave Rosalia with that... that filth, taking advantage... I can't even bear to say it."

"If we can bring down his master, Uguzzoni, he will have no backing. And Uguzzoni, after all, bears the real guilt for this. He allows his bailiff to rob the farmers and to cheat him, and doesn't look too closely as long as he gets enough income from his estates. It starts and finishes with Uguzzoni: Cortino is just a minion."

"A minion who has my sister in his power." He was still shouting.

"Tommasino," I continued. "If you can find me the proof that Uguzzoni is part of Lambertazzi's plot, whether or not it involves the Archbishop, I swear I'll destroy him. Get that proof, and together we will rescue Rosalia – and we'll make Cortino pay for everything he has done."

There was a heavy silence as Tommaso fought to bring his emotions under control. Then he looked at me in that searching, reproachful way he had. "Damn you, Luca. Lorenzo. You disappear from my life and leave it empty. Then you return, out of the blue, and turn it upside down. Damn you." And he left.

Was I shamelessly manipulating my friend? I feared I was. Yet what could I do? Loyalty to my master and to the city in which I had made my home demanded that I find the proof of Lambertazzi's treachery. Allegiance to Bologna? Yes. Curiously, when I searched my conscience, I found I really did care about that city. Its vibrant governance was chaotic, certainly, yet seemed nonetheless to afford ordinary people a voice, not to mention protection against the extortions of the powerful such as Lambertazzi.

But what of Tommaso? I knew that, if he were able to find the proof we sought, he would put himself at great risk. At the very least he might lose his employment, if discovered: yet discovery would lead him into far more danger. So complex and dark a plot did we suspect that anyone endangering it would lose not merely his livelihood but, in all probability, his life.

There again, if he could do it without being detected, and next we went to rescue Rosalia from her enforced servitude, would that not amply repay him for the risk he was taking? It was hard, so hard, to balance and calculate those arguments. I fidgeted throughout the afternoon, so much to Paolo's exasperation that he eventually barked at me, "For the love of God, Lorenzo, sit still. You're like a cat on hot bricks!"

I determined to have a walk around my old haunts. Paolo advised caution: "What if you're recognised? The fact that you ran away all those years ago might cause you difficulty: and in any case it would draw attention to you. We need to be secret." I half reassured him by promising to keep on the mask that was protecting my healing nose, and also to keep my hood up. It was a cool enough day to warrant that.

He declined to accompany me, declaring somewhat mysteriously that he "had a call to make". He would not say more, leaving me with the strong impression that he was going to visit a girl, and would not welcome company. So I wandered around the old city, pleased to be back on my own feet and even looking into the cathedral to revisit the carvings that had fascinated me all those years ago: I made a nostalgic return to that pillar on which was carved the Martyrdom of Saint Lawrence, San Lorenzo whose name I had taken and for whose protection I now prayed (an unusual act for me) as I pondered our next move.

As darkness fell I returned to the inn, and was joined shortly after by Paolo, still mysterious about where he had been. Eventually, when we were so hungry that we were about to order food without waiting for him, Tommaso joined us. He looked troubled, and his manner was nervous. "I have found out a little for you," he declared, "but I can do no more tonight."

I betrayed my disappointment but Paolo, consistently proving himself a far more effective conspirator than I, expressed his satisfaction. "If we manage to get any proof in our hands, we shall need to leave the city at speed: we cannot do that at night, when the gates are closed. Much better that Tommaso gives us whatever he can find in the morning. With a little luck we can reach Bologna within the day."

"So what do you think you can find us, Tommasino?" I asked my friend.

The troubled look returned to his face. "I didn't believe there was anything in the Archbishop's house. His chamberlain keeps his private documents well away from us clerks, but he does frequently have business with Uguzzoni's steward, and rather more than usual lately. That might be something to do with what you're looking for. I've been doing the household accounts recently, so I told the chamberlain there was some confusion over quantities of *balsamico*, which the Archbishop buys from Uguzzoni.

"I asked if I could go over there and sort it out with his steward, and he agreed. Then he said that, if I went tomorrow morning, I could take a couple of other papers for him, to save him the walk. I don't know if the papers I'll be taking for him will be anything that you're looking for: I doubt it, as I say. But I can try to find something when I'm with Uguzzoni's steward, if he's careless enough to leave papers around – and if his master trusts him with anything so important."

"Tommasino," I said, "don't put yourself in danger for us. This is important, really important: but I couldn't bear to see harm come to you because of me."

"It's a little late for that, Luca – Lorenzo," he replied bitterly. "I ran risks enough just looking through the chamberlain's papers. And if something goes missing from Uguzzoni's place on the morning when I'm known to go there, it won't be long before they come looking for me." He looked into my eyes, "You know I'm not doing this for you, Lorenzo. Not even for the sake of our old friendship. I'm doing it because you've promised to save Rosalia. If I find you the proof you want tomorrow, you can send Paolo back to Bologna with it. And you and I will go and find her. Agreed?"

Of course I agreed. What else could I do? I looked at Paolo. "It shouldn't be difficult if Tommasino and I go together. You can go ahead, and I'll catch you up on the road." He looked sceptical, but said nothing.

None of us was good company. We were all on edge, thinking about the next day. Tommaso's anguish and anxiety were etched on his face, a visage I always pictured in memory as sunny and happy. That I was the cause of that transformation troubled me deeply. And Paolo was exasperated with both of us. Since it was clear that we would not enjoy a sociable evening, we agreed to lay our plans and then part, Tommaso returning to his lodging in the Archbishop's palace. I thought that sounded a grand kind of place to live, until he retorted that the corner of a storeroom he shared as a sleeping space with two other clerks was damp, rank and infested with rats. I retorted that our inn was little better, Paolo and I looking set to share a straw paillasse with two or three other travellers. We saw Tommaso off down the street, had a piss against the wall and went to bed ourselves.

Chapter 30

The next morning, as we had agreed with Tommaso, Paolo and I took up position in an alleyway across the square from the Archbishop's palace. From there we could watch him along his route from the palace, across the square, and down a narrow street opposite that would take him almost to Uguzzoni's even grander dwelling. We had our mounts with us so that, in the event that Tommaso succeeded in finding and giving us the proof we needed, Paolo could get quickly out of the city's eastern gateway and off towards Bologna, while Tommaso and I would head west to Cortino's farm, which Paolo had assured me was only a short distance outside the city.

I was a bundle of nerves but, if Paolo shared my apprehension, he did not show it. "Calm down, Lorenzo," he urged. "You know that Tommaso is unlikely to find anything. And, even if he does, it will not be of great significance to the people here and will probably not be missed. I've always considered this a fool's errand."

I gestured him to silence, as I saw Tommaso emerge from the Archbishop's gate. He looked around him and then strode purposefully across the street, a large satchel slung across his shoulder. Across the square he went, looking for all the world like any other clerk going about his rightful business. When he entered the narrow street opposite, however, his demeanour changed. He looked around him so furtively that, had anyone seen him, they would have immediately have deduced that he was up to no good. Then he shrank into a doorway so that we could barely see him. "Come on," I whispered to Paolo. "He's up to something. We mustn't let him out of sight."

"This isn't a good idea," replied my companion. "We're not meant to be seen."

"No one will notice us. We're just two people leading their horses across the square: we could be going anywhere." Already I was out of the alleyway and manoeuvring to a position where we could see Tommaso more clearly. As we improved our angle of observation, I could see Tommaso now kneeling down, rifling through his satchel, which was open in front of him. Then he pulled out a piece of parchment, which he began to read avidly. Abruptly he bundled the documents back into the satchel, closed it and stood up. Then, instead of continuing along the street to his destination, he turned back towards the square. He appeared to be looking for us.

I was about to acknowledge his interest with a wave, when Paolo seized my arm. "Look!" he whispered. As if from nowhere, two burly men had appeared. They appeared to be arguing heatedly with Tommaso, who was shaking his head, apparently dismissive of whatever they were saying. The next moment the two men had seized him by the arms and were dragging him back towards the Archbishop's palace, from which emerged a figure I recognised. Hurrying towards the struggling group, the Prior's powerful build and shining bald pate marked him out at once.

As the Prior approached we could see my friend wrestle, and hear his protestations. I could tell that Tommaso had spotted us, while his two captors, not to mention the Prior who was shouting and gesticulating, were oblivious of our presence.

I was rooted to the spot, at a loss. Not so Paolo, who leapt into the saddle and spurred his mount across the square towards the tussling group. Taken unawares, the men looked up, startled. Paolo directed his horse straight at the man holding Tommaso's right arm. As it knocked him flying, the Prior and the other guard flung themselves to the side, covering themselves (to my delight) in filth. Meanwhile my friend, exercising both a level of horsemanship and degree of strength that he had concealed from me, seized Tommaso by the arm and swung him up behind him. "Hold my waist!" he yelled as he wheeled his horse and galloped back across the square towards me. "Don't just stand there, you idiot! Ride for the gate!"

Somehow I managed to lift my sore left leg high enough to reach the stirrup and mounted my steed at the first attempt. As Paolo and Tommaso streaked past me, I did my best to follow. As I turned, I saw the Prior, who had appeared as stupefied as I, scramble to his feet and call back towards the Archbishop's palace. Immediately the gate opened and I could see men running into the square. I was unconcerned, as none appeared to have horses: next I became aware of arrows skittering across the square. We were turning into the Via Æmilia and could see, to my joy, that the gate was near, when another hail of arrows passed over my head.

I laughed in relief at another miss, until I heard a cry and saw Tommaso lurch suddenly to his right. He would have fallen, had not Paolo extended his right arm behind him. The horse stumbled a little at the sudden shifting of weight, then righted itself: but as I came alongside I spotted a red stain spreading across Tommaso's back. The shaft and feathered flights of an arrow protruded from his back. "He's hit," I gasped to Paolo. "For the love of Christ, he's hit."

"Keep going!" was the response from Paolo. "We cannot stop here. Tommaso, hold on. You must hold on."

The gateway was empty, unusually so. There were none of the usual wagons or handcarts that habitually blocked the way while their owners haggled and negotiated on the taxes they were required to pay for bringing goods in for sale. And so without slowing we galloped out through the narrow gateway, Tommaso clinging as best he could to Paolo's waist with his left arm, the right appearing to hang uselessly. I clung to my reins and the saddle's pommel, unused to such speed on horseback and in full knowledge of the fact that I had no idea how to control my mount if it chose to do anything but follow.

We were out. The great road stretched ahead of us, and, for the time being at least, there was no sign of pursuit behind us. "We need to stop," I begged Paolo. "We must see to Tommaso. He's hurt."

"Not yet," came the terse reply. "We must put distance between us and the city. Giacomo is waiting for us a few leagues down the road, with fresh mounts, too."

"Giacomo? I thought he didn't come with us."

"He didn't. But I know more than you do about escaping from places. Believe me, we're going to need both him and his fresh horses - even though anyone chasing us should be held up at the gate, for a while at least."

We were yelling at each other to make ourselves heard as we hurtled down the road, which was still unnaturally empty. "How do you know they'll be held up? What have you done?"

"Lorenzo, you're such a simpleton!" We both laughed, partly from relief at our escape, and partly from the sheer exhilaration of galloping to freedom. "Your master gave me a letter for Modena's Podestà, asking that we be afforded every assistance. Don't be offended: she reckoned you had enough to do, persuading Tommaso to help us. So I paid him a visit and gave him her letter. Of course, since Bologna now controls Modena, the Podestà is one of ours, not theirs. He arranged that, if his men saw us getting out in a hurry, they wouldn't allow anyone to pass the gateway without proper authority, having their wagons searched and the like. So there should be a good old blockage in the gate by now!"

I was puzzled. "But how did you know...?"

"Lorenzo, you haven't done much of this. You can't go stealing things from powerful people without expecting trouble. I didn't for a moment think that Tommaso would find anything valuable *and* get it to us: not without something happening, at any rate. So I made preparations. That's the long and the short of it."

I shook my head in amazement, and we galloped on in silence.

After a time, notwithstanding my ignorance of horse-riding, I could tell that my mount was tiring. Paolo allowed his to slow, and mine followed suit. Both were snorting and breathing heavily as we permitted them to walk for a while along the great road which, straight as ever, stretched before and behind us, still without any sign of pursuit. "We should meet up with Giacomo in a league or two, remarked Paolo. "How's Tommaso doing?" he added.

I looked round, to see him still clutching Paolo grimly with one hand, his right hanging uselessly. He was pale, gritting his teeth with the pain. "I'm all right," he gasped. "Just a bit sore. I'm not sure I can hold on much longer."

"Let me have a look at you," I said, and dropped back a little. The whole of his back was red and sticky with blood. "By Christ, Tommasino, it doesn't look good. One of those bastards put an arrow in you."

"I know. Luca, it hurts. It hurts like hell." He swayed, and would have fallen from the saddle if I had not been right beside him. I seized his arm to steady him, and he yelped as I jarred his shoulder. Blood seemed to seep out even more quickly. Now it was running down his back and down the flank of Paolo's horse.

"Hold on, Tommasino. We'll get help in a minute. Just hold on. You'll be all right." He smiled wanly: I knew he did not believe me.

"There he is!" exclaimed Paolo. "There's Giacomino!" Sure enough, there was our friend, standing at the side of the road ahead holding four horses.

He grinned as we approached him. "What kept you, boys? Any trouble?"

We were past joking. "This is Lorenzo's friend Tommaso. He's hurt. Badly, I think."

As Giacomo came alongside their horse, Tommaso fell off it into his arms. This time he hardly moaned at the impact. Clearly he was losing consciousness. "For the love of God, Lorenzo, what have you done to your friend?"

"It's an arrow. Can we pull it out?"

Giacomo laughed harshly. "And kill him? Better to pack some linen around the wound to try to stop the bleeding. All we can do is get him back to Bologna as quickly as we can. Your master seems to know all the physicians in the city. Let's hope one of them can patch him up – and that we can get there before it's too late." I was about to hush him, not wanting to alarm Tommaso: but he appeared unaware of what was happening, groaning and twitching in Giacomino's arms.

"Shit," said Giacomo. "This is beyond me. I don't know what we should do now."

"One of us needs to get to Bologna as quickly as possible," replied Paolo: "That is, if Tommaso managed to steal anything important. I guess he did, or they wouldn't have tried to arrest him. We'll have to ask him." He swung down from the saddle. "Tommaso! Tommasino," he hissed urgently, shaking his head and patting his cheek. "We need to know. Did you get the proof?"

228

Tommaso stirred, the movement causing him to grimace again with fresh pain. "Letter," he mumbled. "Gorra letter. Luca can... read." I tore the satchel open and pulled out the parchments it contained.

"Which one, Tommasino?" I asked. "Which one?"

"It's Lamber..., Lam..."

"Lambertazzi? One from him?" Tommaso nodded as I skimmed through the letters. And there, to my amazement, was a short letter addressed, at the top, to His Eminence the Cardinal Archbishop of Modena. And at the bottom, sure enough, was what I took to be the Lambertazzi seal. There was no time to read it. "Tommasino," I asked. "Is it the proof we need?"

His reply was a sigh. "I think so. Hope it's... worth it. Take it. Mentions Uguzzoni. Make him... pay. Please, Luca. Make him pay. And promise me." His eyes were suddenly brighter, and looked straight into mine. "Swear you'll save Rosalia. Now. Go to her. Promise."

I squeezed his hand. "I will, Tommasino. You know I will. Just don't die on me." But he had lost consciousness.

I was plunged into despair. This was my oldest, closest friend. I had sworn years before that I would never ask him to take hurt on my account: yet I had led him into this. He was dying: I could see the pool of blood spreading beneath him where he lay, the arrow protruding from his back. I still wanted to pull it out, as if removing the cause of the hurt would cure the hurt itself, but Giacomo would have none of it. "Leave it," he said. "And we'll bind cloth around it as tightly as we can to slow the bleeding. It's all we can do," he added urgently.

"But what are we to do?" I cried in anguish. "We cannot ride further with him like this. He will surely die if we try. We have to get this letter to the Magister. That's what we were sent to do. And..." I was close to breaking down, "There's Rosalia. I swore. I promised Tommasino that I would rescue her. Must I betray her too? All I ever do is hurt the people I care for."

In an agony of indecision I buried my head in my hands. Yet I knew what I must do: leave my friend to live or to die; abandon

Rosalia to her sordid fate; and perform my duty for my master and for the city that had adopted me. It was a heart-breaking decision that I could not bear to make.

"You're doing it again, Lorenzo." Paolo's tone was deliberately harsh. "Will you never stop blaming yourself? You're becoming boring."

I blustered in an attempt to justify my intense sense of guilt. "But it's all my fault. If I hadn't involved Tommasino. If I hadn't promised..."

"Nonsense. It's a rough, unjust world, and at least you try to do something about it. Besides, there's an easy answer. How many problems do we have?" I shook my head, unwilling to play games with him. "No? We have three. There's Tommasino here: a girl to save; and a letter to get to Bologna. And how many of us are there? Three. So we share out the tasks. Simple!"

I looked at him in wonder. "But how?"

"Lorenzo," he said gently, putting his hands on my shoulders and shaking me, "We can do this. I'll ride on. You've forgotten Salvatore." I looked at Paolo in bewilderment. "I'm sorry: another little precaution I didn't tell you about. An hour down the road Salvatore is waiting with more fresh horses. All I have to do is gallop on until I find him. If I take two horses from there, I can be in Bologna in hours, long before any pursuit from Modena can raise the alarm or let Lambertazzi know that he's finished. I'll send Salvatore back to you with the rest of the horses. He and Giacomino can look after Tommaso here. They can get off this road and take to the back ways, maybe get a cart to put him in and keep him comfortable till we can find him a surgeon in Bologna. He's bleeding, but he's not going to die yet – not if we can help it."

"But what about me?"

"You, Lorenzo? How can you be so stupid? You're going to ride off and find your lady-love! Go and save Rosalia. That's what you want to do, isn't it?"

Suddenly I felt a semblance of hope. As I nodded my agreement, Paolo leapt to his feet. "I'll be on my way, then. Make him

230

comfortable, and get him off the road. It won't be long before the Archbishop and Uguzzoni get their men out of the city to hunt us down: the Podestà won't have been able to hold them for long. Then they'll be coming hell-for-leather this way. You see that clump of trees over there?" A little way off the road to the south there was a small copse with what appeared a wayside shrine beside it. "Take cover there: I'll tell Salvatore to look out for it and to come to you there. And I'll warn him to keep an eye out for whoever is chasing us."

With that, he sprang into the saddle, no longer disguising his expert horsemanship, and galloped away towards Bologna.

Chapter 31

Giacomo and I set ourselves to the task of moving Tommaso who was lying face down on the ground, that dreadful arrow still protruding from his back. Knowing that he could not keep his seat on horseback, we laid him across the saddle, each clumsy movement causing him more pain, though he could do no more than groan. When it was done, I did my best to spread dirt and stones to hide his blood that had made a dark pool on the ground, hoping that any pursuers would, in their haste, miss the signs that we had stopped there. Next we led the horse slowly up towards the copse that Paolo had indicated. There we concealed ourselves and waited.

Sure enough, it was not long before we saw to the west a cloud of dust rising on the road, indicating a group of horsemen travelling at speed. Soon we heard them, and could count them as they galloped past us on the road. There must have been eight or ten of them, heavily armed and determined. I prayed that Paolo's horse would not let him down and that Salvatore would be keeping excellent fresh mounts for him.

Then there was nothing to do but wait: and it must have been three hours or more before Salvatore arrived. To my delight he brought not only two horses but also a cart. I surmised that he had stolen it, but he was indignant. "No need to steal," he retorted. "Money talks!" Again I marvelled at the preparations made for this adventure of which I had been entirely unaware.

Gently the three of us lifted Tommaso into the cart. He stirred and moaned, as we moved him, but did not speak. His breathing was shallow but even, and I could only pray with a fervour that I had not rediscovered since I had been a small child that God and his angels would preserve my friend and bring him back to me. We hitched my horse to the back of the wagon, Salvatore mounted his and Giacomo climbed into the wagon beside Tommaso. "Take care of him, boys. Don't let him die," I whispered. As they set off, keeping to the back lanes at first but vowing to return to the main road if all seemed safe, in order to get Tommaso to help all the more quickly, I turned my fresh horse in the opposite direction and headed back towards Modena, pushing my mount as hard as I could - or as it would let me.

As I approached Modena I kept my distance, skirting it and keeping well to the south of it, yet always in view, until I found myself on its western side. I looked for the landmarks that Tommaso had outlined to me the previous evening. The convent was easy to find, the sisters working in the fields on the backbreaking labour of ploughing the fields before winter set in. I found the lane to the right, and the small bridge that Tommaso had described, and very soon I was trotting down a gentle slope to what I guessed must be the farm belonging to Cortino, the bailiff of Umberto Uguzzoni and a man I had vowed to kill if he had laid a finger on Rosalia.

A sense of foreboding made me approach cautiously. Any arrival on horseback is a noisy business, so I dismounted, tethered my mount to a tree a little way from the farm and walked apprehensively towards it. The first building I reached was a byre, which I used for cover. Peering round the corner I could see a farmyard, which was much like any other. Chickens scratched around in the dirt, and in a pen to my right a few pigs rooted in the mud. Ahead of me was a large barn, bigger than anything I had seen on the poor smallholding that Tommaso's family rented. Perhaps this was where the bailiff stored the crops and tithes for his master – or, more likely, where he hid the goods that he extorted for himself.

Just as I began to fear that no one was around, almost enjoying a sense of relief, I heard a commotion. Round the corner of the barn ran a young woman, pursued by three men. She was gasping for breath, her face contorted with fear. Her shift was old, dirty and ragged, her feet bare. Her face was filthy, and her hair dark and matted. Even so, there was no mistaking her. It was Rosalia, Tommaso's sister: older, grown to womanhood, but nonetheless the Rosalia I remembered and, I realised with a pang, whom I still loved.

Three men followed her round the corner, rough, oafish and roaring with laughter. They soon caught up with her. One seized her from behind, clamping his arms round her waist and nuzzling her ear. "Come on, my pretty. What about a kiss?" She made no answer, but grunted as she tried to pull away, without success. Why did she not scream? Was that not what a woman did to save herself from unwanted attention? From the look of hopelessness on her face I could guess why she made no sound: she knew that no help would come, no matter how much noise she might make.

The hands moved to her chest. "Nice tits. I like a good pair of tits. Let's have a look at them." His hands moved again to grip the front of her flimsy shift and tear it open. The other two, who had been standing back and watching, roared with laughter, each seizing part of her pathetic garment which was torn from her in an instant so that she stood bared before them, the man behind her still holding and kneading her breasts.

"Don't keep her to yourself!" laughed one of the others. "Pass her around!" At this Rosalia wriggled all the more in the firm grasp of her captor, which was suddenly released as he pushed, almost threw, her across to his companions. She was tossed from one to the other, each groping her a little before passing her on. Again and again: until she spun round on one of them and raked her nails down his face, drawing blood. "Bitch!" he yelled, clutching his left hand to his cheek while, with the right, he fetched her a mighty blow to the head. Down she went, bouncing off the wall of the barn as she fell. "Bitch," he muttered again. "You hold her down, lads. We'll have her in turn. And then," he continued, as he unbuttoned his breeches, "Then I'll take my belt to her and teach her a lesson."

They all laughed again. The other two held her arms firmly down on the ground. Rosalia moaned and whispered with a whimper, "Please."

As I watched in mounting horror, it seemed I had become rooted to the spot. Yet now, as the first man spread Rosalia's legs while she struggled to no avail, held firmly by the two men on her arms and shoulders, I was sprinting across the farmyard towards the group who, in that instant, appeared as if frozen in a grotesque tableau.

I do not think I planned my attack: indeed, I was driven by rage. Yet it was a cold kind of fury, not the maddened, crazed sort that Sordello had almost literally beaten out of me as an emotion that would put me at risk. Moreover, Michele had also taught me well, his lessons painstaking and thorough, if exasperating. So intent on his victim was the would-be rapist that he never heard me coming. The other two men could only look up at me as I seized him by the head, my left hand on the back of it, my right under his jaw. I pulled back and up and twisted his head to the left. As he grunted in surprise I jerked upwards, flinging him to my left.

There was a click as his neck broke, and he fell away, twitching, his breeches around his knees, his erection still grotesquely evident.

In an instant, the other two were on their feet. These were men evidently accustomed to violence, and too quick for me. Immediately one had pinioned my arms behind my back while the second struck me across the jaw, making my head ring and jarring my nose into intense agony. Next he punched me in the stomach once, twice. I doubled over as far as I could and my attacker grinned, preparing to put all his strength into a blow to my head. I used the other's grip on my arms to give me purchase as I swung both feet up and kicked him in the face. With a howl he collapsed while, surprised and unbalanced by my sudden movement, the man behind me released his grip and fell backwards.

I was first to my feet, leapt to the man I had felled and kicked him hard in the stomach, then in the face. Again I kicked him, and again until, his face a bloody mess, he appeared to lose consciousness.

If I had disabled another of my enemies, I was reminded of my remaining opponent by an arm circling my throat, while my head was hammered repeatedly against the barn wall. I flailed my arms but could not shift his grip. The blood roared in my ears, and I knew I would soon black out. I reached for my knife with my right hand, but could not get my hand to it. Desperately I tried to gain some purchase to loosen that vice on my throat, knowing that my efforts were futile and my time limited.

Suddenly the grip was relaxed. A grunt came from behind me. Next the weight of a body fell against me as my assailant collapsed to the ground. I turned and, in amazement, saw Rosalia, naked, filthy, panting and gripping in her hands a great log with which she had knocked my adversary senseless.

We stared at one another silently, breathing heavily. She did not release her grip on her weapon, perhaps wondering whether her rescuer might simply take the place of the men he had disabled or killed and seek to take advantage of her vulnerability. We stood, and we stared.

Eventually I managed to break the silence. "Rosalia," I said quietly.

"Who...? Is it? Luca, is it you?"

I had forgotten I was wearing that damned mask! As I had done when I met her brother, I reached behind me and undid the leather thongs. "Yes, Rosalia. It is I. I'm sorry about the mask: I, I broke my nose, you see." I laughed.

She laughed in response. It was an absurd situation. Two childhood friends meeting again, years later: the woman subjected to a vicious assault, naked and clutching a club; the boy she had known, now a man, a killer in a grotesque mask. There was little to do except to laugh.

What did I expect? I suppose that, ever since I had first begun to formulate a plan for rescuing her, I had pictured Rosalia throwing herself into my arms in gratitude to her saviour. And how would she show her gratitude? To a young man, constantly thinking of girls and the act of love, the encounter had always played out in a similar fashion as I had run over it time and again in my mind.

But I had not planned this outcome: one man dead; another covered in blood and groaning on the ground; the third unconscious; a naked girl, shivering and terrified, her modesty torn away, violated and so nearly ravished. It was not the kind of rescue that storytellers describe. It was sordid, mean, squalid: and in witnessing it, even saving her from the worst of it, I felt myself demeaned and even guilty. There was another silence. Again I broke it. "Rosalia. I came for you. Tommaso sent me."

"Luca. Why? Where is Tommasino?"

I did not know where to start. "He... he couldn't come. I had to come alone. I – and I'm not Luca. At least, that's not my name now. Now I'm Lorenzo. There's... so much to tell you. But we must go. We must get away from here."

She looked down at herself. "Luca. Lorenzo: I have no clothes."

Embarrassed, I realised I was trying to look at her, and yet not to do so, all at the same time. I was ashamed for the girl I loved, had pictured all those years and honoured in my mind. Yet the curiosity, the sheer lust of a young man, was irresistible. I could not help but drink in the sight of that body. Inspiration struck me. "I have a spare shirt in my saddlebag. It may serve as a shift for you."

"A spare shirt?" A hint of her old smile crossed her begrimed, bruised face. "My, Lorenzo, you have risen in the world!"

"Come," I ordered. "We must go." I held out my hand and, dropping her club, she took it.

A bellow of anger interrupted us. We found ourselves confronted by a fourth man. He was much shorter than I but stocky, bald on top with long, lank hair down the sides and dressed in a greasy jerkin. In his right hand he held a billhook, its wickedly curved blade, so perfectly designed for reaping corn at harvest, glittering dangerously in the sunlight. "Who the fuck are you? And where do you think you're going with my whore?"

"You're Cortino," I said, realising in an instant who he must be, and how apt his nickname - Shorty - was. "And Rosalia is not your whore." The determination and courage that Rosalia had shown earlier seemed to desert her. She cowered, and hid herself behind me.

"Cortino," I said again. "You cheated her parents. Took Rosalia into bondage when you had no right to. The law forbids it, and you know it. If you've laid a finger on her..." I felt her stiffen behind me, her hand on my shoulder grip tightly and then loosen, as she slipped away from me. Without looking at her I knew. "Christ, you have. You bastard. You disgusting, cheating, raping piece of shit." As Rosalia shrank further away from me, I drew my knife. Cortino and I circled one another. "I'll slice off your balls and feed them to your pigs," I said.

"I don't know who you are, sonny, but it's you who'll be missing some bits of you." He gestured threateningly with the sickle and then swung it at me. Easily I stepped back out of his reach. He stepped forward and swung again. Again I stepped back, but this time I pretended to stumble: it was the oldest trick in the book, and he fell for it. As he leapt at me I dived forward, rolled inside his reach, seized his right wrist with my left hand and jabbed the point of my knife into his forearm so that he screamed and dropped his weapon.

237

I could have killed him then. I should have done. But I wanted more satisfaction than that afforded by a quick knife-thrust to his heart. I grabbed his jerkin and drove him back against the wall of the barn. I held the point of my blade to his throat, a position in which I had found myself too many times. "So now, Cortino, what were you going to do to me?" It was the remark of a bully, of somebody who had the upper hand: but I hated this man with a passion, had loathed the name and my mental picture of him ever since I had heard about him from Rosalia's parents and seen the grief in their eyes.

"It, it was only a joke, sir. I didn't mean any harm, not to a young gentleman like yourself. And the girl. You can have her. She's no use anyway. You take her, sir. Beat some sense into her."

"You don't understand, do you, Cortino? Animals like you never do. She's my friend. I knew her as a little girl, in a happy family. Before you tore all that apart with your greed, your cheating. And then you took her, and..."

"I meant no harm, sir. It's the way of the world. They don't pay me enough: I have to take what I can get."

"I should kill you now," I said.

"Please, sir, no." His voice was shrill now, his tone wheedling. I looked down, and could see his breeches were wet. In his terror he had soiled himself. Suddenly I felt sickened, disgusted by the scene around me, by what Cortino had done, and by what I had become. I no longer wanted to neuter this man, evil and venal as he was. I did not even want to kill him. I was nauseated by all of it – most of all by my own violence and blood-lust.

I may have loosened my grip on him. Perhaps he sensed that my resolve had weakened. Suddenly he pushed me away from him so that I stumbled and dropped my knife. Then he was on his knees, scrabbling for his billhook. He got quickly to his feet, kicked my knife away from me and stood still, and evil smile on his face. "Tricky young bastard, aren't you? I'd like to geld you, you young pup, and make you watch while I have my way again with this baggage – though there's more pleasure in shagging a cow. But you're quick, I'll give you that: so I'll just tear your guts out and kill you now."

I backed away, hands at my side, poised to take advantage of any slip he might make, but aware that most likely I was about to meet my end watching my entrails slowly empty themselves onto the dusty ground. Then a voice spoke behind me: "Step aside, Luca. I'll deal with this pig." Instinctively I obeyed, and stepped to my right. I turned and saw Rosalia holding a pitchfork like a spear, its wicked twin, long points pointing horizontally at Cortino.

He tried to laugh. "You won't use that, girl. Put it down and I'll be gentle when I have you. Don't be..." She lunged at him, her whole weight behind her improvised weapon. The prongs pierced his belly, and he screamed. He flailed his billhook, but uselessly: he could not reach his nemesis, the girl pushing harder and harder so that blood spurted from his back as the spikes emerged. He stumbled backwards as she kept thrusting until he was forced against a densely-packed pile of straw. Again Cortino screamed, and Rosalia pulled the fork out of his guts, only to plunge it into him again. And again. Finally she drove it still harder, grunting with the effort, so that the points protruded once more from his back and into the straw behind.

We left him there, the kicking and scrabbling of his legs marking his death-agony as he stood, pinned vertical by the pitchfork. His screams turned to entreaties as we walked away. I think he begged us to finish him quickly. But I did not turn back: I could not.

I took her hand in mine as we walked, but we did not speak. We did not even look at one another.

We walked on.

Chapter 32

We walked up the lane to where I had left my horse. Wordlessly I reached into my saddlebag and pulled out my spare shirt. Rosalia slipped it over her head, pulling her hair, dirty and greasy, unrecognisable as the intense red colour that I remembered, so that it fell in a heavy lump down her back. She laced the shirt at her neck and, looking down, saw that it fell below her knees. Modesty was restored.

Heavily I spoke at last. "I'll take you home." This time I could not manage to heave myself unaided into the saddle. After a few attempts, at which Rosalia could not hide her smile, I felt less than ever like a heroic knight riding to her rescue: I had to ask her to cup her hands and provide a step up for me. Finally I succeeded in sliding my complaining thigh over the saddle, took my seat and pulled her up behind me. Her hands gripped my waist, tentatively at first and then, as if finding comfort from holding on, more confidently. We headed north.

I urged my horse to a canter, partly out of sheer prudence in order to put distance between us and an episode which had left two men for dead and two wounded, and partly to get away as quickly as possible from the screams and moans of the dying Cortino. After a while we slowed to a walk and, as our mount ambled along, I found the courage to ask Rosalia, whose slim arms still encircled my waist, how she came to be in the predicament from which (more by good fortune than by any planning or skill) I had contrived to save her.

"It was that pig Cortino," she said after a pause. "When I left my parent's house and went to work for him, I knew what would happen. But what else could I do? Cortino would have returned with men and thrown my parents and sisters off the farm. What would they do then, except starve? Oh," she continued bitterly, "It started well enough. He promised that all he wanted was for me to work for him: that he needed another pair of hands around the farm. His wife was a hard-bitten shrew, and happy to have me slaving for her, for no thanks and precious little food. And so it continued for a couple of weeks.

"Then Cortino started grabbing me when his wife was out of sight, groping my body with those big, dirty hands of his. He'd come up behind me and kiss my neck: I could smell his stinking breath. He'd grab me, you know, between the legs, in all those places... Then he'd say things like, 'Come into the barn. Let's have a cuddle in the hay.' I'd tell him to get lost, that I had to work for him but I didn't have to lie with him.

"Eventually he became angry, told me that he owned me, that I was no better than a slave, and if I didn't please him he would give me to his men to enjoy, and then sell me in the market." She broke off and I could hear her weeping. The arms around my waist shook as her grief wracked her body. I wished I could turn around, at least look at her and provide some comfort: but perhaps it was easier for her this way. She could tell her story and share her feelings without having to look me in the eye.

"You don't have to tell me, you know," I said gently after a while.

"I want to. Oh, Luca – I mean, it's Lorenzo now, isn't it?" I nodded. "I'll try to remember." She continued: "I'm not sure I can tell anyone else. I cannot tell my parents." This realisation brought more tears. Eventually she regained some measure of composure, and continued speaking. "At last Cortino wouldn't accept any more refusals. One day, as I defied him once again, he lashed out and hit me. I was stunned: I know I fell over. I didn't really know what was happening but, when I came to my senses properly, I was bent over a rail in the byre, my hands roped to the hay stall in front. Then I heard him. I looked over my shoulder, and there he was, naked from the waist down, laughing at me. I begged him not to do it, but he pulled up my shift, right up to my shoulders and took me. Took me from behind, like an animal.

"I screamed and begged, but it was no use. And when he'd had me, taken my maidenhead, he left me there, exposed. I don't know how long I was there before he released me: he left me, alone with my shame, for what seemed like hours. I was afraid someone would come, scared that others would see me."

I tried to choose my words carefully, wanting to know the rest of her story, yet nervous of intruding into her shame and grief. "How did... today come about, then? You don't have to tell me," I repeated hastily.

"You might as well know the rest. It cannot be any worse. After that first time he reckoned he could have me any time he wanted. He beat me when I resisted, and I could not keep fighting forever. Besides, he'd robbed me of my virginity. What was there left to protect? So I decided instead that I wouldn't react. I stopped cleaning myself, never dressed my hair. I'm dirty and smelly. I saw how you looked at me: you found me repulsive." I began to protest, but she stopped me. "You know you did, Lu – Lorenzo. I *made* myself disgusting.

"I felt dirty through and through: so I made sure I became the filthy slattern he took me for and, when he forced himself on me, I didn't respond. I just lay there. He hated that. He wanted me to be grateful or, at least, to fight him. When I would not do either, he complained that it was like fucking a sack of grain." Involuntarily I stiffened at her use of the word. She used it to show the depth of her misery was, how raw was the hurt. She must have sensed my reaction, for we rode on in silence for some time.

After a while she spoke again. "I'm sorry, Lorenzo. Did I shock you?"

"Shock me? It is not you who shocks me. I don't know how that animal could behave in that way, how any man could."

Her right hand moved from my waist to my neck and caressed my cheek. "Dear Lorenzo. You're so sweet. I don't think you're like other men. That's why I feel safe with you, I suppose." Safe? I guess she *was* safe with me. My head was a turmoil of conflicting thoughts. As she told her heartrending story, I felt nothing but pity for the girl I remembered from childhood and whom I still loved. Yet, even in these bizarre circumstances, I felt a degree of arousal, hot-blooded and confused young man that I was, and even some jealousy towards Cortino who had possessed the girl who had often been in my lascivious thoughts – when they were not dominated by Livia Lambertazzi.

There was another long, pained silence. Then, before I could prompt her, Rosalia started speaking again. "After a few weeks of this, Cortino lost patience. He said he might as well be shagging a cow, and said he'd give me to his men to see if that would wake my ideas up. I didn't know if it was meant as a threat, to make me respond to him. So, as always, I gave no reaction. He got angry and hit me: though that was nothing new.

"I didn't see him for a couple of days: he was off collecting rents and tithes. And those three came looking for me. They'd always had their eye on me, but never laid a finger on me when they knew Cortino was using me. He must have told them they could have me. So they were just beginning to have their sport with me," she laughed bitterly, "when... when you came for me."

There was another painful silence. In a very small voice she continued. "Thank you... Lorenzo. I'm glad it was you. I couldn't bear anyone else to see my shame. But you're so good, and kind..."

She would have continued, but I cut in viciously. "Good? I left you and your family to all – that. I forgot about you while I was living my exciting life in Bologna. How is that good? I damage everything, everyone dear to me. Even Tommaso."

I regretted the words as soon as I spoke them. "Tommaso? What do you mean? What have you done to him?"

"I haven't done anything," I replied heavily. "But I've brought harm to him. Because of me, someone has hurt him and, Rosalia," this time it was my voice breaking in misery: "I think I left him dying."

"You left him dying? You left him?"

"Not like that. He's with two good friends of mine and, if they can get him to Bologna in time, and to a physician, they will. I fear they won't be in time. Yet I had to leave him: he *made* me. He made me promise to leave him, to come and find you – because he was afraid for you. So you see: whatever I do is wrong. It always is." Now it was my turn to feel the wetness on my cheeks. Her hands tightened around my waist, silently giving comfort.

We found ourselves fording a small river. It was not deep, merely reaching the horse's hocks, but it was enough to seize Rosalia's attention, and change her mood. "Stop, Lorenzo. Stop the horse. I need to get down."

I presumed that she needed to relieve herself, so I was about to turn away politely, but she seized my knee and looked up into my face. "Lorenzo, I'm going to bathe. Wash the filth of Cortino and his men from my body. Promise me you won't peep."

Surprised, and then resigned, I nodded miserably. "You see," this time she managed to smile: "I said you were safe. You don't know how good it is to have you as my protector. But please don't look."

Glumly I spurred my horse up the slope from the river and dismounted in turn. I sat on a stone beside the track we'd been following for an hour and more, and stared northwards. Behind me I could hear her splashing in the water: I thought she was even humming a tune, though I could not make it out. The sun was out, glistening on the stubble of the harvested fields. There was an autumn chill in the air, and I wondered how Rosalia could stay in the water so long, but guessed she was relishing the chance to wash all the dirt and the memories from her body, hoping it would do the same for her mind.

After what seemed an age, her voice came from close behind me: with her bare feet she had made no sound approaching. "That's better!" she commented. I turned. My shirt, soaked, clung suggestively to her body. Her hair, wet and plastered down her back, had nonetheless already regained some of its previous luxuriance. Her left eye was discoloured and starting to close from where one of her would-be rapists had struck her. But her lips were as full and red as I remembered, and she looked better, and more like the Rosalia I had so often called to mind. Yet my memories were of a girl, not of this fully grown, intensely desirable woman.

She was entirely different from Livia, the only other female body I had seen in my young life. Where Livia's had been slight and pale, built delicately as if of fine porcelain, Rosalia's figure could have grown from the fecund earth whose produce I had shared with her when we were children. The slimness of her waist was emphasised by the generous swelling of her chest and hips above and below it. There was an abundance in her form that would have appealed to any man: they captivated me. And I wanted her.

As I looked at her - no, I stared at her - she blushed under my appraising glance. Then I noticed that she was shivering. I reached to the saddle and seized my cloak which I had thrown roughly across it as we made our escape from Cortino's farmstead. "I've been so thoughtless. Put this on." Gratefully she pulled it around her, arranging her hair on the outside of it. "I'm still cold," she murmured. "Will you just hold me, Lorenzo? Please?"

I pulled her close to me, and hugged her tight. My mind was a whirl of conflicting thoughts. This beautiful young woman, so often in my thoughts recently, was in my arms. I had seen her body, all its charms revealed: yet soiled and abused. Certainly I desired her: I could feel my body responding to that need, a young man's lust. At the same time there was a sense of revulsion, which made me feel ashamed. For she was no longer, could never be, the virginal beauty of whom I had dreamed. Nonetheless she was still Rosalia, the girl I had wanted so much to hold in my arms, to rescue from danger, to protect.

Perhaps she sensed my confusion. She pulled away and said curtly, "Thank you, Lorenzo. I'm warmer now. Let us go on."

As we rode on, I told her more of what had brought me to Modena. I confessed how, not entirely unwittingly, we had drawn her brother into conspiracy and then into danger and serious injury. "There is a crumb of comfort," she responded quietly. "If it's as you say, if Tommaso did find something – though I don't understand all this talk of the law - then perhaps they'll come from Bologna for Uguzzoni. And we'll be free of him. As we are of Cortino now," she added harshly.

"I hope so," I replied, trying to banish from my head the picture of the bailiff twitching and screaming, impaled on that pitchfork as his life ebbed away.

Eventually we emerged from the track we were following onto a slightly larger one, and I recognised the road that would take us to our destination, the house where Rosalia, Tommaso and the family had known simple happiness, even amid poverty, until their lives had been devastated. We came to that little rise from which I knew we would see the farm across the valley. From behind, Rosalia put her left hand on mine. "Stop here, Lorenzo. Set me down. I shall walk now."

"But I'll take you there, Rosalia," I responded in surprise. "I'll take you back to your parents. I promised Tommaso I would."

"I'm safe now, Lorenzo. It's... it's better if I go back alone. This will be hard for my parents, my father particularly."

I was nonplussed. "You don't have to tell them everything," I said. "After all, I arrived in time to save you from those three. You can tell them that. They don't have to know about Cortino."

By now she was on the ground, standing and looking up at me with a wistful smile, the hair now almost dry, gleaming in the setting sun. "Do you think my mother will not know? As for my father, he will assume I lost my virtue from the moment I left them. It will not be easy." I looked into her eyes, at a loss. I had not become self-congratulatory, but I had felt some satisfaction in having been able to save her. Now it seemed an empty victory. "Don't be sad, Lorenzo." She put her hand on mine. "I'll always be grateful. You did save me, you know. From the worst, if not from all of it. And you didn't know: how could you?

"Go back to Bologna. Go to Tommaso: don't let him die. I won't tell my parents he's hurt. Send word if you can: if not, I'll understand."

"Rosalia," I could barely speak. But then the words came out in a rush. "Rosalia. If ever you need me: you can find me in Bologna. Just ask for the lawyer's house, the woman lawyer. Down by the river, the Idice. Everyone knows her."

She shook her head. She was sure she would never call on my help in that mighty city, so alien to her. "Thank you, Lorenzo. Thank you for everything. Goodbye. Live well, and be happy."

It was the most final farewell I had ever heard, more absolute even than Livia's dismissal of me in the dungeon. Her hand started to slip away from mine: our fingers touched, then our fingertips. She turned away, and, shoulders back and head high, she walked briskly up the hill that would take her to within sight of her parents' house. She looked back once and then strode on, my cloak wrapped tight around her.

She was humming again, and then broke into full voice as she disappeared from sight, departing from my life. Now I could hear the melody, even the words of the song from our youth that recalled to me our shared love and happiness, *Ti canterò lo meo amor.*

I felt my heart would break. For an age, an eternity, I stared at the road she had taken, now as empty as I felt my soul to be. After what seemed an age, I wiped my eyes, turned my horse around and, with the setting sun on my back, kicked it to a canter towards Bologna.

Chapter 33

The setting sun of the next day was on my back as I rode into Bologna's western gate. When I had left Rosalia the previous day there was little more than an hour's daylight left, and in the dusk I managed to lose my way before giving up the battle and paying excessively for shelter in a farmstead. I slept little in the barn, not least because I distrusted the shifty looks exchanged between the farmer and his wife, and feared robbery or worse in the night.

Bone-weary and tired of the countryside, its villainies and its lack of creature comforts (what an incorrigible city-dweller I had become!), I felt a sense of relief on arriving in Bologna. The streets were busy as always, and I urged my mount through the crowded thoroughfares, desperate to see whether my friend was alive. This time the *gonfalonieri* guarding my master's house recognised me and let me through, one of them moving to hold my horse as I tumbled from the saddle and rushed into the courtyard. "Where is he? Is he here? Where's Tommaso?"

The voice of the Magister, sharp yet calm as ever, came from above, from the little balcony outside her chamber. "Be at peace, Lorenzo. He is here, and he is alive – if barely. Calm yourself and come up quietly."

I did neither: As I leapt up the steps she met me at the top, blocking my way. "Calm!" she said. Putting her hands on my arms (she could barely reach my shoulders), she declared, "I am pleased to see you. So pleased, Lorenzo. I have sent you and your friends into too much peril. Now one has paid a heavy price: yet still I hope the physician may save him. Come in – but quietly."

I just restrained myself from pushing her aside and followed her inside. Tommaso lay on his back: she had given him her own bed. He was deathly pale, his breathing fainter even than when I'd left him. But he was alive, and apparently sleeping peacefully.

"His wound has been treated. The physician," she nodded to the robed man kneeling beside the bed, his ear close to Tommaso's mouth as he listened to his breathing.

The physician stood and bowed to me. I returned his greeting awkwardly. "You did well to get him to us quickly, sir. Your friends have told me how you insisted on speed."

"It was nothing to do with me," I burst out. "His injury is my responsibility, not the business of transporting him to you: that was their doing. Will he live? Tell me!"

"He is very weak, having lost much blood. Yet we have removed the arrow and cleaned the wound. We have dressed it with salves and clean linen, and I believe it will heal. If he survives this night, when he is at his weakest, I believe he will live. In the meantime there is no more we can do: except to pray for him."

"Is there nothing I can do?" I reached to take his left hand. "Tommasino. Forgive me."

"It is as I said. There is nothing you can do. He will not know you, even should he awaken. This will be his night of crisis. Your master and I will stay with him, but he must have quiet."

My master intervened. "Come, Lorenzo. You must tell me what happened, though naturally I know most of it from your friend Paolo. And we must talk of the letter he brought, that Tommaso risked so much to obtain. Come. We will go down."

Back in the courtyard we entered the large room, once a store, where Michele, Mamolo and I slept and where we ate, when I was not attending my master. She sat me at the rough oak table, and gestured to Mamolo to bring food and drink. She would not let me speak until I had fed myself, and then told me what she had learned from Paolo – which was, in effect, the whole story.

True to his word, he had brought the letter, and the other papers from Tommaso's satchel. Meanwhile, Giacomo and Salvatore had made what haste they could with the wagon bearing Tommaso whose life, the closer they came to Bologna, appeared to ebb away. The physician was waiting for them, having been summoned on Paolo's arrival, and congratulated them on the speed with which they had brought his patient. They were just in time, he opined, for him to cauterise and dress the wound, staunching the flow of blood and minimising the risk of *gangraena* setting in and ending his life, if the loss of blood did not do it first.

Learning that my friends had left for their respective homes, I recounted my tale to my master. Naturally I spared her some of the details of Rosalia's humiliation, though I was sure she could picture the harsh reality. On hearing that Rosalia had felled one of her attackers and slain Cortino, whom we had left to die, she raised an eyebrow. "A girl of some spirit, then," she remarked dryly.

"A girl whose spirit has been crushed and destroyed," I replied. "What kind of world do we make where someone can be treated so?"

"A world that is better than it would be if people such as you and I did not try at least to address some of its wrongs," she said quietly. "Remember that: we do make a... *difference*, when we can. That is all that we can hope to do."

I fell silent, preoccupied with my own thoughts. I remembered that I had not even asked what was in the letter that seemed likely to cost Tommaso his life. Would it provide the proof we needed of Lambertazzi's planned treachery to his city, and his conspiracy with the Archbishop of Modena and his associate Umberto Uguzzoni? "The letter, Magister. Is Lambertazzi condemned by his own words?" I enquired.

My master made a face. "It is a... *suggestion*, certainly, but little more, I fear. Even when he does commit to writing, that weasel is extremely cautious. Here: you may see for yourself, though it may test your juristic Latin." She pushed the document across the table towards me. As I thought of Tommaso fighting for his life upstairs, and likely to lose that battle, I prayed that it would be at least worth such risk and loss. Then I read it aloud to my master, translating as I went. Under happier circumstances I might have been pleased with my attempt at an unseen translation: but I had little appetite for pleasure in anything at that moment.

"It is very formal," was my first comment. My master nodded and encouraged me to continue. "To His Eminence the Cardinal Archbishop of Modena." I paused: "I don't believe he was either an archbishop or a cardinal when I left Modena."

"He has powerful friends, Lorenzo: and he has, as they say, done well for himself. Continue."

I read on. "As agreed between our... agents," the writing was not as clear as mine, and some words were hard to decipher, "The bearer of this letter brings to you a sum in silver to the value of four thousand Bolognese Lire. Trusting in your loyalty to our... this is rather flowery Latin, Magister, isn't it?"

She smiled. "It is: he enjoys shaping compliments – or, at least, his notary does, since I doubt that Signor Lambertazzi reads or writes himself. In effect it is saying, 'Trusting in your loyalty to our just cause and to the probity of a man of God...' You may continue."

"... man of God, I ask you to pass one half of the sum remitted (two thousand Lire) to our mutual friend when you are satisfied that the designated goods have been despatched to its destination.

"Upon your assurance that the agreed number of armed men are prepared, equipped and ready to march when called upon, with my summons I shall send to you by the same messenger a further ten thousand Lire of which you will retain two thousand to defray your costs, passing eight to our friend to meet his.

"As friend to my cause and as trusted intermediary, I hope you will accept these poor gifts. Then comes another string of compliments. It ends: written in the hand of *Notaro* Oseletti," I interrupted my reading. "Isn't that the jurist you always describe as an idiot, Magister?" She nodded and grunted. I continued: "And signed by the hand of – my God it's Bartolomeo Bardi: that bastard even incriminates himself for his master! Under the seal of Massimo Lambertazzi."

I looked her in the eye. "Magister, is this sufficient proof? That he is really planning to overthrow the authority of Bologna, bringing in an army from Modena?"

She sighed. "Alas, Lorenzo, it is circumstantially compelling: but not, I fear, hard proof. Nonetheless I shall take it to the Capitano del Popolo, who must learn of it."

"And what of the Gatekeeper? Can he make anything of it? Or act on it?"

She paused. "It is in the... *nature* of the Gatekeeper to accumulate and weigh all such evidence, and he will be... *informed*." She was even more evasive than usual. "But it is as I say: on its own this letter will create suspicion, but not prove guilt of conspiracy. Damn him to hell!" she exclaimed with sudden vehemence. "It is ever thus with Lambertazzi, indeed with all that clan. But he will not like its contents made public. When the Two Thousand meet, this letter may be of greater value to us as a bargaining counter than as hard evidence. We shall have to make what use of it we can: and we shall certainly do better by exaggerating its importance and thereby weakening Lambertazzi's position than by sharing it in its entirety and revealing the paucity of its contents."

She saw that my face had fallen. "I am sorry, Lorenzo. It is a… *help*, but does not give us all the answers. I hope that, with cunning, we may make more of it than it truly represents, discomfit our enemies and thus render it worth your friend's... *sacrifice*."

"Sacrifice?" I was angry. "If it is Tommaso's sacrifice, then it was I who dragged him to the altar and honed the knife for the job."

She put her hand on my arm. "It is not played out, yet, Lorenzo. Do not characterise yourself as the Patriarch Abraham. Besides, even he, having been prepared to prove his faith by sacrificing his son Isaac, was saved at the last from wielding the knife. Tommaso may yet recover: the physician – and you know he is the best in Bologna – will not leave until the outcome is assured. Have faith and be strong: with care and not a little cunning, we may yet make more of this piece of evidence than, on the face of it, it… *purports* to tell."

But I was not yet ready to have faith. I pulled my arm away from her, rudely, and stood up. "It is all my fault. If he dies... I will have to go and tell his family... and Rosalia. Christ's blood! I've brought them enough grief."

"You have brought them nothing of the kind." Her voice was imperious now, austere. "Lorenzo, I admire your humanity and your compassion: but I will not permit you to indulge your tendency to self-pity. You have done no wrong to that family and, if you coerced Tommaso to some extent to obtain this letter, you repaid him in full by rescuing his sister from her... *servitude*. You risked your life in doing it – just as he risked his for you.

"That is what friends do, and also those who search after right, as we are doing. The scales of justice do not weigh precisely in such circumstances. We can only make one decision at a time, always seeking the righteous goal. And that we are still doing." She added still more edge to her voice. "So do not become maudlin and instead focus on what must be done next."

I was confounded. "I must think," I said and went out into the courtyard, hoping that the cool evening air would clear my head.

If I was hoping to regain a measure of composure in the courtyard, I was disappointed. Immediately there was a commotion at the gate. Michele roared that he was coming, and stumped across to it. There was a shout from outside: "Oi! You can't just barge in there!" The call was ignored by a small, blonde-haired figure who burst in through the door crying, "Lorenzo! I must see Lorenzo!"

Michele caught and held her firmly. Something in his calm, almost fatherly manner seemed to have an effect, because she immediately ceased struggling. "Now, young lady, calm down. What'th thith about?"

She took a deep breath. "Sir, my lady has sent me for help. I must see Lorenzo, whoever he is."

I stepped forward. "I'm Lorenzo," I said quietly. "But how would you know my name, except... Who sent you?"

She looked at me appraisingly. Meanwhile I took in the young woman standing before me. She was poorly dressed in a plain shift, and she seemed to have a piece of rope around her neck, like a collar. Was she a serf, then? I presumed she must be: yet for all her mean status, she had a quiet presence about her, and a sense of pride. She was clearly out of breath from running, and her breasts rose and fell with each deep breath, something my male eye could not help noticing under that thin garment.

253

"Sir, if you are Lorenzo, then you must know who sent me. I belong to the household of Signor Lambertazzi."

"So the Lady Livia sent you?" She certainly had my attention now. "Is she in need? Tell me: Why have you come?"

"Sir, she is in dire trouble, but I cannot tell you here, in front of all these people. May I speak to you privately?"

Behind me I heard a snort from my master. "Are we to have no peace?" she snapped. "It has been one interruption after another. Lorenzo, what is all this nonsense?"

Chapter 34

But I had taken the girl by the arm, and led her into the room where I had just been discussing strategy with my master. Then I closed the door, so that we were alone. "Now," I said to the girl. "Believe me, I am Lorenzo, the one you seek. Tell me, what news of the Lady Livia?"

"Oh sir," she said. "Let me explain. I am Laura, and I serve Signor Lambertazzi." A memory stirred at the back of my mind. A blonde girl – was the name familiar? I recalled a conversation about a kitchen slave whom Massimo Lambertazzi liked to bed.

"Laura, you say? Are you perhaps a - how shall I say? - a favourite of Signor Massimo Lambertazzi?"

She snorted in derision. "A favourite?" She laughed harshly. "If you mean does he take me to his bed, then you are right." She coloured. "But do not judge me, sir. An owned woman may not choose how her master uses her. He thinks me fair, and sometimes I consider putting my face into the fire so he no longer thinks so. But... I lack the courage." Her voice cracked.

"I'm sorry, Laura," I replied. "Of course I do not judge you: I have learned a little of the world. And you are pretty. I do not blame Lambertazzi for finding you attractive, though I vow that one day I'll kill that man for all the wrong he has done, including the way he has misused you."

"Oh sir," it was as if her tidings were bursting out of her. "He's about to do still more wickedness. Yes, he's a monster, and it is the Lady Livia to whom he will do harm."

At last we were coming to it. "Tell me," I urged. "Is she in danger?"

"Sir, she's the only one of that family who has ever shown me kindness. When she was younger, and I was only a few years older than her, I served her as maid and playfellow, before I was sent back to the kitchens - and summoned to the Signore's bed when it suits him. But she has always remained kind to me, when she could be. And now, now her uncle is determined to destroy her."

"Destroy her? How?" I demanded.

"It is your fault," she said. "Your fault entirely. I don't know how you have bewitched her, but she has done something foolish, and it's all connected with you. What else can I think but that you have some kind of hold over her?"

"I was imprisoned by Lambertazzi and Bardi," she made a face at the second name. "And it's true that the Lady Livia released me - though at the time she thought her part in my escape would not be discovered."

"I heard something of that, sir," she replied. "There was talk of a prized prisoner. I heard the Signore screaming at my lady that she had betrayed him and he would repay her in full. I did not know what that meant until my lady told me, just now. She was desperate, sir, and bade me find the lawyer's house down by the river and ask for you."

"I told her to send for me here," I explained. "If she ever needed me."

"She needs you now, sir. The Signore is going to give her to Bardi. She says he will give her to him, and insist he takes her by force. And then she will be married to him. But..." she faltered.

"What? Tell me what more."

"This evening, sir. I don't know fully what he plans. But it will happen tonight. And I think the two of them will shame her in some way. And then she will be Bardi's plaything, to do what he likes with. She will never escape that family."

"She told you all this? What does she want me to do? I'll do anything she asks, you know," I added, somewhat lamely.

"She just said that she had little time, that they would do it tonight after dinner, and she might as well end her life. But then she said to me, 'Go to Lorenzo. Tell him he said he would come for me: and now is the time.' They will punish me if they find I have come: they will take the skin off my back, for sure. But I risk this for my lady."

She reached out and took my hand, a bold action in a slave. "Do not let her down, sir. She is strong, the strongest person I have ever known. But this will destroy her. And I fear for her, I fear something worse than even she has imagined."

"What? How can it be worse?"

"Sir, Bardi is looking forward to taking her maidenhead tonight. She... I know she is no virgin. I think you may know that, sir, too." She looked me straight in the eye, so knowingly that I blushed and hung my head. "I thought so: though you were not the first. I fear that will make their vengeance still more terrible. Sir, you must rescue her. I don't know how: but she needs you, and you must get her away from that family."

"I will," I was instantly determined, on fire with passion and obsessed by the thought that the beautiful girl whom I had worshipped from afar and whose flesh I had known intimately was being given against her will to Bartolomeo Bardi, the man I detested almost as much as I hated his master, Massimo Lambertazzi. "But you will have to get me into the house: otherwise I will not get past the gate."

"I will, sir. I believe I can get you in. I know you serve the lady lawyer: can you perhaps bring some papers, a quill and some ink? I will convince them that you are a scribe come to do some work for another of the family. And you'll have to remove that mask if we are to fool them."

"Of course," I replied. I was not sorry to reach behind my head, untie the thong and discard the uncomfortable mask. Next I reached into the corner of that very room and seized the scrip I usually carried when assisting my master. "Let us go now."

I pulled open the door, and ushered Laura out into the courtyard. The members of the household, even the master and Sordello, had been crowding around the door, waiting to discover what was so urgent. "It's Livia," I said shortly. "Lambertazzi is giving her to Bardi, tonight. I'm going to save her."

"Don't be a damned idiot," retorted Sordello. "On your own? Back in that household? You're begging to lose your balls if you go back a second time – or your life."

I pushed him aside roughly. "It's no use arguing," I said. "She's called for my help. I have to go."

"Dear God!" I heard my master's voice behind me. "Is Lorenzo dashing off madly again? Someone stop the young fool!" But there was no stopping me. Pushing Laura ahead of me, I was out of the gate and we were hurrying up the road towards the Lambertazzi towers. I knew I left a commotion behind me, but I did not look back.

I was determined, and heedless of danger. Was it love that drove me? Or lust? Or just a foolish notion that I could play the hero, save the maiden and win her devotion? I fear it was a mixture of all three. Certainly I had no plan in my mind: sheer wild emotion drove me as we hastened along the street to our destination.

We swiftly reached the Lambertazzi towers and, in my headstrong determination to save Livia, I headed straight for the gate of the highest tower, the building in which I had twice been imprisoned. But Laura pulled me to one side. "Not that way," she whispered. "They are too watchful there. Besides, it is not in the Signore's tower that it will happen." We skirted the first tower and passed another until we reached the third of the four that comprised the Lambertazzi *consorteria*.

We gained entry without incident: the men on the gate took little interest in an earnest-looking scribe, hooded to shade my bruised face and waving my writing materials at them. Then we embarked on the laborious climb to the top of the tower. "This was where my lady's parents lived, when they were alive, the Signore's brother and his wife," announced my guide. "And it is where Bardi will live with his new bride – or whore." We must have reached the highest room, just below the roof, when at last Laura turned off the seemingly endless stairs. The apartment was richly furnished with a table, three or four stout, carved chairs, and a fine bed against one wall. It boasted rich hangings on its three sides, matching the tapestries that covered most of the walls. "Hide yourself here," she hissed. "They will bring her to this room. This is where they will do it, shame and entrap her. You must prevent it."

"But where can I hide in such a small room? Besides, what can I do against two strong men?" I was beginning to appreciate the enormity of what I had undertaken, and the near-impossibility of keeping my promise.

"How do I know?" she snapped, her ingrained subservience momentarily forgotten in her anxiety. "My lady seems to think you can work miracles. So work one!" She pushed me into a niche on one side of the room: there was a door which, I guessed, must lead onto one of the many wooden links between the towers.

"What if someone comes through this door?"

"They won't," she replied. "They rarely come from that tower. They'll bring her in through that door there," she nodded to a similar doorway on the other side of the room. "The Signore has been keeping her locked up in his own tower, which is how she could speak to me. I must go before I am missed." Again she looked me in the eye. "Do not fail my lady." And she was gone.

Once more I was left alone at the top of a Lambertazzi tower, without any clear idea of what to do. But this time I was not a prisoner: I was armed with my knife; and I was determined that no harm would come to the Lady Livia Lambertazzi, even if it cost me my life.

I laugh at my young self now, as all old people must do: laugh, or cringe in embarrassment, or perhaps a mixture of the two. But I was hot-blooded, in love with not one but two women, or at least with the idea of them; and, notwithstanding some of the ordeals I had already endured in my short life, I still possessed that bravura peculiar to the young that convinces them that they are somehow invulnerable.

It was not long before I heard a creaking sound from beyond the door in the next wall. I had crossed enough of those bizarre walkways between the towers of the great families to know that it signalled the arrival of at least one person, though the noisy complaint of the timbers suggested a significant weight. Sure enough, the door was flung open and crashed back against the wall of its niche. The great bulk of Massimo Lambertazzi, that central figure in my canon of hatred, heaved himself through the door. He was pulling something, or someone, behind him. Then I could see that he held in his right hand a rope tying two delicate, white female wrists, instantly revealed to me as belonging to Livia.

As always my heart leapt for passion and longing – and then in alarm for her, for he was indeed dragging her unwillingly into the room. Instead of one of the finely embroidered costumes in which I had always seen her previously, she was clad only in a thin shift, finely stitched, yet sheer and flimsy, almost transparent against the light of the window.

His captive fell to her knees, her hands perforce stretched out towards her uncle, who still grasped her bonds: yet it was also an attitude of supplication. "Please, Uncle. I beg you..."

"Enough!" I knew that voice and its tone of fury. Indeed, I had rarely heard any other tone but anger from that enormous body. "I have indulged you, Livia. I have pampered you, laughed at your whims and your airs, and loved you as a daughter. And this is how you repay me. I will not suffer treachery – not without retribution."

"But, Uncle." It was still recognisable as the voice I had heard, that of a spoilt and petulant child, yet now there was a hint of desperation added to it. "I did it for love of you. I feared that the lawyer would seek vengeance if you mutilated her servant. She is a dangerous woman: I feared for you, Uncle."

"You did nothing of the sort, Livia. I do not understand that strange mind of yours, but something made you let that boy go, in defiance of my wishes. Perhaps you desired him? Did you? Did you pleasure him? I hope you did not. For your sake I hope Bartolomeo finds you a virgin. I should not like him to be disappointed in his bride."

"Of course not, Uncle." I admired her coolness at that threat. "But Bardi? Why must it be him? I thought you would find me a suitor from one of the other great families."

"Because you have disappointed me, Livia. Because I can at one stroke reward my faithful servant and teach you the need for obedience. Besides, you should be honoured: he comes of a great family in Florence."

"And is an exile on account of his own treachery there. I will not marry him."

I could not clearly see what was happening from my hiding place, but I heard a smack as, I surmised, his right hand connected with her face. "Enough. You will do as I instruct you. And you will do your duty in giving pleasure to my friend and loyal counsellor Bartolomeo. If you do not," I could just see Livia from my hiding place, and now saw her uncle's right hand knotted in her hair as he pushed his face close to hers, "If not, I promise you this. You will wear a hempen collar and become a slave in the kitchens. And there you will oblige all the men who care to use you. You know I will do this, Livia. Do not defy me. "

There was no answer beyond a sob. It was clear that even Livia's repertoire of entreaties and manipulations had failed. "But if you please Bartolomeo, satisfy him and obey him, at the end of a month you shall be married. He will become a member of our family, you will be a dutiful wife, and no shame will come to you. Such is my forbearance: seize the opportunity I offer you for redemption."

There was a pause, the silence broken only by Livia's tears. Then Lambertazzi spoke again. "But first, there must be punishment." Again, Livia started to speak, to entreat, but was cut off. "There will be pain. Bartolomeo will assert his authority before he possesses you. He will tame you. You will learn a lesson. And I will see it done."

Chapter 35

Livia cried out as he dragged her further across the room and hauled her to her feet, still by the rope binding her wrists. Reaching to the bed, where the frame supporting its hangings was attached to the wall, he looped the rope around it. He was almost at full stretch so that, once her hands were secured, she was on tiptoe, stretched uncomfortably, helpless, entirely vulnerable.

Lambertazzi ran his hands down her back and felt the roundness of her bottom through the shift. His fury seemed to have left him, and his voice dropped to a contented rumble. "I had thought to enjoy you myself, to make that your punishment." Still he fondled her behind, stroking and feeling it with his enormous hands. "But such things are not good within families, and give rise to scandal. Besides, sometimes one must make sacrifices for a friend: and Bartolomeo will consider himself well rewarded. So, now we are ready for him."

Livia remained silent. Lambertazzi lumbered across to the door, opened it and bellowed down the stairs. "Laura! Here! Where is that blonde bitch?" he added, muttering to himself. Soon enough came the sound of her footsteps up the stairs. Breathless she entered the room, bobbed a curtsy and said, "I'm here, Signore."

What was I to do? When should I intervene? I stood, concealed, as if spellbound by this bizarre, horrific scene that seemed set to take on still more nightmarish proportions.

The door through which Lambertazzi and Livia had appeared opened again, and there was the other focus of my detestation, Bardi, dressed as always head-to-toe in black. He ignored the girl stretched against the wall, but bowed to Lambertazzi, who greeted him warmly.

"Ah, Bartolomeo. Here is the girl, my gift to you. I trust she will please you: she knows what will befall her if she fails."

Livia remained silent. "As always, Signore, you are excessively generous to me," Bardi replied with another bow, that oily, silky voice making me shiver as it always had.

"Nonsense, Bartolomeo. This is the least I can do for you. Yet," his tone changed to one of menace, "The girl must be punished before you have your pleasure. She must suffer for the wrong she has done, and learn obedience. She is ready. The whip is on the bed." Livia gave vent to a gasp of dismay, but Bardi seemed unaffected.

For the first time he turned to her. "Livia, beautiful lady," he murmured. "Your pain will hurt me, too. Yet a woman must understand who is her master, and it is my privilege to teach you that lesson." She said nothing as he put his hands to the hem of her shift and slowly lifted it up above her beautifully rounded bottom, to her shoulders and over her head, tucking it under her chin so that her entire body was exposed. Gently he ran his hand down her back to her buttocks. "Only a few moments of pain, my lovely one," he continued, "And then the pleasure of man and woman conjoined." His voice fell to a whisper, caressing her ear. "I have desired you for many years. This night will be memorable for both of us, when I show my love for you."

In a tiny voice, Livia whispered back: "If you love me, then why would you hurt me?"

"Because your uncle insists: and because a woman must learn obedience. The lesson will be valuable for you, Livia. You are wayward, but I shall correct you, out of love. Be brave for but a few minutes: then I shall bring you not pain but pleasure. It is the price of your becoming mine."

"The price?" Her old spirit returned to her as she spat out her reply. "It is I who will pay that price – and pay it dearly – when I suffer your *correction*. I despise you."

His face contorted with anger. "Then I shall derive as much pleasure from that correction as from taking possession of your body afterwards." The normally smooth voice now hissed: "Make no mistake, *my lady*: I shall bend you to my will."

"Get on with it!" There was urgency in Lambertazzi's voice as a strange noise came from the other side of the room. From my hiding place I could just see, around the other side of the hanging covering my niche, his gross figure standing against the wall. In front of him knelt Laura while his enormous hands almost obscured her head, which he was moving ungently and rhythmically, backwards and forwards. To my astonishment I realised that he was using her for his gratification while he witnessed his niece's torment.

There was a crack and I nearly betrayed myself with the start I gave. Bardi had brought the whip down across Livia's back, its impact leaving a red mark on that flawless white back. She made barely a sound. A second time he struck, and this time she screamed, unable to stifle her reaction to the pain.

I could no longer contain myself. Pushing aside the hanging I strode across the small room and, as Bardi raised the whip for a third stroke, I grabbed his wrist and tore it from his hand, turning him round and punching him on the jaw. He staggered back against the wall as I reached to my belt and drew my knife. "Bardi," I snarled. "This time you pay." How melodramatic I was, and how ill-prepared! Leaning back against the wall, he kicked me in the stomach, propelling me across the room, back into my niche where I flailed and became entangled with the hanging.

As I righted myself, I saw to my dismay that Bardi was holding a sword: I had not noticed that he was armed. Lambertazzi stood as if stunned, but Bardi's voice cut across the silence. "Signore, get away from here. I will deal with this intruder. And this time the celebrated jurist's choirboy will receive no second chance." Lambertazzi pulled away from the girl kneeling in front of him, slapped her across the head to get her out of his way, pulled his robe together and heaved himself through the doorway.

"So, Lorenzo." Bardi's voice was still even, urbane, and he smiled as he spoke. "You have returned. Is this an attempt at some kind of heroic rescue? Perhaps it is true then: did you couple with Livia the night she released you? I hope you satisfied her, that it was worth what you and she will suffer. For I shall gut you now, and while I take my pleasure with her she can watch you die, slowly and in agony." Livia made not a sound, her forehead pressed against the wall, but I could see the grief and pain wracking her body as her naked shoulders heaved.

Bardi advanced on me, and I backed away, but in so small a tower room I had retreated only three or four paces before I could go no further. I pointed my knife towards him, puny and ineffectual as it looked in comparison to his sword, and used my left hand to pull the hanging from over the door. Its fixings parted easily, and I wrapped it around my hand to form some kind of shield while never taking my eyes off Bardi's face. "That won't help you," he said as he smiled and then leapt at me, feinting once, then twice and then slashing the blade across at head height.

In all that practice with Sordello, I had never faced a sword: but the room was small and Bardi could not make full use of the swing of the blade, while my training was in fighting up-close, hand-to-hand. I rolled under that sweep and stood again, keeping one of the corners of the bed, with its upright and hangings, between us. He swung again, but this time the bed limited the arc of his stroke and, using my improvised shield to protect my left arm, I pushed out towards his sword and ducked in under it. I jabbed my knife at his right arm and caught his hand, causing him to cry out and to drop his weapon as his blood sprayed.

My movement carried me into him and my right shoulder caught him in the stomach. We tumbled to the floor in a confusion of arms and legs. I managed to hold onto my knife, and, as I rolled away and regained my feet, he scuttled across the floor, on the point of seizing his sword once more. The small blonde figure of Laura interposed itself: she kicked the blade away, out of his reach and across the floor to me. As I picked it up, he regained his feet. This time it was I who was smiling, but he seized Laura and held her in front of him as a shield.

"She's no use to you as a shield, Bardi," I sneered. "I'm double-armed, and you are at my mercy." He said nothing, but flung Laura across the room towards me. It was all I could do to avoid impaling her on one or other of my two weapons and, as I flung my arms to the side, she crashed into me, knocking us both off our feet. The door banged shut, and Bardi was gone.

Laura and I were left sitting on the floor, both staring at the naked figure of Livia, two red wheals beginning to show on her back. Laura was instantly concerned. Leaping to her feet and rushing over to her, she quickly pulled Livia's shift over her head and allowed it to fall down her back, covering her marked flesh. "My poor lady," she crooned as she stroked her hair, "My poor lamb." I picked up my knife from the floor where I had dropped it and cut the ropes that held her mistress's hands above her head. Livia turned to me and said simply, "Lorenzo. You came."

I shrugged: "You sent for me."

"I hoped you would: but I wasn't sure. I have been wrong about many things." Her voice was as normal and unforced as I had ever heard it. Gone were the petulance, the wheedling and the coquettishness. My heart was full and I wanted to – wanted to do what? In truth, I was unsure. To hold her? To make love to her? To be angry with her for putting herself at risk? It was all of those, and none. So I shrugged again. Then I realised that matters were far from resolved.

I turned to the slave. "Laura, you must take your lady to safety, before those bastards return with help. Take her back to my house, give her to the woman lawyer, the one we call the Magister: to no one else, you understand? The men at the gate will let you in. They know you now. Take her now and..." I reached up and tore down one of the hangings from the bed, tenderly wrapping it around Livia's shoulders. "Keep her warm. Keep her safe. Can you get out of this house without trouble?"

"I'll find a way. Thank you, sir. You have saved my lady."

"Go," I said. "I have two men to find and kill."

In truth I did not know which of the two I wished to kill more. But my heart was hammering, my blood was up, and I wanted revenge on both: revenge for what they had done to me, what they had threatened to do to me, and what I had only just prevented them from doing to Livia. They must be made to pay.

I held the door as Laura, one arm around her, the other holding one of the many candles that had lit the room, shepherded Livia to the stairs and down the first flight, cooing to her comfortingly as they went, their bare feet making barely a sound on the stairs. They made an odd pair: but it was dark, and I prayed that the streets of Bologna would be quiet and that their passage would attract no attention.

I was unsure where to go next, but reasoned that Lambertazzi would have hastened to the safety of his own tower, even if he had been obliged to take a circuitous route. So, reckoning that I might as well be fully armed, I picked up Bardi's sword and opened the door through which they had all entered. Even under my slight weight the bridge shook, illuminated by the usual torches at each extremity, and I traversed it as quickly as I could. The door at the other end was unlocked, so I seized the torch from above the door and found myself in a tower that was strange to me. Guessing that Lambertazzi would have to climb in order to reach his loftier retreat, I found the stairs in the corner of the modest room in which I found myself, and started up them.

To my joy, I rapidly found myself in the well-appointed chamber where I had sung with my hastily assembled troupe of musicians only days before. I opened the door I remembered and looked across the wooden span. Sure enough, there was Massimo Lambertazzi's own tower, some three or four storeys stretching above the connection from these inferior edifices. I was just starting on that crossing, a path which had so nearly proved fatal to me on two previous occasions, when I was hailed from the third tower, to my right.

On the top of that shorter building stood my friends Paolo, Giacomo and Salvatore, waving their torches and hallooing. "Lorenzo!" shouted Paolo. "Thank God you're alive! We thought you'd done it this time!" Why were they making such a noise? I put my finger to my lips to gesture them to silence: the last thing I wanted to do was to warn Lambertazzi that I was about to invade his retreat. "Don't worry about the noise!" came the reply. "We're here to arrest Lambertazzi and Bardi. The Capitano himself has come to take them. They're on their way up his tower now. We thought we'd try to find you: that little girl Laura told us you were in this tower."

Relief flooded me: I was no longer alone, and the presence not only of my friends but also of the Capitano and a sizeable force explained why I had not found myself confronting a small army of Lambertazzi's men summoned to his aid. He may have called for them: but they could not have come, even had they wanted to.

"I was down there," I laughed, "But Lambertazzi and Bardi both got away from me. I'm after them now. Come across to this tower: but go one at a time on the bridge. I don't trust it. I don't trust any of them," I added, as the catwalk I was standing on, even narrower than the last, lurched under me. "Who's covering the fourth tower, then?" I asked. "That one over there?"

"Sordello and some of the Capitano's men," shouted Paolo.

The towers were so close together that we could almost conduct a normal conversation from one to another, even though my friends were some way below. At that moment, a door opened on the fourth tower, and there was Sordello raising his torch as if in salute. If the Capitano was indeed climbing the stairs with his men, he had closed off the other route out of Lambertazzi's tower. There was no escape for him that way: so, if he were in his private lair, I would have him.

Chapter 36

I ventured out again onto the walkway, hefting the sword in my hand and wondering if I could adequately wield something so much longer and heavier than I was used to. At that moment yet another noise erupted. From a lower window on Lambertazzi's tower a head emerged. It was the Capitano del Popolo, who immediately recognised me. "Is that Lorenzo? I'm glad you're still alive, you young fool! Where is Lambertazzi? We're here to arrest him."

"I'm not sure, Signor Capitano. But I think he'll be in his chamber - a couple of floors above you." He waved in agreement, and barked orders at the men behind him: I could just make out their shapes and the moving lights of candles and flaming brands at the windows as they made their way up the stairs. At that moment the door at the far end crashed open, and my quarry appeared.

Heaving himself through the narrow doorway, Massimo Lambertazzi put one foot and then both on the walkway which swayed and groaned under him. With his left hand he clutched the handrail: but in his right he too held a sword, which he brandished at me threateningly. "Still alive, you young bastard? Not for long, though." He shuffled towards me a quarter of the distance, then half, his fat features illuminated and rendered still more malign by the flickering torch at its midpoint.

Maddened by my lust for revenge, I laughed at him and waved Bardi's sword in turn. "Come on, then, Lambertazzi," I shouted. "I'm ready for you! I'll skewer you with Bardi's blade!"

"You puppy!" he returned. "I should have killed you long since. I'll put an end to you now." He edged ever closer. This was the longest bridge between the cluster of towers, and certainly the least stable, but Lambertazzi needed to cover only some ten cautious paces to reach me.

Keen to fight him, I urged him onward. But Sordello, still two towers distant, clearly thought me in peril and bellowed across the gap: "Lambertazzi, you piece of shit! Leave the boy: I'll come and kill you myself!"

"No! Sordello: stay there! I'll finish him." I shouted, but too late: he had disappeared inside the building.

As the timber rocked and complained beneath Lambertazzi, I laughed mockingly and pointed my sword at him. For the first time he appeared uncertain: he glanced behind him and saw that the other tower, now Sordello had left it, was unguarded, affording him a means of escape. He turned awkwardly and started to hasten back towards his own tower: but that moment the first of the Capitano's soldiers appeared at the far end. First one, then two stepped onto the bridge: a third, then two more. It swayed and twisted as their weight was added to that of Lambertazzi.

"Get back, you fools! It will not take all of us. Get back!" There was a note of alarm in Lambertazzi's voice as the platform swayed ever more wildly.

Beyond his men the Capital del Popolo could be heard. "Signor Massimo Lambertazzi!" he bellowed from behind his soldiers' torches. "I have a warrant against you. Come back!"

At that moment I looked up and, at a window above the Capitano, caught sight of Bartolomeo Bardi, just discernible in the darkness that almost obscured him. As I stepped back into the doorway to gain a better view of him, something whistled through the air. I felt a sudden, sharp pain in my left shoulder and found, to my puzzlement, that I could not move. I looked down: the hilt of a knife was protruding from my shoulder. As I tried to move forward I felt a piercing pain. Whether it was a lucky throw or superb marksmanship, I had no idea: but I was pinned to the door behind me.

In shock and alarm I let go both the sword and my torch. The weapon fell awkwardly and I cursed as it slipped off the edge of the building and spun away, following the guttering flame into the darkness below. I put my right hand to the hilt of the knife in my shoulder, and tried to pull it out, but the pain was so great that I could not: nor could I stifle a cry of anguish.

Observing both my plight and the hesitation of the soldiers at the far end, Lambertazzi regained his confidence. He changed direction again and, almost jauntily, approached me once more, directing his weapon towards my throat. Helpless as I was, I could only watch as, now only a couple of paces away, he prepared to plunge his sword into me: as if in a trance, I found myself wondering what that penetration would feel like. The first three soldiers followed him along the plank, and a few more made to follow: yet they were too far away to save me.

The bridge complained again, and the Capitano pulled back the two closest to him. As I looked in mortal fear along the beam, to Lambertazzi and beyond, it began slowly to lurch to the right. The rail to which the enormous man's left hand had appeared clamped pulled away altogether from the stonework at the far end. His savage grin turned to a rictus of terror. He dropped his sword and seized the right-hand rail: but now the entire span was contorting and bucking under him. It was slipping away from beneath my feet, too. Only the knife through my shoulder held me safe (though it made me howl) as my feet scrabbled to gain purchase on the stone boss that until a second before had supported the massive truss.

The entire construction was disintegrating. As the woodwork shook itself one last time, Lambertazzi let go of the rail, which now afforded him no safety. He appeared to be running uphill while the entire platform was fragmenting. Somehow he gained purchase on a remaining fragment of the structure and hurled himself towards me, stretching his arms almost unbelievably to seize in his huge hands first one, then the other of my flailing ankles.

Now, momentarily, the knife through my shoulder supported the weight of both of us, causing me to shriek my agony once more. There was uproar as Paolo, Giacomo and Salvatore burst into the room behind me and wrenched the door open, pulling me with it and, now dangling desperately down into the void, Lambertazzi still clinging to me.

"Lorenzo," shouted Paolo. "What the hell are you doing? Christ!" I could only groan in anguish, but he took in the situation at a glance. He and Giacomo each seized me under my arms while another hand, presumably Salvatore's, grabbed my collar.

I tried to kick Lambertazzi's hands from me, but his weight stretched my legs straight below me, my body distended as if on the rack. I looked down into his face: it was filled with horror, his mouth open, pleading. Even had I been able to kick him away, I knew at that moment that I could not have brought myself to.

I forced the words out, one by one, though I could barely think for the fiery spasms coursing through my torn, pierced shoulder still, impossibly, nailed to the door by the knife which ground against the bones of my shoulder. "Paolo. Take... his... hands."

"What?" he replied. "Are you crazy?"

I shook my head, though that hurt too. "Take... his..." Before Paolo could argue further, my boots that I had so prized, now tightly pinioned in Lambertazzi's remorseless grip, started to slip from my feet. His hands were grasping empty air: first my boots fell away and, next, the torchlight caught Lambertazzi's panic-stricken face, his mouth opening to scream as, with the last of the timbers, he too tumbled over and over into the darkness, his fine robes billowing as he wailed his last despair. Beyond him three of the Capitano's soldiers also plunged earthward with the collapsing bridge, shrieking in dismay, while their commander and another of his men managed to seize the arms of the last two who, legs flailing as mine had done, were somehow dragged back to safety.

As we watched in sombre amazement, we caught sight of the black figure of Bardi in a window only one floor above the Capitano, whom we could still just discern within the doorway. We roared across the gap, pointing to the floor above him: grasping what was happening, he moved towards the stairs. Meanwhile Bardi swung himself out of the window and leapt across the gap to the catwalk that connected it to the fourth tower one storey below. It was a massive jump, crazy enough if undertaken in daylight, and all the more risky in darkness where he could not have a clear view of his target. He landed on the extreme edge, and his feet slipped: he disappeared from sight so that for a moment it looked as if he had met the same doom as his master.

Yet somehow, implausibly, one hand clasped the rail. The other joined it. Then we could see Bardi as he managed to swing his legs back to safety, finally manoeuvring his body onto the bridge. As we bellowed our hatred he waved at us ironically, then made an obscene gesture in our direction. The Capitano and his men now found themselves a floor too high, and although they yelled

272

at Bardi and even threw the odd knife, he quickly regained his feet and dashed into the next tower. I cursed Sordello for leaving his post there, apparently out of concern for me: but the damage was done. We had witnessed the literal downfall of Massimo Lambertazzi, but his lieutenant had slipped through our hands.

There was more pain as, while the others held me fast, Paolo wrenched the knife out of the wood of the door. Slowly we made our way down to the ground. Searching in the darkness, I retrieved my prized boots, wiping the blood from them on the hem of Lambertazzi's rich robe while trying to look too closely neither at the mound of smashed, crumpled flesh that had once been my enemy, nor at the remains of the Capitano's men who had lost their lives in similar fashion.

If I was too dizzy with hurt and shock to speak much, Paolo filled the silence while he explained volubly, with frequent interruptions from our two friends, how he had come to my rescue. I had, it seemed, left the house in uproar as I followed Laura in search of Livia. My master and Sordello, convinced that I had gone to place my head wilfully into yet another noose with an inevitable and fatal consequence, had swiftly decided that the only hope of saving me was to take the Lambertazzi letter to the Capitano del Popolo and convince him that it might furnish sufficient proof of his treason.

As Sordello left to complete that mission, he had bumped into Paolo who was returning to the house to see whether I had been successful in my mission to free Roslaia. He in turn had gathered our friends and, while the Capitano gained entry to the Lambertazzi tower by dint of authority and force of arms, those lads had bluffed their way into the lesser tower by playing on their old acquaintance with some of the wagon-crews from their trips to Modena.

The rest I could work out. At last, as we approached my master's house, I was overcome with weariness. There were faces in front of me, those of Michele, Mamolo, my master herself. Giacomo and Salvatore too crowded around me, supporting: yet I felt they were hemming me in, suffocating me. I knew there was something I needed to know, but my mind was not working properly. My master's face came closer to mine, pinched with weariness and worry. "Lorenzo," she said.

I remembered what I wanted to know. "Tommaso? How is Tommasino?"

"He lives," said my master. "But you are hurt. Come, let me tend that wound."

"I'm all right," I retorted. "I just need..." And then I was falling. I felt I was myself plunging from the top of Lambertazzi's tower, spiralling into that abyss, over and over as he had done, as if forever.

Chapter 37

The pain awakened me, a burning, searing sensation in my shoulder where the knife had penetrated. I opened my eyes. My master was washing the blood from my body and sponging my brow and all the while humming words of comfort: childish, meaningless things that were nonetheless soothing, her singsong voice – surprising in comparison to her croaking tone day-to-day - taking me back in memory to my first arrival in her house.

I knew my injury was less grievous than on that occasion: nonetheless the pain was keen as the physician – was he here again? I wondered distractedly – interfered with my wound. As I moaned and then swore, both of those tending me smiled. "I see you have lost none of your spirit with the blood that you shed, Lorenzo," said my master with a smile. "Your wound is clean, and the physician is applying unguents before he binds it up. He is not worried for you. Indeed, I have seen you in worse shape – the first time I met you."

"I suppose you have, Magister. And I had no clothes on then!" I laughed, and the movement caused a shaft of pain to course through my shoulder and body. Yet it still felt good to be alive. "Magister, did you know? My boots, those marvellous boots."

"I know. What of them, except that you preen yourself when you wear them?"

"No, I don't!" I was indignant.

"Of course you do! You strut like a peacock, Lorenzo." She put her hand on my good arm. "And I love you for it."

For a moment I was abashed by her rare display of affection. Then I recalled what I wanted to say. "They saved my life. Lambertazzi, he…" I tried, but I could not continue.

"Tell me when you're feeling stronger, Lorenzo," my master replied gently. "It will keep. You are wounded, and must rest in order to heal."

Something about hurt and healing stirred my memory: where had I seen the physician binding a wound? Memory flooded back and, with it, anxiety. "Tommaso. How is he?"

She responded with a smile. "You will soon be able to ask him. He is sleeping, as you must. But it seems the crisis is past, and that he will live – thanks to the good doctor here," she added, nodding respectfully to the physician. "Now you *must* rest." And I did. As my wound was tightly dressed in clean linen and the pain eased, everything became indistinct, and I drifted back into sleep.

I felt that I slept fitfully, though probably I woke little. Nonetheless, every time I stirred, there was my master watching over me, wiping the sweat from my brow and the dribble from my face. I slept through the next day and night without really stirring.

It was daylight, and I was awake. As I tried to move, I could feel stiffness and a slight pain in my left shoulder, but it was nothing unbearable. I rolled onto my right side and tried to sit up. My movement attracted the attention of someone across the room. I was in the master's chamber, lying on a mattress on the floor. My master was standing over her bed on the other side of the room, tending to someone else, and talking.

Immediately she became aware that I was awake and came over to me. "So, Lorenzo, you have returned to us! How do you feel?"

It felt hard to speak at first, and the words emerged thick and slurred: yet everything seemed quickly to return to normal. "I feel... I think I am well, Magister. Though I need to piss."

She laughed. "That is good, then. Shall I help you to stand?" My left arm was bound across my stomach so that I could not move that injured shoulder: she took my right and helped me to my knees and then to my feet.

"I was just speaking to Tommaso," she said quietly.

Tommaso! I had forgotten him again! But for once I did not indulge in self-recrimination. I knew I had been wounded, significantly though not dangerously: I had been also on the edge of exhaustion. Now I felt well, strong, hungry and in need of relieving myself. With my master supporting me on one side, I walked slowly across the room as my head cleared. And there was my old friend: he was still desperately pale, but his eyes were open. And he smiled at me. "Luca." Another smile. "Lorenzo. I must remember your new name." The voice was faint and feeble: but it was unmistakeably his.

He was still occupying the master's own bed, so I sat on the edge of it and took his left hand with my right. "Tommasino. Thank God. I was afraid I'd lost you."

"Lost me? Heavens, no. Who would stop you doing stupid things... if I weren't here?"

It was clear that even to speak was costing him a great effort, yet there was one more thing I needed to say to him. "And, Tommasino, I must tell you. I found Rosalia: I found your sister. I did what you asked me, Tommasino. I found her, and took her back to your parents. She is... well enough, though she has been through a bad time. I did do that for you, Tommasino. I did what you asked."

He smiled again, and his hand squeezed mine: the pressure was barely discernible, but it was there. "You don't have to keep reassuring me, Lorenzo. I didn't doubt you would. I knew you... Rosalia." He smiled again and closed his eyes. My master's hand on my back and shoulder urged me away. "We must let him sleep. He remains perilously weak. He lost much blood: and recovery will take time. But he *will* live. The physician assures me of it. Besides, he is in my debt, and knows he must not fail me!" I looked at her, and we both laughed, knowing that, as always, she was not exaggerating: the number of people in Bologna who owed her a debt, not necessarily a pecuniary one, was incalculable. "Come, Lorenzo," she said. "I will help you down the stairs, where clean air and the company of friends will act as a cure for you."

We were just at the top of those rickety stairs that led down into the courtyard when another memory returned to me. There should have been someone else being tended in that house. I turned to my master. "Livia? What of the Lady Livia? Did she not arrive here?"

"Ah," commented my master. "She did arrive, curiously wrapped in curtains and accompanied by her little blonde servant," she said. "But she is not here now." She caught my urgent, enquiring glance. "I found her... *alternative* accommodation. She is safe and well, and little the worse for her ordeal, if somewhat... *chastened*: but I thought it... *better* if she were not here." She looked me in the eye. "I think you know that in your heart, Lorenzo."

I was silent as I pondered the situation. Should I be angry? Bereft? I pondered for a moment, and found myself feeling, more than anything, empty. I nodded. "I expect you are right, Magister. You always are."

"You know that is not true, Lorenzo. But in this case I think perhaps I am," she added kindly and, taking my right arm, helped me safely down the stairs.

It was good to rejoin my friends and comrades, and to allow most of the household to return to its old rhythm. Yet, though my body healed - as quickly as ever, it seemed - my spirit was troubled. Tommaso was so weak that it pained me to see him. Our conversations remained necessarily short, and from time to time he lapsed into feverish periods. At such times, when life again threatened to slip away from him, the physician was called and there were grave discussions between him and my master.

As for Livia, I could never learn anything of her. My master and the rest of the household were tight-lipped, simply reiterating the bald fact that she was somewhere safe and that it was better if I did not know where. They implied that they were keeping her safe from her own family, notwithstanding the fact that the death of Massimo Lambertazzi and the disappearance of his advisor Bardi must have largely reduced any threat to her. I suspected that my master was keeping her away from me: or, perhaps, protecting me from further entanglement with her.

She was frequently in my thoughts as I recalled that pale flesh at the mercy of Bartolomeo Bardi. And, because I was a young man, I could not help but fill my head with fantasies of being reunited with her and receiving the gratitude due to her rescuer. In my vivid imagination her ways of expressing that gratitude were invariably carnal: what nineteen or twenty year-old boy or man – I was never sure which I was, or how I was regarded in the master's entourage – would think in other terms?

As the household returned to normal, leaving me to live quietly and allow my wound to heal while beginning to assume the lion's share of caring for Tommaso, I became introspective and morose. Not allowed out, I even missed the climax of my master's crusade to end slavery in the city. I was not deemed strong enough to cope with the crowds that descended on the city's main square for that rare meeting of the *Due Mila*, the council of the Two Thousand. Sordello accompanied the master for her protection, though the Capitano del Popolo sent men to accompany both her and Master Rolandino to the *Consiglio*, so they were never in danger.

Besides, the threat to the new law from its leading opponents had largely dissipated. Without Massimo Lambertazzi they were fragmented and disorganised. After his literal fall the Geremei, previously the only one among the great families to support the move to emancipate the city's six thousand slaves, persuaded several of the other magnati that the offer of compensation was a generous one, to be seized with alacrity.

Master Rolandino, so my master reported to me, translated and read aloud the letter we had intercepted from Lambertazzi to the Archbishop of Modena. It was not, as my master had attested, absolute proof of guilt but, now that he was dead, it was strongly suggestive to the Two Thousand that the great families might close ranks and try to seize power: thus the Council was swayed, as she had hoped.

Lambertazzi's eldest son, Roberto, had attended the Council, dressed in mourning. He did his best to refute the allegations and turn them back on Master Rolandino: but he gained little credence. Indeed, the Two Thousand ordered that messengers be sent to Modena's Podestà to express Bologna's extreme displeasure at the involvement of both the Archbishop and Umberto Uguzzoni in such a conspiracy: both (it was later reported) were discovered to have left Modena on urgent and prolonged business in Rome.

As for the cache of weapons, it was never found. Paolo went with the Capitano to identify Lambertazzi's men so that he could question them. But the foremen from those wagon trains had made themselves scarce when their master fell. With a wry smile the Capitano had commented, "We never had a case against Lambertazzi. He would have produced endless witnesses to attest to his innocence."

"So why did you storm his house with a warrant for his arrest?" asked Paolo.

Still smiling, the Capitano said, "Because the Magister asked me. I am in her debt as many others are, for reasons that you do not need to know. It was a bluff, pure and simple. And, fortunately for all of us, Massimo Lambertazzi was convinced, and panicked."

"But why at that moment? Why did you go that very night to the Lambertazzi tower?"

"The Magister insisted," he replied. "She was worried about that young fool Lorenzo, who'd got himself into trouble again. I've never met anyone with such a capacity for getting himself in a mess!"

Naturally there was merriment back at the house, at my expense, when Paolo recounted the story. He seemed to be a more frequent visitor than ever, now firm friends with Sordello and his troupe and often sent on errands by my master, causing me some pangs of jealousy. And, after the legal triumph, naturally my master and Maestro Rolandino were beside themselves with juristic satisfaction at seeing the *Liber Paradisus* enacted in the city.

For my part, however, I felt somewhat apart and excluded, and could not shake off my gloomy mood. Christmas came and went, Mamolo cooking several sumptuous meals at which Sordello generally joined us, though at that time of the year he was frequently in demand as a troubadour – and a highly-paid one, at that.

The master returned to her usual pattern of life, dividing her time between lecturing to the university's students and acting for the guilds, the merchants and, once again, a number of the families. My shoulder had healed, and I played my part once more as scribe, though always I would hurry us home to see how Tommaso was improving.

He was healing, yet with aggravating slowness. By New Year he was sitting up, and we would talk sometimes for as much as an hour before he would need quiet and sleep again. We talked of old times, of our happy days of friendship in Modena, of his family, even of Rosalia.

I confess I was not wholly honest with him about her: how could I tell her brother of the abuse and rape she suffered at the hands of Cortino? So the stories I told focused mainly on my rescue of her from those three would-be rapists. I even made him smile when I described how she felled one of my assailants, though I forbore to tell him precisely how Cortino died. He must have guessed that there was a darker side to the story, but neither of us felt ready to explore it.

Still my bleak frame of mind persisted. I could tell that my master recognised it, and I sensed that it irritated her: but we did not discuss it. In that winter we were busy together with legal work and life had resumed its former pattern, apart from the time all the household devoted to Tommaso's gradual recovery. He was able to get out of bed now, and walk around the house and courtyard, though he generally needed to lean on someone and had the occasional fall when he tried to do without. If my mood was black, he was returning to the sunny temperament that I remembered. He began to make himself useful, too, helping Michele with the household accounts.

Michele had habitually kept a tight hold on the master's money, running the household's finances mainly on the basis of spending as little as possible, except when she scolded him for his meanness. I had always found Michele a stubborn if lovable old cuss, but Tommaso seemed able to charm him into allowing him to help with the money, allocating specific sums to particular purposes.

Even Mamolo began to grumble less about what he was allowed to spend on food, and we certainly ate well, sometimes under the master's pretence of needing to feed Tommaso and me up – though, after being painfully thin for months, my old friend was already regaining the round face that I remembered from our childhood, grinning beneath his mop of curly hair.

One day I returned with the master from her lecture in the square, a chilly one on a grey, sleety February day, and found Tommaso, as was usual by then, sitting at the table in that downstairs room we men now shared, working on the master's accounts. "Oh, Lorenzo," he said. "I have a message for you. Indeed, an errand. A lady has a message for you," he said with a mischievous smile on his face.

I was immediately all ears. "A lady? What's the message? Is it from Livia Lambertazzi? What does she want? Does she want to see me?"

Tommaso smiled again, infuriatingly. "Calm down! I wasn't told: just that a lady sent you a message. You are to go to that *albergo* just inside the northern gate." He gave me the name, which I forget: a different building stands there now. "The messenger said that a room is booked for you there, that you are to stay there tonight, and all of tomorrow if necessary, and wait for word."

"What do you mean, wait for word? Is Livia going to come to me? Will I see her again?"

Tommaso made a face. "I don't know, Lorenzo. That's what the message was."

"And who was the messenger? It wasn't Livia herself? Did she send Laura?"

He looked puzzled. "No," he replied. "It was just... just a boy with a message. But the name, Livia, the place and the time were quite clear. So Michele gave him a coin and he went off happy."

"And when am I supposed to go?" I was beside myself with impatience and curiosity. Would Livia come to me? My mind ran on, inevitably. Would she offer herself to me? Would I know that wonderful body again?

"Calm down, Lorenzo," he admonished me again. "If you leave now, you'll be there long before dark: it's not far. Then you can wait and see what happens. It sounds rather intriguing to me!" He had a wicked smile on his face now.

"Damn you, Tommaso. I think you're enjoying this. What am I to make of it?"

"Learn a little patience, Lorenzo. Stop cudgelling your brains and thinking so much about everything. Just go, and see what happens. And I'll see you about this time tomorrow."

So I went. The whole household seemed acquainted with the arrangement, Michele and Mamolo smiling and winking as I left, even my master giving a knowing smile from her balcony.

Chapter 38

I reached the albergo without incident: I had passed it often enough while running behind Michele's horse, building up my strength and speed when I first joined my master's household. It was more comfortable than most hostelries, perhaps attracting the better sort of traveller from the cities to the north: Ravenna, Mantua, even Venice. I was expected, and was shown to a private room with a table, two stools and a bed. A boy brought a tray of cold meats, bread and wine which he left on the table. I observed that there were two platters and two cups for the wine: but no one could tell me who would visit me, or when.

I have never been good at waiting, with nothing to do: perhaps it reminds me too much of my various periods of imprisonment, shorter or longer. On this occasion I could not be still, but paced the room. At last, I could not say how much later, there was a knock on the door. I rushed to it, and wrenched it open. In front of me was the diminutive figure of Laura.

"Signor Lorenzo," she said, with a little curtsy.

"No one calls me Signor anything!" I replied. "But I thank you for your courtesy. Just call me Lorenzo and," the words burst out me before I could stop them, "Tell me of the Lady Livia. Am I right in guessing that you still serve her? Did she send you? Tell me, is she well?"

She smiled patiently. "If you would just let me in, sir – Lorenzo," she chided me gently, "I might be able to answer all your questions."

"I'm sorry," I said. "Since I received the message from her: or was it from you? Whichever it was, I have been beside myself."

"I can see that," she responded, again with that warm smile.

"But I'm forgetting myself," I felt bad about ignoring the rules of hospitality. "Will you sit and take something to eat and drink?"

"I will. Thank you. Just some wine for now."

I poured us both a cup of wine, but could only sip at mine once or twice until I had to ask her again. "So what news of Livia? *Do you serve her still? How does she fare?*"

She smiled. "I do serve her, sir: Lorenzo. She is well: and safe where she is. She would have preferred to see you," I nearly leapt to my feet. "As I say, she would have liked to see you," she put her hand on mine, "But you must understand that she cannot. To do so would lose her the protection she enjoys. So she sent me instead. She asked me to bear you her greetings, and her thanks. You saved her from a terrible fate, she says, and she will never forget it. As for me," her tone changed, "I would thank you not only for saving my lady but for killing that monster who ruled my life and treated me as an animal. And for saving me from that slimy Bardi who abetted him as his whoremaster."

I was surprised by the expression of her own gratitude: I knew I did not deserve it. "It's true I saved the Lady Livia, with your help," I said. "But I didn't kill Lambertazzi, although I helped to bring about his downfall." I grimaced at the memory of my enemy swaying drunkenly on the collapsing bridge: clutching at my ankles and threatening to drag me down; finally plummeting, screaming, into the blackness below. "In the end I never touched him: he fell. As for Bardi, I only scratched him: you know he escaped. I guess he's left Bologna by now, but he'll go somewhere else and make mischief there."

"Yet, Lorenzo, you don't understand what else you did. I know because everyone's talking about it: have you not heard what they've been saying?"

"Heard what?" I was bemused.

"The new law. There are no more slaves."

"I know that: it has been my master's great work, but I had little to do with it. I was not even there at the time: I was hurt, and they would not let me out."

"You're too modest. What you did to Lambertazzi," still the venom entered her voice when she mentioned his name, "Meant that, instead of preventing the new law, the families accepted it. All of us who were serfs know the part you played in that. And we are all in your debt."

I shook my head. "You attribute far too much to me."

"Nonsense!" she replied. "You have no idea what this means to me, what it means to us all. My name is written in that great book. Every one of us who were slaves can now see our names inscribed by the notaries: even though we cannot read them, we know they are there! It is a wonderful thing. The notary, that big man everyone's talking about, he showed me, pointed to the writing that he said is my name. Look!" she put her hand to her neck: "No more do I wear that filthy rope round my neck to show that a man owns me. No man may bend me to his will or use me as his whore, unless I choose it."

I did not know what to say. "I'm glad," I said. "You're no longer a slave. Yet you still serve my lady: why?"

"I serve her out of love. Oh, I know she's fickle and difficult: and she likes to play games with men and make them dance to her tune. But she is as kind to me as ever, and I serve her gladly. I would die for her," she concluded.

"But now she must pay you, if you serve her?"

She laughed delightedly. "Yes, she does. Or, rather, the family who keep us pay me. Not a great sum, but I have my own place to sleep, not the stinking bed of a man who uses me how he likes: and I am fed and clothed. And that is why I came to thank you."

I was puzzled. "But did the Lady Livia not send you?"

She adopted a patient expression, as if she was talking to someone rather stupid. "Of course she did. She asked me to find you and to thank you for saving her, to say that she would always be in your debt." Her tone became more earnest. "Lorenzo, please don't hope that she will ever be yours. She cannot, and will not be. That is why I may not tell you where she is, and you must not follow me when I leave you. But she will always remember you."

I nodded glumly, understanding all too well, while Laura continued urgently. "But I wanted to thank you myself, Lorenzo. You changed my life when you saved hers. I too will always be in your debt and," she coloured a little, "I do not know how to thank someone like you. You're young and handsome: at least, you are now that you're not wearing that horrible mask!" Now she was teasing. "And you live among all those fine people, not in my world. But I owe my new life, my good fortune, to you: and, even if my mistress cannot thank you in person, I can."

She stood up from the table. Now her face was still redder. "Sir, Lorenzo, I..." She stopped speaking. Her hands went to her throat and undid the woollen cloak she was wearing: she tossed it onto the stool on which she had been sitting. Her hands went to her throat again and fumbled with the laces that tied the collar of her dress: it was plain, again made of wool, but clean, and warmer and less ragged than the poor shift she had worn as a slave.

I stood up. I swear I tried to stop her. I put my arms on her shoulders and said, "Laura, there is no need to do this. I accept your thanks. You don't have to do any more to prove your gratitude."

She pushed my hands away, stepped back and let first her dress fall, then her linen shift: and she was naked in front of me, the contours of her body accentuated by the light of the one candle that the inn had provided. "Let us get more heat from the fire," she said coyly, and knelt in front of the fireplace as she pushed more logs onto it from the pile at the side. Her body glowed in the firelight. She was short but well rounded, with wide hips, a full bosom and a skin that was relatively unmarked. No wonder Lambertazzi had desired her so much, and so often.

She turned back from the fire and came towards me. I was still standing, astonished. "Lorenzo, I will pay that debt. No one is making me do this. I wish to give myself to you: because I can; because I am free to do this by my choice; because I am fond of you and I know that you're sad. I talked to your friend Tommaso."

I started. "He told me it was a boy who came."

She laughed "I asked him to, silly: I told them all at your house. I'm pleased they kept my secret. Even my lady does not know what I am doing: she thinks I am away from her tonight because I must make sure that I am in the book of freed slaves. But I have already done that. Lorenzo, I know you cannot have my lady, and I know you loved Tommaso's sister and think you have lost her: what was her name? Rosalia?" I nodded. "I know I cannot replace either of those women you have loved. But let me make you happy, just for one night. You must stop being sad and be yourself again."

She stepped close to me and unlaced my jerkin. "Sit down," she said, "And I'll help you off with your boots." When I protested she silenced me. "I've done it enough times for other men, Lorenzo. I can manage once more."

She stood me up again, and helped me out of my breeches. Then my shirt: and I too was bare in the glow of the firelight, facing this pretty, generous, willing woman.

She ran her hands over my body and down my back. I felt her fingers tracing the ridges and furrows on my back, the scars from that terrible whipping years before in the tower that had belonged to her master. She turned me round, and traced the lines more closely in fascination. "Is that what they did to you, Lorenzo? Those two beasts?" I nodded. "I think you have suffered more from that family than ever I did," she said: "Come, hold me tight."

So I did, holding her close to me, though in my inexperience I was unsure how to hold a woman against me when my all-too-evident physical desire put a barrier in the way. She laughed and pulled me down on the rug in front of the fire. I kissed her on the lips. I kissed her nipples, her belly. Then I was between her legs, my need pressing, demanding. Her skilful hands helped me to enter her: but I was too far gone. Within moments I was spent.

Like many a young man before me, I felt foolish and ungenerous at leaving her unfulfilled. She hushed me and giggled, "I should be flattered, Lorenzo: pleased that you desired me so much. Come, don't be embarrassed. It happens to young men the first time," she looked knowingly into my eyes, "Or even the second?" It was my turn to blush, and I nodded miserably.

Her hands reached up held my cheeks, "Oh, Lorenzo! Tommaso told me you take everything too seriously. How lucky you are to have such a friend! Listen to me: stop worrying. We can make love and have fun. We can even laugh about it, you know!

Making love is quite a silly business: it's always messy, awkward, and often it goes wrong, mainly because you men are so anxious about it. And then, people talk as if women are not supposed to enjoy it: women of a certain class, at any rate. But I do, I really do: when it is my choice. And you are my choice tonight. Now, why don't we eat, and drink some wine in front of the fire, just as we are? And then we shall make love again – and laugh!"

I am not sure that ham, sausage, bread and wine have ever tasted so sweet to me. I did not love Laura, but I admired her. She was confident, brave: after all, she had summoned me to rescue her mistress. And she was generous, giving herself to me out of gratitude, freely and without reserve. Moreover, she was right: I found I could laugh, too.

When we had eaten, she asked teasingly, "Shall I come and sit on your lap?" I was hardly likely to demur. She did, and my desire returned rapidly. But this time, without the urgency of the first time, she encouraged me to explore her body, to feel, to kiss and to lick. "Take hold of me properly, Lorenzo!" she said impatiently. "I'm not made of glass, and you're not going to break me! I'm a woman, and I need a man to hold me: to feel me, desire me, want me!" She encouraged to me to feel her breasts: to weigh them, fondle and caress them; to explore her whole body with my hands and my lips.

Thus she taught me something of what women like, of what they would like us men to do more often, though we rarely do so because we are so driven by our own selfish, male needs, behaving more like bulls with the herd than humans with feelings. Again those explorations, kisses exchanged, and embraces culminated in front of the fire, the ecstasy this time both shared and satisfying. It must have been very late when she took my hand and said, "Let's go to bed and sleep. But not too long: we have only this one night."

I protested that I was sure I could not satisfy her again. She smiled and said, "Lorenzo, there's a great advantage to being young, even to being inexperienced. Your body doesn't know when it's had enough!"

And so we slept a little. What a wonderful thing it was, to sleep that first time pressed against the warm, soft flesh of a woman. Ever since that night I have considered it one of life's great pleasures. Now long accustomed once more to sleeping alone, I still miss the feeling, sometimes aching for that particular form of companionship. However, in my old age I do not want a woman, however lovely, to lie beside me only because she is paid to: though I confess I have been tempted on occasions.

It was still long before dawn, and the fire had died down to a red glow, when I felt her lips on my stomach, kissing it, her tongue exploring my bellybutton. Then it moved lower down my body. At first I was repelled by the sudden memory of what she was required to do for Lambertazzi while he was watching the torment intended for Livia. But she pushed my hand away, saying (in a muffled voice), "I've told you, Lorenzo. I choose to do this. No one will *make* me do it again: I do this out of affection for you." And then her lips and her tongue were busy and, within a short time, my arousal was complete once more.

Only later, perhaps long after, did I understand the true nature of her gift to me. To be sure, no young man is likely to refuse the offer of a night spent with a willing, good-looking, experienced woman. But she knew too that she was educating me in the ways of love: she taught me to be tender and considerate, not greedy or predatory. I have never been a great lover, but I hope she made me a thoughtful one – and generous, as Laura was to me.

More food and drink arrived with the morning. We both ate sparingly, and knew without speaking that we did not need or want to make love again. Indeed, I was entirely sated: yet suffused with a warm glow, a sense of fulfilment as well as of gratitude to the warm-hearted young woman.

"Now I must leave you, Lorenzo. I must return to my mistress."

I wanted this encounter to continue forever. "Don't," I said. "Stay with me." I had a sudden inspiration: "Why don't I marry you, Laura?"

She laughed, bent down to where I sat and kissed me full on the lips. "No, Lorenzo. You are sweet, and kind. But I am too old for you: I must be twenty-five or more. And I have been used and misused by too many men: spoiled goods, as they say. I'm lucky to have a mistress to serve and a roof over my head. You know, I feared I might find myself in a brothel when my slavery came to an end: too many girls have been thrown onto the streets by those who used to own them, so freedom has not been good for all of them. But I am in a good home, and I count my blessings."

As she finally laced up her dress and then her cloak, she looked me in the eye. "I really do count my blessings, Lorenzo. And you should, too. You have good friends, and a kind master. You have the undying gratitude of two fine women: and of a poor, common one. Even if you have lost all of them, you can carry that knowledge in your heart. Don't give up! So warm a person as you will find a woman you can love – and who will love you. Love will come to you, I'm sure of it. You are *very* lovable, you know."

I tried to speak, but she hushed me. "Stop being sad. Go back to your friends, and enjoy your life. Keep learning all that law with your master. Don't stop singing. And value your friends, for they all love you: Tommaso, Paolo, all of them. Don't forget that. Goodbye, Lorenzo." She kissed me on the mouth, her tongue searching mine and beginning to excite me once more: then she left.

I sat there, still naked, shivering now in the cold of the morning, and thinking, perhaps more furiously than I had ever done before.

Chapter 39

I was shaken out of my torpor by a knock at the door. Embarrassed, I pulled on my shirt. Outside was a boy with, unusually, a written message. I was needed at once at the Palazzo del Capitano del Popolo: there, it read, my master, Maestro Rolandino and all the scribes they could muster were busy inscribing the names of the thousands of slaves freed by declaration of the *Due Mila* in what had become, as its author desired, the *Liber Paradisus*. At least the task would keep me busy, I thought, so I dressed, stuck my head under a fountain outside to clear it and set off into the centre of the city. I tried to pay for my night's board and lodging, but was informed that it was all taken care of: the landlord would not say by whom.

Less than an hour later I presented myself at the Palazzo, and was ushered upstairs, averting my gaze as usual from the corpses hanging on gibbets all the way up the grand staircase. Maestro Rolandino greeted me affably, and my master was unusually chatty. "My, Lorenzo," she commented, "You look as if you've barely slept!" I could not decide whether she knew how I had spent the night and was mocking me, so I looked for a twinkle in her eye: typically, however, she gave nothing away. On the contrary, with the usual comment, "We have much work to do," she set me to work.

I had half expected to see a line of the thousands of slaves who were being freed presenting themselves and adding their names to the roll: but that was not the case. The former slave owners had submitted lists to the *Comune*, and we had merely to copy the names in. It was wearisome, tedious work, and it was dusk when we finished. My head ached, and my fingers were black with ink.

"Come, Lorenzo, let us go home," said my master. "Master Rolandino is dining with us tonight, and I hope that you will join us at table."

"Yes, Lorenzo: let us eat and drink together," added her colleague warmly. "You have done much for the Magister, for me and for this city these last weeks."

Flattered, I thanked both of them, and we made our way home, stretching our backs and hands and complaining of cramped muscles from the day's writing. The two eminent jurists were still swapping anecdotes from the final debate of the Two Thousand that I had missed and for once, hilariously, they were neither discreet nor modest in their expressions of pleasure at their achievement.

A thought occurred to me, a loose end that I had still failed to tie up in my mind. "Magister," I asked, "Now that this episode is closed, what of the Gatekeeper? Will he reveal himself? Or will he continue to manipulate the city, all of us – even both of you?"

Master Rolandino harrumphed and made evasive noises: but my master stopped, took me by the arm, and turned to face me. "Lorenzo," she said, "I think it is time we were honest with you. Did you believe that we were as ignorant as you of the identity of the Gatekeeper?"

"No, Magister," I replied. "I assumed that you purposefully kept me in ignorance: not because you did not trust me," I added hastily, "But so that the truth could not be forced from me. Although you once asked me to find out who he was, I never believed that you did not know."

"As usual, Lorenzo, you see through my... *prevarications*. You are right, of course: I have truly desired to protect you. But now, are you sure you want to learn his identity? Doing so might yet lead you into peril."

"I do, Magister: for I feel I have walked in the dark long enough," I added reproachfully.

"I believe you have, Lorenzo. You have earned my further trust in this: I owe you my honesty. The Gatekeeper is..." Her colleague coughed loudly, but she gestured him to silence. "No, Rolandino, dear friend. He does indeed merit this revelation. Lorenzo, the Gatekeeper does not exist. He is an invention. If anyone, he is the Maestro Notaro here, and I. When we found ourselves deep into conspiracies and stratagems, we felt we needed some form of... *protection* from our enemies. So we concocted the notion of a shadowy figure who controlled us and to whom we reported, rendering us to our opponents merely pawns in someone else's games rather than their authors. And, to a large extent, it was a successful ploy: after all, we are still alive! Though, in my case, that is thanks to you," she added.

I stood astonished. For years I had felt that it was the name of the Gatekeeper that had led me into some of the terrible situations I had experienced: and now he was revealed as someone who existed only in my master's imagination. Should I be outraged? Angry? Then I saw the brilliance of the notion, and the absurdity of resenting someone who had never existed. I stared at my master, who returned my look anxiously. And then I burst out laughing, roaring at the humour of a conundrum that had long vexed me but had now vanished in a puff of smoke. My master began to chuckle, and then Master Rolandino, and soon the three of us were embracing and bellowing with laughter, attracting curious glances from passers-by.

Eventually we regained our composure, and my master urged us to walk on. "We must get home," she said, though she failed to explain why there was any particular hurry. I was about to open the courtyard door for the two of them in my usual way when she stopped me, and instead knocked peremptorily. "Let Michele admit us tonight," she said.

The gate was thrown open, and in we walked, to be greeted by an extraordinary sight. A great fire was blazing in the courtyard, crackling and throwing out light and heat. It illuminated a long trestle table set up there, and around it were gathered, in short, all the people I counted my friends in Bologna: Sordello was there with his two fellow musicians, Andrea and Filippo; Paolo, Giacomo and Salvatore, my three drinking companions; even Mamolo, clad in apron and wielding a large ladle, was smiling, while behind me Michele cackled, "Come in, come in." The seat at the head of the table was empty, but to its right, propped up comfortably with cushions in a large chair, sat Tommaso. All were smiling at me, grinning and laughing.

I followed my master to the head of the table, and pulled back the chair for her to sit. But she put her hand on my arm. "No, Lorenzo. Today the place of honour is yours. I shall sit at the other end with Master Rolandino."

Confused I sat down and turned to Tommaso. "What the hell is going on?" I asked.

"It's a celebration, you donkey!" he replied.

"Of what?" I asked, still blind.

Tommaso's exasperated answer was drowned out by the rich baritone of Sordello, who proclaimed, "Lorenzo. This banquet is in your honour. Through your bravery and sacrifice – I might even say heroism, but for the fact that you might become big-headed – you have saved the city from strife and occupation, preserved your master from murder, rescued two women to my knowledge from ill-treatment or worse – oh, and we like you! We count ourselves privileged to be your friends." All raised a cup and toasted me: "To Lorenzo!"

I was dumbfounded. And speechless. Tommaso leaned towards me. "Say something, Lorenzo, so we can get on and eat. I'm famished!"

His silly comment, the sort only an old friend can make, shook me out of my stupor. I stood and said, "Friends, for so you all are, the privilege is mine. Since I came to Bologna, and more than ever in the last few months, I have learnt what friendship is. Indeed, what love is. And, if I have achieved anything worthwhile, or even taken risks (most of which the Magister tells me were foolish and poorly calculated), all was done out of my regard for the friendship and love all of you have shown me. From the bottom of my heart, I thank you."

I sat down to hearty applause and the feasting started. I'm sure we all drank more than was necessary or wise. We ate magnificently. Two or three courses in, Mamolo proudly announced that the next dish was my (and the Magister's) favourite. I retorted that it could not possibly be, because my dish of choice was prime lean beef, fried and doused in balsamic sauce: "But, as we all know," I said, "There is no *balsamico* to be had in Bologna."

"There *wasn't* any to be had," roared Paolo, laughing as he said it. "But, while we were raiding Lambertazzi's house, mainly to rescue you from your crazy escapade, the Capitano's men came across a hoard of barrels of the essence."

I was astonished, mouth agape. "What's up, Lorenzo?" laughed Paolo. "Does the sauce mean so very much to you?"

"No. Well, yes: but I've just understood something. Ages back, all that time ago, when I was serving at table in Modena... You remember, Tommasino: help me out!"

He chuckled too. "I would, Lorenzo, if you made any sense!"

"I'm trying to! We knew they were plotting to create a shortage of the *balsamico*: just to make Bologna uncomfortable. But it never occurred to me that Lambertazzi had built up his own secret hoard. The old bastard was swimming in the stuff, when no one else in Bologna could get hold of a drop."

"Till now," retorted Paolo. "The Capitano leaned on the new head of the family, Roberto, to release it, and at a fair price too. I believe he suggested that the gesture might make his family a little less unpopular with the Popolo. And I, well, I confess I persuaded Salvatore to liberate a barrel that night, while we were bringing you home."

My amazement increased as, out of the shadows, stepped the Capitano del Popolo himself, his wine-cup raised. "I salute you, Lorenzo. You saved this city from an unwelcome invasion and seizure of power, and you removed the ringleader without the need for a messy trial." He held up his hand to stifle the company's applause, adding, with a roguish smile, "Most important, however, you led us, albeit inadvertently, to Lambertazzi's hoard of *balsamico*. Though," he hesitated for mock effect, "We may all regret that you didn't call that little plot to mind somewhat earlier. In Bologna we'd have hanged him for that crime alone: everyone here knows that life is simply unbearable without the essence!"

There was more laughter, and we tucked into Mamolo's finest creation yet: I swear there was even black truffle in that magnificently rich sauce, though Mamolo merely smiled mysteriously when I asked him. Later on, as the fire kept us warm even in the chill of a February evening, we talked and joked until late. Then, inevitably, we started singing. Sordello and his troupe led the way, and I knew all the songs by now, and the descants. Later still, looking to my right, I noticed Tommaso leaning over and speaking to Filippo, who handed him his rebec.

"Come, Lorenzo," he said. "Let us see if I can still play this thing."

"You'd better, Tommaso," laughed Sordello. "For my boys and I will be heading off to France in the spring: I am summoned to return to Duke Charles's household. So if Lorenzo is to continue his career in music, he will need a new band!"

"You're leaving?" I asked Sordello. "Already?"

"Lorenzo, I've been here nearly a year. I too serve a master, you know. Besides, you have learnt the trade: and that other trick of it, gathering intelligence while you play and sing. Remember: you've learned from an expert!"

I laughed. "That I have," I replied: "From *the* expert! So we shall have to get Tommasino a new instrument."

My master cut in: "That will be my gift to him, a paltry gesture in relation to the debt I owe him – that we all owe. Lorenzo, we must be up betimes tomorrow: there is much work yet to do. So let us get on with the singing."

Tommaso started playing. It was as if those years in between had fallen away, the tone of the little instrument sweet and warm as he played one simple folk song after another, the rest of us joining in as we recognised them. He looked pleased at our applause, and then looked across to where I was standing, near the fire. "Is it time, Lorenzo? Shall we sing the song now?"

I did not need to ask which song. As we sang it my heart leapt. Memories crowded my mind of those happy times in his family, my first meeting with Rosalia and the magic that occurred between us when we sang. Then I thought of all the hurt and wrong I had encountered: the damage done to that girl whom I had rescued from servitude and abuse, and our grievous parting; the love, lust and loss of Livia; the men whose lives I had taken, almost casually; my ordeals at the hands of the Prior of Modena and of Massimo Lambertazzi; the monstrous activities and horrific death of the latter; the moment when I thought my dearest friend would die of the wound he received while carrying out a plan of my design; and, above all, the loss, through all of these and more, of the final vestiges of my innocence.

The tears ran down my face: yet I was glad, and unashamed. They flowed from joy as much as from sorrow. It was as if they were washing away the pain and the doubt, even the misery that had gripped me since those recent adventures.

I lifted up my voice, and as I did so it seemed my soul and all its hurts were at last beginning to heal. Tommaso and I looked into each other's eyes, each knowing the other's thoughts, sharing our pleasure and our sheer love of the music as we sang together.

Ti canterò lo meo amor...

The End

HISTORICAL NOTE

The mid-Thirteenth Century was a turbulent time in the part of Italy we now know as Emilia Romagna. In the previous century the Holy Roman Empire, which, under Emperor Henry V, claimed overall sovereignty of the region, had granted it a degree of autonomy. The League of Lombardy rose against Frederick Barbarossa, and Bologna (which had long sought to create itself a free *commune)* joined that rebellion in 1164. After the Peace of Constance (1183) Bologna began to expand rapidly as a major trading city, partly thanks to its canals, and powerful families began to build themselves the tall towers for which the city is still famed, though few remain at full height.

Under Frederick II the Empire came into conflict with the Papacy. In Italy the so-called Guelfs, essentially Lombards, sided with Rome against the Ghibellines who supported Frederick. After waging wars in Italy for three decades, where individual city-states declared themselves for or against him, Frederick's forces were defeated at the Battle of Fossalta (a few kilometres north of Modena) in 1249. It was not a decisive victory in terms of ending the wider conflict: but the Emperor's son, Enzo, was taken prisoner and remained in comfortable captivity in Bologna until his death in 1272. Modena, a Ghibelline city, thus came under the control of Bologna, its Guelf neighbour and enemy.

Frederick died in 1250, and there followed an interregnum of more than twenty years, during which claimants to the throne constantly emerged. This story is set in that chaotic time where a power vacuum allowed city states to war with one another while, within them (notably in Bologna), powerful families vied for overall power - with one another, with the rising merchant classes, with the Guilds being formed to protect trades and craftsmen, and with the Companies of Arms, the so-called *gonfalonieri*.

The University of Bologna claims to be the oldest university in the world (certainly the oldest in Europe, and the first to describe itself as *universitas*), dating its origin to 1088: it received a Charter from Barbarossa in 1158. As *Magister* Bettisia Gozzadini explains to Lorenzo, it grew from a centre for the study of law, founded upon the famed *Codex Justinianus*, part of the *Corpus Juris Civilis*, in effect a compendium of Roman law set down by order of the Eastern Roman Emperor Justinian in AD529. The text was rediscovered in Italy in the Eleventh or Twelfth Century: one source puts the date at 1070, and locates the Codex in Bologna, which suits my story very well.

Bettisia Gozzadini is a genuine historical figure. Born in 1209 to a noble family, she graduated in law from the *Studium* of Bologna in 1237, is reputed to have worn men's clothing (and, in some accounts, a veil) to disguise her beauty, or at least her gender, and is thought to be the first woman to have taught at a university.

Maestro Rolandino de' Passageri, her close friend in this story, is also a historical Bolognese jurist. The son of a ferry-keeper (hence the name, and thus of peasant stock), he was of a similar age to Bettisia Gozzadini, born in 1215. In 1255 he completed his *Summa totius artis notariae,* his summary of the complete art of the notary, which remained a standard text for centuries, and in 1257 was one of four notaries who wrote the so-called *Liber Paradisus*, the Book of Heaven, in effect a legal document outlawing slavery or serfdom in the city. In the story I have ignored two of the other three notaries, and credited Gozzadini as working with him on it. He became heavily involved in city politics, was instrumental in the repeated exile of the Lambertazzi family and, on his death in 1300, was honoured with a monumental tomb in the square beside the Church of San Domenico, alongside three of the other great *glossisti* (commentators on and teachers of the law) from the early years of the university.

The character of Massimo Lambertazzi is fictitious but, as I mentioned above, in the later Thirteenth Century the powerful family of that name was repeatedly exiled from Bologna after attempted coups. His villainous accomplices, Bardi in Bologna, Uguzzoni, the Bishop and the Prior in Modena, are my inventions. I hope I have not heaped calumny on the sainted memory of two worthy churchmen of the period!

Sordello was indeed one of the great troubadours of thirteenth-century Italy. Born in Goito, Mantua, he led an adventurous life, spending many years in the service of Duke Charles d'Anjou, one of the claimants to the throne of the Holy Roman Empire. Some of his texts in Provençal French survive, but all his Italian songs are lost. The main square in Mantua is named after him.

Lorenzo is my invention, but his initial kidnap is by no means far-fetched! As a choirboy, Renaissance composer Orlando di Lasso is alleged to have been stolen away by rival choirs - not once, but three times.

With so rich and chaotic a world to inhabit, Lorenzo will return.

Bernard Trafford

13321712R00176

Printed in Great Britain
by Amazon